The Mystery of the Missing Persons

By Deborah DR Kralich

ISBN 9781942542001
TX8003785
The United States of America

This is a fictional work. The names, characters, incidents, events, places and locations, are solely the product and concept of the author's imagination or are used to create a fictitious story and should not be construed as real.
See Author's Note on page 360

Table of Contents

Part 1

1 *Histories*

I couldn't wait to start school. I had just one reason. I already knew how to read. I was waiting for them to teach me to write so I could write my book.

I had begun my first short story in September when I had started first grade and had finished it in October. It had been a good story, about a bank robbery in which a teller, Mary, was shot but recovered and the bad guys were caught like in most TV shows. But, although I had enjoyed writing it, it was a long tedious process because I had no choice but to print the entire story, six pages, in pencil.

My mother had read it and looked unhappy. "Why does Mary get shot?"

"She gets well," I had said defensively. I had been embarrassed. My mother did not like my story. I didn't understand. I loved watching old movies on TV, made when my parents were young that were not comedies and this story was like those, I believed. But she had looked worried about it. My mother worried a lot and I didn't want to cause more anxiety. I had dropped my plans to take it to Mrs. Anderson.

In fact I had gone back to my room and torn it up. I had plans for my real book, but I had kept them to myself. Now I was unsure.

What would my mother say about a mystery? I wondered.

"It's my turn to say prayers tomorrow," I said. It was now November and I had secretly begun writing my book. It was untitled, in the early stages. On notebook paper tucked in a pocket folder. Characters were still being developed. Plot was not yet formed. "Can I say the **Hail Mary**?"

"I don't know." My mother looked more worried. "What prayer do you usually say?"

"Most everybody says **Our Father**, but sometimes some of the kids say something different."

"Let me talk to Mrs. Anderson," my mother said, "and make sure it's all right."

"It's also going to be my turn to read something out of a book I like," I said. Every morning we started off class with a student led prayer. Then the student read an excerpt from his or her favorite book.

"I don't think you can read Nancy Drew," said my mother.

"Yes I can! Matthew Waterston has already read the Hardy Boys."

"He read a whole book?"

Most of the kids read such short little books that they could read the whole book in just a few minutes. Every morning it was usually the same prayer and some boring little kid's book. I believed we needed some variety.

"No, Mrs. Anderson let him read a couple of pages that she picked out."

"Then I wish you would read from *Little Women*."

"Umm, I haven't finished it." My mother had given me *Little Women*. I hated to tell her I didn't like it much. It was boring. I knew she had not read it since she did not read for entertainment.

"Ok, take one of your mystery books to Mrs. Anderson today and let her pick something out and ask her about the Hail Mary and I'll call the office and make sure it's Ok."

It was. When I said the **Hail Mary** that Friday morning only a couple of the other kids said it along with me. I knew Mrs. Anderson was not Catholic but she was nice enough to say it too, tearing up as always during prayers. Before, she had announced the prayer would be different and explained that the other kids did not have to say it with me. They mostly didn't.

When Matthew had read from the Hardy Boys it had been funny- the kids had laughed. But they didn't like what I read. They didn't laugh even though it was funny, too. I knew they liked Matthew and most of them didn't like me. Matthew's father owned the neighborhood grocery store and they all knew his whole family. Mama never took me grocery shopping. She and Aunt Worthrose went together when I was in school or she left me with Aunt Worthrose when school was not in session.

But Matthew enjoyed the mystery story excerpt, I could tell. He even tried to say the **Hail Mary,** though he obviously didn't know the words. He liked me, he was my boyfriend. And I had my best friend

Vickie Bianchi. They were all I needed.

We were going to paint murals on the wall. The school was brand new and the walls were very empty. It was about to be Thanksgiving and the mural was going to be about the history of America. I was really excited. I was going to get to paint. My mother would not let me paint at home unless I painted in the garage because it messed up the house. And it was always hot in the garage, or cold, so I had decided I wasn't going to paint until I grew up and had my own house. But here was a chance to paint right now.

"Please let me paint the teepees, Mrs. Anderson," I had pleaded, previously when the project was announced. I knew that most of the scenes of the mural were going to be painted by the older grades. Our grade was going to do just the easy parts. Knowing I did not have a chance to get to paint any of the people, I had tried for teepees. Mrs. Anderson was the English teacher so she had to get permission from the art teacher, Mrs. Hopwell. "I'm going to do my best," she had said, with an encouraging look as she had wiped away her tears. "Glenn wants to paint the horses and he is very good at that."

Glenn might have been the boy I liked but massive freckles and spots on his face made him unpleasant to look at despite his very blond hair.

"I know just how I'm going to do the teepees." I had it perfectly in my mind.

"Show me how you're going to paint the teepees," she had added. So I had taken a piece of paper and I had drawn the teepees and then had explained how I was going to do the painting inside.

"Well," she had said, smiling with more tears in her eyes. "Well, I'll see what I can do."

Now the big day was here. I still did not know if I was going to paint the teepees. Just after lunch we lined up by the doorway, then Mrs. Anderson pulled Glenn and me both out of the line.

"Victoria, Glenn, you two are going to get to paint– Victoria- the teepees, and Glenn- some horses nearby. Mrs. Hopwell is going to take you to that section which has already got the sky and the ground on it so you won't be with the rest of our class. Behave yourself, make me proud." She smiled kindly and sniffled, wiping tears away before they fell on her cheek.

So Glenn and I went with Mrs. Hopwell and she showed us where she wanted the teepees and the horses, gave us the paints and we got to work. We were working side by side pretty far away from the other children so it was quiet and we were both concentrating really hard. I was making beautiful teepees. I had just finished coloring in the center of one that was particularly good when suddenly we heard the POP! of the loudspeaker. It was typical of the principal to interrupt us so nobody really stopped painting at his first words of greeting- which were always "May I have your attention, please-". His voice did sound a little different than usual. But it was the words he said next that had everybody stop, even I stopped painting my teepees and just held my brush up in the air.

"President Kennedy has been SHOT." The loudspeaker POPPED again. The principal said the word "shot" like he could not understand its meaning. In the hallway there was total silence.

Then POP! once more. "I repeat, President Kennedy has been SHOT in Dallas. As soon as we know more I will break in again." POP! Off the speaker went.

Rapidly I turned back to finish my teepees as I suspected this was going to interrupt my painting. I glanced at Glenn's horses, they were all brown and close together, faces unfinished, but they looked like good horses indeed. But Glenn did not paint anymore.

"Poor President Kennedy," said Glenn. Glenn's massively freckled face looked very sad.

"Hurry up and finish, children, finish up and put up your paints, we have to go back to the classrooms," said Mrs. Hopwell hurriedly, running a little from spot to spot where there were students painting.

And so we did stop. I had gotten three tepees painted. They were good. Two more started, they were good but I wanted to add more detail.

Back in class we sat in silence, everybody keeping very still in their desks. Mrs. Anderson stood in front of us. She was quiet too. For once, she did not cry at all. Then we all jumped a little. POP!- but no greeting- no greeting at all, instead the principal said, "President Kennedy is DEAD." A few more moments of silence but no POP. I could hear the loudspeaker was still on but nobody was talking. He said again slowly, "President Kennedy is DEAD." POP! It went off.

We sat silently in class until we were dismissed to go home early. I just knew we would never get to paint anymore on the mural again but at least my book was waiting for me at home. The whole school was being dismissed at the same time instead of the older kids going home later. Many in the hall were crying. Grownups were talking.

When we left the parking lot we got away from the crowd since our car was going the opposite direction of all the other kids' cars.

Mama had the radio on in the car. She never did that. She hated any noise when she was driving.

"President Kennedy was shot today as his motorcade left downtown Dallas, Texas. Mrs. Kennedy jumped up and grabbed Mr. Kennedy as she cried. 'Oh No…' "

"Some of the grownups at school said the colored people killed President Kennedy," I said.

"Who said that?" Mama asked.

"I don't know," I said. "I don't know them. They were in the hallway."

"Don't believe everything you hear,"

"I didn't. That's why I asked you."

We were home in a just a few minutes. The TV was already on and Aunt Worthrose was there. I looked at the TV but the man talking was unfamiliar. I wanted to see a picture of President Kennedy. I knew he was handsome but I couldn't quite remember what he looked like.

"…It appears to have taken five minutes for the stricken President to arrive at the hospital.…"

I knew a little about President Kennedy. He was two years younger than Daddy. He was Catholic. He had a daughter my age, Caroline, and a son who was still a little kid. His wife was younger than Mama. President Kennedy had been in World War II like Daddy, only he had been in the Navy. He was Irish, not Italian like Daddy was. And President Kennedy was handsome, not as handsome as Daddy, but more handsome than most men.

"Witnesses said they saw a man with a gun in the window. They say he was a white man… he was white then…"

"June Rosette," said my aunt, who was standing in front of the

TV paying strict attention. "They said it was a white man, a white man, thank the Lord for that."

My mother was beginning to prepare dinner and I was torn between going to my room and writing, or staying and watching TV.

"...Vice President Johnson will now be sworn in and serve out the remainder of the late President Kennedy's term which runs until January 20, 1964 little more than year and a half from now...Beyond that we don't know..."

One man would be talking, then suddenly the screen would change and another man would be talking but still no pictures of President Kennedy or his family. I wanted to stay and see. I had an idea. The rule was all my stuff had to stay inside my room except books to read. There was no exception, even for paperwork. But today was different. Maybe I could get away with more.

I dashed down the hall to my bedroom, took off my socks and shoes and my stiff dress. I put on old shorts and a shirt that I wore around the house. I pulled out my book which was in a pocket folder and brought it and a pencil back into the den.

"Homework?" my mother asked from the kitchen as she was preparing to cook.

"Sort of," I fibbed. "Can I sit at the table with my folder and paper?"

Actually I never had homework. I did it all in school before the bell rang. But I hoped I could disguise my book as homework, so long as nobody paid much attention. I sat at the dinette table which took up most of the space between the kitchen and the den. Only a short counter separated the kitchen from the dinette and nothing separated the dinette from the den, except the den was longer and the TV was in the part that was not visible from the table. So I could hear, but not see, the TV.

"Tell me if they show a picture of him."

"Ok, do you need any homework help?" My aunt could see me where she was sitting now on the couch.

"She never needs help," said my mother, banging pots and pans. She could see us both over the counter. "The teachers say she can do all the work without any assistance. She just needs the directions."

"...President Kennedy was assassinated today ... the President, cradled in his wife's arms, was rushed in his blood spattered limousine

10

to a hospital where attempts to save him were in vain…The president was 44 years old…"

"No pictures yet?"

"No, just do your homework, I'll tell you," said my aunt. My mother continued working in the kitchen. She avoided looking at me.

"…later two Roman Catholic priests were called to the hospital…"

I got to work on my book. The TV people were just repeating the same thing again so I tuned them out. I had not decided on a title but I had already written most of Chapter 1. And with all the adults being distracted over the President's death, I had high hopes of finishing it tonight.

My characters were very interesting. I was quite proud of them. I gave them names, hair color, eye color, height and age, sometimes weight. But then on the TV they started saying new things. I stopped and listened.

"… A policeman was shot to death minutes after the President was killed, near the scene of the assassination…"

Then they would pause a minute and the screen would be blank and then another man would appear.

"…At the hospital…right now police are clearing a corridor and the President's body will be brought out on a gurney…"

In my mind I could see people dividing in the hallway to make room for the gurney. I knew exactly what that looked like.

"…Mrs. Kennedy at no time collapsed nor did she give way to hysteria…"

"Victoria, I don't know how late your father may work, I am going to go ahead and feed you as soon as the food is ready," my mother was saying. Her voice had a high pitch to it that usually indicated she was angry with me or my father but today I knew it was because the President was dead.

"Ok, just a minute," I said. I was in the middle of a sentence. I was distracted by my supper being put before me and having to hastily close my folder and hide it. I dropped the pencil on the floor. I rose slightly, put the folder on my chair and sat on it. I listened while I ate broccoli, hamburger meat, and mashed potatoes.

"Can I have a Coke?"

"No, milk." Mama set a tall glass of milk before me.

"... *Mrs. Kennedy and the President's body were escorted out of the hospital by police officers. In spite of the horrific experience she has been through, she had not been hysterical, she had managed to control herself and keep her head...*"

I pictured that scene in my mind. I could almost smell the hospital odor. I got up and went to see the TV just in case they showed a picture real quick.

"Finish eating," my mother prompted me. "I have an apple pie for dessert or pineapple cake."

"*...Russian radio reports that the extreme right wing element is believed responsible...*"

"Oh, Lord, June Rosette, do you think it could have been the KKK?" said Aunt Worthrose. "That will be worse than if it is the coloreds."

"Why can't I have both?" I demanded, rapidly getting back to the table.

"Victoria, choose one," said my mother. "I swear I don't know, Worthrose, God help us."

"Because, Victoria Irene," said my aunt. "You are getting too fat."

My mother sat a piece of pie and a piece of cake down in front of me without further comment. I did feel a little guilty, I was getting a little fat. We were all three silent as I ate both desserts.

"They are showing his picture now," said my aunt.

I got up from the table and went over to stand in front of the TV. *Ok, yes, I recognize him now.*

"*...at the White House it is a normal school day for the President's little girl and her classmates...*"

"How can she be at home and school at the same time?" I asked.

"I remember," said my mother, as she cleared off the table, "hearing that, because she was the daughter of the president, Caroline went to school at home, with her mother and baby brother right there, just in different rooms. I was so jealous, she gets to keep her children at home while I have to send you out every day."

"Will Caroline have to go to a different school now?" I asked, fetching the pencil from the floor.

"I don't know," said my mother.

"Victoria, when do you go back to school?" asked my aunt.

"I don't know." I put my book back on the table and opened the folder back up.

"They let them out as soon as it happened today, I think they are going to let the children stay out through Thanksgiving, I'll know more Monday."

"That's good, best she be at home, nobody knows what may happen next."

"...*Thousands of high school students had cut classes to see the President and his attractive wife...Mrs. Kennedy, wearing a stunning pink suit with a matching pink pill box hat ... "*

I knew it. Thanksgiving would be over before we got back to school. We would never finish the mural. I would never finish the teepees. Well, I was proud of the ones I got done.

"*...Late word - police have little doubt that Oswald is the President's assassin. Oswald was reported to have a Russian wife...*"

"Did they say he had a Russian wife?" My mother came back over from the sink where she had begun to wash the dishes, her hands still gloved and dripping.

"Yes, June Rosette, I think they did!" My aunt sounded excited. "Glory be! There won't be a civil war if it was the Russians."

"*... has two children, Caroline, six, and John Jr. age almost three... Earlier this year Mrs. Kennedy gave birth to a third baby who tragically lived just a short time before dying...*"

"I didn't know they had a baby that died," I said. I watched them talk about the President and Mrs. Kennedy with more interest.

"Yes," said my mother. "He died like Rosalind Renee."

I thought about Rosalind Renee, my parents first baby. Rosalind Renee had died two days after she was born in 1945, 12 years before I was born. She would have been my older sister if she had lived. We used to visit her grave all the time at a cemetery where they had a lot of big statues. But we didn't go very often anymore.

"*...the children are here at the White House. They have not yet been told of their father's death. They are with their nurse...*"

Wow, I thought. *I know her father is dead but Caroline does not. I know it before she does.*

"...The First Lady showed remarkable self-discipline, there were no hysterics..."

I moved to the couch with my book.

"If the Russians are behind it, it won't be as bad as a Civil War but it will be World War III!" said my aunt.

"Well, Vic's too old to go this time and his back is too bad anyway," said my mother.

"Why is a Civil War worse?" I asked.

"Because they would fight here in America, not overseas," said my mother.

"June Rosette, they will have Clyde back in the Navy if it gets bad enough." They looked at each other and laughed a little. Uncle Clyde was a real old man with solid gray hair. Then they became somber again. "Drake will be in the thick of it though," my mother said. "Talinda will be left alone again."

Their youngest sister Aunt Talinda was married to a World War II hero, Uncle Drake, who had been in the Marines many years. The army made Daddy work on the airplane engines rather than go fight. But Uncle Drake had gone to fight the Japanese and been wounded and got the Silver Star. He was still in the service and they lived far away and I did not know them. But we were all very proud to have a World War II hero in the family. We had a big picture of Uncle Drake, in his uniform, and Aunt Talinda, wearing a fur coat, on our end table in the living room.

"There's dark days ahead all right. Well, all we can do is trust in the Lord." Aunt Worthrose embraced my mother and then went home to cook dinner for Uncle Clyde. Mama went back to the dishes and I started writing again.

"... those old enough to remember the death of Franklin Roosevelt, so near the end of World War II, just months from seeing victory, will tell you that, where ever you were, whatever you might have been doing when you heard of the death of President Kennedy that is a moment you will never forget..."

"Do you remember when President Roosevelt died?" I asked.

"Certainly," my mother said. "But it was different, they didn't shoot him. He died of a stroke, like my mother."

"…now we have live coverage…"

At last. Mama quickly switched off all the lights so the TV was the only thing lit in the house. I got off the couch and we stood together very close, watching the dark blurred images on the screen.

"See. There it is," Mama said. "There's the plane." And I could clearly see the words on the plane- The United States of America.

Despite the crowd of people in dark suits and uniforms madly scrambling about in the small screen, I could see Mrs. Kennedy behind the casket. They were helping her out, she practically had to jump. I could see her clothing clearly. She walked a short ways and got into the ambulance. I saw the dark stains on her skirt and legs. So this was the woman who didn't have hysterics.

They were taking the President's body to the White House. We sat down on the couch and I continued to clutch my book.

"…All programs canceled this evening until further notice… we can be sure none of us will ever forget where he was or how he felt when he heard the news this sad somber day…"

Mama and I fell asleep on the couch. Frequently we watched TV together at night when Daddy was working late. Mama and I would be curled up on the couch together, watching anything we liked from variety shows to old movies. They had better shows on late at night.

We woke up later - Daddy had come home. The television was still talking-

"…Jackie brave composed, self-disciplined…"

"We are closed down until Tuesday at least," said my father. "I was trying to finish up the job so I didn't hear much. They were talking at work like a Mexican did it."

"No, they think they've got who did it. He was white. A communist. He even lived in Russia for awhile with a Russian wife. He also killed a police officer," my mother said.

"Johnson has never been anything but a crook," said my father. "But they're all crooks, so what can you do?"

"God only knows what's going to happen to this country now, the coloreds are trying to take over and the Communists are trying to take over. We could have another Civil War."

"The coloreds just want to live in peace and make a life for their families just like us," said my father. "We're not going to have another Civil War. But it won't come to that. This is still a free country. This country will survive. No matter what."

"It's way past time for bed. We are scaring Victoria with this kind of talk. We need to get her in bed." She cut the TV off.

I felt wide awake and was not scared at all. I had seen enough war movies on TV to know we could defeat the Russians just like we beat the Germans.

"Are we going to get to see what you're working on someday?" my father asked as he got me off the couch and carried me to bed.

"It's not finished." I clenched my book defensively, sort of sitting on it, as Mama helped me put on my pajamas.

Besides I knew they didn't really read books like I did. They only read the newspaper.

"She's not supposed to be doing that at this age," my mother said worriedly. Afraid she might make a grab for it, I quickly thrust my book in my dresser drawer, climbed in bed and allowed myself to be tucked in. I felt a warm wonderful glow. Chapter 1 was finished. As soon as they left I retrieved it and pulled my secret flashlight from its hiding place and reread it.

Chapter 1
Special Delivery

"I'd better be going," said Jane Lee Kape, Barbara Kay Scott's 17 year old cousin. Barbara is 17, too. Her orphaned cousin Maria Isabell Maine, called Belle, who lives with her, is also 17. Jane is black headed and Belle is blonde. Barbara is brown haired.

"Well, bye then," said Barbara cheerfully. It was obvious she wanted Jane to go.

"Barbara!" cried Mrs. Ellen Scott, her mother. "Mind your manners!"

"Won't you please stay a little longer, Jane?" She inquired.

Belle, the quiet type, didn't say anything, but she too, wanted Jane to go.

Jane was pretty but that didn't make up for her being selfish. Her parents, April and Raymond Kape, gave her anything she wanted. That was well enough but she didn't have to brag so much about it. Jane was always trying to boss Beth and Barbara because she is a few months older.

Barbara's father, Christopher Scott, of the Scott and Starfield Detective agency, was away on business.

"No, I'd better get going," Jane said, looking narrow eyed at Barbara. Jane had come right after breakfast. Now it was time for lunch and the girls were very tired of Jane's boasting.

Suddenly a clap of thunder filled the air and rain came pouring down in sheets.

"Oh good, it's raining," said Belle.

"Oh no," cried Jane. "I left the top down on my car. It will be soaked!"

Jane's car was very new it was a shiny pale green Plymouth convertible. She's had it for about three months, she got it for her 18th birthday. "Dad will kill me," Jane moaned. "What can I do?"

"Here take this umbrella and go put up the top," said Ellen.

"Go out in the rain! Why, I might get wet!" Spoiled Jane was horrified at such a thing. "I won't do it."

"It will be ruined," said Barbara, ruefully. "It's such a lovely car too."

"All right, I'll do it," sighed Jane, ruefully. She took the umbrella and hurried out the side door and pressed the button which lifted the top of the car. For a moment the rain came down so fierce that she had to sit in the car. As it did not let up, she backed out of the driveway, brakes squealing as she barely missed a tree and roared down the road.

Barbara uncovered her eyes. "One of these days she is going to hit that tree!"

"I know," agreed Belle. "Her and her temper! Oh boy!"

Barbara giggled. "Uncle Raymond will kill her for ruining her car!"

"Yes," agreed Belle. "If he hits her once she'll die a thousand deaths!"

"Girls," snapped Ellen. "I'll not have you making jokes about Jane, after all she is your full blood cousin!"

Barbara and Belle moaned.

Just then the doorbell rang.

As Belle opened the door the postman called out, "Special delivery for Barbara Kay Scott."

"Thank you," Barbara said as she took the letter. "I wonder who it's from."

"Open it," said Belle.

"Why don't you wait until your father comes home," suggested Ellen. "I'm sure he will want to be in on it."

"Ok."

"Oh," moaned Belle.

"You can wait, Belle," said Barbara.

"Dinner."

Barbara and Belle sat down to some spaghetti and cheese and steak.

"Mmm," said Belle.

"Mmm is right," agreed Barbara. "If you keep this up mom, we'll be as fat as Jane!"

"Jane is not fat," said Ellen.

Both girls looked at her skeptically.

"Just oversizingly plump," Ellen added.

"Hope we don't have any interruptions," said Barbara.

She had barely got the words out of her mouth when the doorbell rang again!

"I'll get it," said Belle. She opened the door expecting to find someone there. Instead she gave a shriek of horror! "Oh, Barbara," she cried. "Come here! I think I'm going to –" with that Belle fainted!

I need to put Belle in the female hysterical column, I thought.

When I wasn't writing I liked to make lists and put things in columns- like all people with blue eyes, all with brown eyes and so on. It was a good way to keep track of all the relatives on each side of the family. There were so many it was hard for even me to memorize them all, especially the ones I didn't see often or had never met.

I decided that was a good idea for my characters also. Rather than being vague images, I could put them in columns according to their characteristics. I didn't really have any of these columns finished but I like to start them.

Barbara, of course, will be in the self-disciplined column.

I did not want a blond blue eyed heroine or a red head but a brown haired, brown eyed girl like me. And I wanted to call her Victoria badly but decided against it. It wasn't done. This was fiction, the characters could not have the names of real people. I had called my first Barbie doll Barbara. Despite now having several more similar dolls, Barbara was still my favorite. The other dolls could keep their company names but my black hair ponytail was too sophisticated. She deserved to be called Barbara. The name gave me good feelings.

So I named my fictional female detective Barbara. Yet I did not really name Barbara, the brown haired, brown eyed character, after the doll with black hair and blue eyes. I was aware of the comparison and that there was some sort of intangible link. But mainly I chose the name Barbara because I thought it had a lot in common with my name. It had multiple syllables, it ended in 'a'. It was a formal adult name that was plagued by a childish nickname. Despite being beautiful in sound and print, it was unappreciated.

So Barbara Kay Scott became my character.

The last and middle names just came to me from nowhere. I never knew anyone by those names. I didn't even know any real person named Barbara.

Just like all the fictional female teenage detectives looked different on every cover of every book I had, so I envisioned Barbara Scott being portrayed differently by every artist who drew her for the covers of my future books. Someday I might even draw her for one myself. This was only going to be the first of many in the series.

I gave Barbara Kay Scott a family and a mystery to solve. Of course, I did not want to steal anything from any of the mystery series I had read.

That would take all the fun out of it.

I didn't even see Barbara Kay Scott as a potential competitor for teenage mystery detective genre heroines. She just wanted to join the group.

As I started my prayers, feeling sleepy now, I hoped I had stayed awake long enough to sleep later Saturday morning.

On Saturday mornings, if I got up early, I was expected to watch cartoons.

Each weekend I dreaded the time waiting for breakfast having to just sit, hungry, watching the stupid shows.

This morning it didn't matter anyway.

"No cartoons today," my mother greeted me when I came into the den the morning of November 23, 1963.

A pleasant surprise, No stupid cartoons, I thought.

She said, "I hope you're not too disappointed. But it is because President Kennedy was killed."

Yeah!

I didn't like most cartoons anymore.

I was slowly cutting back on them as much as I could get away with.

It was a slow battle. I was expected to think they were funny.

There were a lot of supposedly funny programs on TV that had real people but I didn't like most of them either.

Even more surprising, this morning the TV was already on and Daddy was watching it again. The TV was almost never on except when I had to watch it. Daddy worked almost every day, sometimes he was off on Sundays and we went to church. But not very often. He usually came home every evening though often very late.

Sometimes Mama would take a break from her housekeeping to watch a program with me but Daddy rarely watched anything except Ed Sullivan and **Bonanza**. Mama and I were expected to watch those two

20

shows with him every week, and unless he was working late, we did.

I hated them.

"Daddy's off this weekend because of the President," said my mother.

I noticed then Aunt Worthrose was back too, silently watching the people speaking on TV, her arms folded, her upper body slowly rocking back and forth and a pinched expression on her face.

"You need to watch this too, Victoria Irene," said my father. "This is history."

I had not realized they liked President Kennedy so much. I had heard the story of how Daddy had voted for Nixon and that had made all his family mad at him because Kennedy was the first Catholic who could become president.

This was not unusual. Daddy's family was usually mad at him, and him at them, for something.

"Can I have my book?" I asked, being deliberately vague.

It normally bothered them when I read books and watched TV at the same time.

I had earned that right by repeatedly answering questions about the content of both correctly time and time again over the years.

But it still bothered them and I had to ask permission, frequently threatening to refuse to watch TV if they didn't let me read at the same time.

But this time- "Of course," they all said, almost at once.

Wow, jackpot, not even a dissent.

I went back to my room and got my notebook and pen. Just to be on the safe side I brought **Little Women** also, to try to take attention away from my writings. I could pop it open and read from it if necessary for subterfuge.

To my delight, I got the couch all to myself because my parents and my aunt preferred to sit in hard chairs they brought in from the dinette and placed very close to the television, closer than I was ever allowed to sit because Daddy said the rays from the TV were harmful and Mama said it could hurt your eyes.

And I had never seen Aunt Worthrose come and watch TV with us before, she only ever watched Lawrence Welk at her house with Uncle Clyde. Sometimes I watched with them when I visited.

But today Daddy ignored the deadly rays and Mama didn't care about her eyes and Aunt Worthrose was there with us.

So I was behind them, almost alone on the couch, writing when they thought I was reading.

I got Chapter 2 done before lunch.

Chapter 2
A Warning

Ellen and Barbara laid Belle down on the couch.

"I'm going to see what's out there!" determined Barbara. "Mom you stay with Belle. I'll be right back."

Barbara went to the door and looked out.

Whatever Belle had seen was gone!

On the ground were footprints of a woman's high-heeled shoes!

When Barbara came back in Belle was sitting up on the couch still as white as a sheet.

"Then what did you see out there?" Barbara questioned her with a puzzled expression on her face.

"Barbara don't question her now!" Ellen said. "Can't you see what a shock this has been to her? Come dear, you had better lie down."

Ellen and Belle went upstairs leaving Barbara to figure out things for herself.

Barbara went back outside unmindful of the pair of eyes watching every move she made and of the rattlesnake waiting to be let out of his cage to bite of the plans made for her in the future.

Belle came and said she was ready to tell Barbara what she saw.

They went inside together and Belle said, "Well there was the horrible thing. It was so frightening it made me faint. Well there was a red sign with black letters and it said,

BEWARE
BARBARA SCOTT
YOU
AND
YOUR
FAMILY
ARE IN
DANGER

"It had brown edges. It looked like it was written and colored with a magic marker. At the bottom there was a very funny little mark sort of like this."

Belle took a pad and pencil and made a mark like this:

x

"Was there anything else?"

"Yes, do I have to tell you?" pleaded Belle.

"No, you told me enough for now," said Barbara kindly.

"Barbara, didn't you see it?" asked Belle.

"What?"

"The thing."

"No, all I saw was a woman's footprints."

"A woman's footprints!" exclaimed Ellen who was vacuuming the carpet.

"Yes," said Barbara. "Right out beside the walk."

"Let's go see," said Belle.

"Ok, come on."

Ellen cut off the vacuum and followed the girls out into the yard. Ellen was very proud of her intelligent daughter and her feminine niece. Although Barbara and Belle are very sensible, Jane was more practical even though she was somewhat spoiled. Ellen loved them all very much. Unknown to Barbara, Belle, or Jane, April had had another child. A son who would be 21 if he had lived.

Outside, Barbara went exactly to the place. Then she gasped,

23

The woman's footprints were gone!

What was going to happen next?

I wasn't sure but I sure was proud of my characters. They were turning out just like I wanted them to.

Barbara, the beautiful clever amateur detective, Belle, her orphaned cousin who looked up to her, and Jane, the annoying cousin who was sure to get some lessons from Barbara. Plus I had made Barbara's father a private detective. I figured that was indeed clever. He could be gone without explanation, working on a case. I knew Nancy Drew's father was a lawyer, always around, dabbling in her cases, and I didn't want to copy that.

Belle was a character who would frequently have hysteria, always need attention, thrown into Barbara's family by fate. I used Jane as a name because I did not like the girl characters that had a boy's name, I did not think girls should have boy's names. Boys should have strong names like Victor, Christopher, or Clark. Jane was going to be unattractive, at least at first so her name would be plain. Most of my girl characters would have more beautiful names like Barbara, Caroline, Jacqueline...

"Victoria!"

"Yes, Daddy?" I sat up straight at once.

"Pay attention, the new President is speaking."

Lyndon was a strange name for a man, in my opinion. It sounded like a girl's name, almost more like a last name. It was a name I would not use for any character in my book unless I did use it as a last name.

He didn't talk long and it was soon back to the commentator who was talking about President Kennedy's brother Robert.

Robert. Now that is a beautiful name. I thought that was the best name I've ever heard for a man.

"It's a shame Bobby Kennedy can't just take over and become the president instead of old Johnson," Aunt Worthrose commented.

I agreed. He certainly was better looking.

"It wouldn't be right. He wasn't elected," said my father.

Aunt Worthrose stayed through lunch, saying Uncle Clyde could make himself a sandwich. They had closed his company also and

24

he was home, like me and Daddy.

"He won't starve if I'm not there to make lunch one day." She added, "Clyde said we should send the family of the police officer that was killed some money. What do you say, Vic?"

"They hardly mention him," said my mother resentfully. "He had a family, too."

"Ok," said my father.

"We should send President Kennedy's family some money, too," I said.

"No, honey, they don't need any money," said my mother. "They have plenty of money."

"It's a damn shame," said my father.

"I know," said my mother. She was crying just a little. "Right here in America, after he had traveled all over the world, even to Germany, Africa, to be killed right here in America. It is a damn shame."

"At least it was not here in our city or our state," said my father.

"Thank the Lord for that," said Aunt Worthrose. "Dallas and Texas will be tainted forever. This is America. Things like this don't happen in America."

"I'm tired of reading," I said. "I want to play fashion dolls."

I was getting bored too.

The TV was repeating a lot. They were talking more and more about Lee Harvey Oswald and showing him on TV.

He was quite uninteresting.

I wasn't in the mood to write now. I wanted to resume playing. All this week my dolls were having a beauty contest and it was not finished.

But my father wanted me to watch it all.

So after lunch I received rare permission to bring toys into the den. I spread my dolls out on the couch, my black haired ponytail, Barbara, always won, of course. She beat brunette Midge, blond Midge and the blond bubble every time. I wanted a blond ponytail but with those four female dolls, the boyfriend doll and the rest of the family, my parents were resisting.

Baby dolls were populating my room in ever increasing numbers. They were just in the way as far as I was concerned.

Whenever I got the chance I dumped them in the bottom of my closet.

I still treasured my paper dolls but they were put away in my drawer.

Barbie was the only doll for me.

Barbara, the black haired ponytail had been with me since Christmas 1961, a supposed gift from Uncle Clyde although I did not remember him giving it to me.

At first, I put her away as a curiosity, still preferring paper dolls that had lots of clothes. But it wasn't until I looked at the booklet advertising clothes available that I realized her potential.

I had wanted all those beautiful clothes.

I had gotten several outfits including **Enchanted Evening** and **Theatre Date** with the doll. But the real prize, **Wedding Day Set**, was my one desire.

Knowing that Mama somehow sort of disapproved, I figured cultivating my relationship with Aunt Worthrose was a good plan for getting it.

It was hard to remember that she had not been an everyday part of my life until after the tragedy in 1962.

II *Recollections*

We had not always lived in the new brick house, next house closest to Aunt Worthrose. We had lived in a city neighborhood when I was younger, in a white wood house like the old houses near us now. My first memories were at that house, which now seemed like another world.

During that time we often went all the way across town to visit Rosalind Renee's grave, then to visit my grandmother who lived in a big brick house with beautiful furniture and golden curtains, along with her daughter, Aunt Florrie, who had been left by her husband because she was off (so said everybody), and Aunt Florrie's son, Christian, who was 15 years older than me.

I was always given a new book to read so I would sit still and be quiet. There were many, many rules to follow at their house. I could not play or touch anything. I could not mention anything about Aunt Florrie's problems, her divorce, or Christian's father, who had been killed in Korea. Above all I could not tell that we also went to see his second wife, a person I knew as Aunt Jolene. It was a secret. I could not tell that I played with his daughter Eva, who was my age, and his son, Victor, three years older, who was my father's godson.

I was proud that I knew secrets and that I could keep them.

They are Christian's half brother and sister but Christian does not know them. He never sees his brother and sister. I know his brother and sister but he does not.

I smiled with satisfaction when I thought about that.

I could not say anything at all without trouble, really, when I was at Grandmamás house. I could not touch anything or make a move without asking first. Yet I was always excited to go to Grandmamás house for the trip was an adventure. Traveling there was like going through another world. We had a bright blue and white 1956 Chevrolet with the dark blue interior. I had just recently gotten too big to sit in my father's lap while he drove, so now I occupied the spacious back seat. We went through downtown where there were very tall buildings and strange looking people. Daddy knew different ways to go and he delighted in trying new routes every time.

27

Once, on the way, we went through a very dirty neighborhood with old houses that all looked alike and were very small and close together. Other larger buildings on the way looked like they were going to fall down. Except a larger brick building with stained glass windows. The church was the only nice looking thing about this neighborhood.

"I thought I'd show Victoria where we had our store," said my father. I knew my father and late Uncle Chris Romano had owned a hardware store together before he left Aunt Florrie. Then my parents had worked in the store alone. But after I was born they closed it and Daddy went to work on airplane engines so Mama could stay at home with me.

"This neighborhood has gotten nothing but worse," said my mother. It was hot and we had the windows open. I was in the back seat on my knees looking out the window enjoying the air blowing in my face.

There were no people on the street but one little girl. She stood alone, barefooted in a simple dress that hung from thin shoulders. Her hair was sparse but stuck out in spots, accented by a single bow. I recognized what she was from television.

"Look!" I yelled as the wind was loud. "There's a ni-."

My father glanced back at me in alarm. My mother reached over the seat and pulled me away from the window before the second syllable sounded. "Don't say that! Don't call them that!"

"Why?" I was puzzled. I thought that was correct.

"Where did you hear that word?"

I tried to remember. I couldn't. I didn't know.

"Probably from your relatives," said Daddy.

"Don't start about my relatives," said Mama. "Yours aren't any better."

"Victoria, don't ever say that word, it hurts their feelings," said Daddy.

"Oh, well, what do I call them?" I was still puzzled.

"Negroes," my father said.

"Or colored people," said my mother. "That is a bad word meant to insult them."

Oh, Ok I can see that. If Negro was the correct word, the other was a corruption of the name. It was wrong, it wasn't the right word. I felt just the same about the name Vickie. It was Ok for people actually named Vickie, or wanted to be called that, but my name was Victoria and I felt very insulted whenever people got my name wrong.

"There are names just like that for Italians," my father said. "Wop and dago, guinea."

This was more confusing. Words fascinated me. I had my own dictionary and I sometimes read it like a book. How were those words related to the word Italian? I asked as much.

My parents seemed at a loss for an answer but finally my mother said, "Well I heard someone say that Italians in a bunch move and sound like a flock of guineas. But I don't know about the others."

"Very funny," said my father.

"Just what I heard," said my mother, with an innocent voice. She giggled a little. Then after a moment they looked at each other and both laughed. We had arrived.

"Victoria, don't say anything about our conversation, don't talk about anybody," warned my father, as usual.

"And don't touch anything," my mother said. "Just read quietly."

We got out of the car and went inside. The house was cool and dark but to avoid touching any of Grandmamás valuable objects we spent our entire visit in her screened in porch with no airconditioning. I read while the grownups talked, trying to ignore the discomfort. The visit didn't last long, they never did. Christian would come in and speak, then go to his room. Daddy would talk awhile, Grandmamá would talk some, Mama would watch me, then Aunt Florrie would come in and Daddy would abruptly get up and say he had to go and we would leave. This visit was no exception.

On the rare occasions that Grandmamá came to our little house, such as my birthdays in Februarys, Christian and Aunt Florrie were always with her. I liked Grandmamá. I didn't much like Aunt Florrie, who always wanted to hug and kiss me too much, but I loved my cousin Christian. He was very dark and handsome. He made the birthday parties more fun. So I had been thrilled one summer evening when my mother told me Grandmamá was coming for a rare summer's eve visit to our house. We would be opening up the big living room so that the single airconditioning in my bedroom could cool the whole house.

"Your Aunt Florrie and Christian are not coming tonight. Your grandmother is being driven over with some friends. They are staying with her while they visit from New York."

I expressed my disappointment that I would not get to see Christian.

"While Christian is not coming, there is going to be somebody with her that might interest you," my mother told me. "This couple staying with your grandmother also brought their daughter. Her name is Alexandria. She's 22 or 23 years old."

"She's grown," I said, not very interested.

"Alexandria is an only child like you, I haven't seen her yet but they say Alexandria is very beautiful, exceptionally beautiful. Beautiful like a movie star. And her parents are rich."

This perked up my interest slightly. The criteria for beautiful was very strict in 1962. Not very many people qualified, although I was only five years old I already knew that. My mother had been very beautiful and blond when she was young, but there were not very many beautiful women around.

My mother's words did not prepare me for the sight of Alexandria when she arrived at our small house. Daddy had placed all our chairs in the living room in a semi-circle and the visiting grownups in them faced me while I sat on the ground. Daddy sat on the couch behind me and Mama perched on the arm of the couch next to him.

Alexandria was in the center of the semi-circle, and in the only armchair. Grandmamá was on one side of her, balancing her short plump body in a dinette chair, and Alexandria's parents, larger old looking people, were on the other side of her. She was dressed for the evening in a short poufy strapless semi-formal light colored taffeta dress with a darker satin belt at the center. She had jewelry at her breasts and jewelry around her neck and around her wrists, and glittering rings on her fingers. Fur around her shoulders. Delicate stiletto heels and hose encased toes peeking through. She had beautiful long hair, not dark brown like mine, but a lighter exquisite color that was almost reddish but not quite. It was dialed in a swirl in the front with long curls pinned in the back. She had perfectly white skin with expressive, large dark eyes, copper colored shadow, long lashes and dark brows, and bright red lipstick framing beautiful white teeth. She was animated and expressive and she laughed a lot. All she lacked was the tiara crown. She was a princess come to life.

I totally ignored my grandmother after brushing off her welcoming kiss. I barely glanced at Alexandria's father just noting that he was old. I did note her mother, whom my grandmother called Alma, was a tall chunky woman with lots of big chunky jewelry. And like my mother she wore glasses. She did have on a matching jacket and shirt which I somehow knew was expensive. Alexandria was friendly to all, the center of it all, and during the course of the conversation would occasionally give a friendly word or gesture to the little girl sitting at her feet.

They didn't stay long. Daddy tried to talk them into staying longer, he offered them food and drink. But they declined. I knew he didn't like that.

"Oh, we've got other plans, we've got to get back across town. We're going out to dinner." My grandmother addressed her words to my father.

So in what seemed like an instant, they all said goodbye, Alexandria and her parents, how happy they were to have met us, and to have seen my father again. How they wished they had more time in the city that we could all get together for a longer visit. But they were due to go back to New York in a few days, and Alexandria's schedule was all full.

"She's here to find a husband," said my father, when they had left.

"And what's wrong with that?" my mother said. "She'll be a beautiful bride." And in my imagination I could see Alexandria in a beautiful bride dress with the tiara embedded in her hair amidst a long flowing veil.

I had been to a wedding when I was a real little girl and try as I might I only had two brief memories of it, one of a long line of people dressed in beautiful clothes that I was carried along and introduced to each one. I had to shake hands with all the men and let all the women kiss me if they wanted to. I didn't like the kisses. Some of the women shook my hand instead, that was delightful if they had on gloves. The other memory was of the bride, the wide skirt of her long immaculate white dress, the glitter on the bodice and sleeve, her pure white gloves and the tiara in her veil. It was a brief but exciting memory of a touch of magic. I tried to recall more but I could not. But now I pictured Alexandria as that bride and her lovely face behind the veil made the memory complete, if somewhat imaginary. She would be a beautiful bride.

"That girl is 22, looks like that, and not married yet? They're banking on a catch, looking to set her up with some money. Well, the old lady will fix her up if she can," said my father, "like she tried to fix me up."

"Don't refer to your mother that way in front of Victoria!" My mother spoke sharply.

My father looked at me and grinned sheepishly. I knew he had forgotten I was there. He came towards me and laughed. "You'll find out."

"Vic!" My mother's usually soft voice cracked like a whip. "Victor Christopher! Vittorio!"

"Ok. Ok. Time for bed." He picked me up and swung me up high, that didn't happen too much anymore seeing as his back hurt a lot. My hair flying, I squealed with delight.

"I've got to go to work in the morning. This is all the high society I could stand for one night anyway."

"Watch your back," said my mother, glaring at him.

He dumped me on my bed with a bounce. My mother followed and shoed him out of the room. Each night, when I went to bed, my mother took my long hair and curled it into a bun and pinned it at the back of my neck, so it would not bother me while I slept. I had to sit still for this. After our visitors left, I was put into my pajamas and I was struggling to sit still on my bed as my mother put my hair in the bun. I could see myself in my dresser mirror and Mama as well as she worked with the bobby pins.

My mother took great satisfaction in my long hair as most of the women in her family had been able to grow long straight hair. But her own hair was thin and wispy, slightly wavy, and never grew very long.

"Victoria, even though your hair is dark brown it's just as

32

beautiful as Alexandria's, long and silky. I wish I had hair like that," my mother commented as I watched us in the mirror. I was looking right at my own face, studying my dark brown eyes, sparse but even brown eyebrows, seeing Mama in my side vision when the phone rang. She kept one hand on the bun and expertly reached and grabbed the big black phone receiver without dropping a pin.

"Hello," she said, then she held the phone receiver slightly away from her ear. To my astonishment, she dropped her other hand and let my hair fall. She had never let a bun fall on purpose before. I quickly reached up to try to hold it, pushing bobby pins into my scalp, still watching in the mirror as I heard her call my father and he came into the room. Something was wrong and I stopped being sleepy and started being excited. My mother talked to my father only a minute and he left the room. She hung up the phone.

"You have to get dressed," said my mother, her voice becoming sharp again. "We have to go somewhere."

"I don't have to go to bed?" I said, elated, but hardly able to believe it. Bedtime was absolute in my house.

"No, we're not going to bed," said my mother, apprehensively. As she removed the pens and threshed out my hair, her hands trembled.

"There's been an accident. We have to go to the hospital," she said.

Daddy took the phone to the other room and was dialing it.

"Your grandmother, Alexandria and her parents," said my mother. "They had been going out to eat and there was a car wreck."

"Florrie and Christian were in it too," said my father, still on the phone. "I'm talking to Vince now. It was right in front of the house. Chris saw it, they're on their way. Let's go."

My father had the car out of the garage in just a moment, we left the garage doors open in our haste. Instead of the back seat, I sat in Mama's lap and she held me in her arms as we picked up speed.

"After they left our house, they went by my mama's house and picked up Florrie and Christian." Daddy related what his brother Vince had told him. "They left to go out to eat, but my mama forgot the money, and they were going back to get it. And when they turned left to go into the driveway they were hit. Chris happened to be there, he was standing in the yard and he saw it all. Vince said the driver was drunk.

33

A teenage girl ran her car up into the yard and barely missed hitting Chris too."

"What about Christian?" I asked.

"Was Christian driving?" asked my mother.

"I don't know. He was up walking around, Vince said, and so was Florrie. Mama was thrown from the car."

"Alexandria was in the middle of the front seat?" asked my mother, somewhat hopefully I thought.

"No, doesn't sound like it. I think her mother was in the front seat in the middle. Christian has a license. He's old enough to drive."

My mother gripped me very tightly, so much so that I squawked. She loosened up a little but not much until we got to the hospital. We ran across a parking lot to the Emergency, my parents sort of bouncing me along between them. Through automatically opening double doors, we swept into a small room that had a few people standing around doing nothing and a uniformed nurse behind a counter. We stopped short, uncertain we were in the right place.

"Where are the people hurt in the car wreck on Universal Dr.? Some of the people in the car are family members," my father told the crisply uniformed nurse. She was dressed just like nurses in the movies.

She looked up at him with an expression that somehow betrayed indifference and surprise at the same time.

"They haven't gotten here yet," she said, sounding like she did not know what to do about this turn of events. "You've beaten the ambulance here. They are on their way."

My father looked confused as he stepped back from the counter but in only a few moments we heard the siren of the ambulance and ran back outside the double doors into the darker parking lot. We stood just outside the emergency entrance doors and saw the ambulances arrive and began to unload the victims. And at almost the same moment Uncle Vince came up behind us.

"Our mama was thrown out of the car, she hit the fencepost," said Uncle Vince. He was crying.

Just then several people ran from different exits of the hospital in panicked to the first ambulance. The drivers jumped out and the back doors flew open. A stretcher came out and we followed it through the double doors, passing the counter, into a big hallway where more

34

people were hurrying back and forth. Then we turned around and saw a second stretcher behind us. The men carrying that stretcher came in running and we had to stand back and let the stretcher pass. The second ambulance was behind the first and there were so many people by this time, we were pushed back by the surge of people and got slightly lost in the crowd. We got separated from Uncle Vince. Somewhere, flashbulbs were going off with a loud POP! My father inquired of another uniformed nurse about his mother and was directed down another hallway to a row of gurneys. By this time we were behind so many people I could not see anything but the legs of the people in front of me.

"Lift me up, Daddy!" I begged, "I wanna see!" as I often had at a parade, or show or even on just a clear day. "I can't see!"

I was too big for Mama to carry and Daddy had his bad back. Usually the only time I got a lift anymore was at a parade where there was a fence or post to prop me against. With all these tall people in front of me, I became very afraid I would miss everything.

But this time Daddy picked me up and let me see.

On a gurney parked between other empty gurneys, was my grandmother. She was not crying, but rather writhing, not an inch of her still. She was strapped down. The black straps blended with her perennial black dress, which she had worn since my grandfather died before I was born. I knew she did not know anyone was there or she would have not been writhing like a snake. She would have been attempting to control herself. There was no one attending her, no one near the gurney. Everyone had rushed off again.

Suddenly there was a bustle of excitement in the hallway and we all had to move again. The crowd opened out a pathway without being directed as if a person of royalty was coming through. People dressed in white uniforms, with caps on their heads, were quickly pushing a gurney passed us. Now on my father's shoulders, I had time to take a good long look as they went by.

"It's Alexandria," my mother whispered, but I heard her. And indeed it was. They rushed her right in front of us, no longer running but walking very rapidly. I got a good look at her face. Her lovely hair was gone and white bandages were wrapped around her head covering the top completely. She was covered to the neck by the sheet, positioned slightly on her side towards us so that her beautiful features were completely visible as she went by. Her eyes were closed. Her eye makeup was still intact. She was just as beautiful as she had been hours before when she had been in our house, except her hair was gone. I knew there was no way it could have stayed under those bandages. They must have cut it off. She did not look distressed or in pain, as my grandmother did, and even as she was enduring a bumpy hectic ride through the hallway, she did not move at all. The expression on her face was peaceful and there was even a hint of a slight smile. I was amazed at the contrast between her and my grandmother.

The gurney disappeared through another set of big doors and my father put me down.

I pulled on my mother's skirt and expressed my distress that Alexandria had lost her hair.

"They're taking her to surgery, because her head got hurt in the wreck," said my mother, bending down so I could hear her. "Her hair will grow back when she gets well."

The hospital people then turned their attention to my grandmother and took her much more slowly into another room. Daddy picked me up again and I snuggled my head on his shoulder and closed my eyes for a minute.

The next thing I remembered, I woke up in a strange house with a vaguely familiar woman, standing over me.

"You remember me, I'm your Aunt Worthrose."

"There was a bad car wreck," I started to explain. I figured I must have fallen asleep at the hospital after seeing my grandmother and Alexandria.

"You're going to stay with me. Your grandmother needs people to stay with her at the hospital until she gets better," my aunt said without emotion. "Your father's gone to work, though your mother is still at the hospital with his family."

Aunt Worthrose was unlike anyone I had ever dealt with at that point in my life. She did not carry on about how cute and wonderful I was. When she told me to do something, somehow I knew I needed to do what she said or there could be bad consequences. But interestingly enough, most of the time what she told me to do made perfect sense. Very late that night, but before Uncle Clyde got home from working as a watch guard, Mama came and got me, but very early the next morning took me back to Aunt Worthrose.

I spent another day with Aunt Worthrose and we talked together like grownups, like no one else had ever talked to me except Mama and Daddy, of course. And, unlike them, she also left me alone for long periods of time. That was strange and wonderful. She gave me colors and paper to draw on. Mama did not come back that night but early the next morning she was there.

"Your grandmother died," she said. "You have to stay with Aunt Worthrose one more day. Until after the funeral. I'm sorry, Worthrose."

"It's all right. What about the girl?" my aunt softly said to my mother, taking her by the arm and leading her away from me.

"She never woke up," whispered my mother, beginning to cry.

My aunt put her arms around my mother.

"What happened, June Rosette?"

"The car hit broadside on the passenger side towards the front. Alexandria was sitting in the front passenger seat. She took the brunt of the crash. The old lady thrown into the fencepost in the yard.

"I don't know why it took so long for the ambulance to get there, we got to the hospital before they even arrived and we were farther away."

"Ambulances don't rush to that part of town, even the higher class part," murmured my aunt.

"Afterwards at the hospital, the mother was sitting alone. After they had all been brought in and were being worked on. Florrie and Christian were being treated in emergency rooms. They took her husband back for x-rays. Vince and Chris were with the old lady. Vic had left to bring Victoria here, she had fallen asleep. It was way past her bedtime. I was too nervous to drive." My mother paused guiltily glancing at me. Then she resumed.

"They had taken Alexandria into surgery. So I was the one that stayed with Alma in the waiting room while they were operating on Alexandria. I had just met her earlier that day, but there I was, holding her hand while her daughter was having brain surgery. Telling her don't give up hope."

My mother paused again and took a breath.

"But she didn't have any hope. 'My baby is dead,' Alma

repeated over and over to me no matter what I did, 'I saw. My baby's dead. Oh no, oh no, my baby is dead.'

"And she was dead." My mother sobbed on my aunt's shoulder.

My aunt guided my mother to the sofa, still holding her as they sat down. "You did the best you could, June Rosette. You prayed with her?"

My mother took another deep breath, trying to control herself.

"I tried, you know the Catholics only know the **Our Father** and the **Hail Mary**, but I tried. I prayed them."

My mother was sobbing again and my aunt was holding her tightly. When my mother cried and talked at the same time her voice became very high pitched.

"And then, Worthrose, she told me what it was like and it was just like I had been in the car with them.

" 'I was looking the other way,' Alma said, 'I had just looked down that road and seen nothing, But a sound like the wind made me turn and I saw the car hit at the same time I heard the awful sound of metal contacting metal.' "

Suddenly I could see it too, just like a movie.

In the review mirror, I saw for an instant Florrie, Grandmamá and Christian's faces of fear and trapped desperation. Then, just the second before the full impact, I somehow saw Alexandria's face reflected for a moment in the transposition of the highlights, the side mirror and the window glass, her expression of shock and surprise. Alexandria's face still so beautiful, and then the glass flew in at them like shards of ice and the metal came in, broken and jagged like rocks, flying everywhere, yet not making a mark on Alexandria's lovely face, the bench seat buckling and metal slamming her from behind...

"And Alma said," my mother was continuing, " 'I was protected by the body of my child. I was protected by my child.' "

"Now, June Rosette," said Aunt Worthrose, "think of all the pain and suffering in life that girl was spared."

"Chris, he saw it all," my mother sobbed some more. "He's just a boy, so young to see all that- his mother-"

"He's a grown man, married with babies. He'll cope. He'll get over it. Our mother died, we got over it."

"Not like that! We didn't have to see her killed like that!" my mother cried harder.

"And they told us at the hospital she would be all right. They didn't even have a nurse stay with her. We had to furnish somebody to stay with her." My mother scaled back her sobs and spoke angrily. "They asked me but Vic had to go back to work and I said I had to get Victoria. I told Vic she was going to die. I didn't want to stay with her because I knew she was going to die. We saw people in the countryside, when our mother nursed them during the Spanish Flu, shake and sweat like that and they always died. But the hospital said-" here my mother's voice became mocking, " 'no, she just needs rest. She just had a shock and has broken ribs.' So Chris stayed with her. He was with her when she died."

My aunt was silent, then she said, "well, her suffering is over. All the hard times in life behind her."

"And that beautiful girl, she never knew what hit her. I think she was dead from the beginning. I think her mother was right." My mother gulped for air. "We saw her just as they were bringing her into surgery and she was already white. How can a mother live with that? I had my baby two days. During those days I never dreamed my baby would die. To have a daughter 22 years, then taken away like that. It would be unbearable."

"Well, nothing like that is going to happen to Victoria," my aunt reassured my mother. "Now you see just how precious she is."

My mother rose defensively. "I know, I know. She's just so much like them. And I need you to keep her for now. I know. It's hard." My mother wiped away her tears, looked at my aunt and rolled her eyes slightly.

"She can't help that." I wasn't quite sure why the conversation was turning to me as a subject but it made me feel good and quite important.

"I know, I know. Victoria is mine. Nobody is ever going to take her away from me. I love her more than anything in this world." My mother clenched her jaw together when she said that.

"You just remember that. Think about that poor dead girl. All the years she had before her. But remember, June Rosette, all the heartache of this world, she'll never know any more unhappiness and sorrow. Who knows what lay ahead of her if she had lived? Maybe nothing but pain. It's those left behind who are to be pitied."

"I know. If I were her mother I'd just kill myself."

"No, you wouldn't. There's justice to be had. Did the police talk to Vic's brother? Will there be an investigation? What are they going to do about the funeral?"

"They are taking her body back to New York to bury her. No one is going to investigate. Chris said the driver was speeding. She never slowed down. But who is going to believe him?" Giving the details of the wreck itself seemed to calm my mother down and my aunt relaxed her grip on her.

"Drunk?"

"Yeah, that's what we think. She wasn't even hurt, the bitch." My ears perked up, that was a bad word but I was not sure of its exact meaning.

My mother stood up.

"They should put her in jail."

My mother laughed bitterly. "They won't. She's the teenage daughter of a politician. She had a license. There's no proof she was drunk. Alexandria and the old lady were just dagoes, after all. They won't do anything." They were no longer whispering and I knew Daddy would be mad if he heard that word. But I wasn't going to tell.

So I spent the day of my grandmother's funeral with Aunt Worthrose. I knew that my grandmother had been my last grandparent alive and I should be sad. But I was sadder about Alexandria. She had been beautiful and she had never gotten to be a bride. However this was my first opportunity to see much of Aunt Worthrose's house. As much as she would let me, I began exploring.

She had a small house with a large colorful garden. The house didn't have central heating and air. It had a bigger kitchen with the table and chairs actually in the kitchen, a formal dining room, living room, and two bedrooms and two bathrooms, one each for her and for Uncle Clyde, who worked for the oil company as a watchman. Uncle Clyde only lived in the house, it had belonged only to her.

She still had all her furniture from the 1920s, making it much more interesting than ours. The dining room table was beautiful like Grandmamás furniture but it was older and darker. She had a big credenza that matched her dining room set. I loved the plastic jewel handles on the credenza. I asked if I could take them off and play with them.

"Certainly not. That furniture came from California," she said. "When I was young I bought it from some people who bought it from the man that killed the Lindbergh baby. So it's really valuable."

"Who was the Lindbergh baby?" I failed to see how a dead baby could make furniture valuable.

"I forget how many years have passed," said my aunt. "You don't know. Well, it was the child of Charles Lindbergh, a famous airplane pilot, the man who first flew an airplane across the Atlantic Ocean. His baby was kidnapped and killed by a German in the 1930s. It was the most famous crime ever. I've got a news clipping about it somewhere."

"Why would anyone take a baby?" I didn't see where a baby would be much use, it couldn't do any work. "Did Daddy ever work on Lindbergh's plane?"

"To get money for its safe return, but they killed it instead. No, that was too long ago, your father was just a child then. He didn't grow up to work on airplane engines until World War II. Oh, here it is."

Aunt Worthrose showed me a news photo of a chubby blond little boy.

"Why did they kill it?" I studied the photo with interest.

"I guess they were afraid they would be caught with it and executed. They executed the German killer for it anyway and since then a lot of children have been kidnapped for money ransom because it gave the criminals the idea. They talked about it too much all over the country."

"Did they have another baby?" I asked, thinking of Rosalind Renee and how my mother never had another baby.

"Oh, yes, they had several. Mrs. Lindbergh was young."

So my grandmother and Alexandria were in heaven with Rosalind Renee and the Lindbergh baby.

Mama and Daddy had told me Rosalind Renee was in heaven even though she didn't get a chance to be baptized because nobody knew she was going to die. I had been baptized as a baby in case I died unexpectedly, too.

"Rosalind Renee had been born but had died with her whole life before her," I told Aunt Worthrose.

"Yes, that's right. Life's miseries were spared her. She's in a better place."

"So while she lived, and is now in Heaven, she is not here with us, her family, because she had died," I explained further to Aunt Worthrose.

"That's a very good way to see it," said Aunt Worthrose.

I knew from Rosalind Renee that death did not only mean the dead person went to heaven but that they did not get to finish their life on earth if they died young. *People who die too young or from an accident or war or otherwise unexpectedly die with at least part of their lives before them, so when they should have been living their lives on earth, they are gone. They couldn't be here.* All of that was harder to explain so I just thought about it.

"My grandmother died," I told Aunt Worthrose's husband, Uncle Clyde when he came home from work. "She will not be back again."

Uncle Clyde never said much, he patted me on the head and went to his bedroom.

"You still got me," Aunt Worthrose said, as though that should be a source of great comfort.

"You could get killed in a car wreck too," I said matter-of-factly.

"Victoria Irene, I will not ever be killed on car wreck," she said, very confidently. "I can't even drive a car. I don't have a license. I don't ever go anywhere unless I am forced to."

I had accepted this as fact and went back to drawing pictures. I was feeling disappointed I wasn't going to get to go to Grandmamá's funeral. I had felt it would be interesting.

"Victoria Irene, are you listening to this? Or are you daydreaming? I want you to listen to this, this is history!" My father's voice blared at me, knocking me back to 1963. I straightened up guiltily. The TV was rolling and playing static while it was switching from one man to another again. What was going on? Oh yes, President Kennedy had been killed and now they were talking about his killer.

"...*More about Lee Harvey Oswald, Communist literature was found in his house...Oswald lived in an addition on the outskirts of the city...*"

"Oswald lived in an addition," I announced to show I was paying attention. Most of the kids who went to Fairvine lived in two additions near the school. Fairland Addition had smaller houses, Water Oaks had bigger houses. The houses in the Fairland Addition were only a little smaller than our house, Water Oaks houses were bigger. Fairland Addition houses had attached garages in the front. Our house had the attached garage on the side so the front of our house was not messed up by the garage doors (so said Daddy, who hated garage doors in the front). And our house was all brick whereas most of the Fairland houses had some brick on them, but they weren't all brick like ours and a lot of them were much farther away from the school. Water Oaks was even farther away. Even though across the main road, the shiny new school with the bare walls was built so close to us that I was not allowed to ride the bus.

"I think he just rented a house," said my mother. "He wasn't a homeowner."

"People rent houses in Fairland Addition," I said, thinking of at least one classmate who was a renter. His parents were also divorced. The rest of the class knew that was very strange and regarded him with sympathy and curiosity at the same time. He didn't talk much.

"Not very many in Fairland Addition," said my mother. "And I'm sure hardly any in Water Oaks. They are all white collar workers."

"Any airplane pilots?" I asked, remembering all about the events of the Lindbergh kidnapping. I had found out more about Colonel Lindbergh since Aunt Worthrose had told me after my grandmother's death. There was a book about him in the library at school. It was mostly pictures showing how strangely he dressed. I believed airplane pilots wore white shirts, even if their coats were blue that still would make them white collar workers.

"Yes, there is a pilot living in Water Oaks," said my mother. "Two, I think or one might just work for the FAA."

I'll find out what that is later, I thought as I pushed my dolls aside. I started Chapter 3, keeping one ear tuned to the TV in case Daddy was inclined to focus on me again.

Chapter 3
Kidnapped!

"They're gone!" Barbara was so shocked all she could say was, "they're gone!"

"Hump," snorted Belle. "There never were any there!"

Ellen had already turned around and gone back to her vacuuming.

Unmindful of that Belle turned to go. Suddenly out of nowhere a hand clapped over her mouth dragging her into the bushes!

Barbara was still in a trance. "They are really gone! But I know some were there, I saw them. Footprints just don't disappear in thin air."

When she turned around Belle nor Ellen were there.

"Apparently they went inside to the house thinking I just imagined the footprints," she thought ruefully.

In fact she wasn't so sure she did see any footprints after all.

Then she went into the garage to take out the garbage.

As she entered in the kitchen she saw on envelope which she stuffed in her pocket.

"Where's Belle?" asked Ellen.

"I don't know. I thought she went with you after I

discovered the footprints were missing."

"No, she stayed with you when I went back to the kitchen."

"No, she couldn't have. When I turned around she was gone," insisted Barbara.

"Maybe she went for a walk," Ellen suggested. "But then she would have left a note."

Barbara suddenly remembered the envelope she had stuffed into her pocket. She got it out and said to Ellen, "This must be the note she left. It says-
DO NOT CALL POLICE
YOU WILL NEVER SEE
MARIA ISABELL AGAIN.
A   AND   S."

"Good God!" gasped Ellen. She was very pale.

"Kidnapped!"

"Barbara, we must contact your father at once."

"But, Mom, we have no idea where Dad is, much less how to contact him. Anyway," she added. "It was all probably one of Belle's pranks."

Barbara said that to reassure her mother but she herself didn't believe a word of it. Belle never played pranks.

Ellen sensed this and said quickly, "I'm going to call the police."

"But, Mom –"

"Barbara." Ellen's voice had a warning ring to it so Barbara said no more.

Ellen talked for 30 minutes to the policeman that Chief McBlend sent over.

The policeman then went to scout around.

Jane came over then and was shocked to find that Belle was missing. Her surprise was so genuine they were sure Jane had nothing to do with it.

"Oh I wish Dad was here," mourned Barbara.

Just then there was a knock at the door. Barbara

opened it to find 3 policemen there. One of them said, "We found your cousin's sweater on a back alley street!"

I put down my thick pencil. My hand hurt. I had written enough for one day.

"You do know you are letting her have not only all her papers, that book, but all those toys on the couch," my mother complained to my father.

"This is just for right now," said my father, still looking at the TV. "I want her to remember all this."

"I think that's enough for tonight," said my mother, and she turned the volume of the TV all the way down. "They are just going on and on and repeating everything. Nothing else will happen until tomorrow."

"Well, what are we going to do?" asked my father. "We certainly don't want to go driving and be away if something happens."

"We could play Monopoly," I suggested.

They looked at each other. So we did, until Mama got tired of it. I still wasn't sleepy so Daddy had a yawning contest with me. The object of that game was for me not to yawn no matter how many times Daddy did. I was pretty good at it. I could go for a long time. I sat on my hands and clenched my teeth while he yawned loudly. I was doing really good. He had yawned at least nine times before I lost the game. Both of us laughing, he scooped me up and carried me to bed.

I was up early November 24, 1963. We went to an earlier Mass than usual which was oddly full of people and shorter than usual because there was no music. As soon as we got back home, Daddy turned on the TV as Mama began making spaghetti. Mama bought her noodles but she made the sauce from scratch. We had spaghetti every Sunday but that was the only Italian food we ever ate because Daddy did not eat cheese.

I got back on the couch and started working.

"Pay attention. If you want to keep your dolls and writings in here, you have to pay attention," Daddy warned.

I put the book down for a moment.

"...*Here in Washington the body of President Kennedy will lie in state later …In Dallas, Lee Harvey Oswald is to be transported to a newer jail … we will have a live report..."*

"You've got it on a different station," I observed.

"Change it back," said my father.

My mother did so and my father said, "Watch, they are taking the President's body from the White House to the Capitol building."

A lot of soldiers were lined up on the television and in the midst of them was, at first it looked like a cannon, but then I saw it was just a wagon like a covered wagon with no cover and it only had two wagon wheels and a flat top with short sides and two other wagon wheels in front attached to it by a big stick.

What were they going to do with that? I wondered.

"They'll put the casket on the caisson there - see it-"

"Why?"

"So they don't have to carry it all the way."

"…in Washington there are skies bright and clear…"

It may have been clear there but the TV was very fuzzy and it was hard to see. When the picture rolled and went blank for a moment then I went back to my book. Daddy started towards the television set.

"Don't mess with the fine tuning," said my mother. "You'll make it worse."

"It's back," said my father. I glanced up, then away again. The picture had snapped back- only instead of the soldiers and horses, there was a crowd of people, with hats on, moving around rapidly. I continued with my writing.

"Switch to Dallas Texas...There is Lee Oswald- POP!-He's been SHOT, HE'S BEEN SHOT! Lee Oswald has been SHOT! There's the man with the gun... panic here...the assassin has been shot...by a man in a suit...deputies have called for a doctor... Oswald will be transported to a hospital...it is pandemonium-"

Somebody shot Lee Harvey Oswald. I wasn't paying attention so I missed it, at least the actual shot. I saw all the men scrambling. I heard the word pandemonium, I had just learned that word recently so I knew what it meant. I put everything aside and watched alertly. As much as these people repeated themselves they were bound to show it again. And they were going to! Just as it began- *POP!*-

Then another 'POP' with a slight sizzle at the end. Not the same

'POP' as the gun, for Daddy had jumped up and cut off the TV.

"Take Victoria in the other side," he directed. "She shouldn't see this."

Oh really! I was supposed to sit there and watch all these old men talk on and on but when something interesting happened I wasn't supposed to see it!

"I want to see it, I will miss seeing Caroline," I wailed as Aunt Worthrose dragged me away by the hand, down the hall. I really wanted to see the shooting but I thought complaining about not seeing Caroline would be more effective in getting this decision reversed.

"Turn the TV back on and cut the sound down," my father ordered my mother. And to me he called, "We'll let you come back when Caroline appears."

I was upset. I had left my book on the couch. Suppose they started reading it. "Don't mess with my stuff," I yelled as Aunt Worthrose shoved me in my room.

"We won't touch anything," said Aunt Worthrose, leaving me there. "Your dolls are safe. You can come back in just a few minutes." She shut the door. With no other kids around, it wasn't the dolls I was worried about.

What am I going to do? I was lost. There was nothing to do.

I opened my closet and looked at the creepy stupid looking baby dolls all stacked up in there. I shut that door. I pulled open the drawer of my desk that held my old paper dolls. I had two bride sets, one bride wore a bride dress tinged with pink, the other a bridal gown tinged with blue. They fascinated me, I knew both gowns were supposed to be white but the artists had to use some color in them because white on white paper would not show up. I handled them with care, they were getting so old. I had just picked up a bride when my mother came in.

"Come on back," she said. "The procession is starting."

Back in the den, I paid more attention, afraid I might miss something again. The whole thing had gotten more interesting.

"... Now the casket appears... John Fitzgerald Kennedy, 35th President of the United States..."

I could see Mrs. Kennedy with a long mantilla veil on, like the ones Mama and many other ladies wore to church, although not always black.

"The children are not wearing black," said Aunt Worthrose, mild surprise in her voice. I could not tell if she disapproved.

They obviously had on lighter colored clothing than all the adults around them.

"Why is John John wearing a dress?" I asked.

"That's the way little boys dress up," said my mother. "And it's not dress, it's a kind of a coat."

"The music is beautiful. What is it?" I was in awe. I didn't recall hearing such beautiful music before.

"Doesn't she know these songs?" asked Aunt Worthrose.

My mother shook her head and started to speak but Daddy motioned her to be quiet.

"...*Jackie will walk behind the casket to St. Matthew's Catholic Church ...*"

The reporters stopped talking for a while as the soldiers and horses walked with the president's coffin down the wide streets. Then the TV abruptly rolled again.

"Dammit," said my father.

We could still hear it, but the rolling went on and on.

"...*to report than Lee Harvey Oswald was himself shot ...*"

Daddy jumped up and changed the channel.

Jacqueline Kennedy and Caroline appeared on TV and knelt at the late President's casket.

I imagined the colors on the flag, the red, white, and blue like the flag in front of school. I watched Caroline Kennedy kneeling at her father's coffin, fascinated, I wondered what color her dress coat was.

"When she gets married, she won't have her daddy to give her away," I said.

"No, she won't," said my mother, tears in her eyes behind her glasses.

"Poor little thing," said Aunt Worthrose. I couldn't see any tears behind her glasses. Aunt Worthrose rarely shed tears. "Don't worry, Victoria, your father will be there to give you away when you get married." My father looked at her strangely but did not tell her to hush that time.

49

"…More about Lee Harvey Oswald…"

"We are missing the coverage in Washington so they can talk about him," said my father, exasperated. And he changed the channel again.

"It was assumed this would be the only major news event of the day but Oswald was shot and killed…"

My father changed the channel again.

"Everything happens for the best," said Aunt Worthrose.

"He died from it? Oh my God, they actually killed him too," said Mama. "What can that possibly mean?"

Nobody seemed to know.

"I don't understand," I said, feeling very grownup by joining in their confusion. My parents stayed silent but Mama did get up and clean house a little.

"They shouldn't talk about Oswald even if he is dead," said Aunt Worthrose. "He should be a pariah. They should never again mention his name."

Then Daddy attempted an explanation directed at me.

"Oswald killed Kennedy because he did not have as much money as President Kennedy and his wife was not as pretty as President Kennedy's wife," Daddy said. "And Oswald was a Communist, he liked the Russians and he killed a policeman. Another man killed Oswald because he had really loved President Kennedy and he admired policemen. That man was afraid if Oswald stood trial he would get off and get away with it."

"Jealousy," said Aunt Worthrose, rising, "is worse than anything in the world, even worse than hatred. This world is getting worse and worse. It won't be long now. The Lord will come soon. Well, I need to get on home and fix Clyde his supper. After a sandwich for lunch he'll have a conniption fit if I don't get supper on the table soon."

She went home, briskly walking in the November sunshine back to her house.

"It won't be long for what?" I asked, after she had gone.

"Never mind," said my mother.

"She thinks the world is going to end soon," said my father, smirking a little.

"Will you keep quiet?" said my mother, going into to the

kitchen to prepare our supper.

I hope the world doesn't end before I get my book finished. Make that my whole series of books.

I said a quick prayer to that effect. *There, that should do it,* I thought.

I knew I was supposed to pray for other people, but I couldn't help praying a little for myself also. I had heard in church that to be close to God you had to be poor, so I prayed that if that was true, I should be poor. However, if it was not true, if I could be close to God without being poor, I prayed not to be poor. But one prayer I really meant and sincerely hoped would be answered favorably, I repeated each time I remembered to pray.

Please God, don't let me have a boring life. Amen.

After supper, Aunt Worthrose came back with a thick black book in her hand. I looked at it curiously, I knew, like my parents, she did not normally read books for enjoyment. But I was again transfixed by the TV because this time they showed it all again with a lot less talking. We watched it all again like going to the movies and sitting through the movie twice, only without distraction the second time.

"This is part that we missed earlier," said my mother. Immediately after the casket arrived, Mrs. Kennedy was standing with both children, then only Caroline was visible.

We all paid rapt attention. Mrs. Kennedy was just about to turn, she waited for a wreath to be carried to the casket. President Johnson accompanied the wreath and bowed. Then he went back to stand with Mrs. Kennedy and Caroline. The TV showed a close up of Mrs. Kennedy.

"Jackie has on black gloves and Caroline white gloves," I said.

"John John has disappeared," said my mother.

"Probably got too much for that poor little boy," said Aunt Worthrose.

"Shush," said my father.

Mrs. Kennedy led Caroline by the hand as they left the assembly line and walked up to the casket, Mrs. Kennedy kissed the casket and Caroline put her hand under the flag and they knelt briefly and then walked back to stand with Robert Kennedy. The beautiful music began again.

"Victoria, here is the words to that music," said Aunt Worthrose.

"It is a song asking God to protect the men who risk their lives going out on the ocean to make their living or defend us in the Navy," said Mama.

She took out the book and I read the words as the music played.

...For those in peril on the sea...

"Tomorrow will be the President's funeral," said Mama. She rose and went to clean the kitchen. "Let's cut it off now."

"There will never be another time like this," said Aunt Worthrose. "We are entering the end times."

I looked forward to it with interest. *I wish I was older so I could remember President Kennedy better. In fact I wish I had been young like Mama and Daddy during World War II,* I thought.

Mama banged the dishes loudly. She did this whenever she did not like what was being said and/or wanted the TV silenced. Daddy cut the TV off. Aunt Worthrose departed again. I turned back to my book. Despite all the distraction of the TV happenings, Chapter 4 was done. I reviewed it for errors.

Chapter 4
The Knife – Stabbed

Jane suddenly burst into tears. "Oh," she sobbed. "Why Belle? Why couldn't it have been me?"

Ellen put forward a hand to comfort the crying girl.

Barbara was astonished. She had never before seen Jane cry!

When Jane looked up her face was very tear stained.

"I had better be going," she said. "Call me if you need me."

For the first time in her life Barbara did not want Jane to go. For once the two girls sought comfort in one another. Although they had been rivals to each other they both had loved each other and Belle dearly. Now they were to show their love for one another for the first time. It started when Barbara begged, "Jane, please stay. We need you."

"Well – well, I guess. I could stay if it is all right with you, Aunt Ellen."

"Oh yes, it's all right with me," said Ellen, who was somewhat shocked and pleasantly surprised with Barbara and Jane's attitude toward one another.

Jane called her mother, April, who not only said that Jane could stay but that she would come over herself. As she came in the door a knife whizzed past her tearing the flesh from her arm!

Perfect. This book is going great! Time for bed. I slept soundly that night.

I was up early Nov. 25, 1963, but not early enough to beat Mama and Daddy and Aunt Worthrose who were already back in place in the den in their chairs. I had cereal, then went and got my book and climbed up on the couch.

"*... continuing live coverage of the funeral of John F. Kennedy...*"

Mrs. Kennedy was leaving the White House to go to the capital to get her husband's body. She and the two brothers of the President came out of the White House. There was another motorcade. Down the broad street again with the Capitol in the background middle.

The commentator went silent as the widow and the president's brothers walked inside the Capitol and knelt at the coffin. I could barely see the tops of their heads beyond the backs of the soldiers that were directly in front of the cameras. I noticed one brother making the sign of the cross.

Then the family rose and backed away from the casket for quite a distance before turning and walking out beyond the huge huge columns and down the steps. The coffin appeared in the doorway. The band struck up.

"Is that song in your book?"

"No, that's just instrumental songs they play only when the president is in the room."

Then the music became softer. Aunt Worthrose started turning the pages of her book.

"Fairest Lord Jesus." My mother prompted her.

Fairest Lord Jesus!
Ruler of all nature!
O Thou of God and man the Son!
Thee will I cherish,
Thee will I honor,
Thou, my soul's glory, joy and crown.
Fairest Lord Jesus!
Ruler of all nations!
Fair is the sunshine,
Fairer still the moonlight,
And all the velvet starry night
Jesus shines brighter Jesus shines purer
Then all the angels in heaven's sight

"I'm surprised at all these good Protestant hymns for a Catholic funeral," said Aunt Worthrose.

"Just wait," said my mother. "There's going to be a Mass. You won't hear any good hymns then."

For a long time there were horses and soldiers, sailors, and the casket on its carriage, marching and rolling down long wide streets. Aunt Worthrose showed me more songs but they were songs about America and I knew them from school. But to my surprise I recognized one song I heard often on cartoons.

"That's a lament for the dead," she said. "It's hundreds of years old. I don't know if it has words, they don't sing them if it does."

Sometimes the music would stop and a solitary bell would toll, then the music would start over again. Always the drums beat on.

Finally they arrived. Then bag pipes started to play sounding different than all the music before.

Jacqueline Kennedy got out of the car and came into better view. Her long dark veil was capped by a black hat. Her black gloves made her arms extra long. She wore black hose that were barely transparent like the veil which barely showed her beautiful features in grief behind it.

"…Prominent among many foreign dignitaries is Charles de Gaulle, World War II hero, now leader of France…"

"Look, there's de Gaulle," my father said.

"Is that really him?" asked Aunt Worthrose, with admiration in her voice.

"It's him," said my mother. "He looks a lot older. Isn't he about the only one left except Eisenhower?"

"Hirohito is still on the throne in Japan," my father said. "You'd think the Japanese won the war."

I failed to see the attraction of this elderly tall man with a big nose. Heads of state did not look much different than other people except some wore war uniforms. *It is Jackie who looks different,* I thought. The bagpipes played again.

The casket arrived at the foot of the steps of the church. Caroline and John joined their mother. She held their hands and proceeded up the steps, into the church. This church did not have a plain wood altar with a simple curtain behind it like our church. It was a much larger church with columns and the altar was very large and had elaborate embroidered cloth and large candles. Another difference- there was an American Flag sort of behind the altar. There was no American flag in our church.

As the priest intoned on in the background another beautiful song began to play.

"What's that song? Find the words to that one, Aunt Worthrose, I cannot understand that man singing it."

"That's the **Ave Maria**," said my mother. "It's not in English, it's not in that book. It's a hymn to the Virgin Mary."

While the priests and singers were performing at the same time, the TV commentator occasionally explained the Mass in short bursts of English. There never was any such explanation at our church. We had to figure it out for ourselves.

Finally after much more ceremony that seemed to be just repeating stuff, they played a song we sang in our church, **Holy, Holy, Holy.**

"I know that one," I announced, when Aunt Worthrose pulled out the hymnbook. "And that one- it's- **Holy God We Praise Thy Name.**"

They were playing that song as they carried the body down the steps.

"I'm surprised," said Aunt Worthrose to my mother, who shrugged her shoulders.

Outside the church, the casket was loaded in the wagon again. John walked around to the front of his mother. Then she pulled him back. She bent over to him and he straightened up and saluted as the casket went by.

I believed it was almost over but no, there was another long march to the cemetery. During this they played the same songs over and over, **Onward Christian Solders, America the Beautiful,** the beautiful **Death March**. Daddy still wanted me to watch it. Fortunately I could watch and write at the same time.

"Look at that scenery," my father said. "Look at Arlington Cemetery. Don't you know it is beautiful in color. We ought to go visit there someday."

"Why does it look like that?" I was thinking of the cemetery where Rosalind Renee and my grandmother were buried. Because she was just a baby, Rosalind Renee only had a concrete stone on the ground with her name on it but my grandmother was buried with my grandfather beneath a life size statue of the Virgin Mary.

"That's a military cemetery and all the gravestones have to look alike, except for special officers and the Unknown Soldier," said my mother.

Then when they finally got to the cemetery they started playing **The Star Spangled Banner.**

"We have to stand up for that song." I said remembering music lessons in school.

Mama, Daddy and I stood up. Aunt Worthrose said she didn't have to because she was so old. I made a mental note to ask my music teacher about that.

Then there was another long ceremony. I went back to my book on the couch half listening as the priest talked in English on and on. I noted as I wrote when they said the **Our Father,** then later, the **Hail Mary**. Then later the **Our Father** again! I couldn't always understand the priest even though he was trying to speak English.

"What country is he from?" I asked.

"He's from New England," my mother said.

That was confusing. I could understand him when he said "In the name of the Father, Son and Holy Ghost" and made the Sign of the Cross, but other times his words were just a blur. Finally he spoke clearly again a nice prayer they had repeated several times.

I am the Resurrection and the Life.
He that believeth in Me, though he were dead, yet shall he live;
And whosoever liveth and believeth in Me shall never die.

Then a soldier was playing a bugle.

"That is **Taps**- what they play when a soldier dies," said my father.

"Do all soldiers get a military funeral like this?" I was inadvertently thinking about Daddy and Uncle Drake, plus Uncle Chris Romano who was already dead.

Eva Romano won't have her father to give her away when she marries, I thought suddenly. That had never occurred to me before.

"No, not usually unless they are killed in the war or have a high rank. Your late Uncle Chris Romano had an all out tribute, he died in the service of his country even though it was Korea, not the World War," said Daddy.

"But no matter when or how they die, they all get a flag," my mother said.

Mrs. Kennedy had the flag under her arm and she approached a soldier and beyond him we could see her bend over and light the eternal flame. The commentator was talking again about how wonderful she was because she did not have hysteria. I thought she looked fascinating in her dress with the long black veil. All widows should dress like that at funerals. I expected she would always wear black just like my grandmother had.

She took Robert Kennedy's arm and walked away. President Kennedy's funeral was over. The children were not there, I realized for the first time. Apparently they had not come to the cemetery. If I were Caroline I would really be mad about having to miss that. I hoped she was getting to see it on TV like me.

"Thanks for letting me watch this with you all," said Aunt Worthrose. "I'm going on home now. I've had enough. The poor man is dead, nobody can help him now. Lord, help us all."

I wondered why Aunt Worthrose thanked us for letting her be with us as she had an open invitation to walk down the road to our house at any time. And most every afternoon after school I could look out the front living room window and see her tall thin form striding toward our house.

We might never have lived next door to her if my grandmother had not been killed and left Daddy out of the will. That thought just popped into my mind somehow. Maybe I had heard that said before.

What a stranger Aunt Worthrose had been then, now she was a daily part of my life. And now getting to watch President Kennedy's funeral on TV almost made up for not going to my grandmother's funeral.

I summed it all up in my mind. *John F Kennedy, who had been President of the United States, had died with a lot of his life before him* (the adults were all saying). *He should have lived to see his children grow up. Alexandria, a stranger to me whom I had seen only one day, had had most of her life before her. Rosalind Renee who would have been my sister had died with all her life before her. Uncle Chris Romano had died for his country* (inexplicably this seemed more acceptable to the adults than the others).

My grandmother had been much older than all of them, but she had died with some of her life before her also. She might have lived to see me grow up and be a writer.

I had not yet started school and begun to write when she died. Now I had just completed Chapter 5 of my first book. It was sad that people died but I felt proud and happy about my book.

Chapter 5
Stiff Jones

Although the knife just grazed her, the impact of the knife and the realization of what had hit her made April faint, about the same time as Jane did.

When Jane fainted Ellen screamed as loud as she could. Only Barbara kept her senses. First she applied first aid to April's arm, then she called the ambulance and Ellen's doctor, Dr. Andistone.

Then she slapped her mother who was still in the hysterical stage. Then she tried to revive Jane. This proved to be a difficult task. Jane had hit her head hard on the coffee table as she fell. Finally she was able to get her to the sofa and lay her down.

The arrival of the ambulance and the doctor brought Ellen to her senses.

The doctor revived Jane and examined April's arm. He carried her upstairs. Barbara was sure that he took at least an hour in examining her. He came out to praise Barbara for her first aid and he went back in again.

Ellen seemed sure that Dr. Andistone knew his business. He had been recommended by one of her oldest and dearest friends. Barbara was not so sure. He certainly was old to be a doctor. He looked about 60 but he claimed to be 70.

He called Barbara upstairs to stay with April just then so he can go down and report to Ellen and Jane.

He said that April was in a mild state of shock and that Raymond and Jane could take her home from the Scotts tomorrow.

"Ellen, Ellen, come here, come here please."

"Excuse me, doctor," said Ellen, as she smiled.

"Oh boy," thought Jane. "Here we go again."

"Well I suppose I must 'cuse someone as charming as ya, ma'am," said Dr. Andistone.

A rock interrupted his speech as it came down crashing through the window. Jane ducked as it barely missed her. She picked it up and said, "Aunt Ellen, this rock has a note on it."

Just then a louder crash came from upstairs.

Jane gasped.

"What happened?" cried the doctor.

"Something's happened to April." Ellen jumped to conclusions.

"What's all the noise about?" asked Barbara hurrying down the stairs.

"What was that crash we heard?" asked Dr. Andistone.

"Oh!" said Barbara feebly. "I knocked over the study lamp. What was the crash that nearly scared Aunt April to death?"

"A rock with a note on it came through the window!" said Ellen.

"What did it say?"

"Let me see," said Ellen. "Oh yes it said –

THE KNIFE IS
JUS A LITTLE - HA-HA-HA- GIFT FROM
ME!
STIFF JONES!
HA-HA-HA!

IV *Beginnings*

During the Thanksgiving holidays, longer this year due to the President's death, my parents had arranged for me to meet my secret friend, Claudia, who was eight years older than me. My mother had given me some instructions before she got here. "Claudia's mother died recently and she had to come from Oregon to live here," said Mama. "She's only got her grandfather who is very old and very poor. So don't say anything to her about her family. It's like the other secrets Mama and Daddy tell you." I understood. I was good at keeping secrets.

Claudia and her grandfather came in through the front door, unlike most people who came to our house, who came in through the side door coming from the garage. We would leave the garage door open whenever anyone was expected. The front door was for strangers who rang the bell and we told them to go away.

But these people were obviously expected. Her grandfather was very old and frail looking, stooped over so that he was almost as short as Claudia herself. The grandfather only came a few steps inside our house and sat in the chair close to the front door. My mother embraced Claudia and drew her inside with me. The grandfather greeted us politely then began speaking with my father.

"Victoria, would you like to show Claudia your room?" My mother guided us down the hall to my bedroom. I spent the next few hours showing Claudia everything I had. She was the perfect playmate, she showed lots of interest in everything and touched nothing. She let me talk most of the time and agreed with everything I said.

Claudia came over every weekend and began to spend the night on Saturdays. Claudia was a little overweight like me. So we had a lot in common. I liked Claudia. She was very quiet and very sweet to me. And I didn't have to share my toys with her like I did with other girls that came over. She was too old for dolls. Claudia continued to come over almost every weekend, the exception was special weekends and holidays, and spending Saturday night all through the first grade. On those days, my mother would sleep in the room with my father and Claudia would take my mother's room so I didn't even have to share my bedroom. Daddy usually needed to sleep alone because he needed not to be disturbed when he slept because he worked so hard. Mama had trouble sleeping. She stayed up a lot at night.

But Daddy did not mind when Claudia came, he was always delighted to see her even if he had to give up some of his rest. He would take us to the old ice cream parlor downtown where we would have chocolate sundaes while he talked to the waitress who had a beautiful smile. She would always give us a free cookies to take home.

"Your house is so big and the bedrooms are so large," Claudia said to me one time. "You are so lucky to live here and have all this room."

In addition to our three bedrooms, we also had a big den where the television was, a dinette attached to it, a bar separated the dinette from the square kitchen. There was a long hall to the bedrooms and on one side of the hall was the living room where the front door was and where we always had the Christmas tree and special events. There was a bathroom off Daddy's room. It had only a shower. There was another at the end of the hall that had a bathtub. "Some of my relatives live in bigger houses," I said, thinking of Daddy's side of the family, then I thought about houses in Mama's family- those all only had one bathroom, "but some live in smaller houses."

Claudia did not say anything about her house. Claudia did not live in our neighborhood or even in our school district.

"I live in a district inside the city limits," she said.

But she did not tell me where.

Our new neighborhood was very different than the old one in the city. We didn't live in an addition, like Lee Harvey Oswald did, and also most of my friends on the other side of Silver Brook, nor an old dirty area like where my father had once had a hardware store, not even a neighborhood with Italians in large brick homes like my father's family.

We lived in a place where houses were spread apart and although the houses were older, the land was clean, there were lots and lots of trees, we had ditches instead of curbs and the land bordering my aunt's property was still dense woods. Aunt Worthrose owned 10 acres of the land that went from our street all the way back to Silver Brook, the main road. Our neighborhood was really old.

Our house was the first new house built on our side of Silver Brook in many years, since the war. We had first moved to our new neighborhood in the summer of 1961, just a few weeks after my grandmother's funeral. Most of the houses were old wood houses like my aunt's. Only ours, and three new houses built down a newly cut side street, were brick and new.

Aunt Worthrose's house was on the other side of her land, so that all of her property going all the way back to Silver Brook was like a humongous backyard in which she grew innumerable flowers and bushes.

How we came to live there was that soon after my grandmother's death we found out that Daddy had been left out of the will, so Aunt Worthrose gave my parents a half acre on the corner opposite where she lived and they built a new house facing the same street. Our house was 1200 square feet and it was all brick. It had cost $11,000. We were going to live near Aunt Worthrose and we would not see my father's relatives very much anymore. Mama was happy about that.

Our house was outside the city limits and so was the new school, which was called Fairvine. It was in its own school district, not the humongous city district.

"A small district with a good reputation- neighborhood schools," it was called. That was very important, my parents said. And it had just been finished right before I started first grade.

Kindergarten, which was only nine weeks that summer before real school started, had been a disappointment. It was in a little temporary building while they were still working on the great big gleaming school. We didn't get to eat in the cafeteria. There was noisy construction all the time, not enough chairs and we had to sit in a circle and cross our legs and that hurt my back. We spent a lot of time practicing the position on our knees with our arms behind our heads that was going to save us when the Russians attacked. Every time an airplane flew over the school we had to assume the defensive position. That hurt my back, too. A lot of airplanes flew over our area all the time. At the end, we did get to go to the cafeteria. But we still had to bring our own food and the walls weren't finished.

But on Labor Day weekend of 1963, when Daddy had a day off

for a change, we took a drive back to Fairvine to admire the school before classes started that Tuesday.

"This building was done just in time," said my mother. "They were able to have the screening class so they could see which children would be in the advanced class and which would be in the slow class."

"Victoria is going to be in the smart class, right?"

"Yes, they were actually upset that she could read so well," said my mother.

I did not ever remember not knowing how to read. And I had an extra good memory.

We drove in the front circle driveway where I would be let out for class. "I still cannot believe they built such a beautiful school so close to us just in time for Victoria to start first grade."

We drove on by my school, beyond a lot of houses to a larger school that had beautiful white columns in front. Fairvine Junior High. I marveled at the tall columns, I couldn't imagine being old enough to go there.

"It's because they built the additions. I don't like it that so many people have moved in just across Silver Brook. I wanted to be more in the countryside," said my father. "But I guess the schools are a good thing for Victoria. Education is everything now. Nothing is more important than she gets a good education."

And then we drove deeper into a wooded area on a narrow road, passed larger houses and stopped before a huge building that was three stories and had staircases and balconies on the outside. Mountains were visible in the background. It was beautiful. "This is where you will go to high school, Hereald High." said my mother. "Hereald Memorial High to be accurate. Named for a war hero, it was built during World War I. This school district's been here a long time, the city is just now catching up to it. There is another elementary school that is real old too, but fortunately the brand new one is closest to us."

"Wow!" *What a grand building, what fun it will be to explore it.*

"Not for a long, long time, will you be there," said my father. "If the area continues to grow, maybe they'll build a second high school that will be new before you grow up. Then after that, you will go to college."

We drove back to my school and went around a side street

towards the back. The road in back was not finished. "Your school will be even closer when they finish that road. This is going to be a great place for you, Victoria. Look at that play yard. You are going to be very happy here. There is even airconditioning in one of the rooms, the music room." my mother marveled. "At the Guidance meeting, they said every class will go to music once a day."

She was right. We had a heat wave that fall. So once school began, we all learned to look forward to our 15 minute class in the music room so we could cool off. Otherwise, we spent all day in one large, hot room, except there was recess for 30 minutes where we played games outside and lunch in the big lunchroom, which had now had a stage with a curtain that was always closed. We had rotating teachers who came to our class at different parts of the day, for art, math, and English.

Mrs. Anderson, the English teacher, was there in the mornings and again in the afternoons so she was called our "anchor" teacher. We had the best windows in the school, Mrs. Anderson said, but when she opened them the breeze that came in did not help. It was hot and dry. We didn't have uniforms but we all wore our best school clothes, the girls in crisp dresses with shoes and socks and the boys in pants with button-up shirts. In the mornings, we were all fresh and bright, the girls competing colorfully for the prettiest dress of the day, but by afternoon, we all looked wilted and damp no matter what we wore. I loved school but by afternoon, I couldn't wait to get home to our central airconditioning.

My best friend in class was Vickie Bianchi, who really was named Vickie, not Victoria and she hated to be called Victoria just as much as I hated to be called Vickie. People should be called by the name they want to be called, we both agreed. And best of all she was Italian like me, even though she had blond hair. We were great friends and I did not need any other friends but her.

Vickie's only drawback was that she was gone out of town every weekend. Her father had to live and work far away from home and every week she and her mother traveled to be with him. So she could never come to visit my house. She could be a school friend only. My mother tried to get us to talk on the phone but I didn't like talking on the phone. I never could think of anything to say and neither could she. We did spend all our free time at school together. Our teachers let us sit together in class and work together on everything. We sat together at lunch and during recess played only with each other, ignoring all the other kids.

Mr. Qurand was principal. He was a big tall muscular man with crew cut yellow hair. He was always interrupting class to make an announcement on the loudspeaker. A big horn was mounted in front of every class and it POPPED! when it came on and conveyed his voice very loudly at least twice a day. "MAY I HAVE YOUR ATTENTION PLEASE!" was the way he began every announcement. (Except that one time.) And it POPPED! when it was over and shut off.

Most announcements were for the grownups but sometimes we got a lecture, usually on behavior. Then there were the dreaded name calls for kids who had misbehaved- "John Doe, come to the office!" was always the way they were phrased. And the name inserted was usually a boy. We all knew that to be called to the office was to be punished, usually by spanking, for very serious misbehaving. But I had no fear of my name being called. I never misbehaved. I was a good student.

Mrs. Anderson was my favorite teacher (I loved her even though she cried a lot in class, she cried when she read stories, she cried when I kissed her, she cried when she was hugged, she always smiled as she cried).

"Mrs. Anderson has a daughter the same age as you. Her name is Jayne," my mother told me. "But she could not be in the advanced class this year. Her father, Dr. Anderson, and Mrs. Anderson, Jayne and all her brothers live in Water Oaks, over by the high school. I hope you and Jayne can be friends."

All the other kids I liked lived in Fairland Addition. They all thought living in an addition was superior to living where I lived, on the other side of Silver Brook, because an ice cream parlor and a movie theater was going to be built nearby.

Daddy informed me they were wrong, it was just the opposite.

"You could have built another house between our house and your aunt's house," Daddy said. Our house had survived a tornado which came right after we had moved in that summer. Then we didn't have any airconditioning for several days. Daddy drove us to see the destruction in some of the other neighborhoods. It was horrible. Houses were all mangled and torn apart and there were no trees left in the neighborhoods we saw.

Daddy said, "The new houses in the Fairland Addition will not survive the next tornado, the way they were thrown together, building them with nothing more than matchsticks for wood. They'll never survive a bad storm and if one of them catches fire, they are all going to burn up."

When we got back to school after Thanksgiving, the mural was gone and the walls were bare again. We practiced shielding ourselves from the Russians in the empty hall. We knew the Russians would drop the atomic bomb on us and it was important to get on our knees and hide our heads when they did.

The Christmas tree and the ornaments we made caused our room to be more cheerful than the halls. Mrs. Anderson smiled through tears as we hung our handmade ornaments on the tree. She looked very pretty, except for a large bruise on her arm that I noticed when her sleeve slipped down as she reached to put the top on the tree.

Soon we recessed for Christmas, and again the main road, Silver Brook, divided me from all my friends except for three who also lived on our side. One girl was a year younger than me. She lived down the road the other way from Aunt Worthrose who was friends with her grandmother, who stilled lived there too, and worked in the school cafeteria. Her name was Alyce and she went to our church.

Down on Silver Brook, just passed Fairland Addition, before the freeway was our church. We had never gone to church before moving to the property and we didn't go unless Daddy was off on Sunday, which was not often. I liked to go because I was working on memorizing the Latin words. I liked the songs too. Some of them were in English. I memorized them after one time singing them.

Alyce's family was at church every Sunday that we went. Alyce had a lot of older and younger brothers and sisters. Too many to count. She had come to my house to play a couple of times. My mother told me I had been invited to her house and although my mother preferred for me to play at our house, I needed to go or it would not be polite.

Immediately when I entered Alyce's house, I knew something

was very wrong. It had a terrible smell. Alyce's brothers and sisters ran around unsupervised, some of them still wearing diapers. I didn't want to play with any of Alyce's toys, they were all visibly dirty. I recognized some of the baby toys as having been mine once, but now they were disheveled and nothing I would ever touch again. The beds were unmade and the sheets were pulled down towards the floor, with pillows seemingly tossed at random. I had never been to such a place where everything was in chaos. There was food and what seemed to actually be trash all over the place. There were dirty dishes on the table.

Our house was always perfectly neat. Only with extra special permission, was I allowed to bring my toys outside of my bedroom. My mother made the bed every morning, the dishes were always washed. Clothes were immediately washed and dried and put away as soon as we took them off. The floors were always as clean as the kitchen counters. We ate only at the table and there was no eating anywhere else under any circumstance. Never had I had a bite of food in my bedroom, trash was never anywhere in our house except the trashcan and it was emptied religiously. Our house always smelt of pine sol oil and Mr. Clean, if it smelled of anything at all. Aunt Worthrose's house was equally clean, even though it was old, it never smelled musty.

Fortunately, it was a nice day and Alyce's mother was happy when I suggested we play outside. Playing outside wasn't an option with the other girl on my street. Cindy had asthma and she was very fat, much fatter than me. She could never close her mouth and her nose was always stopped up. Her house was very clean but playing with her was very boring.

And this year, there a new girl, Valery, who lived down the newly cut street, Foam Meadow, in a brand new house. She was not allowed to come to my house, I had to go to her house. But we were not allowed to play in her room which had lots of white lace on her bed and teddy bears with satin clothes. All we could do was sit in her den and watch television. So I didn't want to go back there.

My mother was very excited that more new houses were going to be built on our side of Silver Brook. This was because of an elderly widow who was carving up her land into lots. Her name was Mrs. Longhem. She lived further back in the neighborhood, in a large old wood house with beautiful antique furniture.

I knew a secret about Mrs. Longhem that even she didn't know. She had cancer. Her children, who were also adults, didn't want her to know. Mama and Daddy had told me so I knew. But she did not.

Daddy had thoughts about buying one of Mrs. Longhem's lots. But they had been too expensive and then, of course, Aunt Worthrose gave him our spot to build our house.

Mama was pleased that we would have some more neighbors in the coming years and hopefully I would have some more people to play with. Daddy was pleased that the lots were so expensive that it would take people who had a lot of money to buy them and build houses on them. Foam Meadow was at a right angle to our street, Curving Branch, ending just to the left of our house. So the side of the corner house facing Foam Meadow was directly across the street from our house. Unfortunately, Mr. and Mrs. Miller, the elderly couple that built that corner house had no children or grandchildren.

"Maybe if you get to know Valery better at school, she will be given permission to come here and play," said Mama.

"I have no way to get to know her, I never see her." Since she had not been there for the screening kindergarten, she was not put in my class.

"Don't y'all play together on the playground during recess?"

"Yes, but that is my time with Vickie," I said. "I don't have time for other kids then."

We mostly spent recess inside playing board games when the weather turned cold. Mrs. Anderson had her arm injured and in a sling for awhile when school began again after Christmas, so she needed help and my mother volunteered. She and Mrs. Anderson became friends and she went with Mrs. Anderson to her other classes when the teachers rotated midday. They arranged for Jayne to come to my seventh birthday. I got lots of new doll stuff and also a record player with some records.

I had not seen Claudia since before President Kennedy was assassinated, but she was there for my seventh birthday that year. I had been told to tell that she was a friend of a neighbor if anyone asked where she came from, but no one did. Also there were Connie Vaccaro, back from Europe, Eva and Victor Romano, Ruth Marino, and

Theodore Rossi, Jr. Happy as I was they came, I wished my mother's family were there also.

I had numerous first cousins on my mother's side of the family but we only knew Uncle Buford's children, Pamela, Cliff, and Clark. All the others were way older than me. One, Uncle Clement was already dead although his wife, Aunt Geraldine, still alive. My mother wrote her letters often. While my mother also exchanged letters with her other brothers and sisters, Uncle Buford was the only one we ever saw besides Aunt Worthrose. Pamela was an official adult. Cliff and Clark were younger than Pamela but older than Christian Romano, so they could not be playmates for me. But they were fun to be around on the rare occasions I got to spend time with them.

While my mother barely knew some of her brothers and sisters, my father was in close touch with some of his first cousins. They were all men. Aunt Florrie was the only girl in the whole generation of either side of his family. My father, his brothers and first cousins all vaguely resembled each other. Only Daddy was extremely handsome, although the other men were all taller. They were nicer looking than most men their age. However their wives ranged from beautiful dark Italians to plain dumpy dyed blondes. I had to call them all "Aunt" and "Uncle" even the cousins, who were not my real aunts and uncles.

There was Uncle Chris Marino and Aunt Thelma, Ruth's parents. There was Uncle Vince Vaccaro and Aunt Concetta. Most of my father's first cousins were a few years younger than him like his brothers, but Uncle Vince Vaccaro was actually a few years older. But their daughter Connie was my age and was one of my favorite playmates. There was Uncle Leo Esposito and Aunt Theresa. Their son was Leo, Jr. had brain damage from a bicycle accident when he was a small child. They didn't come to our house though, we just went to theirs so I only had to see Leo, Jr. there, thankfully as I found him rather creepy. He was almost grown and not at my party. Connie Vaccaro was first cousins with Leo, Jr. and she was at my party.

Theodore Rossi, Jr. was almost a stranger to me. I had only met Theodore and his parents once or twice and did not know their names but I figured I would have to call them aunt and uncle when I found out. While not my first cousins, Ruth and Theodore were first cousins to each other. Theodore and Ruth, who were dropped off together, brought me presents, but mostly ignored the rest of us, and sat whispering in a corner the whole time.

I knew children of a divorced dead uncle by marriage and his second wife were not really my cousins, but in addition to Connie I enjoyed playing with Eva and Victor most of all. Eva had several fashion dolls like me and we loved to visit each other and play. Victor officially didn't play dolls but he was always there to supervise us and actually played unofficially.

I took Connie, Eva, Victor, and Jayne to my bedroom. Claudia watched us for a while, then went to spend time with my parents. Jayne had been sulky under Claudia's watch. As soon as Claudia left, Victor, Connie, Eva, and I had to stop Jayne from damaging my dolls. She immediately snatched up my blond bubble and tried to pull its hair.

"You must not know how to play teenage fashion dolls correctly," said Eva. I was grateful to her for insisting Jayne surrender the bubble, which fortunately had very sturdy hair and was not damaged.

I quickly put away my ponytail and handed Midge to Jayne.

"You can only play with that one," I said.

"I don't have to play with any," said Jayne, loudly. "I want to listen to the records."

"Don't you have fashion dolls? You would not want yours damaged," said Eva.

"Stupid dolls," said Jayne, and made a lunge for the bendable leg doll I had just gotten as a present. I had left it unprotected when I had secured Barbara. But Victor blocked Jayne who was yelling at the same time and, by this time, Mama had come in to see what was wrong.

"Why don't you all go play in the garage? Victoria has some bowling pin toys that haven't been opened yet." My mother herded us out to the garage.

"Aw I wanna hear the records," Jayne griped.

"They were a gift from my family in the countryside who couldn't make it to the party this year," I announced. I knew Pamela, who I liked much better than anyone there, was not far away but just didn't come. I really wished Pamela was not already grown.

"If I acted like you, my father would paddle me with a paddleboard," said Connie to Jayne. "My daddy cares how I behave," she added proudly.

How strange, I thought, *just like the boys at school when they are sent to the office. And occasionally a girl would get paddled too...*

Jayne did not reply but she behaved better after Connie told her that. Mama put the record player in the garage and we heard the records while we bowled. Rather than bowl with us, Ruth and Theodore called Aunt Thelma and she came and got them.

As consolation, I got to spend the next Saturday at Connie's house. Connie was the only person I knew who had more doll clothes than me. Claudia was visiting frequently but stayed with my mother at home when my father dropped me off. Claudia didn't mind, she wanted to be with my parents, she said. Other times at my house, Connie and I played dolls all day long and Eva and Victor came over too. As winter deepened, I spent several more Saturdays with Connie, Eva and Victor while Claudia spent time with my parents.

But the visits tapered off by the time spring came with its cool mornings and hot afternoons. Connie was sent to Europe to visit her grandparents and go to school there. Eva and Victor were required to play outdoors when the weather was good and Claudia's grandfather needed her at home more. At school, Mrs. Anderson no longer needed her sling so my mother no longer came, except to drop me off and pick me up.

Our classroom, now almost as familiar as home, had settled into a pleasant spring routine of prayers, songs, reading and arithmetic with breaks for art projects and everyday lunch and recess. After reading each day, the boys ritualistically rose from their seats and raised the windows to let in the breeze. One bright afternoon in April we were busy with reading when the loudspeaker went off - POP!

"MAY I HAVE YOUR ATTENTION PLEASE? Your attention! This is an emergency! A funnel cloud has been spotted to the southeast of the school, dipping and headed in our direction. Take emergency preparations at once! A tornado may be imminent. I repeat. A tornado is imminent!" POP! the speaker went silent.

Almost immediately the light from the windows faded and we lost the brightness of the sun.

"Quickly, boys! Help us close the windows. Girls put all the desks closer together towards the opposite wall."

The room became chaos as we scrambled to obey her. And as soon as we started moving, the overhead lights went out as the electricity failed. The metal on the desk legs clanged against the floor and each other as we hurled them closer together. The light still coming from the windows turned into a gray glare. Some of the quicker boys had one or two windows lowered but before all the boys could even get to the windows, the howling wind sent a cold draft of air into the room and sheets of rain started blasting in.

"Get back, children, get to your desk and assume the position!"

The girls crouched between the desks as the boys ran toward us. We all wiggled into our heads down, knees tucked under chest position. We weren't supposed to look but I peeked as our math teacher ran into the room, closing the windows as Mrs. Anderson grabbed a roll of tape and started putting tape on the lower window panes as she jerked them down, cringing each time the sheets of rain struck. The window panes rattled noisily. Then the howl of the wind increased to a terrible noise and one of the upper window panes shattered. The other teacher screamed, slammed down the last window, and ran out of the room.

Glenn suddenly sprang up and ran to Mrs. Anderson. She left her roll of tape dangling from a window, grabbed Glenn and placed herself between him and the wall of glass, just before it began to shatter. As wet glass flew into the air and showered the room, she forced Glenn under her desk and crouched in front of him. Some of the kids started screaming. More windows broke, those taped had shards of glass just hanging limply. The higher panes showered us with more glass and water. We all ducked as far under our desks as we could get, correct defensive positions forfeited in an instant for more secure cover.

The abandoned roll of tape swung wildly. Then the strand holding it broke and it flew into the room like a missile, striking the wall opposite the windows and bouncing off the top of a desk near me with a loud thud, then landing under the window it had once clung to.

Then the storm stopped as suddenly as it had started. The kids who had been screaming stopped. The wind and rain vanished.

Mrs. Anderson came out from behind her desk, pulling Glenn out from behind her and slowly returned him to his desk, the glass crunching under their footsteps on the way. We all got up slowly, gathered around Mrs. Anderson, shaking off glass and water, some had only gotten a little wet. We were all quiet except there was a little whimpering. Then Mrs. Anderson brushed us off, lined us up and marched us out into the hall, crunching more glass rhythmically as we left the battered room. No one was hurt.

The sun was shining again by the time I got into the car with Mama to go home. She looked a little strange.

"We had a tornado," I told her.

"I know. I was out here waiting in line to pick you up. The tornado picked up my car and turned it sideways. When it was over I had to back the car up and straighten it back out."

"Our windows all broke," I said. "But nobody was hurt. Not even Mrs. Anderson when she saved Glenn."

"All the cars were strewn out of line, some facing one direction, some facing another. I felt my car being literally lifted off the ground," said my mother, as if she still could not believe it. "But none of the other drivers got hurt either. None of the cars were even scraped... God was certainly with me today. I don't know what to make of this."

I didn't either. "Best discuss it with Aunt Worthrose. She'll have a prediction."

"When it was over we were all just like trying to parallel park at the same time coming from different directions," said my mother to Aunt Worthrose, trying to describe the scene.

But Aunt Worthrose had only seen a rainstorm, which she welcomed for the sake of her flower garden. She didn't even know there had been a tornado. The swift storm had struck the school minutes away but only thrown a little beneficial rain towards the direction of our homes. There were only a few small tree limbs down anywhere near us.

"It's a sign from God," said Aunt Worthrose. "But I don't know what it means. 'His mysteries to behold,' the Bible says."

As first grade drew to a close, very disappointing was the news that my friend, Vickie Bianchi, was going to move to Louisiana at the end of the school year. But she was so happy that finally she and her mother were going to be with her father all the time that it was hard to be sad about it.

The last day of the first grade, I kissed Mrs. Anderson goodbye (she cried) and Vickie and I had a hugs and kisses farewell promising to write and be friends forever.

Just after that I got sick and had to have surgery. Somehow I knew this was serious, since my mother relented and let me have another doll that wore wigs and lots more clothes. I still did not have what I really wanted most- the wedding dress set.

"We can't find it," my father said. "It's not in any store that sells toys on our side of town."

"When I had my tonsils out, it was in a countryside doctor's office with no anesthetic. That bride dress costs over $5.00, more than the dolls," my mother said. "That's too much. The dress I wore when we got married didn't cost that much. People on this side of town don't spend that kind of money on toys."

I was beginning to lose hope that I would ever get it.

Aunt Worthrose paid Alyce's grandmother to make some clothes for my dolls. But while they were pretty, they did not fit right. She had made a substitute for a black and white dress I wanted and it was not the same. I desperately hoped I was not going to get a substitute for the wedding dress. I begged my mother for the real wedding dress.

Instead I got a red nightgown to wear to the hospital to spend the night before my surgery. My mother thought I should be just as happy with that as if it were the wedding dress.

I remembered being strapped on the gurney and seeing the ceiling go by as I was wheeled into the operating room. I tried to keep my eyes open but as soon as the doors closed so did they.

When I woke up I was strapped to the bed. My parents and several other people were in the room. Uncle Chris was there and his face was the first I remembered seeing clearly. I remembered thinking that I was not supposed to be seeing much of him again. But he was there and I felt embarrassed because I could not get up and greet him properly. Then he reached over the bed railing and shook my hand below the strap and asked how I was doing.

I told him Ok and then he stepped back and my parents came forward. Daddy had something in his hand and I reached as far as I could to try and take it, knowing immediately what it was. He placed it on my chest where I could barely reach to caress it.

It was the wedding set! I would never forget how beautiful it looked, the white gown covered with lace, the veil with the pearls! The necklace, the bouquet, the garter! All there! And I noticed the dress had long sleeves and the gloves were short. Different from the drawing in the booklet I was sure. But that was Ok.

"Who's this from?" I asked, suspecting Uncle Chris because he was there. *Or Aunt Worthrose might have sent it.*

"No, honey. It's from us, your mother and I," my father said. "Uncle Chris just picked it up for us on the other side of town."

I was loved. I felt a surge of joy. I gazed at the wedding dress happily. Now I knew the truth, the real truth about how my parents felt about me. I was loved. They wished the best for me. They wished happiness for me. They had confidence I would grow up Ok. This was as clear a demonstration as they could possibly ever make. I felt very, very loved.

When I got home from the hospital, my parents had sat down to have a talk with me, which happened a lot, it usually involved a grownup secret that I was to never talk about, but this talk was different. There was news.

"You're going to have a sister," said my mother.

"How would you like to have a sister?" asked my father.

Now, I knew, 12 years before I was born, Rosalind Renee had only lived two days. But when my parents talked about other brothers and sisters they usually asked did I mind that I didn't have any, and I did not. One time, they had talked about adopting a child. I said I didn't want to share my room or my toys. And I didn't hear anything else about it after that.

"I don't want to share my dolls," I said.

I just got the bride dress.

"How would you like it if Claudia became your sister?" asked my mother.

I didn't have to think about that too long. After all, Claudia didn't want my dolls and didn't want to share my room. I didn't really have any objection.

"Victoria Irene, you realize if we adopt another child, that child would share equally in your inheritance and we would have to spend an equal amount of money on her as we do you, so you might wind up with less in life," said my father, very seriously. I communicated that this was not a problem for me so long as I did not have to share my dolls and I got to keep my bedroom to myself. As usual, my parents swore me to secrecy when discussing grownup stuff.

And as always, I kept those secrets. I had never told anybody that Mrs. Longhem had cancer even though she was still alive. I never talked about the will.

One thing did occur to me though… Perhaps… "Could Vickie come back and be my sister, too?" I asked, without too much hope. But why not take a shot at it?

"Vickie Bianchi has two good parents," said my mother. "Plus she is your age and you would have to share your dolls with her."

"Oh." Oh, well, Claudia was probably the next best choice, even if I didn't love her like I loved Vickie. *Maybe I will love her someday,* I thought.

In such a short time, first grade was over. Vickie was gone. I had my surgery and got the wedding dress set and a new sister! And I had finished Chapter 6 of my book.

Chapter 6
A Mysterious Sign

"Aunt Ellen, Mom wants you!" came a voice from the top of the stairs.

As Ellen started up the stairs Dr. Andistone said, "Ellen don't ya' tell Miz Kape about the rock, it might upset 'er!"

Dr. Andistone and Mrs. Scott had been friends for one year. Dr. Andistone is from the North and is 70 years old! Mrs. Scott is 45.

"Mom," said Barbara. "I'm going to do some sleuthing!"

"All right but be careful," warned Mrs. Scott, "Belle is missing and April is injured, so be careful."

"I will."

As she came to the spot where Belle was standing,

she saw a funny sign, it looked like this:

u

The sign, although Barbara did not know it, meant that Belle was still alive! It was for a man who was to kidnap Barbara.

Just then, Barbara heard a hissing noise behind her. She turned to see a huge rattlesnake ready to strike!

Yes, I was very proud of my book.

It would be a very long time before I would be ready to show it to the world.

First, my mother would get to read it this summer and now Claudia as well. And then when I learned longhand and finished it, I was hoping to show it to my new English teacher during second grade.

But first, there was a long hot summer looming.

End of Part 1

Part 2

V *Devotions*

Although it was not supposed to be a secret, I had stopped telling people I was adopted.

My parents had told me that being adopted meant that I was really, really wanted. So I naturally concluded that children who were not adopted were not wanted. They were accidents. One day in first grade at school lunch, I had voiced this opinion to Glenn.

"My parents wanted me," I had said. "Because I was adopted I know that."

Usually so quiet, Glenn had scowled at me. "I'm tired of hearing you say that. My parents wanted me, too. It is not nice of you to say that we weren't wanted."

He was so sure and so angry about it that I had paused and thought things over. Maybe he was telling the truth. Maybe some kids were wanted by their parents even if they were not adopted. Maybe it was possible both things were true. But there was a more important reason that I stopped telling anybody.

Whenever we met somebody new, or even saw somebody that we had not seen for a while, they almost always made a big deal of how much I looked like Daddy. Mama and Daddy would always get embarrassed by this and hasten to tell the person that I was adopted. Sometimes the person would just stare at me. So I decided to tell Mama and Daddy it was a good idea just not to say anything about it.

"Let's just pretend that I'm not adopted at all," I said.

"Of course, she's right, Vic," said my mother. "It's really nobody's business."

"It's just that we have always wanted to be very open about your adoption and let everyone know it is not a secret," said my father.

"Why would an adoption ever be a secret?" I asked, thinking how special it made me.

"You see, we know a couple who adopted a baby, raised her without telling her, then after she was 18 someone told her she was adopted. She left home and they have never seen her since," said my father.

"Why would she do that? They don't know where she is?"

"Well, she was angry they deceived her," said my mother. "See they were both Italian and she was Italian and so she looked like them. No one would have ever dreamed she was adopted. So they were betrayed by someone close who knew. They know about where she is but she doesn't have to have contact with them if she doesn't want to. She's grown."

That seemed an extreme reaction. It sounded to me as if the girl did not have good sense. Of course, adopted children often grew up to look like their adopted parents, my mother had told me before, but everybody didn't know that.

So, from then on, whenever anybody mentioned how much I looked like my father, we just smiled at each other and one of us would say, "Yes, you are right, just like him." And instead of feeling embarrassed, everyone felt good.

My mother had told me she adopted me because my first parents were very poor and had too many children. Although, she didn't talk about it as much anymore, when I had been little, my mother had loved to talk about the story of my adoption.

I was born in Catholic Hospital and I was delivered by Dr. Moscado, who was baby delivery doctor to all the Italians that my parents knew. I had been born to poor people, who had many other children and could not afford to keep me. I had been cared for by nuns until I was three days old and Mama and Daddy had come to get me. It had cost a lot of money to adopt me and I was chosen from among four babies, because I was the prettiest.

Not being little anymore, and having seen how Claudia's adoption was being arranged, I was beginning to question this neat story. I asked Mama to tell me again about my adoption. Each time she told it I was a little older and had understood what she was saying a little more.

This time I had some questions prepared.

"We have to go to church tonight remember? It's the special night."

"I know, but we have time, I know my prayers. Have we told Father Mallett I'm adopted?"

80

"No, he doesn't need to know."

"Tell me the story again. Please." I used the tone of voice that implied I would be a lot less trouble if she just did it.

"Ok," she sighed. "You were born at Catholic Hospital and we came and got you when you were three days old. There were four baby girls up for adoption and we picked you because you were the prettiest. Your daddy said you were the prettiest baby he ever saw." My mother was trying to stick to her story but her hesitation was tale telling.

I questioned this statement first. "Babies all look alike. How did you know which baby to get?"

She hesitated. "Well, actually when the nuns told us there were four baby girls up for adoption that had been born in just the last five days, your daddy said to them 'I want the baby that was meant for us.' "

"How did you know which baby that was?"

"Well, you see, we knew about you before you were born. Dr. Moscado delivered you. He had told me I would probably never have another baby so I wanted to adopt. But your father didn't. He always said he only wanted his own children, his own flesh and blood. But Dr. Moscado told me he had a mother that had to give up her baby and he thought I would be the perfect mother for you. I told him Vic would never agree, but he said he would talk to him. And he did."

"Daddy agreed?"

"Yes, I was shocked, but then I knew God meant for us to have you."

That made sense. "Ok, go on. The next part about the money."

"It cost a lot of money to adopt you," she said, "All our savings. That's why we didn't get a new house until we did, we had been saving for a new house, we had to start saving all over again. So I know your daddy really, really wanted you or he would never have agreed."

"So why did it cost so much money. How much did it cost?"

"Well, about $10,000," said my mother. "We had to pay the hospital bill, over $1100, we had to pay a lawyer more than $2,000. We had to pay a separate lawyer for you, we had to pay a third lawyer for your biological mother, I forget how much, and we had to pay the judge. Your daddy was already working seven days a week then, and he had to take off on Sunday and go to the judge's house to take him $3,000."

I knew what that meant. "Daddy lost overtime."

"Yes," said my mother. "He was mad about it."

"And about those parents were too poor to keep me?" I deliberately was openly skeptical.

My mother hesitated again. "Well, I never believed that story. It didn't fit with what Dr. Moscado said. And honestly, I knew some people who adopted a baby and they got the same story. I think that's what they tell everyone."

"She wasn't married?" I didn't say it but we both knew who I was talking about.

My mother looked as guilty as if it were her that had borne a baby without being married. "I think so," she said softly. Then she earnestly reassured me that it didn't matter.

"Hmm," I said, thinking, *true, it really didn't matter*. I had no interest in my "real" mother. Mama was my real mother as far as I was concerned. I loved her, loved her people. I even loved the countryside although I wasn't there very often. But my adoption was a good story and maybe I could use it in some of my future books.

"And, Victoria," she added. "From the day I took you home, that bitter cold winter day, when you were a baby and we lived in the old house, those were the happiest years of my life."

"I was told childhood was supposed to be the happiest years of your life?" That's what everyone was always telling me. "Weren't you happy when you were a child?"

My mother's eyes misted and she got up and walked away. She spoke, but this time not really to me. "My mother and father loved me and my younger brother and sister. But I had to work in the fields as soon as I was old enough to walk. I had to pick cotton like a slave every day, and watch my baby sister and brother at night. My mother had baby after baby and was always sick and Papa had to work in the coal mine at night and in the fields in the day."

"Where was Aunt Worthrose? Did you not have enough to eat?" I asked, thinking of all the children in Africa who were starving because I did not always eat all of my food. (I was beginning to question that, too).

She wiped her eyes and turned her attention back to me. "Worthrose and my other older brothers and sisters were already gone by then. Yes, we had food to eat, because we had a farm, but nothing else. No clothes but rags, no shoes in the summer. But we were more fortunate than many because we did grow food. Your late Uncle Chris Romano was hungry when he was a child. I asked him once why he married your Aunt Florrie, her being the way she is. He said- 'June, I saw all that food in that bakery and I thought, well she's beautiful, and can't be that bad, and there was just so much food.' That's not why I married your father. I didn't marry for food or money. I wanted a lot of children of my own. If I knew what I know now. I'd never have married. Never get married, Victoria."

"Why not?"

"Marriage used to be forever, now the men can divorce their wives and leave their children anytime they want to. Most men are cheats. You could wind up like Aunt Florrie or Aunt Concetta."

I was imagining a group of men cheating at cards or otherwise stealing to make money. Then it came to me. Connie had more fashion dolls and clothes than I did.

"Uncle Vince Vaccaro and Aunt Concetta have plenty of money, don't they?" I asked, thinking especially of Connie's Cinderella teenage fashion doll ensemble with the plastic glass slippers that I didn't have. "Is Uncle Vince Vaccaro a criminal?"

"Certainly not! I don't know where you get these ideas. Uncle Vince Vaccaro is an honest hardworking man. He makes good money because he is a fireman. He would never take anything that didn't belong to him. And Concetta comes from a very wealthy family."

"What do you mean by cheat then?"

She glanced at me and took a deep breath. "He cheated on Concetta before the war by dating other girls. I know because he was your father's running around buddy. They would take off on Friday nights and go to dancehalls and meet girls. I know they did it because I followed Vic one night. When I found that out, I told your father I'd kill him if I ever caught him at it again."

The idea of my father going to dancehalls and dancing with pretty girls was not that shocking to me. After all, Mama would not have been able to dance, since she was Baptist then. I thought it was interesting that Daddy had such a colorful past. I pictured him dancing with a bunch of girls around him, waiting their turn. He was so handsome that was easy to imagine.

My mother was glaring at me.

"Daddy should not have done that," I told her, dutifully. "He doesn't anymore, I sure." For some reason the image of the pretty smiling ice cream parlor waitress popped into my head.

"Yes, but Aunt Concetta caught Uncle Vince Vaccaro doing it again and she is divorcing him."

"Oh? She threw him out of the house?"

"Yes," said my mother, some admiration in her voice. "She threw the bum out. She is keeping Connie, of course. She wants full custody. Connie was Concetta's miracle baby. She was going through the change of life when she got pregnant with Connie, having never before been able to have a baby. Her family got her medical care that I could never afford. Connie was born premature, but she lived.

"Now that they are gone, I guess I can tell you this. Concetta and Vince Vaccaro were the couple who were abandoned by the child they raised because they didn't tell her she was adopted. Then right after the girl broke off with them, after they had raised her from an infant and cared for her all her life, the little wench, that's about when Concetta got pregnant with Connie. It was like a double miracle for Concetta."

"Whatever happened to the adopted girl? What was her name?"

"Her name doesn't matter, she changed it legally, first and last. We don't know. But rumors were she somehow found her biological mother even though that is strictly against the law, she- you would never do that would you? You would never abandon us and try to find your real mother?"

"Of course not," I said thinking how stupid that girl must be.

"Concetta was afraid Connie was being alienated and she would abandon them when she grew up, too. Concetta claims Vince paddled Connie frequently against her wishes." Mama paused. "We may not see as much of them as before. I heard Concetta is going to marry someone else and he will marry his girlfriend, who is much younger. We don't know the man and woman they are going to marry."

"Oh?" *Connie hadn't seemed to mind that she was paddled occasionally. She always talked about how wonderful both her parents were. Aunt Concetta must have been having a little hysteria about that,* I thought.

I would miss Connie. I thought Daddy would miss Uncle Vince Vaccaro too. Mama seemed to think it was Ok that Aunt Concetta had found someone else to marry.

"Is Uncle Vince Vaccaro going to become a Baptist?" I had been doing a column of Baptists versus Catholics and I wanted to know if I needed to switch Uncle Vince Vaccaro to the Baptist side.

My mother laughed. "Why do you ask that?"

"Well, it is a sin to get a divorce if you are a Catholic, but not a Baptist," I said, remembering what the priest had said one time when he gave one of his speeches in English during Mass.

"Some of the things the Catholics say are not quite right. But the Baptist don't get everything right either so-"

"I heard Father Mallett say divorced Catholics could never get married again or they were exiled."

"Excommunicated. Baptists do not like divorce either," she said. "And the Church of Christ will also kick you out, too. They did - to - um one of my family members."

"I thought your whole family was Baptist."

"No, originally my family was Church of Christ. Back in Kentucky. Except for your Aunt Worthy Rose, your Uncle Buford and Aunt Nelwyn and their kids, and your Aunt Talinda and Uncle Drake, my other brothers and sisters are Church of Christ as were my parents, when they were alive."

"You were Baptist, but your parents went to a different church? How did you get to be Baptist?"

She looked at me as if trying to decide if she should tell me or not.

"Come on, tell me."

"Well, I told you, we were very poor. On Sundays though we didn't have to work in the field, Buford, Talinda, and I would go out and play. In the summertime we would go in search of watermelons. It was extremely hot and dusty, so we'd go off the main road to the watermelon patch and steal a watermelon and eat it right there in the field. A little further down from the field was an old Baptist church. It was just a shack in the woods."

She paused. "Just an old shack- it was a colored Baptist church. They sang and shouted so loud we could hear them in the watermelon patch, while we were eating our watermelon. One day before I could stop him, Buford took off across the field toward the church.

"Talinda wasn't much more than a baby, so I had to carry her, she couldn't run very far. When I caught up to Buford, he was hunkered down on the side of the church, peeking through one of the stained glass windows. They weren't very dark windows, so we could see through them pretty well. Well, we ran off after we watched a little bit. But the next Sunday we came back earlier and watched them again a little bit longer. Then the third Sunday, we got there right after the service started.

"We were, all three of us, so absorbed in watching that we didn't see a couple of the colored men sneaking up behind us. When we heard them, we jumped up. I was scared to death. Buford took off running but one of them caught him. I grabbed Talinda, who was starting to cry and backed up against the wall.

" 'Help,' Buford was screaming. 'They are going to kill us.'

" 'Shush, be brave.' I didn't scream or cry, I looked them right in the eye. Buford was hollering and squirming but the other man held him tight.

" 'What you want me to do with him, Pastor?'

" 'We saw you out here watching,' said the preacher. 'It's really hot out here, and you all look tired, why don't you come in and sit down? We've got some visitors.'

" 'Shut up, Buford! Shush, Talinda! Haven't you got any pride?' I was ashamed my little brother and sister were acting like babies. I was going to stand up for us. If they killed us, we had to be brave.

" 'Pride goeth before a fall, little Missy,' said the preacher, blocking any escape, but he didn't touch me. Talinda shut up but kept squirming in my arms. Buford was still yelling but the other man took him farther away. 'That young un is bound to be getting pretty heavy by now. Why don't you come in and put your burden down?'

"The preacher stepped back out of my way. 'Yous can go on now if you really wants to,' he spoke to me softly.

"Talinda started crying again. But I told her to shush. I held my head up and carried her around the corner and through the doorway. The colored man carried Buford in behind me, and Buford shut up as soon as we entered. The people in the pews were all staring at us as we walked all the way to the front. All the seats were full. The people in the front pews moved out to make room for us. The preacher sat us down in the front row right in front of the fan.

" 'Yous just sit there while we finish our worship and after we will git something for you', he told me.

"We sat there while they sang and prayed some more. We didn't have a fan at home. We didn't have electricity. It was heaven to sit in front of that tall fan. They had a block of ice behind it to help the air be cool. Then I saw they didn't really have electricity either but the fan was rigged some way into some wires that were on the floor draping over the sill of an open window."

My mother paused. She seemed to be scrutinizing me for my reaction.

"They tied onto the electricity illegally," I deduced.

She smiled at me. "Well, I don't know, they might have been given permission, there were some rich people's houses not too far away. Someone may have given them permission to run a cord to the church."

"What then?"

"After the service they gave us some sweet bread and cider."

"Is that all?"

"Well, instead of stealing watermelon, we'd go to the colored church service on Sunday mornings. They always had something to eat and we always got the front row right in front of that wonderful fan. If someone got that spot first, they would move as soon we came in. We were welcomed there like nowhere else and believe me, they know how to preach, and they know how to sing, better than anybody. Better than any white preacher or choir I've ever heard and certainly a lot better than these Catholics."

I pictured my mother a child of 10 or 11, her younger brother, maybe eight or nine and toddler sister, the three children alone, surrounded by all colored people, a large group of them singing and praying.

"Then you joined the church?"

She hesitated again. "I was baptized."

"Was Aunt Talinda and Uncle Buford?"

"No, your Aunt Talinda was baptized later, in the white Baptist church. They were too young at the time, the colored preacher said, but he baptized me. Buford was too ornery, he refused to be baptized."

"So, then you started going to white Baptist church? Your parents were willing to take you even though they went to the Church of Christ?"

She hesitated again. "My parents did not go to church. By this time, they were too poor, they didn't have clothes to wear to church. But when the rich people at the white Baptist church found out what was happening they asked my parents if they could send a carriage for us kids. The white church was too far away for us to walk and everybody was afraid of the KKK, they rode the mountains in their white robes terrorizing the countryside those days, so we could not keep going to the colored church."

I knew who the KKK were from the movies. I knew they dressed like ghosts and carried burning crosses.

"Did the white church have a fan?"

"They had several fans in the ceiling, they had real electricity. And they always fed us. But it wasn't the same."

"What did the white church look like?"

"Oh, it was beautiful, and the people who went there lived in mansions. I wound up cleaning house for some of them, times I wasn't needed in the field. They all had great big old two and three story houses with rugs and long curtains that fell on the floor. They took all day to clean and then I would get 50 cents. I'd have to give it to my parents. They needed it for clothes."

She paused.

"To their credit, they did send a carriage every Sunday for many years for the three of us kids. And they gave us church clothes until we got too big to wear what their children grew out of. Talinda had good clothes for a long time."

"Wasn't the KKK during the Civil war?" It suddenly dawned on me that the historical context was confused.

"They came back in the 1920s. I guess the Civil War KKK were the ancestors of those in the 20s."

"Did any of your ancestors fight in the Civil War? Some of the kids at school have said their ancestors fought for the Confederacy. They said if mine did, I could be a Daughter of the Confederacy."

"Yes, I had some relatives in the Civil War." She looked oddly guilty as if admitting it made her uncomfortable. "Not ancestors exactly, my grandfather was too young, but his older brother and my grandmother's brother fought in the Civil War, one of them was killed and one of them lived to collect a pension. And I don't remember which was which. They were not direct ancestors, so you can't join any groups that way."

"So you did join the white church?" She seemed happier talking about that.

"Not exactly, they lost interest in me and Buford when we grew up. But, as I said, they baptized Talinda. A few years later she met Drake there, one time when he was home on leave from the Marines, visiting his family, and he married her when she turned 14 in 1933. Papa was mad, but he got over it. She's been gone with Drake wherever they send him since, except when he was in the Orient during World War II. She came home then," Mama said. "When I left home in the 30s, I started attending a Baptist church here in the city, until I started dating your father."

"At church, the priest said if you're not Catholic you go to hell when you die." I had been meaning to bring that up, I been worrying about this at night since I loved all my mother's family, even the ones I didn't know well, because she loved them, and I did not want them to go to hell. Heaven would not be quite as good if family members were missing from it. I thought perhaps this was one of the times the Catholics got it wrong and the Baptists were right. I hoped.

My mother looked angry. "Don't pay any attention to that. It's not true. The only people who go to hell are those who do not believe in God. We're all the rest of us Christian. It doesn't matter which church you go to."

"Then why did they say that? Who doesn't believe in God?"

"I don't know, honey, and it's not just the Catholics, the Baptists and the Church of Christ says the same thing. They all say that only they can go to heaven. It caused a big argument in my family, too. It's wrong. And it's all the criminals who don't believe in God. And Communists, like the one that killed President Kennedy. And the Nazis and Hitler didn't believe in God. They all went to hell. But it is wrong to say you have to belong to one certain church to be saved, but they do."

I was disappointed that the Baptists were that way too. I wondered who in my mother's family still belonged to the Church of Christ. Now I was going to have to redo my columns, which would turn it into a chore. I rarely had to do anything over and when I did, I didn't like it.

"They say it because they don't want people going to a different church and not giving all the money to them." My father had come home without us realizing it and had been listening. "It's all about money," he added.

"Not always, they're not all like that," said my mother. "Anyway, we all worship God. You cannot hold what people in the church do against God. They are not the same thing."

I had an afterthought. "When did Aunt Worthrose become Baptist? When she married her first husband or Uncle Clyde?"

"You know, I don't know. I didn't have much contact with her from the time she left home until I came to the city and that was several years later. You'll have to ask her. And it wasn't because of her first husband. Sam Harp was a Quaker."

I had never thought about Aunt Worthrose's first husband before now. Nobody had ever said anything about him.

"Did he leave her?" I asked. "Did they get a divorce? Is he missing? Why was he forgotten?"

"No, honey, of course not, Sam Harp died in the late 40s. They were married more than 20 years."

"He was killed?"

"No, no, Sam Harp had heart trouble, he just died. Your aunt remarried a couple of years later. Uncle Clyde is Methodist. Although he doesn't go to church. Aunt Worthrose follows her own mind. Worthrose never became a Methodist and she was never a pacifist like Sam either."

"Sam Harp was a good man," said my father, as he went down the hall to change out of his work clothes. "Don't let anybody ever tell you otherwise."

Methodist. Quaker. Church of Christ.

I was astounded. How much more work was this going to be? I would need many more columns.

Or maybe I could just call all of them Protestants. Yes!

That would be simpler and much easier. I would relabel the columns- Catholic and Protestant.

"Could we go see that church where you were baptized the next time we go to the countryside?" I asked, imaging the colored people in there singing and shouting, thinking, *that must be an interesting sight.*

"Oh, honey, it's not there any more. It was just an old shack, if it is still there, it's abandoned and rotting away."

"How much time do we have before we have to be at the church tonight?" My father called down the hall.

"About three hours, plenty of time," my mother replied to him. "Victoria, go and study your prayers- you have to say them correctly tonight. I need to go fix dinner now."

I went down the hall to my room and pulled out my book.

Chapter 7
The Shack in the Woods

Jane hurried out to tell Barbara supper was ready and before Barbara could warn her the snake struck!

"Oh!" cried Jane as she felt a sharp bite on her leg!

Staggering with pain, Jane managed to cry "Barbara, help!" and fell to the ground!

But right now Barbara needed help, too!

Right now Barbara was strapped to the back seat of an automobile, bound hand and foot!

She could not scream because she was gagged!

"Hey, Barbara," the driver gloated. "Remember me? Stiff Jones! ah ha, ha, ha."

"You an' this ole car are agoing deep down the river. Ha ha ha."

What he meant is that he would jump out of the car and the car and Barbara would roll down into the river!

What he didn't know was that the ropes around Barbara's wrists were becoming looser!

Soon he jumped out and raced towards the woods

and at that moment Barbara's wrists came free!

Even though Barbara's feet were still bound she managed to get to the front seat of the car. She opened the door and jumped!

She tumbled 2 or 3 times.

"Oh," she said, getting up on her feet. Because her feet were still bound she sat right down again!

"I better get these things off my feet."

It took her some time to get the ropes off her feet.

"I better report to the police. Too bad I didn't get his description," murmured Barbara all in one breath.

Instead of doing this, she wandered about in the woods until she saw a rotten wood shack.

Suddenly she heard the murmur of voices!

"There's someone in that shack," said Barbara half aloud.

Instantly she began to creep on her hands and knees up to the shack.

The voices were clear now. "What did you do with that Scott girl, Jones?" A man's voice demanded. "And your car?"

"That ole car o' mine is a deep down in that ole river. That ole Scott girl is a supposed to be with it. But she done 'scaped!" said Jones.

"What?" cried the other man.

"Stiff Jones," came a woman's voice. "I'm surprised at you."

"I a sorry, Addie," said Stiff. "You're my wife an–"

Barbara waited to hear no more. This would make a good story to tell the police!

"If only I had evidence," thought Barbara.

She broke a piece of wood off the house and raced as fast as she could towards home!

After dinner, as it turned dark, we went to church. I had never been to church in the dark before. I tried to walk quietly in the sanctuary but the heels on my shoes, so easily drowned out at school, clicked sharply on the church floor. No one was in the church except my parents, Aunt Thelma, her daughter Ruth, and the priest.

I saw the priest anoint my mother with the water and oil. Then she and my father went with him into the very back corner of the church. Aunt Thelma took Ruth and I up closer to the altar. I wanted to stay in the back and hear. The priest was saying I could, but Aunt Thelma would not let me go, telling me I had to sit still and be quiet.

"It'll be your turn soon," said Aunt Thelma. And sure enough the priest called me back shortly and I said the prayers I had memorized- The **Our Father, Hail Mary, Act of Contrition,** and **The Apostles Creed.**

"You did very good," said Father Mallett. "You can start attending classes in the fall. If you know your prayers that good, you can go to the second grade. You won't be behind the other kids even though you didn't go last year."

"Yes, you did very well," said Ruth, with sincerity. The other adults agreed.

There was nothing easier than memorizing words and I wondered why they were so impressed. After all, I had only memorized, not written anything.

After visiting the church since before first grade, we had joined officially and my mother was now baptized in the Catholic Church and my father and mother were now married in the Catholic Church. Their first marriage had not been in any church. They had eloped before the war to a courthouse because my mother would not become Catholic then, which was one of the things that had made my grandmother mad and she had left my father out of the will. Or so my mother said.

My mother had explained her change of mind. "I'm going to become Catholic now, so that our family, me and you and your father, can all go to the same church."

After this, during church, when other people got up and went to take Communion, my parents did too. My father had always been Catholic but he had not taken Communion until my mother could do so also. I still had to wait, I had to go to CCD first. Aunt Worthrose didn't go to Mama's baptism. Mama told her all about it the next day.

"So, June Rosette, if Vic doesn't really like the church and I know what you think of it, why join it now?"

"Victoria needs to go to church. All children need to go to church. Where are we going to go? We visited other churches, it was obvious after the first two or three times we were not welcome. I guess we could go to a big church downtown and get lost in the crowd, but with the way Vic works, it will be just me and Victoria many Sundays. I don't want to have to drive downtown. I'd like a church we can get involved in. The Protestant churches around here want the white collar workers in Fairland Addition and Water Oaks for members. When they find out we live on the other side of Silver Brook and that Vic is an Italian, well-"

"Why don't people like Italians?" I asked. "Aren't most Italians rich and famous or at least rich?"

"Not most, just a few," said my mother, abruptly switching her attention from her sister to correct me. "There are the famous Italian entertainers, singers Dean Martin, Frank Sinatra, Perry Como."

"I know who Frank Sinatra is," I said. "He was in **Never So Few**." That was a World War II movie I had seen on TV. It was one of the best World War II movies ever. So he was Italian.

"You like the war movies. But you never watch the westerns or the gangster movies do you?" Lately my mother rarely paid attention anymore when I watched TV during the day. She frequently went into Daddy's bedroom to talk on the phone. We had an extension Daddy had put in all by himself without the phone company knowing.

"In the gangster movies all the bad guys will be Italians like all the bad guys in the westerns are Indians," she said.

"I never watch them," I got enough westerns with the weekly **Bonanza** requirement. "I'd like the gangster movies except they tell you who did it from the beginning. I like the mystery movies where you don't know until the end, like my books. But there is not many of them. The only way I usually watch a different type of movie is if Frank Sinatra is in it."

"He's a singer too," said my mother.

"I don't have any of his records," I said.

"I noticed you never play your records. I thought you didn't like music."

"Oh, I loved the music at President Kennedy's funeral," I said. "But the records you bought- I can't understand all the words." I had no interest in songs I couldn't understand.

"I have some old Frank Sinatra and Dean Martin records somewhere. I'll find them."

Aunt Worthrose had not followed the conversation and did not comment about music. Instead she said-.

"It won't be long before these lily white people will all have a lot more than Italians to worry about. What did we fight the war for? The Nazis might have well just won the war. What's happening in this world?"

"It looks to me like," said my mother, "they want to go back to what it was like in the Depression. We were separate but equal then all right, everybody separate and everybody poor as a church house mouse. Why anybody would want to go back to those times, I'll never know."

"It's all this civil rights," said Aunt Worthrose. "It's making everything worse. It's backfiring. What kind of people go to this church? Any Italians there Victoria could get to know?"

"No, they're all white, well, except for a few better class Mexican families."

"Maybe still it is better than no church at all, for Victoria, at least."

"I'll have to make the best of it. Anyway, after all this, it may not last, Vic particularly doesn't like this priest."

"Why not try other Catholic churches then?"

"Oh, we can't," said my mother, with a touch of sarcasm in her voice. "This is the church we are assigned to. It's just like the schools, you have to go to the church that is closest to you. You don't have a choice."

My Aunt Worthrose turned around and stared at my mother for a moment, eyes wide behind her bifocal glasses.

"You're kidding, June Rosette," she said incredulously.

"Nope, that's the way it is."

"You've got to be joking."

"No, no, I couldn't believe it myself, but that's the rules. You have to get permission from the bishop to switch parishes and there has to be a good reason for it. Usually, I'm told, they turn you down. They want you going to the church closest to you."

"Why I never heard of anything like that in all my life! But what about all the Mexicans that live just north of the freeway? Surely that is the closest Catholic church to them?"

"Oh, they've got their own little church over where they live, with a priest that speaks Spanish. Sometimes they use our facilities for special events but they don't come to church with us."

"Well, I don't know anything about Catholics, Vic is the only Catholic I've ever known."

"Well, now I'm Catholic too." My mother laughed, a little bitterly.

"You know now that Mrs. Longhem is selling more lots down Foam Meadow, before long it won't be such a stigma living on this side of Silver Brook. Someday there will be some churches right here in this neighborhood. Good Protestant churches."

"We'll all be dead and buried before then, I'm afraid," said my mother.

VI *Diversions*

On the way home from church the next Sunday we stopped at the new ice cream parlor that had just opened up right across Silver Brook, between our house and Fairvine. It was very old fashioned, Daddy said, and the waitress there was very pretty and smiled at Daddy just like the waitress at the old ice cream parlor downtown. I thought it was a very happy place, small but bright and colorful with high counters that had busy happy people behind it. We felt welcomed. We really liked it.

However, we did not visit the parlor again immediately because shortly after, we went on vacation in the car. Mama would have liked to fly but, although Daddy worked on airplane engines, he refused to fly in planes unless his bosses made him. Daddy said you could not see any good scenery from a plane.

Although I couldn't take my book for fear it might get lost, I was given plenty of paper and pencils. We drove a long way to Texas to a place called Six Flags where we met a Japanese couple on vacation really from Japan, which amazed my parents as we had been at war with them such a short time ago. But we were all very friendly and there were more rides there than at the fair at home.

Then we went to Dallas to see where President Kennedy had been shot. There was a statue of his head there, among a lot of flowers. At first we thought someone had broken it because it had holes in it. Then we realized that was to represent where the bullets struck.

When we first entered Texas I had been disappointed that nothing really changed when we crossed the state line. I expected Texas to be much different. So I didn't pay attention to the scenery on the way home, which annoyed Daddy. I was thinking about the rest of summer ahead. I had a plan.

Paper in hand, the next morning after vacation I put away all my pride and literally begged my mother to teach me longhand and let me use a pen or at least a thin pencil. Maybe if my mother knew how many stories I had to write, it would help. And begging in front of my father usually worked.

"I have lots more stories to write," I complained. "But the big pencil hurts my hand and takes so long. It is such hard work printing every word letter by letter."

"Later, not yet," said my mother as she served my father breakfast.

I repeated my request, trying to be more dramatic.

I NEED to learn to write longhand.

"Why not teach her?" my father demanded, as he ate.

"No," said my mother. She turned towards me. "Victoria, I'm not going to teach you longhand. Fairvine Guidance Group already criticized me because you could read before you started school and could print your ABCs. I don't want to have to be talked to like that again."

"Why don't they want her to learn?" asked my father suspiciously.

"There's a certain age and grade level that they are supposed to learn each thing, and it throws off the rest of the class and the teacher if they are taught too soon," my mother reported. "The Guidance Group has already made the decision on how to proceed with cursive instruction. They will be using bright blue fountain pens in the third grade to begin the practice of calligraphy. We will have to get her certain pens with special cartridges designed to make the ink flow just right. It is very important that she have beautiful handwriting."

"Oh." My father continued to look suspicious, but was silent as he finished his breakfast. "Why should that be so important? That doesn't sound right." He sighed.

"It is especially important for young ladies who might need to get a job someday. I talked to them about it before school ended. The teachers said writing too soon could cause her to malform her letters and never have good handwriting."

"They may not be as smart as you think. Look at Mrs. Anderson," said my father. "I don't see where she is so smart."

"That's just gossip coming to Worthy from Alyce O'Kelley's grandmother in the school's kitchen from who knows how far down the line. But as for the pen, regardless, I'm the one who will get chewed out over it, so there it is."

"What do you mean about Mrs. Anderson?" I asked.

98

My parents exchanged glances.

"She had a baby. Jayne has another brother," Mama said quickly.

I felt sorry for Jayne about that. Jayne had several older brothers, one her own age- a twin and now a younger one. Sad, but I really wasn't interested. I returned to the mission at hand. "At least give me a thin pencil."

"No and that is final. You heard what I said to your father. Only a thick pencil, no longhand until the class is ready for it."

"Why can't she have a thinner pencil at least?"

"The Guidance Group teachers say it is very important that she be able to erase her mistakes. Thick pencils make soft impressions that are easily erased. She cannot mark things out, if she does, she has to start all over again. They really don't want her to do any writing at all except in class. But I don't know how to stop her. That's all she wants to do."

"Well, I have to go to work or I'll be late," said Daddy, and the conversation ended. Daddy was now occasionally working all day and night and the next day. On a few occasions he was gone for three or four days. His job was now to figure out why the airplane engines did not work right. He was so good at his job that his company was flying him to a different city to work on bad engines there, even though he didn't like to fly.

"Stop cleaning house and play with me," I would beg Mama when my dolls were not enough to keep me happy and my hand hurt too much to write.

"You can just watch TV until I'm finished," she would say. Mama cleaned house in the morning. She would have it all clean by lunch. She didn't like me to help her clean. She said I messed up more than I helped.

"There's nothing on," I would reply. "I'm bored."

"Why don't you just play dolls? You drove me crazy about playing fashion dolls, now that I let you whenever you want, you don't want to."

"I do, but not all the time!"

"Don't you have any more books to read?"

"No, I've read them all, twice." I could now read a mystery

book in two to four hours depending on its length and complexity.

"I wish we had a library closer than downtown." My mother sighed. "These books have gotten so expensive."

"If I write my own books, it doesn't cost as much," I ventured.

"Play your records."

I did like to play the old records Mama had found. Aunt Worthrose had also found some magazines with pictures and stories about Frank Sinatra and Dean Martin.

"They are too old for you. You know they are the same age as your daddy is," said my mother, when she saw me examining their pictures and reading the stories about them, which took maybe two minutes.

"Daddy is just as handsome as Dean Martin," I said.

"From what I have heard about them, he may look more like Dean but his personality is more like Frank's," said my mother.

"Why didn't Daddy go to Hollywood and become a movie star like Dean Martin?"

She laughed. "Well you know, back in the 30s when we were dating, a studio did come to town and held a little fair of sorts, where they were looking for people to go to Hollywood. Me, your daddy, and Florrie were actually interviewed. But Florrie and your daddy, while they had the good looks, they were too short."

"Even if Daddy is short, couldn't he have been a singer?" I asked.

"He doesn't sing," said my mother.

"Oh yes he does, I heard him sing in church," I said. "He sings good."

My mother stopped her housekeeping and looked at me. "When?"

"Not too long ago. The priest asked for just the men to sing a verse. I told him to sing and he did. You had gone to the ladies room. He sang good, too. People were looking at him. But he stopped when you came back. It was time for the women to sing their verse then anyway."

"I have been married to your father 24 years and I have never heard him sing a note," she said and threw down her duster. A little cloud of dust burst from it. I sneezed.

"Maybe I could be an actress," I said, after recovering from the dust. "Or a singer."

My mother choked a little as she coughed. "I have another idea," she said, as she fetched the vacuum.

My mother's idea was that I should take piano lessons. I was so smart that surely I would be a good piano player. Maybe a concert pianist.

Daddy immediately bought me an antique tall upright piano. We put it in the living room. I loved it, as furniture. It was much more attractive than the Early American style furniture that was all over the rest of the house. That country style furniture, though it was all new was just ugly. I longed for a crystal chandelier to go with my antique piano. But our hanging light fixture in the living room was wooden, shaped like a wagon wheel and had tiny brown lamp shades on it instead of beautiful crystals. I hated it.

We drove a long way across town to the piano teacher who had a lot of other students at the same time. She taught us the scales. It was torture, not because of the playing, but because the piano teacher smoked and my head hurt all day after every lesson. Nevertheless, I tried my best to play every day because it made my mother smile.

I did learn how to decipher some of the musical notes and decided to try my hand at writing a few lines. I believed maybe the Virgin Mary would like a song written for her in English.

Mary O Mother Oh Pray for Me
By Victoria Grasso

Mary O Mother oh pray for me
Who many times have offended thee
O Mary O mother O Virgin most pure
O Mother of Jesus Christ Our Lord
O Mother of Beauty most tender to see
I deeply humble myself before thee.
Verse 2
Mary O Mother O Pray for me
My dearest love I give to Thee
O Ho-ly Virgin Most De-Vine

All Ho-ly, All Pure art thine
All Bea ut i ful art thou to see
Mary O Mother O Pray for me!

I thought about showing my song to Father Mallett. Father Mallet was friendly to some people, but not me. I suspected that Father Mallett didn't like me. Maybe there would be another priest I could show it to someday.

I did not have time to play the piano when Claudia came over but many weekends she canceled at the last minute. Because most of my weekends were reserved for Claudia whether she came or not, I didn't get to see Eva and Victor anymore. Now that she was going to be my sister, Claudia seemed to be even more of a secret than ever before.

And with the Vacarro family broken up, seeing Connie was no longer an option.

"As soon as we can tell people about Claudia, we will have Eva and Victor over again," Mama promised, but with a new condition. "I'm afraid to drive that far so your father will have to be available to go pick them up and bring them here for you to play with them. Your Aunt Jolene has gotten a job. She is working for a hospital in the cafeteria just like Mrs. O'Kelley Senior works at Fairvine. Her income for being a widow was cut and she had to go to work for money. She leaves Victor and Eva alone weekends. You certainly cannot go to their house with no adult supervision."

This was sobering news. All my class had felt sorry for Pete, the boy at school whose mother had to work. And even more for Marva whose parents were divorced and her mother worked all the time. They were both so quiet. I wondered if Victor and Eva would become quiet like them, too.

"Remember not to tell people about Claudia yet. I am so glad I can trust you on these things. Remember our story about her being a neighbor's friend's daughter?"

"I remember."

"Her grandfather wants her to spend more time with us before we start the adoption proceedings. Then we will have to bring in a social worker from the state and eventually go to court to change her last name," my mother said, and bit her lip as if anticipating all this was stressful. "Try not to worry about it."

I'm not worried about Claudia, I thought.

The odd thing was I rarely thought about her when she was not there, same with Ruth Marino. I'd almost forgotten her but when Claudia canceled yet again, my mother contacted Aunt Thelma. That Saturday we all went shopping at the mall. Aunt Thelma liked to drive so she came and got us. But I hated shopping because I always had to try on clothes that were labeled "Chubby Girls". Ruth wore normal sizes. She had a lot more to choose from. Aunt Thelma was preparing Ruth to go to several girl only camps that would take the rest of the summer.

After hearing Ruth describe what the camps would be like, I stopped complaining about the piano lessons. But after a few weeks the instructor told my mother my hands were too small, so mercifully the lessons stopped.

Then Claudia's grandfather told us she was going off to vacation with relatives for the rest of the summer. She would not be back until school started after Labor Day. Daddy was still working every weekend so I still couldn't see Eva and Victor, now stuck at home by themselves.

I hoped we would fetch them when Daddy finally had a weekend off. But instead, we went to an Italian festival where we accidentally ran into Uncle Chris, Uncle Vince and their families in the midst of a huge crowd. It was a friendly reunion. Then I had to go and kiss a really, really old lady who couldn't speak English. And she had bad breath.

"If it's so important for me to have somebody to play with, why can't I ever play with my real first cousins?" I asked, when we got home, trying to remember the fun encounter rather than the old lady.

Mama seemed to truly smugly enjoy this conversation. At first. "Well, Vic, give Victoria an explanation."

He glared at her. "We can still see Uncle Vince's family sometimes. Maybe. But they live across the mountains."

"Why them?" asked my mother, with a little taunt in her voice. "Why them and not Chris's family?"

"Do I have to say it straight out?" He glared at her. "You take a good look at Chris's girls? Do you think other people won't see? Do you think people are blind?" He paused. "Vince's little girl looks like her mother."

"You could've consulted with me first before you said that. Are you forgetting how smart she really is?" I wasn't quite sure why my mother was now angry, but she was.

"She's a little girl. She's book smart but she's a little girl. She should not have to have an explanation for everything!" My father turned to me. "Ok, Victoria, it's because of the will. It's because they won't give me my part. Let's just leave it at that." He glared at my mother again. "Do you think I want it this way? Do you think this is what I want? This is the way it has to be. For your sake. For Victoria's sake. Let's not this discuss it anymore. It's final. Period."

My mother and I glanced at each other. We could see he was getting mad. It was time to drop the subject. My real cousins were all at least two years younger than me. So it really wasn't that important.

But Mama still had hopes for my social life.

"Mrs. O'Kelley says you can come and play with Alyce. She's invited you especially."

Back again to the neighborhood kids.

I thought about Alyce's house. "Tell her I can't go, "I pleaded. "Alyce can come here but I'm not allowed to there."

"I don't think Alyce is going to be allowed to come here again until you have visited her. It's been a long time. What am I going to tell her mother?"

"Tell her I can't come. Tell her I'm being punished."

"They'll think it's me, that I'm a snob," she sighed. "Oh well. What can I do? Valery has gone to summer camp like Ruth. What about having Cindy over? Her mother has a new baby, you cannot go there."

Remembering Cindy's asthma, I said. "I'm not letting her into my room. We would have to play outside in the heat."

"You know she cannot do that."

"Then tell her the same thing, that I'm being punished and can't have any company."

My mother sighed and rolled her eyes again. "Well, I've run out of possible playmates and ideas," she said, and went back to her housework.

Maybe I can get to work on my book now, I thought. *I need to*

104

remember not to complain about being bored again.

"I have another idea!" My mother had finished cleaning the kitchen before I could get going good.

On no! What next?

My mother got a small table for me and set it up in the den. I sat at that writing table and had to write my numbers clear through from one to 1000.

"Before school let out The Guidance Committee teachers had recommended I have you do this sometime during the summer before second grade began." she said. "This will really get you into numbers."

1,2,3,…34,35,36..435.436...689.690...997.998...all the way to 1000. Every single number. In pencil. I wrote them big so it took several pages. It took several days. It made her really happy when I finished. My hand ached.

"I am so proud, I can report this to the group in September. And I know they will approve!" She picked up the written pages of sequential numbers. "You don't mind that I take this work and keep it safe do you?"

"Oh, no, that's all right."

You can put it in the garbage as far as I care, I thought.

That chore over, I got back to my writing. But not for long.

She bought me math "fun" workbooks and sat down at the table with me to work math problems. She was good at math and she liked it. I let her do all the math work and just watched. Whenever she left me alone I would sneak my book onto the table and print, hiding it under the math books.

My arm constantly ached from printing. One morning, my mother was up walking about house, picking up stuff and dusting, trying to keep quiet, thinking I needed silence to work at math.

I was also trying to be as quiet as possible, slipping my thick pencil behind the math books to print on my story under them. I would print a little, glance out of the corner of my eye at her. She seemed to be glancing out the corner of her eyes. Sometimes our glances caught and we hastily looked away. This could not go on.

I have to tell my mother I am writing no matter what the consequences.

I prepped for a big argument. If I yelled loud enough like

Daddy, and then cried at the end, I knew I could win. I shoved my chair back from the table turned around and looked up at her. She put down her dust cloth.

"How is it coming?" she asked nonchalantly.

"Come and see." I pushed my chair further back, pushed the math books aside, stood up straight and revealed my work.

To my surprise she took it well and calmly said, "I thought that's what you were doing perhaps. I guess it's all right."

I was ecstatic. I sat back down and buried the hated math books with my papers.

"Mama, read my story," I demanded, emboldened by my victory. "Remember, it's just the first draft." I let her read all I had written. Chapters 1- 5.

"You know your Uncle Vince's middle name is Raymond," said my mother, when she finished.

"I forgot. So what?" I replied, impatiently. I wanted to know how I had done.

She has not caught that while her name is June, I named one of the characters April, I thought.

Then again, April was not based on my mother, nor was Ellen. I wanted them to both to be like my mother and like Aunt Worthrose at the same time but really not like either one altogether.

This was fiction!

I divided the chapters of the book out and drew up a table of contents and character list. I was worried about the name Jane Lee Kape. I had named Jane before I ever heard of Jayne Anderson, before I ever knew Mrs. Anderson had a daughter. I knew I should not name characters after people I knew but Jayne Anderson's name had an Y in it -J A Y N E- so I figured that was all right since Jane Kape's name was spelt J A N E L E E K A P E.

No one can think I based Jane Lee Kape on her, certainly not.

That was the fun part of writing- making up your own people who might be kind of like people you knew or read about but were all different. I was enjoying my characters but I still had to figure out to what else was going to happen in the story.

"You have so many books you could read again. And there's lots more we can buy you. Why do you have to write your own? That's so much work and you know you're too little to get them published or anything. Who is going to read them, the other kids at school? Do the other kids at school write books?"

This was a good question. I had often asked the other kids about what they wrote. I told them I wrote stories and asked them if they did too. Most of them said yes, they did, but whenever I suggested an exchange they said no. Or if they said yes, they wanted to take my stories and then give me theirs later. I wasn't going to do that.

"I don't know," I finally replied to my mother's question.

"Do you think you are going to be a detective when you grow up? Or a policewoman?"

"No, Mama, Barbara Scott is just a character. She's make-believe."

"Are Barbara, Belle, and Jane like imaginary friends?"

"No," I was frustrated that my mother did not understand. I never thought about the characters except when I was writing the book. "I don't have any imaginary friends."

"It is all right to have an imaginary friend," she said. "I did."

"I don't." I never had.

I have enough real people to deal with, I thought.

"Which of the girls are you in the book? Barbara?"

"You don't understand," I said, getting more impatient with her, although I tried to be kind. "None of them are me. They are characters. Like in the movies and on TV they are just make-believe."

"Where do you get your ideas? What is going to happen next? What is going to happen to the missing girls?"

These last questions pleased me even if I didn't know the answers yet. I was making this up as I went along. I didn't want to reveal that I didn't exactly know what was going to happen in the book.

"You'll see, I don't want to give away anything yet. I'm almost ready with the next chapter." I turned back to the table and got back to work, printing on laboriously. Then I had a thought. I had a good start but no title. I had a vague idea of what was going to happen, but a title would give that structure. After some thought, I believed I had it.

"**Barbara Kay Scott Mystery Series - The Mystery of the Missing People** is going to be the title," I announced to my mother, who was now cooking in the kitchen.

"I don't think that sounds right," said my mother. "People does not sound right. How about 'Persons'?"

I thought about this a while. I didn't necessarily agree but I was so happy to have someone to read my book and help a little, I didn't want to reject her advice. Maybe persons did not sound so bad.

Persons. I wrote it out. ***Barbara Kay Scott Mystery Series -The Mystery of the Missing Persons.***

"That sounds better," my mother said. ***"The Mystery of the Missing Persons."***

Hearing her say it out loud convinced me. *Yes!* I thought, marveling that my mother was right and being suddenly hopeful that she might be more supportive than I had previously hoped.

Barbara Kay Scott Mystery Stories- The Mystery of the Missing Persons. Perfect!

Chapter 8
The Missing Person

When Barbara got back to town she reported what had happened to the police.

She told that Stephen Jones, alias Stiff, had made an attempt to get "rid" of the pretty young detective and about the shack in the woods.

"Also Stiff Jones had a wife named Addie," Barbara continued. "Stiff Jones is from the south I could tell by his accent."

The sleuth gave him the piece of rotten wood from the shack.

"Thank you, Miss Scott," said the chief. "We've been trying to catch up with Stiff Jones for a long time, Miss."

On the way home Barbara passed Black Oaks Park. On a bench sat a crying woman!

"What's the matter?" Barbara asked sympathetically.

"M-my daughter was k-KIDNAPPED!" The stranger sobbed.

"Did you tell the police?" asked Barbara.

"N– no!"

"But why?"

"Diane will be killed," was the answer she got.

"Why?" asked Barbara.

"Because – because!" The stranger burst into tears!

Barbara learned the stranger's name was Fae Bolman. Her daughter Diane Bolman had recently disappeared. A note was left on her bed. It said:

DON'T GO TO THE POLICE
OR YOU WILL LOOSE EMILY MAY, TOO!
STIFF+ADDIE

"So what shall I do?" cried Mrs. Bolman, "my husband is dead and I have only my two daughters."

"Now, now, Mrs. Bolman." Barbara sympathized with her. "I'm sure everything will be all right.

"I'll take the case for you.

"You know my cousin is missing too."

"Yes, I heard," was her answer.

"I think if we find Belle we will find Diane too!"

"Mother, It's time to go," came a high-pitched voice behind them.

Barbara turned to see a girl about 20 with the most beautiful flaming red hair Barbara ever saw!

"This is Emily May," Mrs. Bolman said proudly.

Emily May had dark blue eyes and a cheery smile.

"How do you do?" said Barbara shaking hands with her.

"My what a pretty dress you have on, Miss Scott."

"Thank you," said Barbara. "And do call me Barbara."

"You may call me Emily and I must go," said Emily May rushing off.

In a few minutes she came back, a frightened

expression on her face.

"I found Diane's sweater on a back alley street," she cried!

I was very proud of the name Bolman. I had made it up all by myself. I took the word bowl and added man as a suffix and dropped the W.

After I had made up the name, my mother and I looked it up in the phone book to see if it was real. It was, but all people listed with that name had two Ls in it.

I was quite pleased that I had come up with something different.

I was sure there were not any people with the last name Bolman spelt that way in the whole world.

VII *Preparations*

We rarely went to downtown. Before we moved, Mama and I had regularly gone downtown on the city bus that stopped right near our old house and would take us to a huge department store. This was before I had to start wearing the chubby girl's sizes and I enjoyed it then. We had many happy shopping trips then, although one time I lost a five dollar bill. But after we moved, the bus stop was too far away and we rarely went. Sometimes Daddy took us although he did not like shopping and would go elsewhere while we were shopping for clothes.

We rarely saw the movies but we went to a lot of musical movies at the theatre since Daddy liked those so much. My parents liked a beautiful ornate movie palace with real comfortable seats that was a long way away downtown. We never went to other theatres. The theatre in Fairland Addition was still unfinished, its foundation sat empty all summer since all the construction workers were engaged in throwing up (as Daddy put it) more houses in the additions at break neck speed (he said).

I thought we were going to a movie one hot day in July when we started in that direction, although I noticed we were not very dressed up as we should be. Then Daddy parked the car and we got out where there were many people walking. We joined them.

It was a hot windy day and after a long hot tiring walk, with many other people all going the same way as us, we were finally seated on a blanket among many other families out in the open field. Most all of the people were white but there were one or two colored families within sight further down the slope. My parents commented with casual interest on this. Every family had their own little space but it was very little. There were ants in the grass and we had to be careful to stay on the blanket and kill them if they crawled up there with us. We had a little bit of food and we each had a drink. I was absolutely miserable. My mother was cross as well. Her makeup was melting and her hairstyle had fallen down. She complained bitterly about the heat. I was less bothered by the heat than by the bugs and the boredom. Only my father remained cheerful and resolute.

"It is going to be worth it," he said.

My mother and I just glared at him.

Suddenly from overhead came a tremendous roar. I saw many airplanes coming at us flying high then diving down directly at us. My instinctive reaction to the noise was to dive to the ground, cover my head, and pull my knees up against my chest. As I huddled there waiting for the onslaught, I felt proud that I had remembered my training so well and had acted at the first moment of danger.

Then I heard my parents laughing at me. I sat up and looked around. A few other people nearby were snickering too.

My father pulled me close to him, my mother was still laughing. "It's just the jet show before the fireworks start. What did you think was happening?"

"The Russians," I replied, surprised that was not what all had thought. I had expected everyone to assume the defensive position we practiced so often at school.

There were extremely beautiful fireworks after it turned dark. The mosquitoes come out after dark also. By the end I had numerous bites, was hungry and thirsty, and then we had to walk a long, long way back to our car and wait for a long time to get out of the parking area. It was very hot in the car just creeping along in heavy traffic. There was no breeze through the windows. Mosquitoes riding home with us buzzed around our ears. My legs hurt.

"Wasn't that great?" said my father. "Did you ever see such colors?"

My mother and I both glared at him as hard as we could but it was too dark for him to see us.

"We need a color TV," said my mother.

We also traveled to downtown when my mother took me to the doctor. She had taken me often when I was little. She worried that I might die like Rosalind Renee. Dr. Plunkett was always very reassuring I was not going to die.

Dr. Plunkett had moved his office further away and to get there on time, Mama had to brave the freeways. Despite her fear, she was more worried about me. A large thick spot had formed on my middle finger, and it hurt, so I was going to the doctor to make sure it wasn't cancer.

"This is a callous," the doctor told my mother, then turned to me, "you do a lot of writing in school?"

"She writes all the time at home and in school. That's all she's been doing all summer." My mother sounded a little exasperated.

"What does she use?"

"This." I pulled the large thick pencil out of my pocket. I tried to take one with me wherever I went in case I got a chance to write when nobody was looking.

"Victoria, I didn't even know you had that in your pocket, you're going to ruin your clothes. Pencil lead is going to get all over your good dress." My mother considered any piece of clothing that had a small spot on it as ruined and she would give it to Alyce's mother right away, along with any of my toys she could get away with, whether they were ruined or not. Other grownup items regularly went into the garbage once they acquired even the most minor blemish.

"I had to make do with old and used stuff most of my life," my mother would say, as she routinely dumped clothes, towels, kitchen utensils and anything else with a minor flaw into the trash can, to be replaced on the next shopping trip or by mail order catalog. "I'm not going to put up with used or dirty looking stuff, now that I don't have to."

Daddy kept all his stuff hidden from her in the backyard barn he had built to be his workshop. But I had nowhere to hide my stuff except my room and could only protect my paper dolls, fashion dolls and my book by constantly proclaiming how important they were and memorizing exactly where they were every morning before I left for school. She knew that if anything was out of place I would know it when I got home.

"Don't look so anxious. Relax. Show me how you hold this pencil," Dr. Plunkett was saying to me, breaking into my worries about my stuff being thrown out or given to charity. The doctor was examining my finger and compared the mark to the pencil. He held the pencil up and gazed at it.

I demonstrated printing with the pencil. He told my mother that was probably causing the problem. My mother explained why I had to use the big fat pen or my future would be ruined, according to the teachers.

"Hmm, teachers," said Dr. Plunkett, rubbing his chin with one hand as he showed me how to hold the pencil differently. "Don't worry, she's all right. I doubt she has a thyroid condition. She just needs to eat less sweets and more fruits and vegetables. As for the finger, tell you what, try to get her to hold the pencil the way I showed and see if that doesn't help, if not, just let her use something else during the summer and give her the fat pencil back when school starts back up." He winked at me.

Mama was feeling anxious and nervous on the way home so she drove on the narrow back streets, avoiding the tangled freeways so we would not have a car wreck. Dr. Plunkett had given her some pills to take when she became nervous. But she could not take them when she was driving.

After a long time, the back streets took us to the back entrance to Water Oaks where our car would then proceed through Fairland Addition and approach our house from the other side of Silver Brook. It was an interesting drive, passing many different types of buildings and I enjoyed the scenery while I toyed with the results of the doctor's visit in my mind.

"Why isn't Dr. Anderson our doctor?"

"Don't you like Dr. Plunkett?" My mother did not look at me while she drove. She kept her eyes on the road. But there was little traffic on these winding back roads so she was relaxed.

"He is nice," I said. "But I thought maybe Dr. Anderson had an office in Water Oaks." I had been told I could not go and visit Mrs. Anderson after school every day next year as she was not one of my teachers anymore. I was too attached, they said. But maybe I might see her at the doctor's office.

"Oh, honey, he's not a real doctor. He's a college professor, he has a PhD, not an M.D.," said my mother. "He teaches psychology at the university."

"What's that?"

"Well that is- um- ah- there are some doctors who treat people who have problems in their- um- mind. But that is not what Mrs. Anderson's husband is, he is not a real doctor but he teaches college students who later might become those kinds of doctors. They are called psychiatrists," said my mother. "You don't want to ever have to have a doctor like that. That's not a good doctor to have."

This was a very strange remark for my mother to have made because it seemed my parents usually thought doctors and teachers were the most important people in the world.

They admired educated people because neither of them had finished high school. My mother had gone to the eleventh grade in a one room schoolhouse. My father had only gone through the fourth grade.

"But Dr. Anderson is a teacher who is called Doctor because he has studied as many years in his subject as a real doctor studies medicine," further explained my mother, who misinterpreted my silence as confusion.

And all this time I had thought he was a real doctor. People need to be more clear about these titles, I thought. *Like in the movies princess doesn't always mean the girl is really a princess in a real country.*

Titles were deceptive.

"Like your teachers are all women, professors are men. A very few women make it though," said my mother. "Let's drive by the high school since we are near it. They have a grand ballroom, I'm told, where they hold the prom every year. You can wear beautiful dresses like your dolls when you go to dances."

And once again I saw the huge antique old building, a truly magnificent structure, which I would one day get to see inside and attend classes. It most resembled an old plantation home, I decided, graceful and elegant like the one at Arlington cemetery that had stood in the background during President Kennedy's funeral.

"Looks like it should be full of antiques and chandeliers," said my mother thoughtfully. "Instead of classrooms. It will be wonderful to go to school there. I wish I had had an opportunity to go to such a school when I was young. As smart as you are, you are going to take the place by storm."

I envisioned the rooms at Hereald High full of such treasures, with old fashioned desks for us and a pulpit for the teachers. But while it was nice to anticipate Hereald High and my bright future, I needed to remain focused on my present mission. For the rest of the drive I silently picked at the bump on my finger hoping to make it look worse.

And when we got home I made a great show of holding the

pencil differently, placing all my fingertips around the pencil thus avoiding the sore spot. But I could not write that way.

"This isn't going to work, you're going to have to give me a pen," I announced, as soon as my father got home from work. "My finger's getting worse."

Later that night, I heard her discussing this with my father. My mother's voice was high-pitched and my father's voice was angry.

"And how much did this doctor visit cost? For a callous? Because she can't have an ordinary pencil or pen!"

"But the teachers don't want her writing with anything else!" was my mother's last protest. "The teachers in the Guidance Group specifically told me-"

"I don't give a damn what the damn teachers want! Who's got to pay this doctor bill? The teachers? Dammit, give her a pen!" was my father's last word.

So I got a pen. A red pen. My mother devised a plan to give me a pen that was as far from a blue fountain pen or thin pencil that she could possibly find. I got a red ballpoint. And it made the printing a lot easier.

Chapter 9
Harold Hall

"What?" cried Mrs. Bolman in disbelief.

"Yes," cried Emily May. "Close to Harold Hall!"

"That's just where they found my cousin's sweater!" Barbara cried.

Harold Hall used to be one of the show places of Black Oaks edition but J. E. Harold and family had deserted the old place years ago when Barbara was only 7.

Mysterious happenings have been going on in the old place. Some people claim it has a ghost!

"Do- do- y-you think, Di- Di-" Mrs. Bolman burst into tears!

"Mother please don't cry," begged Emily May.

Barbara shuddered to think that Belle was in there

too. But she didn't say so!

"I'm going to investigate Harold Hall!" determined Barbara.

Barbara got on her bike and raced towards home.

She told her mother about the latest happenings, and of her suspicion of Harold Hall.

"I've never heard of a family named Bolman," said Ellen as she put the last dish away.

"Oh, they're new here."

"Where do they live?"

"On Oak Leaf Road."

"Have they found Belle yet?" came a brisk voice from behind them.

They turned to see the black haired Jane and her little dog Bleachy. She had already recovered from her snake bite. Bleachy was a cute little Cocker Spaniel with brown fur and black eyes.

"Don't bring that dog in MY house," Ellen demanded sternly.

"Oh," moaned Jane. "He won't hurt anything."

"Nevertheless I don't want him in this house. Tie him up outside or something!" said Ellen.

"How's Aunt April?" asked Barbara.

"Oh, Mom's doing lots better," said Jane.

Jane and Barbara launched into a discussion about Harold Hall and its "ghost".

Finally they decided to investigate it.

Soon they drove off in Jane's car towards Harold Hall.

When they reached the place they saw its once beautiful door was shut.

As Barbara reached for the knob a man's voice said: ' "THIS-S-S IS THE HOU-O-OUSE O-F THE SPIR-R-RITS.

GO-O-O OR DI-IE! '

Just before summer ended my hair was cut for the first time

117

ever and I had my hair fixed at the beauty shop where Mama went every week. The prickly rollers were very painful. The smells in the beauty shop made my head hurt whether there were smokers there or not (and usually there were) and the hairspray stung my eyes. They washed my hair in very cold water and the dryer was very hot. It was horrible.

It was nice not to have to have my hair put in a bun every night. Mama bought me a night bonnet to keep my hairstyle in place while I slept. I took that off as soon as she left the room after tucking me in, so it was not a problem. But soon I realized that Mama planned to take me to the beauty shop every week, every week for the rest of my entire life.

"Would you like go to the bank? We could go to the ice cream parlor afterwards." Daddy looked at me hopefully.

My father had a special day off during the week when the bank was open and he wanted me to go with him. When I walked into the bank holding Daddy's hand, I realized that it was a much different building than I had ever seen. It was not like the grocery stores or the department stores downtown or church, although it was more like church perhaps than any of the others. It also somehow reminded me of the ice cream parlor. I decided it was similar to a church building and an ice cream parlor combined.

The entrance was a glass door. There were some windows on that wall but most of the windows were on another wall to the right. The other walls had huge red granite counters. Also on the left wall was a large steel door that looked like it belonged on a ship. The overall effect was impressive, invoking feelings of reverence and pleasure at the same time.

"It's her first visit to a bank." Daddy was addressing a man in a police officer's uniform who stood near that steel door.

"Welcome to the bank," the policeman said to me, and shook my hand.

Other people came over. They were friendly and welcoming. They seemed to know Daddy well and called him Mr. Grasso with a good deal of respect, even if they didn't exactly pronounce it right. They said Grayso. But Daddy did not correct them and I didn't care. In my opinion Grayso sounded better, actually. After they greeted me, I had a chance to look around and take it all in.

In the middle of the huge room there were tall wooden tables. Behind the tall red granite counters stood very well dressed people with black bars in front of them with little gates in the bars that opened when someone approached. There were lines at the counter but also people walking around, all dressed in clothes even better than church clothes. They all seemed very happy and busy. Then Daddy steered me towards the steel door. The policeman came and turned the wheel and let me see inside.

"This is where all the money is kept," said Daddy. "Not just our money, hundreds of people keep their money here."

Daddy walked up to the counter but I couldn't see anything. The counter was just too tall for me. He talked to the lady behind the counter for a few minutes and she gave him some papers.

"She might work for a bank someday," said Daddy to the lady. "Or she might be a lawyer. She's really smart. She'll be going to college. I've got a savings account here for her, just for that."

The lady looked impressed and came out from behind the granite counter to shake my hand.

"You're a lucky girl," she told me.

"Always save all the money you can," Daddy told me as we left. I knew that was important. He had mentioned it frequently before. I planned to do so whenever I got any.

Daddy never talked much in the car when it was just me and him so I was able to contemplate the experience without interruption. An unbidden thought came to me. *If that is where all the money is, all I would need to do would be to get a job in the bank and to take out a little bit of that money every year until I had a lot of money over time.* I sat back satisfied. That seemed a good plan.

But wait! I thought, panicky, *I cannot do that because God would be watching.* That was a real shame because I felt like I was certainly clever enough to get away with if I tried.

Then the thought hit me from out of the blue – *people who did not believe in God but were clever, might try anything at all. They either didn't know or didn't care that God could see them.*

Somehow from this thought evolved the realization that nothing was safe. *Anybody might do anything at any time.*

I felt suddenly cold and empty. This was a frightening thought.

But then I remembered I was safe because God also watched over me as well as watched me.

The only way to be safe is for God to protect me.

Without His protection anything might happen, like car wrecks. I looked over at Daddy. He was paying strict attention to driving the car, not talking at the same time like Mama did, both his hands firmly on the wheel. He looked very strong and secure. I felt a little better.

I did want to learn more about God. Summer ended and I was pleased to start going to CCD on Wednesday nights. I was to go every week during second grade and at the end of the year I would get to make my First Communion. I did not know anyone in my CCD class. We were seated at a long table on both sides while a teacher, who was the mother of one of the students, talked to us about being Catholic. The teacher changed most every week.

Across from me there was a good looking boy named Kris, spelt with a K - not a C, who laughed and flirted with me and when our eyes met it gave me a little thrill. Each new teacher scolded him but he kept right on doing it. I knew that night that Kris was going to be my church boyfriend. I only saw these kids for two hours a week on Wednesday nights, and sometimes to say hello on Sunday morning if we were at the same service. I never bothered to learn any of the rest of their names. But soon I knew Kris as well as anybody I went to school with.

He became more than my church boyfriend. He was like a friend too, in spite of being a boy. He got me in trouble because after the first time, he always sat next to me and talked the whole time to me. But for once I didn't care if I got in trouble. I found out which service his family attended and insisted we go to that one also so I could see him more. He did not go to my school so there was no other way to see him.

VIII *Detours*

Claudia returned from visiting her relatives and her weekend visits resumed as second grade started.

At Fairvine, my high hopes of learning to write in longhand were at once crushed as soon as second grade class began. The Guidance Group had decreed printing only through the second grade.

So I waited out the second grade with great impatience, printing some on my book but not getting very far. Schoolwork was nothing. I brought mystery books into class, to read under my desk to pass the time.

At first this had caused a problem.

"What's this?" Miss Tucker, an old tall thin woman with very thick glasses was my English teacher now. In fact she was such a good teacher that she taught us all the other subjects, except art, all by herself. Only our art teacher, Mrs. Hopwell again, came to our class, briefly before lunch.

So we were stuck in the room with Miss Tucker most all of the day. Visually she reminded me a lot of my Aunt Worthrose who loved me. But Miss Tucker was a stranger.

"What are you doing?" She towered over me and glared down. I did not think she liked me.

"Reading." I disliked the attention of the class focused on me. I said defensively, "I've finished my assignment."

"Perhaps you could read some of this out loud for us," Miss Tucker said.

I was surprised. I had not expected to be rewarded for my surreptitious reading. Happily, hastily, I went to the front of the class and started reading **The Hidden Staircase**. But I had barely gotten through the first page when Miss Tucker stopped me.

"That's enough." Miss Tucker looked disconcerted. "I see you can read this. But the rest of the class needs to share in the experience. Perhaps you have some books at home you could bring that the entire class could share? One with some pictures and that is not fiction."

I knew just the book and I brought it the next day. It was **Our Flag, a Little Golden Book.** I had not read such books since before kindergarten and had put away the huge stack I possessed except for this one, and one other. I was allowed to read the **Our Flag** to the class and felt it was a great success. They passed it around and looked at the pictures.

Then the next day I brought another favorite, also with many pictures, also nonfiction. I presented it to Miss Tucker with pride. But Miss Tucker, normally stone faced, suddenly looked very upset, almost about to cry.

"No, Victoria, we cannot have this book in class, I must confiscate it and return it to you at the end of the day." Miss Tucker looked down at the floor as she took **The Loaves and the Fishes** away from me and put it in her desk drawer. "The Supreme Court has ruled we cannot mention God in school any longer. This is the law of the land and we must now abide by it and face the consequences."

I did not know what to make of this. I brought no more books to school to share but did notice that from then on Miss Tucker looked the other way when I sneaked my mystery books under my desktop.

I did get in Miss Tucker's good graces with a poem I wrote for the class.

The Statue of Liberty
There it stands, gleaming under the sun
Given to a country so very young.
And when night falls there it stands
Watching over the ocean and all our land.
Under the moon, under the stars.
The symbol of American men near and afar.
There it stands so proud and tall
Earned by men who answered their country's call.
Torch in her hand so lovely and free,
Stands our Statue of Liberty

It was pretty bad. I knew I should like poetry and want to write it but I didn't. However, Miss Tucker loved it. So did my mother and Aunt Worthrose. Since I knew they were both like some of the kids at school who did not like to read, and they only read the newspaper and the Bible, I understood how they could think it was good, bad as it was.

"This is really good," my mother said. "I'll bet you get an A for this." She liked something I wrote. It was bad. She didn't like the good stuff. But she liked the bad stuff. It was a strange feeling. I didn't tell her it wasn't graded because none of the other kids had done anything like it.

"So you've got a spinster school teacher this year for most of your subjects," observed Aunt Worthrose, with interest, after I told her about Miss Tucker.

"What is a spinster?"

"Old maid. Never married. Sometimes by choice. Probably never had an opportunity."

"Like Pamela?"

They both laughed. "She's not quite old enough yet to be called a spinster or old maid," said my mother. "She would have to be my age or older. I think Miss Tucker is maybe older than me."

"But probably younger than me or she'd not be there. She'd be retired."

"Miss Tucker is not much younger than you, Worthrose. And some of those teachers are very young like most of the mothers. Most teachers are in their 30s and 40s though."

"I'll bet most of the other kids' mothers think you're just a little older than them, June Rosette," said Aunt Worthrose. "And most of the teachers think you are much younger than you are. If they knew how old you are, they would treat you with a little more respect at those committee meetings.

"I don't need respect that badly as to tell them how old I really am," said Mama.

While still mourning the loss of Vickie Bianchi, I had taken up with Jayne Anderson as my official second grade best friend. Having Jayne for a best friend made me glad I had Claudia to fall back on. Jayne was not as satisfactory a friend as Vickie had been. She was unpredictable. She was moody and we argued a lot. She was very pretty but I did not think she was smart enough to be in the advanced classes. Mrs. Anderson never dropped Jayne off at our house when she visited. Someone else, who never got out of their car, did. I was forbidden to see Mrs. Anderson but I was expected to put up with Jayne.

Jayne, for some reason, had to spend all night every time she came over. And unlike Claudia, who was given my mother's bed, Jayne had to sleep with me in my bed. Plus, I knew that would mean we would not go to church since Jayne could not go with us, she was Protestant. Since when Claudia was with us, if we went to church, Daddy took her home first, I suspected she also was not Catholic. But Jayne never went home early enough on Sunday mornings for us to make it to church.

"When she moves in for good, will Claudia go to church with us?"

"I don't know," said my mother. "She's almost 15, she may not want to. Or she may want to go to a different church. Either way, we will cross that bridge when we come to it. Claudia cannot come this weekend, shall I see if Jayne can come over and spend the night?"

"I don't want her here," I said. "We can't go to church if she comes."

"I can try to see if any of the other girls in class could come just for Saturday so it would not affect church. I see most of their mothers when I am waiting to pick you up. Some of them have already asked about their daughters coming over to play with you like Sue and Marva did."

I thought about how carelessly other kids handled my dolls. I liked Janine but she just couldn't handle teenage fashion dolls, she didn't know how since she didn't have any. And last month as a "surprise" my mother had two girls over who I didn't know very well, Sue and Marva, without my permission. They played with my dolls together and refused to play with me!

"Only if I don't have to let them play with my dolls," I said.

"Why, you have plenty of dolls, why don't you want to share?"

"Not if I have to let them play with my dolls," I said with finality. "They can play outside in our yard." *And I will stay inside.*

"Now you know they will want to, their mothers usually mention your dolls when they ask." She was right. Word of my many dolls had now gotten around. A few had questioned me at school since most girls just had one teenage fashion doll. Some had none. And I knew that was why most of them wanted to come over. They certainly did not want to play with me.

"I don't need anybody to play with."

For some strange reason I thought about Kris at church. *It would not be so bad to have him over to play. He would be fun.*

"Where does Kris from church live?" I asked nonchalantly.

"He lives across the freeway in a subdivision inside the city limits."

"So he goes to the city schools?"

"No, there was a district already there before they took his area into the city so it remains separated from the city district. Like Fairvine will still be when they take Fairland and Water Oaks into the city next year."

"Will they take us in the city limits?"

"No," my mother said wistfully. "They're stopping the city limits at Silver Brook, just behind us. I wish they would take us in the city. If Mrs. Longhem can sell more lots and people build more houses on them, they might."

"Why is it good to be in the city limits?"

"Well, we would get better police and fire protection and we could get rid of the septic tank and not have to depend on the well for water."

"Does Kris live too far away to come over?" I asked, timidly.

"Yes. And you cannot ever have a boy to come over and play, unless there is a party." She hesitated. "Plus his mother doesn't like me, I don't think. His father is a white collar worker and they are really snooty to us at church."

I dropped that idea. I was not sure about it anyway. Nobody coming over meant I could write on my book in peace all weekend. It was a good thing anyways, as we had a minor storm that knocked out our electricity Friday night, which meant no water, as our well had an electric pump on top of it, and no lights. It was dark and cloudy Saturday morning, so Daddy lit a coal oil lamp in the den. But we would have to do without water until they fixed it, probably not till Monday.

As my mother worked sweeping the house on Saturday, I curled up on the couch, near the lamp, with my pen and began working on my book again.

"How did you have water in the countryside when you were a child without electricity?" I asked.

125

"Oh, we had an old fashioned well that you dropped a bucket on a rope down to fetch the water," she said.

"If we had that kind of well now, we would not be without water when the lights are out," I observed.

"Yes, but then you would to carry water from the well all the time," my mother said. "Let me tell you, that is no fun."

Chapter 10
The Old Well

In her hurry to get to the car, Jane dropped her purse!

Unnoticed by the two cousins, a man came and snatched it up, and ran off!

When they got back to the Scott house Barbara said, "Thanks for the lift home, Jane."

"Oh it was nothing," said Jane. "Bye Barbara."

"Bye, Jane."

"Barbara have you seen my purse?" asked Jane.

"Why, no Jane."

"Oh it's probably around here somewhere," said Jane, but to herself she said, "I probably dropped it by Harold Hall."

Jane did not tell Barbara that she was going to Harold Hall again!

"Boy, Harold Hall sure was spooky!" Barbara said to herself as she hurried up the steps.

"Have a nice day?" called Ellen from the kitchen.

"We didn't learn much," called Barbara regretfully. Barbara did not tell Mrs. Scott about the warning voice that told them to go away!

Meanwhile, Jane was back at the old mansion looking for her purse!

"No voice is going to scare me away this time!" she said, determinedly, then "Oh!"

Jane had fallen in an old well! Luckily there was no water in it! But the 17-year-old girl had a big scare as she hit the bottom of the well!

For about two hours Jane lay in the bottom of the well unconscious!

When she did wake up she had a headache and was dizzy! But soon the dizziness left and she stood up straight.

"Now how to get out of here," Jane said to no one in particular.

She tried to climb up the sides but they were too slick. She tried jumping up but the well was too deep.

The rope, bucket and the top part of the well had rotted away years ago and the walls of the well were only about 10 inches above the ground, so the well was hardly visible above the ground.

Jane shouted for help but soon realized that no one was around for miles within the old house!

"Oh!" said Jane, discouraged. "Why didn't I tell somebody where I was going!?"

She sat there for about five hours and just when she was about to give up hope she heard a far off but clear voice call, "Jane, Jane, where are you?"

Jane shouted with all her might. "Help! I'm in the well!" Then suddenly a rope was dropped down to her. Jane climbed up the rope and was surprised to see it tied to a tree and no one was around!

Just then a hand was clapped over her mouth!

"Just don't get the idea you can make a living writing," Mama said, when I handed her the next chapter. "Very few people ever get books published. It is almost impossible. You have to live in some place like New York and know a lot of important people. And we don't."

"What should I do when I grow up?" I asked.

"Whatever you want that will make you happy."

Writing and painting would make me happy, I thought.

"You might consider becoming a hair dresser. You could go to beauty school and work at the beauty shop. That would be great."

As much as I hated the beauty shop and how bad it smelled and gave me a headache every time I went there, I sincerely hoped not.

Later that night, I woke up, thinking my parents were arguing about my writing perhaps. But that was not the topic of the conversation. I sneaked down the hall and listened. They were not arguing. But they were having a very serious grownup discussion.

"How did this come up all of a sudden?" said my father. "It was all set."

"What if we hire a lawyer and go to court? What if they bring up Victoria?" said my mother.

"June, I told you and told you, nobody is going to take Victoria away from us." said my father. "I told you that eight years ago when we first found out she was expected. Nobody is ever going to take her away. Her real mother does not want her back."

"But what if it somehow all comes out at court?" said my mother.

"But we are the right age to adopt Claudia. No one should object."

"But someone is objecting. The social workers will get involved and I am afraid it could lead to an investigation. You can't trust anybody we know-"

"I know, I know, I know," said my father.

"Do we dare risk it?"

My father sat and thought for a long time. Finally he said to my mother, "No, I don't think we can."

I believed my mother was going to cry but she did not.

My mother looked at him, "I should ring your neck," she said. My father held his head down. "If you ever again –"

"Do you think I would ever do that now that we got Victoria? That's all in the past, I swear it."

"I ought to kill you someday."

He went and put his arms around her. "You won't do that."

"But what if you are wrong. Victoria's real mother comes back and wants her back? You are wrong sometimes you know, not very often but occasionally."

My father drew back, took her gently by the shoulders and said, "Listen, June, we lost our baby, we may have lost this one, but we've got Victoria. She's seven years old now. Nobody can take her away from us."

I was glad about that. The thought of some poverty stricken woman with a bunch of screaming little kids coming and taking me away from my parents was very unpleasant.

They saw me then. I had crept down the hall when their voices fell to hear better.

"You might as well know now," said my father.

"What?" I had some idea of what they were talking about but it was late at night, I wasn't sure I wanted to hear. I started feeling sleepy again...

"Claudia is not going to be your sister," he said.

Oh, that's what this was about. Claudia. I discarded my sleepiness. "Why?"

"Her mother's brother has objected to our adopting her," said my mother. "He is going to take Claudia to Vermont to live with him and his wife. In fact we think they are already gone."

"I didn't know her mother had a brother."

"Neither did I," said my mother, looking at my father.

He shrugged and smiled a little sheepishly. "Well, neither did I."

"It would mean a lawyer and going to court," said my mother. "We cannot afford it."

Their silence after this told me something else. "She's not going to come back?"

"No," said my mother, biting her lip. "The uncle doesn't want her to come back. Doesn't want her to have any more contact with us."

"What about her grandfather?"

"Apparently he would still like to have Claudia here, but he has no money and the uncle has hired a lawyer."

"Oh." I digested this. *So Claudia wasn't coming back. No sister. Lawyers must be scary people and powerful to stop families from adopting.*

I knew I should have been sad but all I felt was a little emptiness and pity. Claudia was missing a great chance to be adopted by my parents. For a brief moment I saw all the wonderful life she might have had with us, growing up, graduating, marrying... I wondered what unknown future without any parents awaited her. I wondered if she knew what an opportunity she had lost to have the best parents ever. I felt very sorry for her.

"I can start seeing Eva and Victor again," I said, trying to look on the bright side.

My parents exchanged glances.

"I'm afraid not," my mother said. "Aunt Jolene has remarried to a man with a really good job far, far away. In a place called Saudi Arabia. They have gone to live there with him."

"Aunt Jolene didn't like working at the hospital cafeteria?"

"No, no, I don't think she liked that at all."

So while entertaining Claudia, who no longer wanted us, we had lost Eva and Victor, and Aunt Jolene.

I was silent. I thought about all the times we had expected Claudia and she had not come. I thought about the times she did come and how we had made her part of our family.

"You still have Ruth Marino," said my mother. "We'll try to get you together soon. It's just been so hectic this year. And my niece Pamela is moving to the city from the countryside. She has gotten a job with a big company and will live in an apartment, not near here but not too far away either."

This did not seem relevant at the time. Ruth was five years older. Pamela was grown. I dismissed that information. I was feeling grateful there had been no busybody relative around to stop my adoption.

"I know you had looked forward to telling everybody about Claudia becoming your sister," said my mother. "You're too young to understand that I need you to know it's important still not to tell anybody about her. We think, maybe, she'll come back sometime and see us in the future. When she's 18 and of legal age to decide for herself. Nobody could stop her then. But we don't know."

Actually I had not ever thought about telling anybody about Claudia even after I was told she would be my sister. That secret was absolute. I was prepared with the neighbor's friend's child story if anyone had ever asked but they didn't. I actually missed seeing Connie, Eva, and Victor more than Claudia and if I could have had anybody back again it would have been Vickie Bianchi, no contest, even though she wasn't a relative.

Mama and Daddy went to bed. I decided not to worry about people I could not see again. I stayed awake and wrote more on my book. I had to decide if Jane was going to be put back into the well.

No, I decided, *time to get Jane out of the well and keep her out.*

She had been there long enough.

Chapter 11
Missing!

Jane fought desperately to get away but her captors were far stronger than her!

She was blindfolded, gagged, and her wrists were bound. Then she was led away.

Suddenly a piece of cloth was held under her nose – SHE BLACKED OUT!

Meanwhile, back at the Kape home, April was getting very worried about Jane's long absence.

Finally she decided to call the Scott home to see if by chance Jane was there.

"Hello Ellen."

"Hello."

"Do you know where Jane is?"

Mrs. Scott said that she did not know where Jane was but that Barbara may be able to shed some light on the matter. But Barbara said she has no idea where Jane is.

April said not to call the police so Barbara went down to the police station and told them.

"I wish to report a missing person," she said to Chief McBlend.

"What is your name, young lady?"

"Barbara Scott."

"Who is the missing person?"

"Jane Kape."

"Her description, please."

"She is black headed, slightly plump, with blue eyes and medium height."

"What was she wearing the last time you saw her?"

"A green turtle-neck sweater, a pink blouse, a blue skirt and black flat-heel shoes."

Chief McBlend sighed, "Boy, one person kidnapped from one family. And one from another family and ONE from ANOTHER family.

"Goodbye Miss Scott."

"Oh, Jane is 17."

"Thank you."

We had my birthday party a month early that year. Daddy was going to be gone a whole month, his company was sending him to Boston to work on an airplane that they could not figure out why it would not fly. He was to leave February 1st and might not be back in time. Claudia was not at my birthday party for turning eight. Connie Vaccaro was not there. Neither was Eva or Vic Romano, who had gone to Saudi Arabia. But because they weren't there, Christian Romano could come and that was a nice surprise. He was really old now but sweet to me and friendly to all. I wondered if he would get married soon. My cousin Cliff, in the countryside, had gone to Alabama for Christmas and stayed because he married a girl there and he was younger than Christian.

Also Ruth Marino was at the party. Pamela dropped by to leave a gift but, being grown, she did not stay. Christian left as soon as the cake was cut, taking his piece with him. But Aunt Thelma stayed for the party this time and helped Mama with the cake. And Aunt Worthrose was there of course.

Jayne could not come for some reason. But there was a girl from CCD class at church, Phoebe Crestman. I did not really know her but my mother had made friends with her mother and they wanted us to be friends. She lived in the old part of Water Oaks so she was in Fairvine district but went to the older elementary built out of wood during the 1920s.

"Phoebe lives just across the street from the line so she has to go to the old school or she would be in your class, which is a shame. Phoebe's mother is the same age as me and we would like you two to get to know each other," said my mother. "Except, well, you must not say anything about this-"

And my mother told me. Mrs. Crestman really wasn't Phoebe's mother, she was Phoebe's grandmother. And her father was really her grandfather. Phoebe's older sister was actually her mother, and I had to keep that a secret because Phoebe didn't even know. She thought her grandmother and grandfather were her parents.

So Phoebe came to my party too. I didn't really like her, I decided. Why couldn't my mother become friends with some of the mothers of people I really did like, such as Kris who I didn't get to invite? But at the end I did not care who came and went. I had asked for new mystery books, Barbies, and doll clothes. I was not too disappointed when a present that was obviously a book turned out to be a biography of Jackie Kennedy. But at the end of the party another present was not what I expected.

"We have a special surprise for you," said my mother as I picked up a teenage fashion doll size box. "A new doll, just like your old ones, only better."

I tore open the present and pulled the doll out of the box. I couldn't believe my eyes.

"She has some beautiful clothes too. Barbie has more than her share of beautiful clothes, now this doll can share," said my mother, picking them up to show me.

But I was not interested in the clothes. I had already pulled the doll out of her box and pulled off her gray jumpsuit. I examined her body closely and fingered her rough curly blond hair. I didn't remember ever before feeling so hurt. I felt insulted too, but I felt more hurt than insulted even. Is this what they thought of me?

This doll had a great big ugly head, too big for her body, and she had short fat fingers and wide fat feet with big toes. Worst of all, most humiliating of all, her tummy protruded out.

"We were hoping you would play with her instead," said my mother.

I started to cry. I knew I was too fat, but I was not as fat as some of the girls. I knew my fingers were too short to play the piano, but did this mean I didn't deserve to have a doll with beautiful long fingers? Did I have to play with this hideous doll because my feet were short and fat and my tummy was not flat?

"What's wrong?" asked my mother, and the others were staring at me in silence. "We thought you might like this doll more because she is more realistic."

How could anyone think such a doll with a big stupid head was realistic? Besides Barbie was like paper dolls, artists' pictures, and sculptures.

She is beautiful the way those things are.

Dolls weren't supposed to be realistic. I threw the doll across the room and demanded I be allowed to play with my dolls. I was terrified they were going to be taken away from me. And I was going to be left with this deformity. And it was a blond!

"Ok. Ok," said my mother. "Go play with your dolls,"

"That's enough, Victoria Irene," said my father, and I could tell he was really angry. "Do what I tell you! Show some respect for your mother and me. You have no respect for your elders, behaving like this. Go to your room until you can behave better. You make me ashamed behaving this way in front of people."

I stopped crying and looked at the doll clothes that came with the ugly doll. They were pretty. I snatched them up. I would see if my doll could wear them. She couldn't wear the shoes, that was for sure. I abandoned my other new birthday toys as well. A toy guitar, stupid games, books that weren't mysteries, dolls that were not Barbie. More baby dolls!

"When you give away my outgrown clothes to the O'Kelleys, you can give them all that stuff as well," I said angrily, and stormed off to my bedroom. I could hear my father yelling at me as I went down the hall and my mother trying to restrain him but I tuned out their words.

After a minute, Ruth followed me to my room. "It is nice of you to want to give your toys to the poor people."

I stared at her in the doorway. What did she know? She was thin and too old to play with toys anymore. She said "mam" and "sir" to every grownup. Daddy had told me only grownups who had done something to deserve respect should be called mam and sir. And grownups that were very very old.

Mama disagrees but what Daddy says goes at our house.

Then I wondered scarily if Daddy had known or approved of this fat ugly doll. Was he ashamed of me, too? I hoped not. I dismissed his angry words easily but this doll was something else. Where had such a hideous thing come from? I had immediately suspected this was Mama's doing but now I was afraid to ask. Mama sometimes went shopping downtown and took Aunt Worthrose on Saturdays when Daddy was home. Could Aunt Worthrose have been in on this? I felt bad for suspecting them all but if they all felt like that about me I needed to know now.

"Ruth has to go now," said my mother, coming up behind her before I could show her my dolls, book or anything. Ruth obediently turned and went back down the hall. "See how Ruth obeys her mother. You embarrass me behaving the way you do. We're going to try to see more of Ruth. Maybe she'll be a good influence on you."

Soon everybody else went home, too. My mother and Aunt Worthrose came back to my bedroom. I saw my mother had in her hand one of the pills Dr. Plunkett had given her to take when she was nervous. But she did not take it.

I was silent. I was still too hurt to speak. How could they think so little of me? I vowed I would try to lose weight but I didn't have a clue how to do that. I couldn't do anything about my feet being wide and flat and my fingers being short but maybe I could find out how to lose weight.

"You like to play with Ruth even though she's five years older. Wouldn't you?" said my mother.

I shrugged. I had nothing against Ruth.

"Here, Aunt Worthrose got you a new doll outfit, she forgot to wrap it," said my mother. Aunt Worthrose did not dispute her. She handed me the pink ice skating outfit. I had wanted that one. I forgot my pain for a moment.

"I told you, June Rosette, that would not work," I heard her say as she and my mother went back down the hall. "She'll never give up Barbie."

Chapter 12
Robbed

When Barbara got back home April and Raymond Kape were there. They looked extremely stern and worried.

"Barbara Scott, have you no respect for your elders?" Mr. Kape spoke very sternly.

"Your aunt told you not to go to the police! Why did you?"

"I– I–" stammered Barbara on the verge of tears.

"I'll tell you why!" screamed Raymond Kape, "because you have no respect for your elders!"

Meanwhile April and Ellen, who stood nearby, were startled. April was about to faint, while Ellen was getting madder every minute!

Just then Barbara burst into sobs and flung herself onto the couch.

Ellen was furious. "It so happens I told Barbara to go to the police," she cried.

Mr. Kape looking somewhat sheepish laid a hand on Barbara's shoulder. He whispered softly in her ear. When she refused to talk to him he got up and went into the Scott garden.

April said that Mr. Kape was very upset.

"He didn't mean it, Barbara!"

She didn't have a chance to continue for Barbara picked herself up and went to her room.

Mrs. Kape and Mrs. Scott went into the garden with Mr. Kape and all three began to talk.

Barbara decided to go sit on the patio.

She sat on the swing thinking of Jane's disappearance.

"She didn't go home after she dropped me off. And she said something about not knowing where her purse was. Of course, she went back to Harold Hall to look for it. I better tell Uncle Raymond." Barbara was so very excited over her discovery she didn't think to lock the door!

"Well it's worth looking into," said Mr. Kape, when Barbara finished her story.

Everyone got into the Scott family car and Mrs. Scott drove off leaving the front door open!

As soon as they got to the old mansion everyone began to look around.

Suddenly Barbara cried out, "Here's a button from Jane's sweater by this old well!"

Raymond, April, and Ellen hurried over to see it.

By the button Barbara found footprints. Footprints of flat heeled shoes coming from the well. A man's footprints coming from the right side of the well and high heel shoes on the left.

IN ONE OF THE HIGH HEEL PRINTS WAS A HIGH HEEL SHOE STUCK IN THE MUD!

From there on there were footprints of a stocking.

"This is an excellent clue!" Barbara exclaimed.

Mr. Kape gasped, "Look on the inside of the shoe."

"Yes!" cried Barbara, "there's some writing here."

The ink was fresh and it said:

K. MARY WATSON, JUNE 16.

K. SARAH HORTON JUNE 17.

"'K. Mary Watson June 16!' Why the Watsons are our best friends," cried Ellen.

"And Sarah Horton was one of my classmates last year," Barbara cried out excitedly.

"We'd better warn them! Let's see today is the– uh– why today is the 16th!"

Instead of going home they drove to 1516 Emrose, the Watson home.

Mrs. Carolyn Watson had been friends with Ellen long before she married.

Mr. Watson greeted them, a worried expression on his face.

They were surprised to see Mrs. Watson crying and Mary's 9-year-old sister Katie sobbing on the couch.

When she looked up she cried out.

"Oh, B-Barbara! Mary's been kidnapped! An' An' Mummy won't tell the police!"

"What!?"

The Scotts and the Kapes learned that a heavily veiled woman had come to the house when Katie and Mary were there alone. She had said that a very important package had come for Mary that could not be delivered and she had come to take Mary to the post office.

"I shouldn't o' let 'er go," sobbed Katie. "And she never came back."

The Scotts and the Kapes left the Watsons and drove to the police station.

After that they drove to the Scott house.

Ellen was going to fix dinner and opened a drawer her best silverware was in. Ellen gave a little scream. "I've been robbed!" she cried out!

I looked at the doll again. Ugly body and hair that it had, I did have to admit it had a pretty face. Maybe that's what grownups meant when they said it was a shame Pamela was fat, she had such a pretty face, she would be beautiful if she was not fat. Suddenly I wondered if it was her idea for Mama to get me that fat doll. But no, she had gotten me a record album with some really creepy looking men on the front. I tossed that into the pile to give to Alyce O'Kelley.

I opened up the book about Jacqueline Kennedy and started to read it. I forgot about dolls and even forgot the party and its disappointment as I read the whole book without putting it down.

IX *Expectations*

That spring I brought the book about Jackie Kennedy to school to show Miss Tucker. But before I got the chance, suddenly we had to get up and leave our desks and go to another classroom. There was no announcement over the loudspeaker but, as we were on our way, the lights went out.

The other classroom was just like ours and except the desks were much larger. This classroom had Venetian blinds like we had at the old house. The blinds were still cracked, giving us some light in the room.

"Children, find someone who can share a desk with you and sit together in the desk," said Miss Tucker.

This was a bizarre command but the other teacher in the room was apparently in on it for she did not object. I found a nice looking older girl and climbed in the desk with her.

"Now, Class, those of you in the back, without partners in your desks, come forward and sit with another classmate nearer the front. We want everyone as close to the front of the room as possible, all desks in the back empty," the other teacher directed.

As this was happening, Miss Tucker went to the windows and closed all the blinds. In a moment, Mr. Qurand popped his head inside the door.

"It's on its way, we are delaying dismissal until it passes," he told the teachers. In this uncomfortable position we rode out the second tornado to strike the school. We didn't see or hear anything this time and when it had passed, Mr. Qurand came back around to tell us to dismiss, since the lights did not come back on that day.

"This tornado was not as bad," said my mother, as I climbed into the car. "It just been raining and windy, I think it actually hit somewhere else. But we have no power again as usual."

Fortunately power was back on the next day as we were going to have guests. The family that now lived in the old house we had lived in before was coming to visit us. They had been renting the house all these years but now were going to buy it.

"The Gonzalez family has several small children," said my mother, in advance. "You can play with them while the grownups talk."

"I may have to play with children my own age but I absolutely refuse to play with smaller children," I said, hoping that was clear. "I am going to sit with the grownups and talk."

My mother sighed and threw up her hands.

"Let her stay," said Daddy.

"Only if you be quiet," said my mother.

"I'll sit on my hands," I said. That was a trick I used to stop talking when needed. Mama often said neither Daddy nor I could talk above a whisper if our hands were tied up.

They entered through the front door. When they got there my mother and Mrs. Gonzalez took the little kids into the den and I stayed with Mr. Gonzalez, Daddy, and another man that Daddy explained was a real estate agent.

"Your father and mother are selling their old house to the Gonzalez family and I am the person that draws up all the legal papers and makes sure it is all done right," he told me, with a smile.

As I contemplated that, keeping my promise to be quiet, Daddy said, "She's real smart. She's written a book."

"Really?" Mr. Gonzalez said.

"That is quite interesting," said the real estate agent, pulling a stack of papers out of his briefcase. "Now-"

"Could I see your book? Did you do this in school?" asked Mr. Gonzalez.

"Yes! No." I scrambled off the couch as I answered his questions and darted down the hall to get my book.

"Now the terms you have agreed to..." the real estate agent's voice trailed off as I went to my bedroom and grabbed my folder.

When I got back to the living room, Daddy and Mr. Gonzalez were signing papers and I had to wait until they finished.

"Here," I said, giving my folder to Mr. Gonzalez.

"This is very impressive." He spoke with an accent. He held it up to the real estate agent. "Don't you think?"

"Um, yes, indeed, now Mr. Grasso if you could get Mrs. Grasso to sign this waiver even though her name was not on the deed..."

"June." My father called towards the den.

"I have hopes my children will do as well in school as your father says you do," said Mr. Gonzalez to me.

I wanted to explain that the book was in no way related to going to school, that school teachers had actually held back its progress because they would not let me learn longhand but I didn't have a chance. As soon as Mr. Gonzalez' small children came towards me I grabbed my book ran to my room and safety at once and shut the door behind me. For a few moments I leaned against it until I was sure they were not going to try to break in.

"She does not ever want to play with anybody," my mother complained after they had left. "She won't talk on the phone. I even offered to pay long distance for her to talk to Vickie Bianchi on the phone but she didn't want to."

"Everybody cannot talk for hours on the phone like you do, June," said my father, unconcerned. "Well, we will start trying to take her to see Ruth as soon as we can."

"I never talk to my friends until after I have all the housework done. I have to have some recreation. As for Ruth, Thelma tells me she has weekend activities for school every week, she's very involved in extra circular activates," said my mother. "I'm afraid it's going to have to wait until school is out."

True to their word, we did start going to see Ruth after second grade let out for the summer. Her father and my father, first cousins, even looked a little bit alike and they had always been great friends. Plus Aunt Thelma had been a white Protestant and had converted to Catholicism just like my mother. So we should have a lot in common, everyone agreed.

But I didn't see how. Ruth was thin, quiet and reserved. Timid even. Nothing like me.

On my first visit to see Ruth that summer right away, despite our age difference, I felt equal, even slightly superior to Ruth. I knew that her parents were not near as well off as mine because Ruth had hardly any toys. While I got the bride dress when I was in the hospital for my surgery, Ruth told me all she got was ice cream when she had her tonsils out. And we lived in a new brick house. Ruth and her parents lived in a small old wood house like the one we now sold to the

Gonzalez family

In her small room, instead of toys or even baby dolls, Ruth had statues of Jesus and the Virgin Mary and a collection of cups and saucers. These things are all breakable so she wanted to play outside.

"Do you know who Jesus and the Virgin Mary are?" she asked, as we were going out the back door. Ruth had a nice backyard that was really like a big garden, very symmetrical with beautiful flowers growing everywhere and she had a sidewalk in her backyard leading from the house to the garage on which we could play hopscotch. There were lots of bushes and green grass and flowers.

We were having a beautiful spring after the storm. It was a very nice day. The sky was very blue with a few white clouds and there was a nice breeze. Usually I didn't want to play outside but today it seemed like a good idea.

"You know who God is?" Ruth uncharacteristically let the screen door slam behind her.

"Have you ever heard Him?"

"Yes, of course I've heard of Him," I told her, thinking about playing hopscotch. "He is in Heaven far away."

"No, I said have you ever HEARD Him?" she said, adding, "God hears your prayers."

"Yes, I know," I said, feeling a little guilty for not praying enough. A vague fear that He might get me some day for not paying Him His due. We did not go to church every Sunday the way we were supposed to. I knew it was because I insisted on it, that I was taken to CCD every Wednesday night. And I insisted on it because of Kris, not because of God.

"God answers your prayers," Ruth repeated, as if she thought I was desperately praying for something all the time.

"I heard that." I was actually thinking of a story I had read waiting in the doctor's office one time about a boy who was going to die and somebody told him to lift his hand and ask Jesus to take him and he would go to heaven.

"When you pray you talk to God," said Ruth solemnly.

"I know that." The story did not make it clear if the boy did go to heaven but I assumed he did.

"And God talks back."

I looked at her skeptically. "He does not talk back."

Stupid, I thought, not verbalizing this insult. Ruth was sensitive and I didn't want to make her cry.

"He can't. He's too far away for us to hear Him." I had no trouble with the idea that God could hear us. Being God, His hearing would be unusually acute. But we could not hear Him, our hearing was too weak.

"Yes, He does," insisted Ruth. "He can talk back and we can hear Him."

I looked at Ruth. She was smiling a little superior smile. This was unusual. Ruth never acted superior. Indeed I had heard my father say she was mousy and whiny. My mother had defended her as always being a good and obedient little thing, unlike me. But here she was, sure and happy about what she was telling me. I took notice.

"God talks back," she said emphatically. "You just have to listen."

"He talks back? You've heard Him?" I knew Ruth was too much of the goody-goody to ever lie and she didn't have enough imagination to make things up. But she was a bit of a jokester on rare occasions. However, if she was serious, she knew what she was talking about, this had to be on the level.

She was still giving me a superior look. She was serious all right.

"But you haven't actually heard Him? You can't hear His voice?" I persisted.

Ruth nodded with great deliberation. "Oh yes, you can," she insisted. And she was so very much more sure about this than I was.

"You just have to listen."

At this point I turned and looked up at the sky, listening very hard. But I didn't hear anything. Yet there seem to be strong rays in the sky pulsating in a way I hadn't seen before, the light was brighter and more intense. The sky was very beautiful but I could not stand to look at it any longer. I looked back to Ruth.

"You have to talk to Him first," said Ruth, as if I should know that already. "He's not going to talk to you unless you talk to Him and He might not answer you right away. Sometimes you have to wait. But if you listen hard enough and wait long enough He will talk back to you."

I looked back at the sky, the rays had gone and the sky was simply lovely with fluffy clouds. This was very important news to me. I believed my parents had told me all the adult secrets. But apparently they were keeping this from me. The adults came out the back door then with our lunch and Ruth quickly changed the subject. But as we sat in Ruth's nice backyard and ate potato chips and sandwiches, I periodically looked up in wonder at the beautifully fluffy clouds and strained my ears.

As a playmate, Ruth didn't really work out. She lived too far away, she had no toys. She was not interested in teenage fashion dolls. Ruth did not want to come to my house. She was always busy with after school activities. I did not like to play outside, she did not want me touching her breakable stuff. I was glad my dolls did not break. Our visits did not become routine. But I never forgot what she said. And I started trying to listen.

Not too long after that, to make up for the fat ugly fashion doll, I finally got a blond ponytail. I examined her with wonder.

"It's not Christmas or my birthday." I said.

"It doesn't have to be Christmas for me to give you a present," said Daddy solemnly. "I can give you presents anytime I want. I can do it just because I want to give you something special. Just because I love you."

The doll was special indeed. Unlike my black haired Barbara, she did not have curly bangs but her hair went around her forehead in a smooth swirl. And it was not really blond, it was pure white.

"That is a platinum blonde," said my father. "Your mother's hair was almost that blond when I first saw her, then in just a couple of years before we married, it turned golden blond after we spent a lot of time in the sun at the beach. I first saw her when I was at a party at a big hotel downtown and I had just ducked down a hall with some girl, when I saw her coming my way, delivering towels to the rooms. She was wearing a black uniform and her hair was silky white curls just to her shoulders. She had sparkling hazel eyes and she smiled at me with, red lipstick against those perfect white teeth. She was the most beautiful creature I had ever seen.

144

"The girl from the party was all dressed up in a fancy gown but she was nothing compared to your mother in that maid's uniform, coming towards me, her arms full of towels…with that smile…"

"Was the other girl, the girl you were supposed to have the arranged marriage with?"

"Who told you about that? Never mind, I know who." He smiled a little. "Oh, my mama arranged a marriage for me. I wasn't having none of that. I met that girl but I never went out with her. She was a nice girl, I didn't have anything against her. Her family was a bit above us on the social scale. My mama was trying to move up. But I was having none of that arranged marriage bull. Nobody was going to tell me who to marry."

"Did Grandmamá arrange for Uncle Vince and Uncle Chris's marriages?"

"No, no, that was so much later when they married. Just a couple years or so before you were born."

"So before World War II there were the arranged marriages but not after?"

"Pretty much. I think it really began to die out after World War I, but my mama was old school. She didn't like change."

"Do you remember World War I?"

"No, not really, I was a little boy. You know your Uncle Clyde was in World War I. He was in the Navy. You could ask him about that."

"Uncle Clyde doesn't talk to me."

"Really?"

"Oh, not because he's mad or anything," I added hastily. "He's always real nice and polite but he is just not interested in me."

"Well, he is in his 70s. And I respect that he's still working as a watch guard at the oil company. Most people retire by that age, but he's not lazy. Some people just don't cotton to children." Daddy hesitated, then looked as if he suddenly understood something. "You know, we were told Clyde got you that first doll, but I guess that was really Worthrose. She's fierce, but in an odd way she's a little afraid of your mother sometimes."

I was comparing the new doll to Barbara, with her black hair and red lips. The doll's eyes were still blue but her lips were not dark red, instead they were beautiful pink. Although she could never win, sometimes she would tie the beauty contest with Barbara. And although she couldn't keep it, she would at least get to try on the wedding gown. And I knew I could never ever dare to let anyone else play with her because her hairstyle was so delicate. Barbara's hair was coarse and touchable but this doll's hair was soft, silky and fragile. I was going to barely be able to touch her myself. She was going to be treated like a queen.

I looked up at Daddy. "Mama still has hazel eyes and wears red lipstick and she still has perfect teeth. All natural she says, since she was never able to afford a dentist when she was young."

"That's right," said my father, thoughtfully. "All her family has perfect white teeth and they've all been poor all their lives. Must be hereditary. But none of the rest of them was a natural blond like her. These dyed blonds don't look anything like a natural blond like she was. You have to go to Switzerland or Scandinavia to find them usually. You know, no matter what you hear about your Mama's people, they're good Christian people. Now, I'm not crazy about them all. But her parents were always good to me, treated me with respect. And her brother Buford, he's the best good old boy I've ever known. He'd give anybody the shirt off his back. Your Aunt Nelwynn may not have an education or fine dresses but she is a fine lady at heart."

I pulled out the **Sophisticated Lady** pink formal with silver trim and the long dark pink velvet coat. That would be the new doll's dress. I put on her long pale pink gloves. I slipped clear Cinderella shoes on her feet. And there was a matching tiara that I could gently slip over her ponytail so as never to mess up her hair. Mama's hair may have turned light brown now that she was older but this doll's hair was never going to change.

"You need something to do," said my mother, when she realized playing with Ruth was not working out. "And we've thought of something for you to do at least part of that time. Aunt Worthrose says you can go to her house in the afternoon and she will teach you to sew."

That was a complete failure.

While I enjoyed talking to Aunt Worthrose and she had beautiful things she had sewn in the past, she could no longer see well enough to teach me. That made her irritable. I spent most the time attempting to thread the needle and I wound up pricking myself with the sharp point over and over again. We mutually called it quits after the second lesson.

However, I did not stop going to her house. I enjoyed being alone with Aunt Worthrose. I just didn't mention to Mama that we were talking instead of sewing. I found I could get really good information from her, whereas Mama would often say she didn't remember if she didn't want to talk and Daddy would usually just say, "the past is the past, we need to forget it". But Aunt Worthrose would talk. Alone with me, she was almost a different person, certainly a much more relaxed and vibrant than when other adults were around. She talked much less about the imminent end of the world, but I wanted to find out what she really knew about God.

I thought about telling her what Ruth had told me. But I thought better of it. However I did try the question- "Do you ever talk to God?"

"Victoria Irene, I pray all the time."

"Why?"

"Because I need to."

"Why don't you go to church? I didn't exactly mean prayer. I mean talk to Him."

"Well, sometimes I do." Her voice sounded a little pained. "Because I'm a sinner. I've sinned so much I cannot go to church."

"Does He talk back? Did He tell you you can't go to church?"

Aunt Worthrose put her finger to her heart. "He talks to me here," she indicated. "And no, He didn't tell me not to go to church. I just know I shouldn't go. I've sinned too bad in my life to go and present myself to the Lord as a good church going woman. I'd be a hypocrite."

"I don't understand."

"I've been mean," she said. "Mean all my life, to everybody and everyone. And I've never taken anything off anybody. I've stood up for myself all my life. And you have to do that, too, Victoria Irene, when you are grown. Nobody else will look after you in this world. You have to take care of yourself."

"At our church they want the sinners to come. They say Jesus will forgive all your sins."

"I've no doubt the Lord forgives all sin. He has forgiven me. But sometimes we cannot forgive ourselves. And don't ask. I'll never tell you. Just let's say I was mean to my first husband and let that be it. And I've been mean to all the children I've ever come in contact with, which isn't many, thank the Lord, except you. For some reason that I don't understand, I love you."

"I love you, too," I said automatically, hoping the conversation wasn't going to be sidetracked by lovey dovey stuff. I continued it without delay. "Our church says you just have to go to confession. Then you can go to church."

"Catholic churches, I think, are all the same," she sniffed. "But Protestant churches can be very different from one another. Like these around here. They want you only if you are lily white. I'm not. I'm just regular white."

"What exactly does lily white mean?"

"Well, I guess it must mean that you look real white like June Rosette, with real white skin and also, unlike her, you can prove it. You can prove your bloodlines are pure white from way back. I guess that's what it must mean."

"Can't you prove your bloodlines? How do you do that?"

"Oh, I know my bloodlines, but I'm not lily white. I'm part Black Dutch."

"Dutch is white," I said confused. "Mama says she's part Dutch. That means Mama is Black Dutch too?"

"No," she said. "I'm Black Dutch on my father's side. He was German. He died when I was eight years old."

"What is Black Dutch?" *I may make a new list of everyone and put them in columns depending on their origin.* The thought of this project made me excited.

"It's a type of German. Our mother's family was part English and part real Dutch- that is from Holland. Her original family came over with the Pilgrims and later married with the Indians, one of our great-grandmothers was a full-blooded Cherokee Indian, that's why I have a long nose and high cheekbones, I took after her. I'm one eighth Cherokee Indian, half Black Dutch- that is German Dutch, and one quarter English and one eighth Holland type Dutch."

I was more confused than ever. With her fair skin and delicate features, how could my mother be a natural blond and be part Indian?

"June Rosette took after her father," she said, as if to answer my unspoken question. "She looks just like him. He was a good-looking blond rascal. But he was a mongrel. His blood and the Holland Dutch on our mother's side must be why she looks lily white. But she can't prove it. She's not a purebred."

"I believed he was Irish." I knew Patterson was an Irish word.

"No," my aunt said. "He could've been part Irish. He didn't know what he was. Patterson wasn't even his real name. He did not know who his real father was." My aunt went to the credenza where she kept the clippings about the Lindbergh baby and brought out some old pictures that were real photographs.

"That's her?" I looked at an 8x10 in astonishment. "She really was beautiful." No one had been exaggerating about my mother's beauty, when she was young she had been as beautiful as Daddy was handsome. Aunt Worthrose showed me another picture.

"This is their wedding day, they came by the house on their way home after they eloped and I snapped their picture."

I looked at my mother as a bride. She was wearing a dark dress with white embroidery around the neckline and a tilted hat. The smile of pure joy on her face was something I had never seen in her before, while Daddy looked just about like he looked right now, maybe little thinner but not much. He was grinning. The hat made her look even taller than him than she actually was.

No wonder they looked so good for their ages now. And while Mama had changed some, judging by all these pictures, Daddy had barely changed at all since he was young.

They were so beautiful, and even now look so much better than everyone else near their age that I can never compete with them. But I am not going to be fat when I grow up. I won't be as homely like Aunt Worthrose but I will be thin. I'll just look normal like most people. I'll be ordinary looking.

"June Rosette and Vic both were plenty blessed by the Lord in the looks department. Your father could have gone to Hollywood if he had not been too short. He is so good looking. June Rosette was equally beautiful back then and she wasn't short. They offered her a chance to go to California back in the 1930s. She didn't want to," said Aunt Worthrose. "You couldn't tell her anything. All she ever wanted to do was to get married and have a lot of children. Yet that was denied her. She couldn't get pregnant but the one time. While I - I never wanted children but-" she sighed deeply, "that is the way of this world, this world makes no sense."

The world makes sense to me, God meant Mama for me. But I did not argue with her.

"Victoria, this is a bad, evil world. I'm glad I never brought any children into this wicked world. No, I never wanted any and I can't have any. Therefore the Good Lord knew what He was doing in my case."

I wondered briefly if she didn't have any because she didn't want any or because she couldn't have any and decided to make the best of it.

I did not think the world was so bad. *So far I've had it pretty good,* I thought, but I still kept quiet.

I did not want her to stop talking.

"Your daddy loves you very much, Victoria Irene," said Aunt Worthrose very seriously. "Vic Grasso is a good man. When your mother's father died, Vic paid for the funeral. And then he helped with our mother's too. It didn't matter to him what class of people they were."

"Why didn't they object to Mama and Daddy's marriage like the Italians did?"

"Cause they were way too poor to object. When your mama brought Vic home, they were happy about it. They hoped June Rosette would be protected and taken care of for the rest of her life. Vic is a hard worker and he doesn't drink. They could see right away he'd be a good provider. And he has been."

"I thought they were farmers." I was more confused than ever.

I thought farmers owned a lot of land even if they didn't have money. Why would anybody think farmers are lower class?

"They were tenant farmers, sharecroppers, they didn't own the land. When my father died he left our mother a big house in the city. Lind Patterson came along and by the time your mother was born they had lost everything. Lind had to farm the land for the landlord by day, and work in the coal mines at night to feed all those hungry children. Here's his picture."

I saw a good looking fair man standing beside a pile of cotton. His features were very comparable to my mother's as a young woman. He was smiling, and although poor and overworked he might have been, he was still handsome and looked happy.

Aunt Worthrose brought out another picture of a very old man with long hair and a long beard.

"This was mine and you mother's grandfather on our mother's side," she said. "He lived to be real old so we got his picture."

As I looked at this picture, another exciting thought came to me. "Was he in the Civil War? Mama said we had some relatives that fought in the Civil War."

"That's right, on our mother's side, at least two of them. Not him, though, he was way too young, but his brother and brother-in-law who were older."

"Do you have their pictures? In Civil War uniforms? What did they look like?"

"I saw the pictures many years ago. They were in gold painted wooden frames. One of the men was a private but the other had bars on his shirt. He was a captain or something. My grandparents brought those pictures from Kentucky when they came to the countryside here, in the covered wagon. But those pictures are all gone now. They were burnt. Frames and all."

"Why?" I was horrified. It was disappointing enough that the covered wagon didn't survive. Surely there was no greater crime than burning a picture that could never be replaced.

"Because we were afraid somebody would see them. It broke my grandparents' hearts to have to burn them but they didn't have any choice, it wasn't worth anybody getting hurt."

"I don't understand." *Photos of war heroes from the past should be family treasures. How could they get anyone hurt?*

"Your mother didn't tell you? Well, Victoria Irene, we were living in way out in the countryside, amidst the KKK. And those were dark blue uniforms they were wearing in those pictures. Our relatives were Yankee soldiers."

This, and the information about my mother's father changing his name, were such an interesting revelations that the next day I found myself doing the opposite of what I normally did. I was confirming something Aunt Worthrose told with my mother, instead of the other way around.

And my mother did confirm. For once she was eager to talk.

"I didn't know about the pictures from the Civil War but I'm not surprised. And as far as my father- his mother left him at an orphanage when he was a little boy. He told me he grew up in foster home after foster home where they farmed him out to work and beat him. Finally he ran away. Later, when he was grown and married, his real mother came to him for him to support her." My mother sounded bitter.

"And did he really change his name?" I asked, thinking he must've done something criminal.

My real mother better not show up wanting me to support her, I thought. *I won't do it.*

"You're not learning much about sewing are you? Yes, his mother was married to a Patterson for a while. Then he took that name and he didn't like his first name. So in the 1920s he started calling himself Lind. After Lucky Lindy, I suppose."

"What was his real name?"

"Hopewell Clarkson."

"What?"

"His first name was Hopewell and his last name was Clarkson."

I could certainly understand why he didn't want a name like Hopewell. That was not a first name. But I grieved over the loss of Clarkson as a last name.

That would've been a great last name. A great pen name.

"That's why I have an older brother named Clark and your cousin is named that as well."

Uncle Clark was one of my mother's older brothers that I had never met.

"Speaking of Clark, your cousin Clark got married last week," my mother announced.

"Really," I was disappointed. "I didn't know he was old enough to get married. Did he run off to another state like Cliff?"

"No, he just got married at home," she said. "They didn't invite people. He married a girl from Jacksonville and moved there."

"Where is that?"

"North of here. We never go there because it doesn't have many shops or attractions and it's out of the way. But her family lives there."

"Will we get to meet her?"

"Soon, next time we visit the countryside. We'll go around to see them."

Chapter 13
Sarah disappears

Barbara and Ellen made an inventory of what was missing.

Barbara's golden band ring was missing, $50.00 from the kitchen cupboard was gone. Mr. Scott's silver ring was missing and Mrs. Scott's diamond necklace was missing.

"Mom, I was just thinking," said Barbara. "Why would anyone want my golden band ring, I mean even though it is pure gold it's only worth $10.00."

"Dear," Ellen sighed, "that is the way of thieves."

After reporting the robbery Barbara decided to call Fae Bolman. Just as she was about to call the phone rang. It was Fae Bolman, she was frantic, Emily May had been kidnapped! Ellen and Barbara rushed right over and tried to comfort to the distraught woman.

But they did not succeed in doing so because when they thought they had her calmed down she would cry, "Oh my Emily May, oh my Diane."

Finally they got her to tell them what happened.

"Well," she said. "Emily and I were working in the kitchen. I went out for a moment and when I was came back all was left was a note saying -

'DON'T GO TO THE POLICE OR BARBARA SCOTT' "

Mrs. Bolman burst into tears.

After visiting Mrs. Bolman, the Scotts went to the police station and gave Chief McBlend a report on Emily

May Bolman.

"Mom," said Barbara, "Don't you agree that we should go see the Hortons? It may be too late to warn them about Sarah."

"Yes today is the 17th."

At the Horton home Ellen and Barbara learned that Sarah was out.

"She was very mysterious about it," said Mrs. Horton. "She just said a man had come to take her to the post office, that she had a very important package that could not be delivered."

Barbara looked worriedly at Ellen. Ellen nodded sadly and knowingly.

Mrs. Horton saw this and said quickly, "Do you know something about Sarah that I don't know?"

"Mrs. Horton –" Barbara began, but she did not finish her sentence for just then the doorbell rang.

"Excuse me," said Mrs. Horton. When she came back she looked as pale as a ghost. The Scotts thought they knew why but they politely remained quiet until Mrs. Horton showed them a note which said–

DON'T GO TO THE POLICE
YOU WILL NEVER SEE SARAH AGAIN
ADDIE JONES

"That's what I was going to tell you," explained Barbara.

She told Mrs. Horton about the others who were kidnapped.

"I'll find Sarah too," she finished.

Suddenly Mrs. Horton rushed up and hugged Barbara with all her might.

"Oh, you dear dear girl," she cried. "You can do it, you must. Oh those poor girls."

By this time the woman was crying hysterically.

The Scotts were about to give up trying to calm

the distraught woman when Mr. Horton let himself in the front door. He dropped his briefcase and rushed to his wife. He laid her gently down on the sofa and opened a desk drawer and took out some white capsules. He was giving it to her as the Scotts quietly left the house.

"Poor Mrs. Horton," said Barbara. "She's had such a shock."

So far that makes Belle Maine, Jane Kape, Diane Bolman, Emily May Bolman, and Sarah Horton." Barbara's eyes became misty, not just because of Belle and Jane but because of all the other poor girls.

As Ellen and Barbara were going home a woman ran right into Ellen.

"Oh, I'm so sorry," said the woman. "Ever since my daughter has been missing. I haven't been the same."

"Your daughter missing? Why don't you tell us about it," Barbara said.

The woman said her name was Fran Denson. Her daughter Kelly had disappeared that morning.

"She wasn't in her bed. All that was there was this

DON'T GO TO THE
POLICE OR HARM WILL COME
TO YOU!   S. J.

"Mrs. Denson, I think your daughter has been the victim of some clever kidnappers that have kidnapped several other girls I know."

After bidding goodbye to Mrs. Denson Ellen and Barbara went home.

"Who could be doing the kidnapping? Besides Stiff Jones," wondered Barbara.

"Don't ask me Barbara," said Ellen, "you know that I don't know anything about sleuthing."

Just then the phone rang.

After talking 10 minutes, Barbara hung up.

"Oh, Mom," she cried out excitedly. "They've got a woman they think is Addie Jones. They want me to go to Jacksonville to identify her!"

The next morning Barbara and Ellen went to Jacksonville.

As they went in to identify Addie Jones the desk sergeant greeted them. "You will be given only one chance to identify her. If you can't identify her we will have to turn her loose!"

"I'll know her anywhere," said Barbara. "I'm ready!"

"All right."

Barbara was led to the cell and looked straight at the woman. Suddenly she cried out, "That's her! That's Addie Jones!"

We didn't ever go and meet Cousin Clark's new wife on our summer vacation because they had already split up and he was back home before we ever got there.

I abandoned the idea of making columns based on people's nationalities. The origin column was too complicated on my mother's side. And on my father's side everyone was simply Italian. Just like the religion column wound up being Catholic all on one side and Protestant all on one side, the origin lists would have just been Italian and Not Italian. I decided trying to categorize real people was a waste of time. Making columns on characters in my book was much more interesting. I could mix them all up, change and categorize them as I pleased.

I got to work on that, taking that work on the road when we went on vacation, to the Grand Canyon this year. I worked on columns of new characters for future books during the drive there and back. Mercifully our summer activities did not include the Fourth of July at the park because Daddy had to work that day.

Much nicer an experience than any fireworks could ever be was the rehearsal for the big event at church right after we returned. I got dressed up in white and put on a veil. I had flowers and a prayer book in my hand and practiced going down the aisle.

Mama had wanted to get me a special formal white dress but

Father Mallett said no, all the girls had to be dressed alike in white robes. But she did get to go and pick out a veil so I could look special when I made my First Communion.

Before the event, Mama took me to the studio to have my pictures made in my First Communion outfit. I usually went to the studio two or three times a year, dressed up, and took good pictures, better than school pictures, which we always bought anyway. But I was very disappointed in the studio pictures this time. The veil looked pretty but the robe just draped and made me look fat. I showed the pictures to Kris Stavich before the church service began.

"It doesn't matter if you are fat," he said, even though he was very skinny. He was shorter than me too, just like Daddy was shorter than Mama. But he was all dressed up in a suit and tie.

I was ashamed. I wanted to tear the pictures up.

"I like the pictures and I want one," Kris insisted.

I gladly gave him a picture since he wanted it. But I decided I was going to stop eating as much and lose weight no matter what before school started. I was disappointed Kris did not have a picture to give me.

It was time to go down the aisle for real, kneel at the railing and take my First Communion. There to watch was Uncle Chris Marino, Aunt Thelma, and Ruth. Once again I recalled Ruth's words about the Voice of God as I went down the aisle. There was one part of the Mass that said-

Lift up your hearts to the Lord
We lift up our hearts to you, oh Lord!
It is right to give Him thanks and praise.

At that moment in my mind I could see my outstretched arms holding my heart up to God, a darkened crust falling away from it to reveal a beautiful red color as it reached his hands. If I could make a painting of it, the image would be captured forever. I burned the image into my memory to assure it would never leave me.

End of Part 2

Part 3

X *Judgments*

If Ruth was right and it was possible to actually hear God speak, then the stories I was being told in CCD about the Catholic saints were not the whole truth. Our CCD teachers varied so much that we never got to know them well. Frequently they would only last one week. Most of them were parents of the students. But they all agreed that when the saints said they heard voices of God or the Virgin Mary, it was all inside their heads.

"That's because the psychologists say that people who really hear voices are crazy," explained my mother, when I mentioned this.

"The only one they agree claimed she heard voices was Joan of Arc," I said, thinking about Ruth and how she did not seem crazy at all. In fact, Aunt Thelma had reported that not only was Ruth doing fabulously academically, she had been elected cheerleader at her junior high school for the upcoming school year, a singular honor considering she would only be in eighth grade.

"They burned her at the stake," said my mother.

"But Joan of Arc still got to be a saint," I said.

"She dressed up in men's clothes, she had to be a little crazy," said my mother, and went to the kitchen to start cooking supper. Aunt Worthrose arrived for a visit. Daddy was working late again.

"My God, madness has been let loose in this world!" said Aunt Worthrose, that evening as she watched the news with us. "This is the vengeance of the Lord. This is the indeed the dreadful end times predicted by the Bible!"

My mother said nothing but she was as white as a sheet as she clutched me in her arms as the three of us watched the television. For once it looked as though Aunt Worthrose may be right.

"*...Our top story... vicious murders in a nearby state...a police officer called to investigate suspicious circumstances at a frozen food storage facility which was closed due to electrical failure. Freezers for storing food were being powered by generators... the warehouse was* *hot, over 95 degrees… to get a burst of cool air the policeman opened one of the refrigerator freezer doors expecting to see packaged frozen foods or at the most frozen butchered meat…*

"The decapitated heads of a man and a woman stared back at him with lifeless eyes.

"The police officer said he slammed the door shut, but the image of those faces staring at him is burned in his mind forever-…The suspect in the murders is on the loose and believed headed towards Colorado…"

Headed towards Colorado! For days it was on the news. Everybody talked about it. Pamela came over explaining that her roommates had all gone to stay with their families and she did not want to be alone. Aunt Worthrose even slept in the bedroom with Uncle Clyde for awhile, something unprecedented since they were both so old when they got married. Nothing like this had ever happened before that anybody remembered. Nobody knew who did it. The police did not catch anybody. They called it the Freezer Murders. And everybody was very scared.

I slept with my mother for a week after it happened, while Pamela got my mother's room. Mama further reacted to this horror by refusing to leave the house without Daddy. Aunt Worthrose just stopped going anywhere. So we had to do grocery shopping for both households when Daddy was available.

Aunt Worthrose was too nervous to keep me. She refused to take any of Mama's nerve pills. So for the first time ever, I got to go to the grocery stores. The small store managed by Matthew Waterston's father near Fairvine was delightful, open and full of sunlight, very neat, orderly and clean. But the other store, Greater City Supermarket, was more fun to go too. It was closer to the freeway and although it was kind of dark and not real clean, the prices were cheaper and it had toys! It had dolls! Records!

"We might as well pay the higher prices at the closer store," my mother finally decided, after I added substantially to my dolls' wardrobes and my record collection was well established. "We are spending more on Victoria by going to the cheaper store than we save."

But my mother found a different grocery store, across the freeway, sort of clean, drab, no toys or records. So we didn't go back to shop at the bright cheerful little neighborhood grocery store with higher prices or Greater City where the good stuff was.

Other expeditions were curtailed as well. The ice cream parlor closed down. Mama didn't even take me to the doctor, the beauty shop, or to get my picture made at the studio.

And she stopped trying to get me to go play with other kids or have them over at my house. We started watching the news every night to see if the murderer had come to our town. After a few weeks I got over being afraid. There were no more murders. The news was mostly about the Vietnam War. But Mama was still afraid to go anywhere for a much longer time. Her nerve pills stopped helping her. The start of school was still a long time away. There was little to do.

So she decided to teach me longhand.

"I hope I'm doing it right," she said, as she pulled out the wide lined papers and the cartridge pens that I had to use. "You'll have to pretend you don't know how to do it when school starts. And if they show you a different way to make any of the letters, be sure and make it the way they show you not the way I'm going to teach you."

It was so easy! Once she showed me how, it was the easiest thing in the world! I could not believe I had not figured it out by myself before now.

The pens and ink cartridges were messy and sometimes leaked so the ink got all over my hands. This aggravated my mother who so hated a mess.

"I'm going to put them away until you need them for school and you can go back to using your ballpoint."

That was all right with me. The next chapter was twice as long and I wrote it in half the time because now I could write in longhand.

Chapter 14
The Enemy Strikes Again

"Are you positive, Miss Scott?"
"Yes, I'm sure that that's Addie Jones!"
"Thank you, Miss Scott, Mrs. Scott. And good day."
Back at home Barbara answered the phone.
"Hello my name is Mrs. John Andrew. I live in

56607 Washington Ave. Please come right over, my daughter Sandy was kidnapped!"

At Mrs. Andrew's house Barbara learned that Mrs. Andrew had two children, a nine-year-old son and an 18-year-old daughter. This morning Sandy, her daughter, disappeared. All that was left with this –

YOU'LL NEVER
SEE SANDY
AGAIN
S. JONES

"The enemy strikes again," exclaimed Barbara in disgust.

"Yes," Ellen nodded tearfully.

"Of course that's it," cried Barbara. She turned to her mother. "Mom, I'm going back to Harold Hall."

Driving Ellen's car, she hurried to the abandoned mansion.

When she got there she stopped short. ON THE GROUND LAY A WOMAN BOUND AND GAGGED. THIS WOMAN WAS APRIL KAPE!

Quickly she untied her.

"Aunt April," she cried. "Are you all right?"

As Barbara helped her to her feet April gasped, "Oh, Barbara we've got to get out of here before those awful men come back!"

"Yes," agreed Barbara.

"I'm so glad I'm not married," said April.

"Married?" said Barbara, "but you are married. You're Mrs. April Kape."

"Barbara," cried April. "I am Miss April Cobbler! You know that!"

BARBARA WAS DUMBFOUNDED! HAD HER AUNT SUDDENLY LOST HER MIND?!

"Let's go to my house, Aunt April," suggested Barbara.

161

"Of course, dear," said April.

When they got to the Scott home Barbara said to April, "Wait right here."

She went to the house and told Ellen about April.

WHEN SHE WENT BACK OUT APRIL WAS DRIVING OFF IN ELLEN'S CAR!

"Wait," cried Barbara. "Wait!"

April paid no attention. She drove to a department store and parked the car.

Barbara, out of breath, ran up to her aunt.

"Aunt April," said Barbara. "I think we better go home."

"Very well, dear. I was just buying some clothes," said April. "You know I have none here."

Barbara started to say something but thought better of it.

Ellen was very relieved that her sister was back at her house but very much concerned over her health.

Barbara immediately summoned a doctor. Dr. Grasson.

"She is reliving her past," he said. "In about a week she will become normal. Just go along with her. And let her think she's not married."

Barbara was relieved but Ellen was worried. Barbara comforted her mother saying, "After all Mom, if Aunt April doesn't remember Uncle Raymond she certainly won't remember Jane and that will cause her less worry."

Ellen thought it over and admitted it was true. "And she will recover sooner too," she added.

April came out just then so Barbara and Ellen had a chance to say no more.

Barbara went to see Sarah Horton's mother. When she got to the door she was surprised to find Mr. Horton awaiting her.

"It's about time you got here," he snapped.

"Where's Mrs. Horton?" She asked quickly.

"Martha is having another spell just because you called and told her that you supposed Sarah was dead. And you are giving up the case."

"Mr. Horton I made no such call," said Barbara, shocked.

"What?" he cried. "I'm sorry then, please tell that to my wife."

After talking to Mrs. Horton, Barbara went home and told the whole story. "Whoever she was she mimicked me perfectly."

"This mystery is getting more dangerous every minute. PLEASE be careful."

"All right, Mom."

That night Barbara looked in Belle's bedroom. Its pink canopy bed was untouched.

On a chair lay her golden evening gown. Her dead parents had given her and Barbara evening gowns two weeks before their fateful trip.

That night Barbara could not sleep. She kept thinking of Belle and Jane. When she finally fell asleep she dreamed that she was running through the Kape home away from Stiff Jones who was running after her carrying Belle's head and Jane's clothes.

Then the dreams changed. She was flying through the air with Chief McBlend chasing Addie and Stiff who were carrying the heads of all the girls who were kidnapped. Barbara screamed, "No no you'll not kidnap me, help, help!"

Ellen came running in the room to see what was the matter. She awoke her daughter and Barbara found herself wet with perspiration. She was surprised to find the sunlight streaming in the window.

"What time is it?" asked Barbara, alarmed.

"11 a.m."

"Oh," she groaned. "I had hoped to get an early

start. I got to go to Harold Hall today."

"No Barbara I cannot permit you to go to Harold Hall by yourself," said Ellen firmly. "It's too dangerous." She shuddered.

"But Mom–"

"No, unless you take someone with you. You cannot go," Ellen declared.

"I know who I'll take. Minnie Foster," said Barbara.

"I thought you didn't like her!" Ellen looked surprised.

"Oh I do," Barbara said hastily and scrambled out the door before Ellen could retort.

Minnie was 16 with blue eyes and blond hair which was rapidly turning brown.

Minnie, being timid at first, was reluctant to go but finally Barbara persuaded her that there was no danger.

When they finally got to the old mansion it was dark and Minnie begged to stay in the car.

"All right," agreed Barbara.

When she was out of sight of the car she quickly glanced around. IN THE WOODS WAS AN EERIE BLUE GLOW! As though realizing that she had seen it, the light flicked out!

Barbara decided against investigating it since she was not familiar with that part of the woods.

The door creaked eerily when she opened it. Barbara sat down in one of the mildewed chairs and it groaned beneath her weight. As the chair showed signs of collapsing she quickly got up. Every board, it seemed, squeaked beneath her feet.

Finally the young sleuth decided she had had enough of Harold Hall.

AS SHE TRIED TO OPEN THE DOOR, BARBARA FOUND IT WAS LOCKED FROM THE OUTSIDE!

I was very careful, when third grade started, to pretend that I didn't know how to write longhand so I wouldn't get my mother in

164

trouble with the teachers. They did have a few letters they wanted done differently and I had a little trouble with that. But that just made it look like I was learning it for the first time.

Still, my mother was not selected to be the third grade parent sitting in on the Guidance Group as she had done in first and second grades.

Even though Miss Tucker had been tall and thin, old and strict, I had begun to like her before second grade had come to end. But I was still very happy to see a most beautiful blond young woman as my third grade anchor and also our English teacher. She was sweet just like Mrs. Anderson, only she was younger. Her name, Mrs. Choy, was Asian, but she was not.

Matthew Waterston was back in my class in third grade but he decided he didn't like me anymore because I had gotten fat. I decided to keep him listed as a school boyfriend because there wasn't anybody else there that I liked. Glenn was still too freckled.

I wasn't surprised not to see Jayne Anderson at the school the first few days. I knew she was supposed to be in my class again. But last year Jayne was so often absent that I didn't think anything of it at first. But then weeks passed, and though I looked for her every morning, she didn't show up.

I told my mother Jayne was missing.

"Jayne will not be back," my mother told me. "Mrs. Anderson has left Dr. Anderson and taken Jayne with her."

"Why? Are they getting a divorce?" I was shocked, thinking more about Mrs. Anderson being divorced like Aunt Concetta and Aunt Florrie than about her being gone. I remembered when Marva in first grade was the only person I knew that had divorced parents and how the class all thought that strange, just a short time ago.

"You must not tell anybody this but, yes, they will."

"Why do people get divorces? I miss Connie. I wish she would come back to play, even if her parents are divorced."

"They have changed the divorce laws so that it is much easier now. Connie will never be back," said my mother. "Her mother has taken her to another country and they are in hiding. None of the family has any idea where they are. Not even Uncle Vince Vaccaro and his new wife. Aunt Concetta's new husband hit her and Connie and they have to hide from him."

I had heard about stepfathers who hit their children.

"Aunt Worthrose said her stepfather had been mean to her and hit her," I said, distracted by thinking about Mrs. Anderson and Aunt Concetta, forgetting for a moment that Aunt Worthrose's stepfather was Mama's real father.

"That's not true! Worthrose is cruel to say that to you! And if he ever hit her she deserved it." My mother appeared to be taken off guard. Her voice was extra sharp.

"Ok," I said, not wanting to cause trouble between my aunt and my mother. *I shouldn't have said that.*

"We all of us got whippings when we were little, mostly from our mother. Worthy Rose need not get so high and mighty. Her own father was no saint." Mama said smugly. "He left another wife and kids to marry my mother."

"What?" *Ooh this is interesting.*

"That's right, he had a bunch of kids with his first wife, half grown, when he met my mother who was just a teenager. Your Aunt Worthrose has older half brothers and sisters she's never known. Did she tell you that?"

"No." What stories they had to tell from the old days. I wondered what else I didn't know.

"Well, after her father died and she married my father, he had to support those kids and eight more that she had with him. She was sick all the time, having 12 babies in 20 years."

"How did she manage to have so many babies? I thought it was hard to have babies," I said, thinking of Mama, Aunt Worthrose, Aunt Concetta, and Aunt Talinda who had no children.

"No, it's easy. Easy for most women, they can't help it, most women just spit them out like cats having kittens." she said bitterly, then added hastily, "once they're married, of course. I was different, something was wrong with me and Talinda, and- and your Aunt Worthrose- she didn't want any."

"But she was married. How could she not help it?"

"Well, there must have been something wrong with her, too."

"I'm never getting married," I said, thinking of Alyce O'Kelley's family. So they couldn't help it. What a nightmare.

166

"Oh, there's a pill now, just invented, they say you can take it and it prevents you from getting pregnant even if you are married. If only they had invented it 50 years ago. Although you can't take it if you are Catholic." She tried to change the subject. "You know, you're lucky your Aunt Worthrose loves you so. She's never taken to any other child."

I thought it quite natural that Aunt Worthrose loved me, and having experienced other children, I understood why she didn't like most of them.

However I said, "Daddies shouldn't spank children, men could hit too hard because they stronger. Daddy doesn't spank me."

"He did once," she said wryly. "You just don't remember. It was at the old house. I made him. You misbehaved so badly in public that I insisted he take action. And then after he did it, he cried. Then he said to me that any spanking in the future, I would have to do it."

"Well you don't have any problem with it," I said. I had a healthy respect for the belt that she never wore, but occupied a prominent place hanging in her closet. It hadn't been used but once or twice since we had moved. But I recalled its frequent sting at her hand at the old house. Aunt Worthrose had said her stepfather used a tree limb when he had been drinking. But I didn't mention that.

"Was Connie's stepfather Italian?"

"No, he wasn't. He is some kind of Greek or Middle Easterner or something. Some foreigner. Very rich. So they will have to hide from him a long, long time."

"And did he drink?"

"He drank too, I heard. Most men do," said my mother. "That's why I started going out with your father. He was the first man I ever knew that didn't drink at all."

"You had other boyfriends? Did they all drink? Why?"

"I don't know, I never understood it." She smiled sadly at me. "I had lots of dates and, yes, they usually would have a drink. But there was only one other man, really. I had a boyfriend from the countryside, a man like my brothers and your Uncle Drake, and I always thought I'd marry him. But he drank."

"So you knew him before Daddy," I asked.

"Oh, yes, he was a cowboy, well not a real cowboy but close to it. He was tall and handsome with blond hair and blue eyes," she said. "He looked a little like Gary Cooper. He was kind and sweet when he was not drinking, and even when he was, he would just be quiet and still, never mean, that I saw. And he wanted to marry me in the worse way but I turned him down. Because he drank. And I knew what could happen. He swore he would quit. But I knew better."

"Whatever happened to him?"

"Oh, he finally married someone else, and he did stop drinking for a while, but then they had a son that died of the polio, and he started drinking again. I ran into him in a store in the broad daylight some years later, and there he was, just as drunk as could be, but still handsome like Gary Cooper."

"Who was Gary Cooper?

"Oh, don't you know him, or maybe, you mainly watch the old war movies, not Westerns, don't you? Um- he was in *Sergeant York.*"

"I hate Westerns. I never watch them. I don't remember a movie called *Sergeant York*."

"I'll make sure you catch it next time it comes on."

"Daddy is handsome like a movie star," I said.

"He looks more like Rudolph Valentino. You would really not know him. They never show any silent movies," she said. "Some of those movies were something else. The men beat the women in them a lot. Some men got the idea from those movies that it was Ok."

"So you think that is what happened with Aunt Concetta's new husband? Is he old enough to remember silent movies?"

"He's older yes, not much older than Vince Vaccaro though. I know Vince used to paddle Connie. But apparently it was much more violent with the second husband and they are now living in fear of their lives. Concetta has wealthy relatives in Europe that will hide them the rest of their lives if they have to, I guess."

"Her father won't ever see Connie again?"

"He's not trying to find Connie, he can't. If he finds her, the stepfather may find her too."

"So it will be like Uncle Vince Vaccaro doesn't even have any children." I remembered about the adopted daughter he lost and now he had lost his own.

"Oh. He'll soon be 60, but he's a man! They can still have

babies until they're practically dead with old age. In fact, I hear Vince Vaccaro and his new young wife are expecting a baby." When she said the word baby, her voice tone went from sarcastic to wistful. "Maybe he will do better this time, if he lives long enough to see the baby grow up." Now her voice was sarcastic. "I don't expect we'll be seeing much of them though. You ended up being right about him not staying Catholic. He and his new wife joined some charismatic church where apparently they don't care how people behave."

He's replacing his old family with a new family, I thought. I felt sorry for Connie. Her real father did not realize he loved her too much to hit her and then she lost him. Any new babies he had would be way too young for me to ever play with.

"What is a charismatic church?"

"Oh, a Protestant denomination like Pentecostal or Assembly of God. I don't know which."

"Protestants?"

She nodded. *Good grief! How many more Protestant types are out there?*

"Everyone now acts as if divorce is a normal occurrence, whatever the reason. I had rather thought Mrs. Anderson would have said goodbye to us, to me, at least over the phone, but I never heard a word from her. I guess something could have happened while we were gone on vacation and she couldn't reach me. It doesn't matter, they are gone."

So while Daddy, Mama, and I had been on our regular family vacation having a good time, Mrs. Anderson and Jayne had vanished from our lives, moved on as if they had never known us. Just as gone as Aunt Concetta and Connie.

Aunt Worthrose had some old movie magazines and I looked up Gary Cooper and Rudolph Valentino in them. Gary Cooper did have that general look of Uncle Drake and all Mama's brothers I had seen or seen pictures of. Rudolph Valentino looked handsome, but not as handsome as Daddy.

Back at school I looked around the classroom. I surveyed the other girls, studying them. I was going to have to pick out a new best friend and I didn't want to rush into anything.

There were several candidates. Julianna Wells was much fatter than me and she was nice. She made no secret of the fact that she admired me and wanted to be my friend. There was a very blond thin girl who was very beautiful. Her name was Julianna too and she seemed nice but she was absent very often. It was hard to make a decision about her. And shortly before Thanksgiving, two new girls came into the class. One was not a possibility. Rita was very shy because her religion prevented her from saying **The Pledge of Allegiance** each morning.

The Pledge of Allegiance was all we said anymore when class began every day. Prayers had been discontinued after first grade, patriotic songs like **My Country tis of Thee** and **America the Beautiful** were eliminated late last year.

Now in music class we sang stupid nursery rhyme songs like in the cartoons. Songs about twinkling stars and mersy dotes, whatever those were. When I complained, my mother got me some record albums with the good songs on them to play at home.

The other new girl in class was friendly in a quiet way. She had just moved into the area. Her name was Carmelita. Most of the other kids did not talk to her but I did.

"Are you Mexican or are you Negro?" I asked, being very careful to use that word right.

"I'm Mexican," said Carmelita. "I was born in America though."

It was hard to believe Carmelita was only Mexican. She was so dark. Darker than Christian Romano. I had heard that when he started school some people tried to get Aunt Florrie to admit he was part Negro even though he was only Italian. But he got lighter when he got older. So I believed Carmelita when she said she was just Mexican. She spoke so softly and slowly, it was hard to tell what her accent was. But she seemed intelligent. And she was nice to me so I put her on my list of candidates to be my best friend.

The girls on my list were the only possibilities since none of the rest of the class was friendly to me at all this year. They all silently hated me in class because I could not play baseball well outdoors. Gone were our fun recess times outside where we played games. We had to go outside in all kinds of weather now, whether it was cold or not, even light rain would not get us out of playing baseball. It had to be pouring to keep us inside. Now, because of President Johnson's Physical Fitness Program, the girls had to play baseball by themselves, separated from the boys. I hated President Johnson.

It was the most stupid game ever thought of, throwing a little ball at someone holding a stick. And I had stopped running years ago after skinning my knees once. When a ball came flying at me, I ducked. Naturally, I did not want to get hit. I didn't mind picking it up and tossing it to somebody else but that didn't please anybody.

Only Julianna Wells and Carmelita defended me on the playground. The teachers who had always supervised and joined in our fun games previously, now hardly paid any attention as we attempted to play baseball. Only one of them would stay outside and yell at us.

I figured President Johnson really hated children to take away their recess and subject them to the horror called P.E. I hoped he wouldn't be President very long. I heard people say they thought he was damaging the country.

He is certainly damaging my life! I wish we had a president who cared about us.

I had heard Mama, Daddy and Aunt Worthrose say President Eisenhower had cared about the people, especially soldiers. And so had President Roosevelt, who routinely had a fireside chat with all the people just as if they were his friends. I did wonder how that worked for people without fireplaces. President Kennedy talked to the people on TV and they thought he also would have become a friend of all the people if he had lived long enough.

President Johnson must not have had a best friend to play with and, now that he is President, he wants revenge on all children because he was lonely and disliked.

The decision on who my next best friend was going to be was taken out of my hands. My mother informed me that from now on in class I was being paired with Julianna Whaels. This was a decision of the Guidance Committee after the announcement about the tests.

The announcement had come out of the clear blue sky. I was walking in the hall with another group of kids going to the school library to return books for the class.

POP! went the loudspeaker. "May I have your attention

please?" Pause, static. "As you know the entire school recently participated in the national IQ testing. We now have the results and are very proud and pleased to announce that two of our students have exceptionally high scores. Both of them are in the third grade and in the same class- Mrs. Choy's class. They are- Julianna Whaels with a score of 154 and Victoria Grasso with a score of 147. Congratulations, girls, well done!" POP!

I looked up in surprise at hearing my name. Several other kids congratulated me. Most of them just stared at me. A couple advanced toward me in an unfriendly way. A teacher I didn't know came up to me, took the books I was carrying, and directed me back to class.

My mother was surprised and happy when I told her about the announcement. She contacted the school for details, before the adults all went home, as soon as we got to the house.

"Why am I supposed to be friends with Julianna?" I asked a few days later. "She's blond." *And thin,* I thought. As soon as school had started I had gained back most of the weight I had lost in the summer. I was beginning to resent thin people a little.

"Don't you like her? Try to get to know her. If she is nice we can have her come and visit you and you can play dolls."

"What about Carmelita?"

"Maybe later, we'll see. I don't know her mother."

I agreed to give Julianna try and invited her over to play.

"Don't talk about the test," said my mother before Julianna came over. "Her parents are upset that it was announced over the loudspeaker. I don't know why, they should be proud. Her father is a geologist so he must be smart too. But they are angry at the school so don't mention it. We just want you and Julianna to play like normal kids."

I had long ago decided the ultimate test for everybody who came over was handling my fashion dolls. She passed the test with flying colors although she did make a bid to play with the ponytails.

From my introductory chats with her at school I suspected she was able to talk intelligently even though she was not any older than me. So I had a few questions for her on her first visit. The type of questions that only brought blank stares from other kids but she had answers. "Do you really have more fun because your hair is blond?"

was the first. That's what they said on the TV commercials. No other girls in our class were as blond as her.

"Well," she said thoughtfully, but with humor in her voice. "I suppose I really do. As I have always been a blond, I cannot judge how much fun I might have had otherwise. That is an unknown. So I can only conclude, therefore, that I do have more fun. I have only one life and I am living it as a blond."

"Do you think you are happier and more well adjusted because you are not an only child?" I had heard that line from one of the substitute teachers.

"Happier? No. My little brothers and sisters are a pain in the neck. But definitely I am obviously more well adjusted than you are. You won't share."

"Ok, I guess that's right. Still, you cannot play with the ponytail swirl."

"Meanie." She stuck her tongue out at me and I replied in kind. From that moment on we were best friends. I did let her play with a new red headed ponytail but I kept a close eye on her.

Julianna was the first other kid I had ever known who also wrote stories. She and I soon planned to trade stories and read each other's. But she was not ready yet. She showed them to me at her house so I knew they existed. For the first time, I got to go visit someone who lived in an addition. My mother finally got to where she would leave the house to take me to Julianna's. Soon she and Aunt Worthrose were shopping again while I was at school, so there were no more Saturday trips to the grocery stores. Instead, Juliana and I traded visits at our houses.

I was surprised that Julianna's house was much smaller than ours, her room half the space of mine, her yard a fraction of the size. Daddy certainly was right about addition houses being inferior. I did enjoy my visits to her house. She did not have as many dolls but almost as many doll clothes. She had a short piano and was still taking lessons so sometimes we could play at making music. But frequently we had to play with her little sisters and brothers. So her visits to my house, where I had no nuisance sisters or brothers about, were much more enjoyable.

It was different playing with her. It was almost like being with a grownup. She understood me and did not get angry when I tried to talk about something interesting. She was as good at games as I was and frequently won. We didn't have to play with toys if we didn't want to. We could just talk for hours about all kinds of things.

We both agreed Matthew Waterston was still the handsomest boy in our class. Julianna said she often went with her mother to grocery shop at his father's store but never saw him there. After several visits, Julianna opened up more. I was surprised to find that Julianna liked Matthew and thought he liked her, even though she was smarter than him.

"Yes, I have liked Matthew for some time but I didn't want to tell you in case you got mad," she said shyly, looking sad. "I treasure your friendship but I really do like him."

I thought it over. "It's Ok, you can have him."

"Really?" She was delighted and brightened up at once. "It's Ok with you? You don't mind?"

"I have Kris at church. He spells his name with a K." I told her. "He's my church boyfriend and cuter than Matthew Waterston."

"What is he like?"

"Oh, he is real thin and has dark hair and he's part German and part French. On the German side, he is descended from the famous ancient musician that they named sherbet after. On the French side, he's descended from royalty!"

"Really, he told you that? Did he tell you he was really rich?"

"He told me about his ancestors, but his family is not rich. They are always broke, he told me."

"That would be Schubert he was talking about. Well, that makes it all more believable. Personally I don't like sherbet. We usually have only real ice cream."

"So do we, but sometimes we get the lime," I said.

"My mother can trace one of her ancestors back to British aristocracy. Since our textbook says that England is our Mother Country, I assume that branch of the family is of superior quality," said Julianna. "But the rest are just Heinz 57, she says. And we never have any extra money either." Her voice became wistful, then hopeful. "Matthew Waterston's father owns the grocery store. So they must have money."

174

"Anyways, you can take Matthew. I'd keep him as a backup but since you want him, he's yours."

"Thanks!" her eyes widened. "Thanks so much!"

We hugged spontaneously. As I embraced her, suddenly I was glad Kris did not know her. It had been a close call. Kris had told me that his family had wanted to buy a house in Fairland Addition. But when his father was transferred, it was in the middle of the school year in first grade, and they couldn't find any houses for sale in the whole addition. So they had to settle for a house farther away across the freeway. That was why he did not go to my school. If he knew Julianna, he might prefer her to me like Matthew did. But he didn't know her.

Julianna thought it was strange that I liked Frank Sinatra and Dean Martin. She looked at my record albums curiously.

"They are old men. Don't you listen to the Beatles?" she asked.

"Who are they?"

"What kind of music do your parents listen to? My mother is a great Elvis fan."

I thought for a moment. "They don't listen to music. Mine is the only record player we have."

"Everybody listens to music. What radio stations do they play in the car?"

I thought harder. "Except when President Kennedy was killed or when the weather is bad, they don't turn the radio on."

But I do remember Mama watching an Elvis movie alone in the den one day. And when I came in, she jumped up and cut it off. When I'm at school and Daddy's at work, she could watch anything and we would never know, I realized.

Julianna looked up and around rotating her head in a semi-circle. "Well."

"Very seldom we all go see a movie. But very seldom. They don't watch much television either, and they don't read books."

Julianna was so stunned by this, she was speechless.

Julianna and I did enjoy the same movies. She was looking forward to the movie theatre close to the school being finished and then we could go to the movies together. She didn't like math although she was good at it. We also agreed that we hated playing baseball although she was good at it as well.

Now that she was my friend, she joined Carmelita and Julianna Wells in defending me when I played badly, which was all the time. I pined for recess even more when I realized that how much Julianna and I would enjoy the games now that we knew each other.

"You always were with Vickie Bianchi at recess and never looked at me or anyone else. And then you took up with Jayne Anderson all the time," Julianna told me, with a little hurt in her voice. "I was stuck with Julianna Wells since her name was next to mine alphabetically. She's nice but not interesting to be with."

I had looked up our old school group pictures to prove that she had really been in my classes all along. Yes, she was in every class but I did not recall her at all before now. I wondered who else I had missed. Some of the kids that had been there since kindergarten had left this year and I had never really known them. Glenn's family had moved so he was missing, too.

"You never miss anyone until they are gone," said my mother, when I mentioned students disappearing.

This insight was a little hard to understand at first but it hit home in December. Mrs. Choy left us at Christmas. In a shocking announcement at the very end of the semester, she tearfully told us she would not return in the spring.

It was the last day of school before the 1965 holiday. I thought it odd that morning when Mrs. Choy arrived wearing a short sleeved yellow jumper dress with no blouse underneath and the hemline only came to her knee. Usually she wore a long sleeve shirt and below the knee skirt or belted dress like most other teachers.

She stood up in front of the class and asked for our attention. I noticed a substitute teacher standing in the doorway. Then Mrs. Choy said goodbye.

"I'm not coming back after the Christmas holidays." She started to cry. "I am sorry I can't come back and I will miss you all very much. You are all wonderful and I love you all and will never forget any of you."

She broke down visibly and cried uncontrollably then. And the substitute teacher came all the way in and led Mrs. Choy to the door where other people were waiting for her. The substitute closed the door and took over for the rest of the day.

Mrs. Choy was gone just like that. She never did say why she was not coming back. As she had spoken, I tried to memorize her lovely face. I realized I had no pictures of her. And as our group picture was taken in the spring, she would not be standing with the class. Just like that she was gone. And my memory would be all I would ever have of her.

"Her husband is making her quit," my mother told me. "That's what I heard. He doesn't want his wife to work."

This made no sense to me.

"Are you sure that is the reason, June Rosette? I've heard other rumors." Aunt Worthrose had been talking to Mrs. O'Kelley Senior again.

"What are you hearing?"

"Why would her husband not want her to work?" I asked.

"Maybe it's the same situation as that other teacher. He's afraid if she stays on word will get out, like it did in that case."

"Why would her husband not want her to work?" I repeated my question impatiently.

"Well, your father doesn't really want me to work," said my mother. She explained-

"He can get jealous if I'm around other men. That's happened in the past. But I don't care. When I was child I worked in the fields picking cotton. Then when I was grown, and came to the city, I worked in the hot laundry at the hotel folding hot clothes till my fingers bled. Then when I got married, I had to work in the store. Finally, after the war, I didn't have to work anymore. And I don't ever intend to work again. I've done enough work to last a lifetime. I have all the work I need. This house and taking care of you."

"And, June Rosette, you do a wonderful job of it," said Aunt Worthrose, sounding especially sincere.

"When your fingers bled, didn't you get blood on the clean clothes?" I asked.

"No one can say I don't do the lion's share of the work around here. I even cut the grass when Vic has to work seven days a week and is so exhausted," said Mama. "Victoria, they just bandaged my fingers up and I went back at it."

177

"No indeed- I mean. Yes. You have worked hard, June Rosette, as have we all. As a schoolteacher she wouldn't be around any other men, except the principal. No principal would ever- I don't think that is it." My aunt turned the conversation back to Mrs. Choy's departure.

"What else could it be? You know how men are. All of them. School principals not excepted."

"I've heard it was because of the little dark girl that came into the class," murmured Aunt Worthrose, looking away.

"I don't think it's because of that child. I know she looks colored, but she's Mexican. She is just dark like Christian Romano was when he was younger. Her family moved just inside the district limits. They are not in Fairland Addition or Water Oaks. She's just one child. A teacher would not leave her job over that. Some man is behind this."

"I heard that they're going to take the district to court because it is 99% white and all the teachers are white. Plus, all the principals and everybody else is white." said Aunt Worthrose. "I heard they may have to go to forced busing."

"I think they have a black janitor now," said my mother.

"I don't think that counts, June Rosette."

"Why don't we say colored anymore. Why do we say black?" I asked.

"Well, they wanted to be called colored for years. Now they don't want to anymore. Because we are called white they want to be called black."

"Of course, it's possible she just quit because she's pregnant if she's pregnant," said Aunt Worthrose. "Mrs. O'Kelley Senior just didn't know. She could have a fatal disease for all we know. One rumor is that her husband is Asian and Asian men never allow their wives to work after pregnancy."

"I don't think she's pregnant," said my mother. "Asian or not, her husband just does not want her to work anymore. Probably doesn't want her to have any money of her own."

"I'm going to work when I grow up. I'm going to be a writer."

"June Rosette, do you think she could have been fired?"

We were stunned into silence at that horrific suggestion. Nothing was worse than being fired from a job. It was total humiliation and most people became alcoholics, I knew that from the movies.

"Victoria, did you hear anything like that?"

I thought for a moment but my mind was blank. Mrs. Choy had been so wonderful, so sweet, so pretty. Surely nobody would ruin her life by firing her.

"Have they hired a new teacher? Have you heard anything?"

On the other hand, I didn't really recall us doing very much English work in class like in the first and second grade where we worked hard at English all the time. We had lots of tea parties, worked a lot in longhand, but not much other class work...

I pushed these traitorous thoughts from my mind. "I don't know." I added, "I don't think we have a new teacher yet."

"You might be a teacher," said my mother. "You can't make a living as a writer. Writers don't make any money. You'd never be able to save any money. No, I haven't heard anything. We won't find out who the new teacher is until after Christmas break."

"Mrs. O'Kelley Senior says that now that Silver Brook is going to be the city limits boundary they might try to merge Fairvine ISD in with the city ISD," said Aunt Worthrose.

"She doesn't know what she is talking about. No they can't. For some legal reason. I know that because Victoria's friend Kris at church is in a district that existed before the city took over and his mother said they were not allowed to take the district, just all the houses are now in the city. That's why they're called independent school districts."

"I hope Victoria doesn't have to be bussed off to another school. Mrs. O'Kelley Senior says-"

"She's just a cafeteria worker, Worthrose, for heaven's sakes."

"She's been right about a lot of things so far. You're not on that committee so what do you hear anymore? Plus, I hear those meetings are petering out anyway. And they've been talking about bussing on the news. Making the blacks and whites go to school together has been the law since the 50s but now that Kennedy's dead and that damn Johnson is in power, they are going to enforce it. Just like they did with doing away with the school prayer and Bible readings."

What about P.E.? I wondered. *Don't they realize how horrible that is? President Johnson's Physical Fitness Program.*

The title was enough to invoke terror, much less the thought that I would have to endure nine more years of it until I graduated from

Hereald High. It was enough to make me consider being a dropout! I prayed daily that something would stop it, at least stop us from having to play baseball.

"Worthy Rose, don't believe everything you hear on the news. Bussing schoolchildren will never happen here. People are not going to stand for it," said my mother. "What kind of society puts such a burden on their children? If we have to integrate with the blacks, there must be some other way."

"Making us bus the children is going to be the way they do it," warned Aunt Worthrose. "The sins of the fathers visited on the children."

"Vic would never permit Victoria to be bussed off. Victoria's education is the most important thing in the world to him." My mother's voice slowly became more stressful, indicating she needed to end the conversation soon.

"He won't be able to stop it."

"Of course he could. She's our child. She has a bright future. Victoria, your father would like it if you became a teacher." My mother's voice ended on a high pitched note and she went to the kitchen and began rearranging her pots and pans.

I was feeling a bit stressful as well.

Oh God! I don't want to be a teacher when I grow up! It would be like being in jail during the day, just going home at night and reporting back to jail the next morning. Teachers cannot even go to the bathroom when they need to.

From what I had seen they could not leave their classroom unless another adult came in to relieve them. They couldn't have food. And one time, when searching the hall for Mrs. Anderson, I had peeked into their private place- the Teachers' Lounge. I had been curious to see it, thinking it would be an elegant beautiful space with plush curtains and soft sofas and antique tables. But it had been a little tiny cramped space that was dirty, had ugly furniture and smelled like the cigarette smoke that I had to endure when we visited my mother's relatives in the countryside. Dirty dishes were everywhere along with abandoned drinks and trash.

I believed their bathroom would be cleaner than our bathrooms but when I peaked in, it was dirtier than ours. Our bathrooms used to be clean, in first and second grade, but they had not been clean like they should be so far this year.

I couldn't be a teacher. I couldn't stand to go to the teacher's lounge. The cigarette smoke would give me a headache all the time. I would be hungry. And I may have to put up with the dirty bathrooms now. But when I grow up I am not going to tolerate dirty bathrooms where I work.

I didn't say anything. I was embarrassed to tell my mother and Aunt Worthrose about the dirty bathrooms at school. I was ashamed for the school. Mama and Aunt Worthrose would have been shocked. They kept their bathrooms so clean. If Mama, especially, knew the school bathrooms were dirty, she would be horrified. When she knew about someone who did not keep her bathrooms clean, she said terrible things about her. I didn't know what she would do. I knew the teachers were not really responsible for the dirty bathrooms but they were tolerating them.

No, I did not want to be a teacher, locked in a classroom all day, helpless about dirty bathrooms, and with nowhere pleasant to go even for a snack.

I went down the hall as Aunt Worthrose left for home. Safely in my room, I pulled out my book.

Chapter 15
Locked In

For a few minutes Barbara almost gave way to panic then reason restored itself.

Her mind darted to who could have done it. Stiff Jones? Minnie? Addie?

Her thoughts were interrupted by loud voice that loomed from nowhere. "Ha Ha Barbara Scott, you fell into my trap!"

Stiff Jones!

Barbara then checked all the windows. To her surprise one was open. She hastily scrambled out and jumped to the ground.

WHEN SHE GOT TO THE ROAD THE CAR WAS GONE!

"So," she thought ruefully, "he locked me up so he

could steal my car." She flopped down wearily on the grass which was cut by the road.

Suddenly she remembered Minnie. She called till her voice was hoarse.

Hoping to find Minnie or a shortcut to the main road she wandered about in the woods.

After an hour she realized she was hopelessly lost.

"Oh, how did I ever get in this predicament?"

Sleepily she stumbled along in the woods. After five hours she fell to the ground utterly exhausted.

Back at the Scott home, Anthony Kape, April, who had recovered when she saw her husband, and Ellen were worrying over Minnie and Barbara.

Minnie's mother and father, who were getting a divorce, were at the Scott home, too. They were bitterly accusing each other that they were to blame for Minnie's disappearance.

Meanwhile Barbara finally found the main road and stumbled through the doorway of the Scott home.

"Barbara," cried Ellen. "What happened?"

"Jones," mumbled Barbara. "Stole car. Minnie gone!" With that she fell unconscious on the sofa.

Ellen immediately called Dr. Grasson.

The doctor said all Barbara needed was rest. "She'll be fine."

Barbara told the whole story to Minnie's parents.

"Oh my poor baby," cried Mrs. Foster, weeping.

There was little Barbara could do for her so she rode the bus back home. As the bus traveled along, Barbara's thoughts turned to the girls that were kidnapped – Belle Main, Jane Kape, Diane Bolman, Emily May Bolman, Mary Watson, Sarah Horton, Kelly Denson and Minnie Foster. Eight in all!

"I wonder how it will all end?" She mused.

I was wondering this myself. I hated to put my book away in the middle of a chapter but I hadn't a clue as to how to end the chapter, much less the book.

"You made a couple of mistakes didn't you?" asked my mother, when she read this part. It was almost time for Daddy to be home.

"What?"

"You have Barbara at her home with the Fosters visiting. Then you say she is riding the bus back home from the Foster house. You must have gotten confused. And what about the girl named Sandy? You left her off the list of missing girls. Should be a total of nine girls missing."

"Oh," I took the pages back and looked at them. She was right.

Well I'll fix those things later, I decided and put the book away for now. I was so enjoying starting new ones, I felt really naughty about that though. But somehow I would work it out. I had plenty of time.

And I was not planning to make money as a writer growing up. I knew now that had to be a sideline to a high paying career of some kind.

"I'll go to work for the light company when I grow up like Pamela."

"That would be a good job for you," said my mother. "She's a receptionist, they make good money. If she would only save for the future she would be Ok when she gets old. But still don't count out being a hair dresser. My hair dresser gets good tips every day."

She went to prepare dinner, happy that Daddy would be home on time tonight.

"That's no job for you, you can do better than that," said my father, when I told him about my plan for a job at the light company. "You are going to college and get a good education."

"Do you want me to be a teacher?" I asked softly, scared to hear the answer. What would I do if he said yes?

"Well, if you're going to get that much education, you might as well be a lawyer."

I felt weak with relief. *Thank goodness!*

"But the light company, they don't pay much more than a waitress."

I knew I couldn't be a waitress. I would eat all the food. And my allergies had gotten worse. I was so allergic to cigarette smoke that we never went to restaurants to eat anymore because the smoke always made me sick after. I was allergic even when there was no smoke like at home, and had to take medicine all time for sniffles and headaches.

My mother still had not given up on one other career option.

"I have found a new piano teacher for you, this one does not smoke," said my mother.

Oh great. Not again!

The piano had sat silent for a time now. It was beautiful. It did seem a shame to waste it.

"You will only go twice a month," said my mother. "You'll like her, she lives in Water Oaks. She was recommended by a good friend of mine."

At last I was going to get to go inside a house in Water Oaks. That was something. The lessons would begin right after Christmas.

I only got one doll for Christmas, actually a redhead Midge with bendable legs.

"Why do they all have red hair now?"

"I can usually get those cheaper," said my mother, in a satisfied tone.

I also got more Frank Sinatra and Dean Martin record albums. As far as I knew I now had all they had ever made. Also I finally got **Gone with the Wind** to read.

And, especially from Daddy, I got a new expensive multicolor pen. It had buttons on the side. Whichever color you pushed, it wrote that color.

Over the holiday break I took some time to reread my book and make some improvements, now that I could write much better and faster. I didn't change much. One character, Dr. Andistone, seemed inconsistent. He had already been replaced with Dr. Grasson as the Scott family doctor. But what to do with the part about him already written? I decided to make him a mere acquaintance of the family for only one year, recommended by a friend, and make his appearance and age ambiguous as if he wore disguises.

That was an idea.

Maybe he could be in disguise...

It took up so much time reading **Gone With the Wind** that I didn't get as much written as I wanted. But it was nice to have a book that was not over with in an hour or two. It was an interesting book. I skipped a lot about Scarlett and Rhett and all the love stuff. And after at first deciphering a little of the dialect of the slaves, I skipped all that too.

The book was long enough without trying to figure all that out.

Reading about the Civil War and how people were affected was very absorbing. The book dragged after the war ended. I wished it had been more about the generals and the battles and how America survived the Civil War than about Scarlett's boyfriends.

The character Scarlett seemed like she was not too bright but I felt sorry for her that the world she was born in had vanished completely by the time she grew up.

I put the book away to read it again later. I planned not to skip all the soap opera part about who loved who the next time I read it, maybe just some of it. I was still going to skip all that ridiculously overdone dialect. I was going to make sure any dialect in my books was understandable. I didn't like the bad words that hurt people either. I was never going to use those in any of my books.

I still found reading music almost as incomprehensible as the dialect in *Gone With the Wind*. I had lessons with my new piano teacher, learning to play a few Christmas Carols. She said it was Ok to play them even though Christmas was over.

I had arrived at her house and at once loved it. Her house did not disappoint me in what I had expected from a Water Oaks house. She had beautiful curtains and furniture. She had a curved staircase coming down into the room where a grand piano stood gleaming.

Her name was Mrs. Lambert. She was almost as old as Aunt Worthrose and her hair was silver gray.

Right after we began she invited my mother in to sit down for a conference.

"Here are the songbooks we talked about on the phone. I want to make sure it is all right for her to learn these songs. She has your permission and Mr. Grasso's permission?"

"Yes, if you want to call my husband…"

"No, of course not, I'll take your word for it."

"So long as there is not any- well, anti Catholic-"

"Oh no, no indeed. None of that, we are nondenominational."

My mother left and Mrs. Lambert sat down with me. "Now we

are going to work from this book," she said. "I will play some of the songs and you will learn them, then learn to play them."

Mrs. Lambert began to play the songs and they were beautiful. I tried to talk her into just playing, instead of teaching me.

But that didn't work and she taught me as best she could.

XI Classifications

I had learned to play several songs from my new song book by heart by the time of my birthday party and was planning to play them for the event. As a player I had become only adequate. But I really loved the songs. We had a substitute teacher still, when it came time for my birthday party. Mama had decided that instead of relying on relatives to come, I should invite my class. We would have the party in the garage, my parents having just painted it and put curtains on the windows. If it was too cold, they would bring in some heaters.

We would invite everyone in the class. Problem was, there were only 24 invitations in the package and there were 27 students in the class.

"I'm not buying another set of invitations, they are too expensive. Surely someone will not be able to come and won't need an invitation," said my mother.

"Rita can't go to parties because of her religion," I said, remembering that Rita had to sit in the library during our Thanksgiving and Christmas parties.

"And the little Mexican girl, she won't be able to come, her parents live too far away and she'll have no way to get here," said my mother.

I wondered how she knew that.

I filled out the invitations and put most everyone's name on them. But I left Julianna's unnamed. She'd be absent from class for sure.

When I got permission to pass them out, I called out each name but kept an eye on Rita and Carmelita. They looked more and more disappointed and hurt each time I passed them by. I handed the blank one to Carmelita. She glowed.

"I'll get you a present even if I can't come," she promised.

I still had one left and everyone had one, except Rita. I looked at the name on the invitation to see who else was absent. *Glory be, as Aunt Worthrose would say.* It said "Riland". I quickly bent over and erased the nd, and crossing the "l" to make it a "t". Messy but effective.

"I had a little trouble spelling your name at first," I said to Rita, smiling brightly as I handed it to her.

"Oh, that's Ok," she brightened, smiling back at me. "Thank you so much!"

That was the longest sentence I ever heard her speak outside of mandatory reading aloud in class. I knew she couldn't come but it felt good to invite her. I wondered why it made her so happy to be invited when she knew she could not come.

"You'll just have to tell Riland's mother he's invited by phone," I told my mother at home.

Riland had no problem coming without a written invitation. Most everyone else came, filling our garage with laughter, giving me lots of cheap presents that Mama could take back later. Most important Julianna was there, she brought doll clothes. Julianna Wells came too and we had to distract her with presents I didn't want, to get away from her. Rita did not come, in fact she never came back to class after that day I gave her an invitation. I supposed her family had moved. Matthew came. But I didn't care, he belonged to Julianna now. A few others, that I did not know well, did not come. But we had about 16 guests, more than any party that depended mostly on family.

I had wanted to invite Kris, but Mama said this was only for school classmates. If I had fought that, then I would have had to invite Phoebe, Cindy, Alyce, and Valery, since they also were not in my school class, my mother said. She wanted to be able to explain to their mothers that was the reason they were not invited, rather than that I wanted as little as possible to do with them. Carmelita did not come but, true to her word, she had a modest present for me the next Monday.

I played the new songs on the piano and found that most of the kids already knew them and thought they were supposed to sing along.

"I have never had to sing hymns at somebody's birthday party before," complained Matthew.

Right after my party the substitute was gone and our new permanent teacher arrived. Our new teacher was strange looking. She had very straight black hair, a very wide nose and large bright teeth. She was very young and we were her first class. She was not from our state. She wore very short miniskirts. But all this was irrelevant to me because at once I knew she didn't like me.

She would not let me come up to her desk and talk to her. She did not like it that I finished my assignments before everyone else. She got angry if I read ahead, passing all the slow readers reading out loud. She would not allow me to raise my hand in class to answer questions more than once. This meant that when Julianna and Matthew were absent, as they frequently were, no one could answer the questions.

Then she got mad at the whole class when, if she had just let me answer, there would have been no problem.

She dressed differently, too.

I wrote a poem for her and it was sort of about her.

The Miniskirt
Oh, the miniskirt
The hardly any skirt.
So far above the knee
For all the world to see.
The girls who wear them
With boots to go along
Laugh at the other girls
Whose skirts are long
They raise eyebrows from coast to coast
But men think they are the most.

But I never showed it to her. I knew she wouldn't like it because I wrote it.

Except my few friends, the other children were now openly hostile to me in class as well as on the playground, making fun of me due to my weight and lack of ball playing skills, perhaps valid observations, but also they made up nasty things to say that had no merit, said them openly, and Miss Bridge did nothing. I even saw her smirking a little.

These, the same children, who had just a couple months before had come to my birthday party, brought me presents and had cake and ice cream and a good time, now openly hated me.

The only other student who experienced hostility from the class at this point was Carmelita. And they never said anything to her openly. They just ignored her and refused to include her in anything they didn't have to. Of course they did that with me and occasionally with Julianna also. But we didn't care, we had each other. Only Julianna was absent half the time now because her mother liked to keep her home and have her do her schoolwork there.

Mama would never let me stay home when I wasn't sick. It did not matter if we missed a lot of school. If we did the work and passed the tests the teachers did not care. There was that many less kids to tend to. But I always had to go anyway. I didn't know why Matthew was absent so much. All the kids loved him no matter what he did, even though he pretty much ignored them all except Julianna. He was Miss Bridge's favorite, too.

"My teacher doesn't like me," I complained to Daddy. I had never before had a teacher that didn't like me. I didn't think it was even possible before Miss Bridge.

"Your teacher doesn't have to like you, she just has to be a good teacher," Daddy said.

All Mama would say was everybody was jealous of me. I knew she didn't understand it was more complex than that. So I didn't know what to do. Without Daddy's support, it was hopeless.

Then everything changed.

We were taking a test. Miss Bridge loved to give tests. It was an easy test. We were all working quietly at our desks, bent over our papers, when Miss Bridge started my way. *What now?* I wondered, looking up at her.

"Victoria, raise your paper please," she said.

I sat back and raised up my paper and looked at my blank desk, confused. As soon as I did this the quiet noise of pens moving and paper shuffling stopped. Everyone was very still. I looked back up at her. She stiffened, nodded at me slightly and said, "Ok, thank you. You may resume."

Then she went to Sue, the student seated in front of me and made the same request.

Looking very upset, Sue raised her paper. And to my surprise I could see another paper was underneath with writing on it.

"Class," said Miss Bridge. "No one move their papers. I will be checking each desk to see who all is cheating."

Everyone, except Julianna, Matthew, Carmelita, and me, had

been cheating. More than 20 students in all, some had been absent so they were also safe.

"Everyone in class today, except the four students not caught cheating, will receive a zero on this test," she said, when she finished. "And this will cause some of you to have to repeat third grade."

An audible collective gasp.

"Silence!" In that one word Miss Bridge conveyed beyond a doubt how deeply angry she really was.

Nevertheless, not a few choked sobs escaped. We were the major works kids. We were the smart kids. To fail would be humiliating beyond comprehension.

I felt ashamed even though I had not cheated, had known nothing about it.

"For many of you, that have been struggling, you still have a chance. I will monitor you all more closely from now on. Cheating is not the answer. I will be speaking with all your parents, except for those four students who were not cheating. I do want to commend you Julianna, Carmelita, Matthew, and-" she swallowed hard, "and Victoria for not cheating. You will receive an automatic A for this test."

Julianna, Matthew, and I would have made As anyways but Carmelita was ecstatic. "This means I'll pass! I'll pass third grade!" she exclaimed in her slight accent, after school as we awaited our parents. "I'll pass, Gracias a Dios!"

"Why didn't you cheat?" I asked just for curiosity's sake. "If you were in danger of failing?"

"Well." She smiled a little. "Pardon my Spanish. It slipped out. I could say I was too honest, but that was not true. They just didn't include me in their plan for cheating. They've been getting the answers off her desk when she wasn't paying attention. They've all been cheating for a while, figuring Miss Bridge was too new to catch them. But they wouldn't let me in on it."

Miss Bridge's advancement in her teaching skills did not endear Julianna and I to the other class members at all.

"It's your fault we cheated," Riland yelled, as the girls separated from the boys on the playground the next day. "You and Julianna Whaels! You're so smart! We hate you! You make us all fail!"

I learned to walk out with Carmelita every day when we exited to the playground so I would not be alone, since Julianna was absent for many days after the cheating scandal incident. Miss Bridge did, from then on, not allow any harassment inside classroom towards us. Nevertheless, Julianna only put in brief appearances the rest of the year. We still played at each other houses most weekends and I kept her up on what went on at school

While the playground harassment was ignored by the teachers, in class Carmelita and I were now ignored to the point of rarely being spoken to. I didn't care if they didn't talk to me but she withdrew into a shell and spoke to no one hardly, even me at times. She did maintain a sweet smile and a glow from knowing she was going to pass now and she would talk normally if I could get her alone, which was rare. Somehow immune, flirting nonchalantly along, Matthew remained beloved by all.

One Friday morning, close to the end of the semester, Miss Bridge was late and the substitute failed to show. The teacher next door was checking on us periodically. I was nervous figuring this was a golden opportunity for them to get at me. Miss Bridge insisted on us sitting in alphabetical order which placed me nowhere near Matthew or Carmelita. So I got out of my desk and went nearer to them for safety after the bell rang and we were still without an adult.

Other students were milling about too, when suddenly we all heard the distinctive clack clack of Miss Bridge's stiletto heels.

Those of us out of place rushed back to our desks. As the door flew open, she strode breathlessly in the room.

"I apologize for being late, Class. And the person expected to cover for a few minutes didn't make it-" Still breathless she stopped slightly bewildered for we were all staring beyond her. While I was not paying attention, someone had scrawled a word in huge letters on the blackboard.

She turned her back to us and faced it too.

An insult! In ALL capital letters!

Miss Bridge stepped back like she had been struck and for a moment I believed she would fall backwards into the kids on the front row. But she recovered her balance and straightened up and turned to us.

Her face was ashen. She looked us over wordlessly, then stepped back, stopping between the door and blackboard.

No one made a sound as she clicked her heels toward the black board, picked up the chalk and erased the word.

She turned back to us, "The word is-" she wrote slowly with the chalk, "is Negro." She took a deep breath. "Now we can continue with the lesson from yesterday…"

It wasn't long before the teachers rotated and she left to go to her other classes. As our math and art lessons proceeded with those respective teachers, the class speculated as to whether she would return in the afternoon to dismiss us, as anchor teachers were supposed to, or if she had hysteria and went home.

I voted that she would return and I was right. She came back in time to dismiss us. She walked back in and held her head up proud. I studied her features. Now that I knew, I could see Negro traits, her wide nose, large mouth, bright teeth. Although she rarely smiled anymore. As we filed out of the room in line for dismissal no one said a word and I observed most heads were down.

She'll be back Monday, I thought. *No hysteria for her.*

"I didn't know she was not white," I said to my mother and Julianna that next Saturday morning, as I was recounting the incident.

"I didn't either," said my mother.

"We did," said Julianna. "My mother is on the Guidance Committee this year, as you know. She said they thought she was passing, but when she checked, the school district did know. She was just very white skinned but you could see the features. She's from Louisiana."

"Oh, that explains it, many of them are very white," said my mother.

"The district didn't want to advertise it. They were left in a situation with Mrs. Choy gone like that. We didn't care," said Julianna, carefully dressing my bendable leg Midge in a new outfit. "But my parents were concerned about her competence. She is very new."

"People have to learn," murmured my mother. "Well, I will leave you two to play." But she stopped in the doorway.

"Who wrote the word?" Julianna asked.

193

"I don't know, I didn't see." I would have gladly told on any of them if I had seen. "Matthew and I were talking and he didn't see either. Carmelita knows but she won't tell."

"It's best forgotten," said my mother, as she exited.

"What do you mean by she was 'passing'? Passing what?" I asked Julianna when we were alone. Obviously she and my mother understood the term in that context. I would rather Julianna have known I didn't understand a word than my mother.

"Oh, Victoria, you don't know anything about some things," said Julianna, and she told me. "That's when black people who are white skinned try to pretend they are white."

"But if their skin is white, then aren't they white?" I figured this was just the luck of the draw, so to speak. If God gave you white skin, you were white.

"No, silly, if a person has any blood relative that is African then he or she is black by law, even if their skin is white," she explained.

I was suitably impressed with her knowledge. I thought of another sort of word that had been puzzling me for a while that I didn't want to admit I didn't understand. I couldn't find it in my dictionary.

"What is the FAA?" I asked Julianna. "Do you know?"

"The FAA? Oh, yes, I know, it is a group of people who want to become farmers. I know someone in that. They get together and do farm stuff and things. They still live in the city but they are hoping to get to be farmers someday."

She spoke emphatically and I was even more impressed with the scope of Julianna's knowledge.

Julianna went with us on a special trip to get our new car right after third grade ended. It was a 1966 Pontiac Executive and it was a cross between grass and mint green on the inside and out. It had airconditioning! We had to go a long ways across town through the freeways, which Mama said were becoming like a spaghetti bowl, they were so intertwined. Julianna and I sat in the back facing backwards all the way, the seats were so deep and wide we could balance ourselves without falling on the floorboard as the car weaved and swayed on the way home. Daddy liked driving this new car really fast.

Then I said goodbye to Julianna for awhile since we were leaving on a long long trip that summer of 1966 to Niagara Falls and Canada. I couldn't work on **Barbara Kay Scott Mystery Series - The Mystery of the Missing Persons.** I was still stuck in the middle of Chapter 15 and I had to leave it at home so it didn't get lost.

But I had fresh paper, my multicolor pen and I could write all the way there and back. I wondered why we were going to Canada to go to a foreign country when Mexico was closer. That would be a good locale for Barbara's second mystery I believed-

Barbara Kay Scott Mystery Stories:
The Mystery of the Lost Painting

Chapter 1 – *Mexico*

Dedicated to my best friend Vickie Bianchi

"Have we crossed the border yet?" Jane Kape asked the conductor excitedly.

"No ma'am. We is comin' toose it now." The Frenchman answered her.

Jane Lee Kape, Maria Isabell Maine and Barbara Kay Scott were traveling together. They are going to Mexico where Barbara was asked to solve a baffling mystery. Since Barbara solved "The Mystery of the Missing Persons", the young sleuth has become quite famous. She was asked to solve the mystery of the disappearance of a lovely painting.

Jane Lee is called Jane, Maria Isabell is called Belle and Barbara Kay is called Barbara.

"Barbara do you think the mystery will be a dangerous one?" Belle asked timidly.

"I don't know but I hope it's as challenging as 'The Missing Persons'." Barbara answered her.

"Well, I hope it's not anyways like it."

Jane, Belle, and other girls got kidnapped and Barbara was asked to unravel the baffling mystery of their disappearance.

Belle's parents Anna and Frank Maine were killed in an accident some time ago.

Belle lives with Barbara.

"I wonder what Mexico will be like," mused Jane.

After they got off the train in Mexico City they looked around for a hotel and finally decided to stay at the Palm Tree Hotel.

"Tomorrow is going to be a pretty exciting day," said Barbara, "tomorrow we're going to see Señor Garcia."

The next day Barbara, Belle and Jane went to see Señor Garcia and heard his story.

"I was a fool," he said. "Si, si. I was a fool. A rich man, he – he fall in love with my granddaughter. At that time I was at my farm. I own miles and miles of woodland. Well now my granddaughter, Maria, she – she no like the richa man, Señor Roberto Garcy. She and a poor boy, they fall in love. Well, one day Señor Peter Camblen, he poor boy, he come to see Maria. Well I geta my gun. Before I shoot, I hear a shot, then I see Peter, he was shot. Maria, she run to him and drag him to the woods. That last I ever see of her or him. The next night someone a break in and steal the only painting I have of my granddaughter. You see Maria is not Mexican, neither is Peter, my son and daughter-in-law are dead. Miss Scott you got to get that painting back. Please."

Barbara smiled. "I'll do my best, Señor Garcia. I may even do better." She smiled mysteriously.

Back at the hotel Barbara pondered over Mr. Garcia's mystery. "You know it's possible that Maria and Peter are still alive," she said to Jane.

"Oh, Barbara, can't you think of anything except the mystery? I want to see some of the sights."

"All right Belle," Barbara grinned and deliberately pushed the mystery out of her mind.

The girls had a marvelous time sightseeing. First they went to a Mexican restaurant and had dinner. Then they went to the Palace of Fine Arts.

After they got home Belle said, "Listen to this. Mexico City is 4,925,000 miles. They grow corn wheat, etc. and the main religion is Roman Catholicism."

"So so," sniffed Jane.

"Don't be jealous, Jane," said Barbara. Jane was Baptist as was all others of her mother's family, the Cobblers, except Belle. Belle at the age of 10 was given a choice of her religion and she chose Catholicism.

Barbara's mother Ellen, Jane's mother April, and Belle's mother Anna had all been sisters until Anna and Frank Maine's death. In their will they had left Belle to the Scotts. All of the Cobblers objected to this as they objected to Ellen's marriage to Christopher Scott, because of religious difficulties.

The Scotts are and always have been very devout Catholics. And when Ellen married Christopher she married the Catholic religion. Then when Belle was willed to them there was a big court battle. All the Cobblers wanted the Kapes to have Belle, all the Scotts- the Scotts. Christopher and Ellen won the battle, and Belle, on the condition that when she was 10 years old she could choose her own religion.

The girls went back to see Mr. Garcia. But they learned nothing more than they knew already.

When they came home the phone rang and the operator said that there was a call for Belle

"Why I don't know anyone in Mexico!" said Belle when Barbara informed her of the call.

Nevertheless the operator assured Belle the call was for her.

"Next state ahead. Time to get out and stretch our legs. Victoria, your mother's going to ride in the back with you for a while," Daddy said. We all got out and he got the rifle from under the back seat and positioned it across the front seat beside him.

To get to Canada and Niagara Falls, we had to drive through a lot of other states on the way, not taking a direct route because Daddy liked to drive and wanted to see as much scenery as we had time for. Sometimes I got to ride in the front seat. Sometimes Mama rode in the front seat and sometimes we were both in the back. Those were the times Daddy had to keep his rifle on the front seat with him.

Daddy had researched the laws and knew which states to keep the rifle on the front seat beside him so it would be visible if the police stopped him and which states he had to put the gun under the back seat so no one could see it. Sometimes, before a state line he would stop the car and unload it before proceeding. Then coming to another state he would load it up again. So sometimes, it was unloaded the front seat, loaded in the front seat, unloaded behind the backseat, loaded behind the back seat. One time he got it out and put it in the trunk. I was strictly forbidden to touch it wherever it was placed, and I certainly did not.

I did ask why we had the gun and he replied, "Because of all the trouble in the country. We have to protect ourselves if there is trouble."

I knew he meant the civil rights trouble but I wasn't sure which side we were afraid of, or if it was both.

But no one ever gave us any trouble and the police never stopped us. I got to stay in motels in different states and swim in swimming pools that were all different shapes. We visited some of our distant Italian relatives who lived near Niagara Falls, saw the falls (they were soooo beautiful) and then started home again going a different way, so it was even more complicated where the rifle should be and when it was loaded. I was glad Daddy had all that under control.

It was a long long drive and I got to write as much as I wanted to. Well, Daddy did complain that I did not look out the window more and see more of the scenery, but when I did, it all looked the same. I had been very disappointed by Canada when we crossed the border. I believed I would get some more ideas about Mexico, just change the local from Canada, but Canada looked just like America. I abandoned **Barbara Kay Scott Mystery Series -The Mystery of the Lost Painting** for the time being.

Well into our trip back, still far from home, we stopped at a small motel for the night. Mama made a special long distance phone call to Aunt Worthrose to make sure everything was safe. It was very expensive to call long distance but Mama felt like she needed reassurance that nobody had yet broken into the house or anything while we were gone.

Daddy and I were sitting on the beds in the room when she placed the call. We had two double beds in the room with a lamp between them. I got one bed and they got the other. Daddy was reading the phone book to see if anyone in the town had our name while I was trying to overcome writer's block again. Daddy had the TV on very low volume, trying to catch the weather report for tomorrow's driving.

"Really!" said Mama to the big black phone receiver in such a tone that made both Daddy and I stop what we were doing and stare at her.

"When did it happen?"

Pause. Daddy reached and cut the TV off quickly.

"Was anyone else hurt?"

We were really paying attention now. Daddy started to get up but Mama shoved him back down and waved for him to keep quiet.

"I see, Yes. Ok. No. Ok, Worthrose. You, too...We will...Yes, mysterious....Yes, it does, yes, Worthrose. Goodbye." She hung up the receiver with a loud click. It couldn't be anything too terrible or she would have been crying and having hysteria but instead her face was like stone.

"Well," she said, slowly. "Well, there was a wreck on the news last night at home. Worthrose recognized the name. It was the girl that killed Alexandria and the old- your mama - uh grandmother- Gabriella."

Her stumbling over the Grandmamás name was agitating. We did know who she meant.

"She kill somebody else this time?" My father asked, angrily, impatiently.

"No, just herself. She's dead. She rammed her car into a freeway barrier. It rolled and pitched over the overpass. She was dead at the scene. It made the news big time because her father is in the government now. You know, she couldn't have been much over 20 years old."

We didn't say anything else. Mama and Daddy decided to cut off the lights and go to bed early so we could get an early start on the next part of our trip in the morning. I curled up with a little flashlight and my paper and pen and started a new Barbara Scott book.

Barbara Kay Scott Mystery Series - The Ghost of Anita Rosbeck

Chapter 1
Anita's Accident

Barbara Scott sashayed her beautiful delicate blue evening dress. Her and her cousin Belle were impatiently waiting for their other cousin Jane Kape. Finally Jane came in the door. She was dressed just like Barbara and Belle except hers was a light pink. Belle's is purple.

Jane and Belle had arranged for a blind date for Barbara.

"I thought you'd never get here." Maria Isabell Maine, usually known as Belle, scolded her cousin Jane. Barbara nodded. "Slow poke," she laughed.

Barbara Scott, Jane Kape, and Belle Maine, are cousins. Barbara, her hair a deep dark brown, Jane, her hair as black as coal, and Belle, a light golden blonde are pretty sight to look at.

They are going to a party where Barbara is to meet her blind date.

Belle's date John Roy Cape, and Jane's date Jim Main picked a date for Barbara.

John Roy, Jim, Belle and Jane know who it is. Barbara doesn't

Belle went upstairs. At the top she took her long rose pink dress and pranced down the stairs.

"Oha, Greetings Queen Barbara, Princess Jane. Tis I, your humble servant Belle!"

Barbara and Jane laughed.

Just then the doorbell rang. "Oh." Jane cried. "That must be Jim, John and D – oh yes, Mr. You Know Whom."

Jane almost tripped over her long yellow gown as she hurried to reach the door before Belle or Barbara did.

Barbara wrapped her white lace shawl around her beautiful sky blue gown. Jane wore an orange lace shawl. Belle wore a deep dark purple one. Barbara's veil is pink, Jane's is white, and Belle's is violet blue.

Jane reached the door first and yanked it open she let in John Roy Sands Cape. Although Jane adored John Roy with his flaming red hair, Barbara did not think him very good-looking. Jim, he was nice looking but not handsome.

With them was a very very handsome man. Was this stranger her date?

Oh how she wished he was! Her wishes were answered when Jim walked up to her with him and said, "Barbara this is Dave Scott. Although his last name is the same as yours, you are not related."

"We may be soon," Barbara thought dreamily.

Things went very well at the party. Barbara talked with one of her best friends Anita Rosbeck. Anita had white hair and green eyes. Her date George Hancock had black hair and black eyes.

The party ended at 12:00 midnight but Barbara, Belle and Jane went at 11:00 PM.

Just as they were about to get undressed – Jane was spending the night – the news came over the radio that Anita Rosbeck had a car wreck and was injured. She was not expected to live much longer.

The next day the girls went to see Anita. They never dreamed that this was the last they would ever see of her.

"Hello, Anita," said Barbara to the pale young woman who is drinking some orange juice.

"Oh, hello, Barbara," she answered meekly

"Hope you're feeling better Anita," said Belle.

"Not much better I'm afraid," she replied

"Oh that's bad," said Belle, sympathetically.

"Yes, yes it is." Anita drifted into a stream of thoughts and her eyelids began to close

Just then the nurse came and said it was time for them to go.

Later that night the hospital called Barbara

I would have to work this out. At first I was going to have Anita killed in the car wreck at once. After all if she were going to be a ghost as in the title she had to die. But then I wanted to write some about her first. Plus I already had an idea for another story. I kept thinking of wonderful titles and stories so fast that I could not get very far on one before the next one popped into my mind.

The next morning the gun had to be in the front seat so my mother was sitting next to me and watching me write as the car sped forward.

My mother asked. "Is it a good idea to start the next book before the first one is finished?"

I stared at the scenery out the window, like Daddy wanted me to, for a minute. "I'm looking at the scenery, Daddy," I called to the front seat. I wanted to make sure I got credit for this for while it lasted.

"Ok, good," he said, then repeated his position- "this is your only opportunity to see this scenery ever in your whole life because if you ever come back it will be changed."

"How are you going to keep track of all these books?" asked my mother.

The scenery was nothing but a blur of grass and trees. I looked at my three ring binder. It had some divider pages in the pocket.

"I'll use these." So I devised a system. I wrote the title and beginnings of the stories as far as I wanted to go as I thought of each one. Then every day I wrote at least one word on each one. Often one word led to another and some of them were getting pretty far along. Barbara and her family members' lives were progressing with each book and I was putting new interesting things about them as the stories went along. I would come back and do the actual solving of the mysteries later.

But I couldn't write all the way there and back so I had gotten some new books to read, including one that was true life. I had found this book all by myself on one of the trips to the farther grocery store while I was still going. I had asked for it and my mother bought it but put it away, telling me it was too advanced for me. Now several months later I recalled it and asked to take it on the trip. And she agreed, saying it might keep me busy.

It was **The Song of Bernadette** by Franz Werfel. It was an extraordinary book made more compelling by the fact that it was true. It was hard to understand. I read and reread it three times on the trip and still didn't understand it all.

However, by the time I had read it the third time I had the gist of it down. Bernadette had seen the Virgin Mary in a cave. No one believed her at first. Then, if they did, they were very jealous that the Virgin Mary appeared to a poor young girl, instead of them. Because Bernadette told everyone about her special relationship with the Virgin Mary, she was taken away by the police and narrowly escaped being sent to jail or a mental institution only because the Catholic Church protected her. But in exchange for its protection the Catholic Church wanted her to be a nun. She had a young man who was her special friend but she had to give him up and be separated from all her family and change her name to a name that was partly a man's name. She had to be the nurse type of nun and work very hard, was sick most of the time and died of cancer. Yet she was happy and it was worth it all because a spring came out of the ground and the water healed sick people.

"The next time the movie comes on TV we'll try to catch it," said my mother, when I showed her the picture of the girl on the cover. "That's not Saint Bernadette, that's the actress in the movie."

That was disappointing. I wondered what the real Bernadette looked like.

"Not thinking of becoming a nun, are you?" asked my mother lightly.

"Well, they did talk about it in CCD and it sounded good, giving your life to Jesus. But then they said that most nuns are teachers or nurses and they have to wear those awful clothes and hose all the time," I said. "So I have ruled it out."

"You don't want to be a nurse?"

"Ooo yuck, no definitely not."

"Well, nurses don't get paid much. What's wrong with being a teacher?"

"Lots of things, and they have to wear hose too."

I had recently been given hose and it itched and stung so bad that I couldn't stand to wear it. I could never stand touching my mother's legs when she had hose on but it was a thousand times worse having to wear them myself. I went back to socks.

But I feared hose looming in my future.

We came home by a route taking us through Washington D.C. We stayed the night there and went to the White House, the Capitol, the Washington Monument (we took the elevator), the Smithsonian, and drove by all the memorials.

Last stop before we left was Arlington Cemetery and President Kennedy's grave.

It was remarkable to see it in color after all this time.

And when we got home there was no more black and white TV for us.

Daddy went and got a brand new Zenith color TV that was also a piece of furniture with a top like an end table had.

The screen was bigger and in color.

Unfortunately the shows in color were still boring.

We found that that we had missed a tornado which fortunately had not done any damage to our area but had damaged a house Daddy owned downtown that I had never even known about before.

"I'm going to have to fix the damage to the roof before the fall rains come," said my father. "I've no choice."

"Maybe we can hire somebody to go fix it. Don't you know anyone?"

"I'll check at work but I doubt I can get anybody," he said.

Something else had happened while we were gone. We had been away from the news and not paid attention to national events. But Aunt Worthrose told us there had been trouble not far away in some of the city neighborhoods when James Meredith was shot. And they were still talking about it on the news.

"Who is James Meredith?" I asked studying the photo of the young, well dressed black man shown on TV.

The television answered my question

…first black to attend University of Mississippi was shot during the March Against Fear…

"Mark my word, they'll kill Martin Luther King just like that," said Aunt Worthrose. "And when that happens there'll be Civil War. This nation won't survive."

"This man's not dead. Worthrose, aren't you 68 years-old? Didn't you live through two world wars and the Great Depression? This country will survive no matter what."

"Don't forget the Spanish influenza. I remember everybody being sick, wondering who was going to die. If it would be one of us," said my mother automatically. Then she jumped a little.

"I remember the 1920s, Vic. You were a little boy in the city surrounded by your own people. You don't know what went on."

"Nevertheless, I don't believe we're going to have the Civil War. The blacks just want to be treated like everybody else. That's all we all want."

"Well, hopefully nobody else will get killed," said my mother.

"And I say amen to that," said my father. "And June, you cannot possibly remember the Spanish flu. I don't. And you are only a year older than me. For God's sakes, that was 1918! You were only four

205

or five years old."

"Oh, they'll be more killings, it'll be worse than the world wars and the Spanish flu," said Aunt Worthrose. "There's dark days ahead."

"I remember a lot of things from when I was four and five."

"No you don't," said my father. "Stay out of this, Victoria."

"Yes, I do. I remember lots about the old house. I remember the wreck that killed Grandmamá and Alexandria. And I remember falling out of my babybed."

"Victoria! What about falling out of your babybed?"

"My rag doll fell over the side," I began.

"Victoria, you cannot possibly remember," said my mother.

"You must have told her, like a story," insisted my father.

"I never did. I've never thought about it! Really!"

"I certainly do remember it."

Quite clearly in fact. *Relaxing, since they left me finally alone with my rag doll, accidentally tipping her over the edge of the bed railing and the ensuing frustration.*

I remembered not wanting to call them back, wanting to get it back by myself, *looking down at it on the floor, not realizing how far away it was, trying so hard to reach it, climbing and then- whap!*

"I remember running into the hallway crying because it hurt and you were both in the bathroom and, Mama, you had to get your clothes on-"

"Yes, you weren't really hurt but it scared us to death-"

"You told her about it."

"Vic, I did not!" She stared at him, then at me. "But Victoria you weren't four when you fell out of the babybed. You were only 18 months old."

"Oh. Oh?"

"You must have heard it somewhere, one of us must have told you."

"I don't care how old I was, nobody told me. I remember!"

They looked at each other and me.

"Well, I have heard of some people who claim they remember way back before it was supposed to be possible, like when they were born," said Aunt Worthrose.

All three of them stared at me again.

"I don't remember that," I said quickly, feeling like they thought I was weird for remembering about the babybed fall.

I don't exactly remember THAT part. I thought hard and tried. But I couldn't. I did have other memories...Bits and pieces...

Best keep quiet about those, I thought.

XIII *Homecomings*

Aunt Worthrose had to go to the hospital to have surgery on her gallbladder, so I didn't see her for two weeks. When she got home, I still could not visit her until she recovered more. So I had to go everywhere Mama and Daddy went for a while. I enjoyed riding in our airconditioned car and was allowed to bring my books along when we went for drives in our new car just to see the scenery. Joyrides, Daddy called them.

We rarely used the old car anymore. Daddy just used it for work. So I was surprised one day when Daddy told me to get in the back seat of that car. I hoped we were not going to the park or to see the Espositos. I suspected as much because I was dressed in shorts and a sleeveless shirt clothes that I normally only wore at home. Then Mama was dressed very casual, too. She never went out in public in her casual clothes, with no makeup, unless we were going someplace like to the park or beach. But we didn't have our swimsuits, so I feared the park. Yet even though it was very hot, Daddy was wearing a coat.

"Where are we going?" I asked, standing up in the back of the old car as we jerked along the road. We were heading towards the freeway. I knew as soon as we picked up speed we wouldn't be able to talk because, with the windows down, we wouldn't be able to hear each other. "Not to the park, I hope?"

"No," said my mother, "we're going to the older rent house so Daddy can fix it. We couldn't find anybody who would do it." And then she spoke to him. "You really shouldn't have to do it now. It might not rain for a while yet."

"I can't wait any longer. She might not be able to pay it all. Then we get back a ruined house. Even if not, she doesn't have anybody to do it for her. She is an elderly lady," he said.

"How did we get another rent house?"

"Your grandmother owned a lot of these houses. It was sort of a business with her. She wanted her sons to come in with her and this one already had your father's name on the deed before your grandmother died. So we were stuck with it. Your daddy has had to keep it up all

208

these years."

"The lady who lives in the house, she's lived there near all her life," said my father, as we were stopped at a red light. "She is named Trudy and if she speaks to you, you call her Miss Trudy. You do not speak unless spoken too, you hear? She's very very old so she deserves respect."

"Otherwise you keep really close to us and don't talk to anybody else that or who might be there," said my mother. "And absolutely under no circumstances do you touch anything. This house will be dirty and full of germs. Your father has not been to this place since all the riots started taking place and we don't expect trouble but we want to get the problem taken care of, the papers signed and get out of there as soon as possible. I have to go along to sign the papers, plus I didn't want your father going over there alone right now. If your Aunt Worthrose had not been sick, we would have left you with her."

"Don't worry," said Daddy. "Nothing will happen. Look here."

I pushed myself up on the edge of the bench seat leaning over to look. Holding the wheel with his right hand, my father opened his coat with his left hand and I saw a pistol.

"And I've got this hammer too," he said. The hammer was on the seat along with a box of nails.

We came to the freeway then and I sat back and let the wind whip me on the long drive across town. The dirty neighborhood was just as I had remembered it from the times we had passed through it on the way to visit my grandmother. Daddy stopped the car in front of a row of houses so small they looked unreal. They all looked exactly alike from the front. They all had a front door and a back door lined up, both open so you could see clear through them from the street to their backyards. They were all wood, painted white, most of them in need of new paint.

"Why do they all have the doors open?" I asked, whispering.

"Because it is so hot, that lets the air pass through the house if there is a breeze. They don't have airconditioning. They cannot afford it and the landlords don't provide it."

We got out of the car in front of one house and as I walked closer to it I could see that it was just one room and a toilet was visible from the front door. A very old lady, very thin with gray hair and thick glasses, greeted my father as he went up to the front door. At first we stayed behind on the sidewalk. Within no time some tall men started to walk slowly towards us, so we went inside also.

"Mr. Grasso, you don't know what this means to me," said the lady. I stared at her. I had never seen a colored person whose hair was gray. I didn't know their hair turned gray.

I looked around the house. There was a broken down couch, a small table and what looked to be sort of a kitchen and a bed that was hanging on the wall. The place was not clean like our house but it didn't smell, as the wind came right through one door and out the other. I kept my arms tightly to my side. I certainly didn't want to touch anything. Other than the toilet being in the room, I didn't see where this was place was as dirty as Alyce O'Kelleys' house.

Daddy used a ladder in the yard and his own hammer. He had the storm damage fixed in no time. Then he, Mama and Miss Trudy signed papers. Then Miss Trudy started towards the front door with the papers and called out. I turned around. The men we had seen in the distance were now just outside the door. They stood silently, staring at us with undisguised hostility. She handed each of them a pen.

"Mr. Grasso, can you make sure that they sign in the right place. I can't see so well."

My father stepped forward having to reach up to each of the men to show them where to sign the papers.

"Here, where it says witness," he instructed them.

Without a word, they each in turn signed the paper.

"Go on boys, then, I have something for you later," said Miss Trudy. And they reluctantly stepped back outside the door.

They, a couple of other men, and some younger boys, were standing in the yard and on the sidewalk between us and the car as we went out the front door. As we started towards the car, we had to pass all of them. As we came to each one, he would step back a few paces as we passed, never taking his eyes off of us. Somehow stepping back the way they did, it was more menacing than if they had stepped forward. We were walking very slowly, staying very close together. Daddy had one hand in his coat and the hammer in his other hand.

Then suddenly from the street, from beyond the other side of our car, a man wearing a hat and dressed in a brown coat, white shirt, dark tie and dark pants strolled briskly towards my father. The man had his hand out a good two feet before he reached Daddy.

"Hey, Mr. Grasso, good to see you, how've you been doing?"

"Oh fine." My father met him halfway. Never stopping as he shook the man's hand, actually picking up his pace a little. We followed and were almost to the car now.

"Haven't seen you around for some time. Mr. Vince and Mr. Chris has so many houses we see at least one of them most every weekend fixing something or other." The man was grinning and he seemed overly friendly. "They always let me know before they come."

"This is my family," my father said to the man, indicating my mother and I. "My wife, June, and my daughter, Victoria."

"What a fine looking family! How do you do on such a fine day?" He bent over slightly and grinned at me.

"Thank you, Mr. Grasso, I can't tell you how much this means to me," called Miss Trudy from the doorway. She had the papers in her hand and she waved them vigorously at us.

My father opened the door and we got inside the car. Mama got in the back with me.

"You take care, Miss Trudy," my father called, as he rounded the front of the car to get in the driver seat.

The man in the hat said goodbye to us and turned away as Daddy started the engine. We drove away from that neighborhood. Not very far away were neighborhoods with fine large brick houses. There Daddy pulled over to the side of the road, took off his coat and put the gun in the glove compartment. Mama got out and got back in the front seat where she belonged.

"Thank God that's over," she stated. "You don't ever have to go back there again."

"If she makes the payments," said my father. "She is supposed to mail them to us by the seventh of every month. If she's late there is a five dollar fee."

"I'll keep track of it," said my mother.

"Who was that man that was so friendly?" I asked.

My father shook his head. "I haven't the slightest idea in the world. I've never seen him before."

"Who knows we were coming here today?" My mother asked

suspiciously staring at my father as he drove. "Who did you tell?"

"Nobody- I - uh- I guess I must have mentioned it to Chris, I mean Vince, I ran into him recently," my father said quickly. He then changed the subject, "Shall we get some ice cream on the way home?"

"The ice cream parlor has closed down," my mother reminded him.

"This is the big city," my father countered. "More than one ice cream parlor in this town."

Chapter 15
Locked In (continued)

"I wonder how it will all end?" She mused. (was the last thing I had written way before our trip to Niagara Falls.)

"What did Mrs. Foster say, Barbara?" asked Ellen, when Barbara got home.

"She was just like Mrs. Horton."

"Poor woman," said Ellen sympathetically, "how can people be so cruel?"

"The big question is: Where and why are they holding them?" Barbara sighed.

The doorbell rang.

Ellen opened it to the postman.

As she reached for the letter he drew his hand back. "This letter is to be handed to Miss Barbara Scott in person!" he snapped.

When Barbara read the letter she gasped, "Mom listen to this:

DEAR BARBARA,
I'M STIFF AND WEARY. I LEFT YOUR HOUSE NEVER TO COME BACK. JUST YESTERDAY I LEFT FOR HOLLAND WITH JANE. HOPE NONE ARE MAD AT ME. NOT DEAD. WE GIRLS ARE HAVING FUN. I HELD DIANE'S PUPPY MONDAY. I'M IN A PLANE. LEFT DENVER TWO WEEKS AGO. HAVE ANOTHER GIRL WITH US. DO BE KIND TO AUNT ELLEN. I WILL WRITE, SOON. NOT KIDNAPPED. MAYBE

TOMORROW I'LL WRITE. MET JANIE TODAY. A WHITE CLOUD JUST FLOATED BY.
ALL SAFE,
BELLE

"But she wrote it in our old code- every second word of the sentence. So it says:

DEAR BARBARA,
STIFF LEFT YESTERDAY. NONE DEAD. GIRLS HELD IN DENVER. ANOTHER GIRL WILL BE KIDNAPPED TOMORROW. JANIE WHITE.
BETH

"I wonder how she got 'Janie' in there?" mused Ellen.

Barbara snapped her fingers. "Remember we used to call Jane 'Janie' to make her mad."

"Yes and she probably told Jones that 'Janie' is a nickname for Jane," said Ellen.

"Or vice versa," agreed Barbara. "I think I'll call the families of the other girls."

Sure enough every other girl had sent a note.

"These are the notes in code –

DEAR MOM AND DAD,
NO HARM DONE. HELP JANIE WHITE. GIRLS NOT BOUND. NONE ARE DEAD. WISH I WAS HOME.
JANE
P.S. FOR BARBARA: I'VE BEEN MEAN TO YOU. MAY NOT GET OUT LIVE. I EVER SEE YOU AGAIN I'LL CHANGE. SORRY.

Barbara burst into tears. "I've been mean to her too!"

When Barbara could stop crying she continued-
DEAR MOM,

LONESOME. EMILY FINE. COLD HERE. GUARDED AT ALL TIMES. UNBOUND AT DAY. ALL HAVE BEDS. STIFF WORRIED ABOUT HIS WIFE.
DIANE

DEAR MOM,
I'M FINE. THREE KIDNAPPERS. ONE GUARD.
MARY

DEAR PARENTS,
DON'T WORRY. STIFF GONE.
SARAH

DEAR MOM,
AM FINE. HAVE GOOD FOOD.
KELLY

DEAR MOM,
ME FINE. HELD AT PLACE. WHERE I WAS KIDNAPPED.
MINNIE

"Mom," Barbara cried out. "We know where they are! Harold Hall is where Minnie was kidnapped!"

I suspected I was getting a little sidetracked with all those notes in code. At first they were such fun to write. Finally though, I got tired of them and stopped bothering to write the coded versions, just the deciphered messages.

"When are these girls ever going to be rescued?" asked my mother, after reading this section.

"I don't know." Secretly I was toying with the idea that everyone might not make it back. Along with murder victims, runaways were on the news all the time these days. But somehow I suspected that would cause trouble. On the other hand, something Aunt Worthrose had said was stuck in my mind and I did want to be realistic. By July, Aunt Worthrose recovered from her surgery enough so I could go and talk to her. So I reminded her about her prediction while she was still convalescing. She was still of the same opinion.

"Why do you think more people will die?" I remembered she had said that. But we had gotten distracted by the focus on my being able to remember so well and I had not had a chance until now to question her about it.

"Because this is the end times, Victoria Irene. The Lord is coming soon. You just read the Bible, it tells you right there." Aunt Worthrose had a huge Bible that she pulled out and showed me. It had beautiful pictures but the pages with the words were too fragile to handle much. She carefully turned the pages until she found the words she wanted me to read.

I read them but they were about ancient Israel, battles between different peoples and lots of violence. Other than the violence part, I didn't understand how this related to what was happening today.

"They are going to desegregate the schools, force the blacks and whites to live together. Mind you, I'm not saying that's wrong, I'm just saying there'll be more killings because of it. Right here in in our area these lily white people are all upset because some Mexicans and a stray Italian or two are moving in their neighborhoods and going to their schools. What do you think is going to happen when the blacks are forced on them? There is going to be killings right there on the school grounds."

I had gotten used to Aunt Worthrose's predictions to the point that I could easily tune them out if they seemed too farfetched. That was the case with this prediction. I became more interested in looking at the beautiful artwork. But the Bible was too fragile for me to handle and she put it away.

I was in charge of the plot in my book, so I decided I would make the sole decision as to what happened to my characters. If I wanted to be realistic I could, but I didn't have to. I could be partly realistic and partly unrealistic if I wanted. I was the writer.

However, Aunt Worthrose soon proved to be right, but only partially. There were more killings, and at a school, but not in the way she predicted.

End of Part 3

Part 4

XIV *Defamations*

College was my future and the future of all of my classmates in the advanced class. We all knew it, it was inevitable and if anything prevented it, our lives would be ruined.

I knew I would live in a dorm with roommates, like Pamela had at her apartment, except I would get no choice as to whom I would live with. Not knowing what college would accept me, I knew I may have to go far away. I hoped more than one might want me so I would have some choice. But I knew for many people it was only one that would let you in and you went there or nowhere.

Despite all the movies that showed college students having romances and parties, I was already dreading it. I figured the academic work would be easy. But with protests growing over the Vietnam War, it seemed college would be more than just a social ordeal, it could be actually dangerous. The news was full of reports where police and demonstrators clashed and students were hurt or went to jail or worse. I was glad college was a long time away for me, hoping the bad times would pass before I had to go. But in summer of 1966 a new danger arose, which we had never associated with college life before.

"What's going on?" I asked.

My mother was viewing the TV with increasing alarm. I had been writing and just came into the den and saw from the expression on her face something was wrong. I stood beside her in front of the TV.

"*...A sniper with a high powered rifle has taken up position at an observation deck of the tower on the campus of the University of Texas. He is firing at persons within his range...We have had reports that at least five people are lying on the ground in front of the tower... We just heard another shot...*"

Right there on the news we could see a puff of smoke from the killer's rifle. My mother cut off the television then. We heard the results later on the evening news- a total of 16 people dead, 14 on the campus, shot from the tower.

"Killing a bunch of people like that, strangers that he didn't even know, who ever heard of such a thing?" my father said.

"He had to have been crazy," said my mother. "And at a college, too."

My parents looked at each other grimly. They also fretted each time there was any news about protest violence at colleges. But they told each other the Vietnam War was would be over by the time I grew up, and all the protests at the colleges would stop by then. But this was something entirely different. The TV news commentator summed it up.

"...*Random mass violence unheard of in this country...This is indeed different than any type of violence this country has seen to date...have to assume this is the act of a mad man and certainly will never be repeated...*"

"Is that true?" I asked. "Does he have to be crazy?"

"That type of thing happens in other countries, but not here," said my mother. "Not in America."

Yet worrisome for the future as it might be, for some reason this horror story did not affect my family's daily life as the Freezer Murders had just a year ago. It was indeed a radical departure from the violence now heard daily on the evening news but somehow it was more like a plot variation on the riots, racial shootings and uptick in regular crime that was the mainstay of the news nowadays. Random mass killing at a Texas college was so far away, so unreal, not something we had to cope with in our immediate present. We put it out of our minds as a bridge we might have to cross in the future after I graduated from Hereald Memorial High School. Like World War III with the Russians, I began hoping going off to college would somehow never materialize.

Far more frightening was the crime drama in our own area that made only local news, and only briefly, for no one was killed. But it hit home hard for us at Fairvine. School started the Tuesday after Labor Day with a happy, but uneasy reunion as we found out our new anchor teacher mainly taught math, not English. But that anxiety paled against the news next weekend that Matthew Waterston was kidnapped.

"He was not exactly kidnapped and he is Ok now," our new teacher, Miss Garter, informed us on the following Monday after it had been all over the news and we knew it anyway. "When bandits robbed the grocery store his father manages, at the same time some of the bad guys went to his house and held him, his mom, and the rest of the family at gunpoint. They thought they would make sure that his dad cooperated and gave the robbers what they wanted."

"Did he?" I asked.

"Raise your hand before speaking, Victoria."

"But did they get the money?" I lifted my hand as I repeated my question in different words.

"Ye-es, but the important thing is that no one got hurt," said Miss Garter. "Victoria, I need to speak with you after class."

We all had admired Miss Garter instantly while at once being in awe of her. She was a polio survivor and had to walk with two short metal canes that were attached to bracelets on her wrists. Her movements about the room made a constant tapping noise which was amplified whenever we walked down the hall.

This day, sitting behind her desk, Miss Garter lectured me about talking to her and my mother had to wait to get me that afternoon. As she spoke, I tuned out her words and studied her. Handicap notwithstanding, she was an unusual person. She was new to the district but she had been a teacher 15 years, she told us. She was much like Miss Tucker, only she was younger and not thin. Her face was not pretty. She wore black rimmed glasses and always wore a jacket that matched her skirt, even when it was really hot. She never took it off. In our unairconditioned environment she had to have been burning up.

"What was that all about?" asked my mother, when I finally got to the car. "The committee has not contacted me about any problems."

She was once again the parent representative for my grade on the Guidance Committee but the group now only met once every other month.

"I don't know," I said. I didn't know any other way to talk to people. Anyway, Matthew Waterston has not come back. The robbers got all the money. Were they black?"

"He's not going to," said my mother, during the short drive home. "If what I heard is true, they are putting their house for sale and Mrs. Waterston is moving into an apartment in another city immediately, until their house sells and they can buy another house. She is afraid to stay in Fairland Addition. They are selling the store to a national chain. I don't know if the robbers were black. The news used to always tell but they don't anymore."

"Why would one house have to sell before they can buy another house?" I asked, noting with pleasure that Daddy was already home from work. "We didn't have to sell our old house first."

Daddy answered. "Some people can't buy a new house until they sell their old one first because they owe money on the house they live in. It's called a mortgage."

"Really? Who do they owe the money to?"

"Um. Usually a bank, sometimes the people who did own the house before, like we sold to the Gonzalez family and Miss Trudy."

"Why don't they just pay cash?"

"Either they cannot, or more likely they want to live beyond their means. They want to buy a bigger house than they can afford. That is very foolish. You should never do that. Never have a mortgage."

"I won't," I said, thinking how right that was. Nothing good could come of owing money to someone else, or worse, a bank, on your own house. "Do we have a mortgage?"

"Of course not."

"Vic!"

"Well, what do you want me to say?"

"Most people have mortgages when they are young, Victoria. Mortgages last 20 years and people get them paid off when they are old so they can afford to retire. Since most of your friends' parents are much younger than us, they probably have mortgages," said my mother. "Anyway, don't expect Matthew back. He's gone for good."

Although Matthew no longer liked me, I felt sad he was gone, especially for Julianna. As far as I was concerned, glad that he was Ok, as of course I was, the robbers might as well have kidnapped and killed him. He was just as gone for me and Julianna as if they had. Next Saturday at our house I was consoling Julianna over Matthew's leaving.

"You're lucky you've got a church boyfriend," said Julianna.

"Why don't you get one at your church?" I asked. Julianna's family went to a big Presbyterian church downtown.

"All we do is go to service there, we don't know anybody."

"Oh," I said.

"Anyway I don't want a church boyfriend. I don't like church. I am an agnostic."

"What's that?" Julianna was the only other kid who kept coming up with words that I didn't know yet. She wasn't having trouble in math either, like I was.

"It means that officially I do not know if I believe in God or not."

This was a new idea for me. It made me feel empty, a little cold inside.

"Atheists officially do not believe in God at all," she said. "But agnostics say maybe there is a God, maybe not."

"How could you not know what you believe?"

"You just can," she insisted, looking distressed that I wanted to pursue this, even though she brought it up. "And I don't know."

"Well, how do you decide?"

"I won't know for sure until I grow up, go out into the world and find myself," she said confidently.

Her voice indicated that if I pressed the point, an argument would ensue. I hated arguing with Julianna. I loved her so much and she did not know how to argue. She always got her feelings hurt and when she cried, it was because she really was sad about it, not for effect. Then she didn't want to play anymore. Her parents had been remiss in raising her, not teaching her how to argue properly. She did not understand arguing was not personal and the objective was to win, not get all emotional.

Fortunately my parents, especially my father, had taught me well. With Mama, I could watch her argue with Daddy and see what not to do. She usually lost. When arguing with Daddy, he would always give me tips on what I should have said or done to win, after he had won, of course. He even sometimes called time out on the argument while it was still happening to point out weak moves on my part. I hardly ever won arguments with him, however using his tips I frequently won when arguing with anybody else. On the rare occasions I did win an argument with Daddy, he would always look astounded at first, and then congratulate me and tell me he was proud of me, even while he was miffed at me for winning.

It didn't make sense to me that Julianna needed to go out into the world and find herself to know if she believed in God. I certainly didn't like the idea of being undecided about God, or anything important, until I was grown and was able to go out in the world. I was no older than her and I didn't feel lost. But I didn't argue with her.

"You should never talk about religion, politics, or money," said my mother, when I told her what Julianna said.

"You and Daddy talk about those things all the time," I said, confused.

"The Bible says, 'the fool sayest there is no God'," she said and changed the subject. "You are going to have a new CCD teacher this year. Two new priests are coming to assist Father Mallett. One is named Father Braun and one is Father Schmidt. They are both coming from the same parish where Theodore Rossi and his family go to church way across town. And they weren't always Catholic, either of them. Isn't Julianna Lutheran?"

"No, she is Presbyterian." I was trying to remember Theodore. I had not seen him in years. We didn't see much of the Italians anymore.

"Then she does believe in God. Presbyterians are good Christians. People who don't are criminals or alcoholics or drug addicts."

Julianna was no fool. She was as smart, even smarter than me. Still as close as we were- and I knew she wrote stories, not just made up lies about writing them like the other kids- still she would not let me read them.

"Julianna writes stories like me," I said, trying not to betray a confidence, yet it was hard not to have someone to talk to about this.

"Have you read any of her stories?"

"She won't let me. She says they are not finished. But I know they exist because she showed them to me."

"Have you ever finished that book you were writing? The long one about the missing persons?"

"No," I said guiltily. "I'm kind of stuck. I don't know how to end it."

"Writer's block?" she asked, with a smile. "Well, you just have to keep writing from what I have heard."

I guess so. I went and pulled out the beleaguered pages. I wondered what Julianna's stories were about as I tried to get past my writer's block on Chapter 15 of ***Barbara Kay Scott Mystery Series -***

Chapter 15
Locked In (continued)

"Mom," Barbara cried out. "We know where they are! Harold Hall is where Minnie was kidnapped!"

That was the last thing I had written.
Has it really been since before third grade ended that I last wrote anything on my main book? I have to stop starting so many new ones or I am never going to finish my first one.
I picked up my pen and continued.

"Then I can't allow you to go out there alone," Ellen frowned.
"Of course not," said Barbara. "I'll call the police."
The chief assigned three men to go with Barbara (who insisted firmly upon going). Lt. Anderson, Sergeant Memoy and Officer Brownlee.
At Harold Hall they found the door open. The place was deserted!
Sergeant Memoy snarled, "What's the meaning of this young lady?!"
Barbara, wordless, stepped through the doorway. Spying a piece of paper she beckoned them to descend. "Listen to this:

BARBARA, STIFF FOUND OUT YOU KNEW WHERE WE WERE. ONE OF THE KIDNAPPERS IS A POLICEMAN. HE IS SARGENT– "

Memoy suddenly grabbed Barbara and said, "Make one move and I'll shoot her!"
In spite of the situation Barbara smiled. "The joke is on you Memoy, the note ended there!"
Memoy had fire in his eyes. "I regret that I can't

take you to join your friends, Miss Scott but unfortunately I have to free the boss's wife!"

"Tisk tisk tisk, don't do anything rash," he chuckled evilly, "Wouldn't want Miss Scott to get hurt."

Barbara felt the cold hard steel press against her neck! "All right take off your guns and drop them at my feet!"

They obeyed.

"March in that room."

They again obeyed.

"You too, Missy."

He locked them in!

There was only a small table in the room.

"If anyone feels faint there is a barred window up here!"

"I don't think it will hold us both," said Sergeant Anderson, doubtfully.

Barbara jumped down.

"I always carry a thermos full of water," said Officer Brownlee.

"I have three sandwiches," said the sergeant.

"And I have dessert," Barbara said. "3 candy bars!"

Suddenly a brown form jumped from a ledge above onto Barbara knocking her against the wall!

To the surprise of the amazed onlookers the whole wall gave forth into what was revealed as a secret passageway!

"Bleachy," cried Barbara. "Jane's dog. Oh Lieutenant this proves that my cousin was here, doesn't it?"

"Yes and look behind you."

Barbara, amazed, impulsively darted into the passageway.

"Wait, Miss Scott, wait," cried Sergeant Anderson. "You don't know what's there."

But Barbara did not stop! She found that it had no door at the end. "Officer, come here, we're free!"

The men raced through the tunnel.

Barbara took Bleachy.

"Come, Miss Scott, to the car!"

"What car?" asked Barbara, bewildered.

"The police car, of course," said the lieutenant.

"It's gone. Memoy must have taken it!" exclaimed the officer.

"Yes and how are we going to get home?" asked Barbara still not losing her head.

"Miss Scott, I must say you are a remarkable young lady. Any other girl would be screaming for us to do something or wouldn't have come along in the first place," said the lieutenant.

"Thank you." Barbara was pleased and she made no secret of it.

"Here comes a car!" said Officer Brownlee. "Maybe we can get a ride."

The man in the car was more than willing to take them into town. He insisted on taking them all the way to the police station.

"We're very grateful," said Barbara. "Thank you very much."

"My pleasure, mam. My pleasure."

There! Just about done. All I had to do was report the crooked cop to the real police and get Barbara and the other girls back home!

"No," said my mother, after she had read it.

"What?" I said, confused.

"You cannot end it with it being the police being the bad guys," she said.

"They are all the time on TV."

"They are not. Anyway, this is a book, not TV," she said. "You cannot have the police being the bad guys."

I had believed I had a great ending. Now it was going to be more work. I scowled, feeling rebellious.

"If you end it this way you cannot show it to Miss Garter."

That did it. I wanted badly to show my book to Miss Garter. I felt her opinion would be very important. Miss Garter was definitely the smartest teacher I had ever had. She was very no nonsense about all our work. When school began she got the class started working immediately. There were no ridiculous activities designed for us to get to know each other. After all, we mostly had known one another for almost four years now. She tolerated no harassment of anybody in class. It was so pleasant not to have to argue with the other kids and listen to their nonsense. Her manner was such that the class obeyed her without questions and with her in charge, I looked forward to a rewarding and fulfilling year of learning.

But events at school suddenly became overwhelming just a few weeks into the fall semester and the scholarly atmosphere of our class was shattered.

"We will be having a group of new students coming to our school," Miss Garter said. "A new teacher has been hired for them and a new classroom prepared. They are all in the fourth grade, so we will of necessity, have contact with them on the playground. You are to make them welcome and play nicely with them. They will arrive in mid October."

I wondered why Miss Garter was making such a strange announcement. Then we heard. During a week of unending October rains they arrived. They were all black. I didn't know how we knew that since, despite looking all around every time we left the classroom, we never saw them as long as it rained. None were put in our class even though the numbers in our class shrank about that same time as several families moved away. But their presence could be felt in the suspense in the air. What were they like? What would we say to them if we ever saw them? Were they the reason why our missing classmates left?

I had thought Carmelita was among those that moved until the second week when it stopped raining and we faced the black girls at baseball. Carmelita was there, on their team.

"When I tried to talk to her, she turned away," I told Julianna.

"Let's try talking to some of the black girls one day when I am there," said Julianna, "and maybe Carmelita will talk to us again."

We did and soon we got to know a girl named Michelle who seemed to speak for all the black kids who turned out to be mostly girls. There were so few boys, that on the playground, the boys were not separated from the girls like us. They were not allowed to run in the baseball games because they could run faster than girls but they were allowed to bat and have a girl run for them. They could hit the ball really hard and it went far, so usually a teacher had to go off the school property to get it. A girl would then go around the bases.

Most of them kept a distance from us but Michelle would come over and talk to us if she could. She especially liked to talk to me between baseball games and this helped me get away from the girls that harassed me because I played so poorly. Soon they realized they played poorly too as they lost every game to the black girls. I smirked inwardly as the black girls laughed and congratulated each other. They would then all fall down in a heap on the ground and the teachers would have to yell at them to get them to get up.

"Why do you like to lie on the ground," I asked Michelle, after a teacher had scolded them severely for it.

"Cause I'm tired, I'm tired before I play and really tired after," she said.

"Why are you so tired?"

"I have to get up at four clock in the morning," she said. "So I'm tired."

"Why do you get up so early?"

"Because I have to catch two busses to get here. One bus takes one hour to get here and the other one takes two and there is time in between them. Some sleep on the busses but I can't."

"That's awful."

"But I wants to come. My daddy says my education is everything. But it is hard here. We didn't have no good teacher last year. Before last year we did. But the good teachers left to teach at the white schools. So I am behind, but I'm working hard to keep up."

"Why did your teachers all leave?"

"More money. They left so they could go where they could make more money now that the white schools are having to hire colored teachers. Except for a few that really love us. They stayed. Now we are gone."

The next week we went back to the recess games of old and never played baseball at Fairvine again. I was so very glad. We did sometimes have to play kickball, a game that we sometimes won against the black girls. But that was not so bad. I could kick as well as anyone.

But one day I got in the way of one of Michelle's kicks and fell down in pain, screaming. It was an obvious fault on her part although not intentional. But it hurt.

At once there was a hush over the playground and the monitoring teacher came running over. So did the white boys who were angrily eyeing the few black boys. Some fists started coming up but there was still no sound except Michelle's voice.

"I'm sorry," said Michelle. "I'm so sorry, Victoria."

Everyone was looking at me as I got up. Getting knocked down had really hurt and I couldn't speak for a moment. The white boys halted their play, slowly came over from their section and stared.

"Are you all right?" asked Michelle persistently, urgently. I noticed Julianna and Carmelita were standing beside her.

"It's Ok, it was an accident," I was finally able to say to the presiding teacher who sighed with relief. Everyone seemed to relax and turned away. But from the retreating white boys came an anonymous call. "Coward! Traitor! The KKK will get you!"

I felt a pang of fear as the others fell away from me and I was alone. Everyone pretended not to hear the insults. The teacher walked away. Then Julianna and Carmelita came to stand beside me. Michelle was still near.

"Don't worry bout him," called Michelle confidently, "He's jus a bully! He won't do nothin." But she went quickly back to her other black friends and they encircled her.

It didn't take long for Julianna to start being absent all the time again. And I was left with Michelle and Carmelita as my only friends. And I only saw them on the playground. I looked for them everywhere whenever we left the classroom. But their class never had lunch with us, never had music with us, never was present in the auditorium when the rest of the school convened for any reason. Their class was at the end of a short hallway that was otherwise used for storage rooms and we were forbidden to go down there. But I did at least expect sometime to run into them in the bathrooms. But I never did.

I had thought the playground incident was closed but it was the only reason I could think of when a few mornings later- POP! went the loudspeaker and the words so dreaded by many (but never me) came out- "The following students will report for discipline to the office this morning - Victoria Grasso, George Pen-" I heard no more names. The sound of my own sent me into a total shock and the rest of the names blurred in my ears. Then- POP! It went off. I stood slowly up. Surely Miss Garter would say something.

But there was only the hushed gasp from the class and I felt suddenly dizzy. But I knew the procedure. Silently I stepped out of my desk and went out the door, passing Miss Garter on the way but she kept her eyes averted and said nothing. I made the long walk down the hall looking at the blank spaces where our first grade mural had hung so briefly. Never before had it been such a long walk. Pulling the glass door open at the office and reporting to the secretary, I was ashamed to face her.

She did not look up.

"Victoria Grasso reporting," I said, hoping she would say it was a mistake, that they got the wrong name.

"Sit down in here. Mr. Qurand will see you soon," she replied, still without looking at me. So it was a not a mistake.

The little office section was airconditioned. It was very small so it was cold. I sat there shivering. The other kids summoned arrived and were let in before me, one by one, to see the principal, some coming back out in tears. No one looking happy. Finally I was the only one left.

I sat there all morning trying to figure out what I did. I decided my only hope was prayer.

I prayed for strength to answer whatever charges were going to be brought against me. I thought of the usual reasons kids were summoned- fighting, not doing their work, absences without excuse. I couldn't think of what I had done, only it must have been something on the playground.

The lunch bell rang. The secretary finally looked at me and picked up her phone for a second. The she put it back down and spoke. "You may go to lunch. Don't just stand there. Hurry or you'll be late for

228

lunch. And just go back to class after lunch."

I had to go back to the classroom to get my lunch so I was still a little late getting to the cafeteria.

Already eating as I sat down with my tray, the other kids asked me what happened.

"Nothing," I said, still a little breathless. "I just sat there."

"Oh, you're lying!" said Riland, after a moment. "You know you got paddled."

"All I did was sit and wait," I protested. But none of them believed me.

After school I was not let out with the other kids. My mother, summoned by Miss Garter, came into the classroom to get me.

"Sit back down at this desk right across from mine," said Miss Garter, standing for a moment on her crutches. "Mr. Qurand has decided to let me handle this problem as I see fit. Won't you have a seat here, Mrs. Grasso?"

My mother sat down uncertainly in an adult chair positioned just to the side of Miss Garter's desk and looked a little frightened.

"Now, Victoria," said Miss Garter, sitting back down and facing me. "Would you please show me the multicolor pen?"

I pulled my multicolor pen out of my folder.

"Where did you get the pen?"

"My-"

"Please don't interrupt, Mrs. Grasso, I want Victoria to answer this question herself without any prompting. Victoria, where did you get the pen?"

"My father gave it to me," I said.

"Now that is not the correct answer," said Miss Garter. "We know what happened and where you got this." She took the pen from my hand.

My mother stood up.

"Please, Mrs. Grasso, sit down and let me handle this. Where did you get the pen?"

"My father gave it to me."

"This is a very expensive pen. No one would give a child a pen like this. Now Mr. Waddingsworth-Smythe had his pen taken from his briefcase and he saw you with this pen and says it is definitely his."

"It's mine."

"Victoria, do I need to get Mr. Qurand involved?"

"Just a minute." My mother, still standing, finally spoke up, "My husband did give her this pen."

"Mrs. Grasso, I know your intentions are good. But if she does not face up to this and admit the theft, there is the possibility she could be suspended and that would go on her permanent record." Miss Garter pointed at me to press her point.

"I didn't steal any pens. I don't even know Mr. Waddingsworth-Smythe and have never been near his briefcase," I said, rising and moving closer to my mother.

My mother grabbed my hand. She was crying. "You will hear from my husband about this." She abruptly jerked me away. I looked back at Miss Garter. She sat frozen, staring after us with her hand paused in midair and her mouth still open.

My mother pulled me down the hall, pushed me into the car, and cried all the way as we went home. I felt very bad that she was crying over something they thought I did but that I did not do. I wondered what I could do about it. Daddy would know. But it was only Monday. Daddy was away working again overnight and he would not be home until sometime Tuesday. I still had to go to school the next day. I went into the classroom the next morning and sat down defiantly. Miss Garter carried on the class as usual and did not pay me any particular attention.

But at lunch she pulled me aside and said, "I need to talk to you alone. I will give you time to eat lunch in class if necessary."

We stayed behind as our art teacher came and took the class to lunch. *This is a set up,* I thought. *What now?*

"Victoria," she said, looking me straight in the eye. "I owe you an apology." She took a deep breath. "I was only acting on the information given to me by a fellow teacher and the administration."

"What information? From who?"

"Be quiet and let me finish. The other teacher's pen was found today. He had left it with a substitute who did not know about this and forgot to remind him that he had left the pen with her until, well until now."

"I told you I didn't take it."

"Victoria, don't answer back."

"But I didn't!"

"The incident is closed. I apologized to your mother over the phone this morning and I am apologizing to you."

"But-"

"I don't want to hear any more about it. Now go on to lunch."

I did but I knew it was too late. She may not want to hear any more about it but she was going to. Wednesday, Daddy did not go to work. This alone would have been enough to make him mad. He took me to school without a word, sent me to class and proceeded to the office. I don't know exactly what he said. But even with the glass door closed and Miss Garter trying to conduct class, I could hear him yelling down the hall. In a few moments Miss Garter was relieved by a substitute and she left, her crutches tap-tapping down the hall. I heard more yelling. Then I didn't hear any more and she came back looking a little shaken but brave.

She's strong, no hysteria, I thought, with admiration.

Mama told me about it when she picked me up. "Your father demanded an apology from the school, your teacher, and the teacher that accused you of stealing. Apparently he didn't think he needed to apologize. Your father demanded to see that teacher. Believe me, he apologized to him and he is supposed to come and apologize to you. Has he yet?"

"No."

"Well he is going to. You let me know if he doesn't. Miss Garter was made the scapegoat for this. He thought he could get away with it because he is a man!"

Each day for a while I waited and each time a strange man went by I thought it might be that teacher who needed to apologize to me but he never did.

A few weeks later I asked Miss Garter about him, casually.

"He's gone, he got a job at another school," said Miss Garter, equally casual. "But while we are on the subject, I need to talk to you about your attitude."

"Yes?"

"You are not respectful of adults and persons in positions of authority," she said. "It was wrong to accuse you of stealing the pen.

Your mistake was talking back when adults were talking to you."

"But I didn't steal the pen," I said.

"Mr. Waddingsworth-Smythe was sincere in his accusation. He really believed you had stolen the pen. It was an honest mistake on his part. He is an adult and you are a child. So naturally I sincerely believed him and did not realize I was accusing you wrongly until later when Mr. Waddingsworth-Smythe's pen was found."

"But I didn't do it!"

"Now see there! You are talking back to me right now."

I was absolutely bewildered.

"What am I supposed to say?" I asked. The question was quite innocent. I really didn't know.

"Well, nothing. You should maintain a respectful silence when an adult is talking to you."

I was silent for a moment. *Daddy always says if you don't defend yourself then you're going to be found guilty.*

Then I said, "In other words I should have let them accuse me of stealing the pen when I didn't do it. Then they would be sure I did it."

Miss Garter sighed and said, "Never mind."

I put the episode behind me as best I could but each time I thought of it, a cold feeling came over me. *Suppose they had not found the other pen.* But two good things came out of it. Miss Garter was friendlier and seemed to like me a little now. And I was so proud Daddy had taken time off work to defend me.

Chapter 15
Locked In (continued)

"Thank you again."

Barbara and the two innocent policemen had just hitchhiked back to the police station. So how could I deal with the bad guy policeman character without making the all the police officers look bad? I had an idea…

"Why the police station looks like it's deserted."

Barbara gasped in astonishment.

"Anyone here?" called Lieutenant Anderson, loudly.

"In here," came the faint reply.

The two men busted down the door and were surprised to see six policeman bound and gagged behind bars. One of the men's gags has slipped a little, allowing him to answer faintly.

Officer Brownlee unlocked the door and began untying the men. Barbara helped. She untied the youngest one first who said, "I can just see the headline now- 'Beautiful young girl comes to the aide of six helpless policemen'."

Barbara laughed.

"I didn't think you could laugh after all you've been through, Miss Scott," said Officer Brownlee.

"What has she been through?" asked an officer.

"We were locked in a small room and Miss Scott found the secret tunnel and got us out."

"Where is Sergeant Memoy?"

"He was one of the kidnappers. He was the one that locked us up."

"Not Tom Memoy! I knew him when we were both kids," said one officer who was about 30.

"Sergeant Sackle! You weren't born when he was a kid!"

"I was, too. We grew up together."

"Lieutenant, maybe Sergeant Memoy was not Sergeant Memoy," said Barbara.

"What!?"

"Maybe he was an impostor!"

"Of course, that's it! He was an impostor!"

Someone knocked. Sergeant Anderson opened the door to find a young sergeant about 30. "I'm Sergeant Memoy."

"Tom!"

"Fred!"

"You were right Miss Scott. Memoy was an impostor!"

"I beg your pardon?"

"Not you, the other one. The one that led us into the trap."

"Led who?"

"Miss Scott, Officer Brownlee and I."

"Oh, is Miss Scott a policewoman?"

"No."

"Ug- yes, hmn."

"I'll explain Sergeant."

"Thank you."

Barbara ended her story with: "Well you see Belle and Jane are my cousins and I just had to go along."

"I see. But where's the chief?"

"They took him as a hostage."

"Oh no! Which chief?"

"Chief McBlend."

"Oh!"

"We had better get you home Miss Scott."

"Do we have to tell my mother what happened today?"

"May we tell your father?"

"Yes," Barbara smiled mischievously.

"Hello, Mrs. Scott. Where is Mr. Scott?"

"He is away on business and we can't contact him. He doesn't know that Belle and Jane were kidnapped," said Ellen.

Lieutenant Anderson looked at Barbara sternly but his eyes twinkled.

"She lied to us," said Sergeant Memoy.

"No," said Lieutenant Anderson." It's just a teenager trick. She never told us her father WAS home."

Finally!

Chapter 15 was finished and the police were exonerated. But

the book was still not finished.

Changing the police villain to an impostor had thrown a kink into everything.

I would have to think of another ending.

XV *Doubts*

The English teacher quit so Miss Garter had to take over English as well as math for our class. I loved it when Miss Garter taught English. She was so smart and I learned from her every time. I longed to take my book to her when it was finished.

I had never made less than an A in English. That did not change under Miss Garter. But on my next report card was a letter I had never seen there before.

I got a C in math. I had never made a C before. I had rarely made any Bs. I was devastated. Mama and Daddy were very upset.

"I don't like math," I said to them. "It's hard."

My mother went to school to talk to Miss Garter. Despite the C, the meeting was much more cordial this time.

"If only she could reveal her talents in math as she does in English. This is the age of math and science." Miss Garter took leadership in the conversation at once.

"She has always had a little problem remembering our phone number. She hates to talk on the phone." My mother was not quite following.

Miss Garter looked annoyed. "Memorization has nothing to do with the new math we teach today. We are teaching students to think." She intoned the word "math" with a reverence that was lacking in all her other words.

"I already know how to think."

"Victoria, we promised you could sit in on this conference if you kept totally quiet," warned Miss Garter.

I put my hands under my hips and sat there.

"As bright as she is, she can do the math. It will just take some effort on her part. Everything else comes too easy for her."

"Well, I have heard of moving children up a grade when-"

"Oh absolutely not, experts don't recommend that at all. Children need to be in the same grade with other children as close to their age as possible. They all need to learn the same lessons at the same stage in their lives. That is vital."

"I see. Well-"

"Try a punishment and rewards system for progress in math," said Miss Garter.

"Oh, I don't think my husband will agree to punish-"

"She needs discipline, academically of course." She added the last hastily.

"Surely she does not misbehave in class?" My mother looked a little too shocked. I wondered suddenly how good an actress she might have been if she had taken that opportunity to go to Hollywood.

Miss Garter hesitated. "Her behavior does not fall into the category of 'misbehavior' but she definitely- has, has- an attitude problem. Yes, I would call it that. An attitude problem."

My mother gave me a look which involved a strange narrowing of her eyes. I knew what the look meant though. This was the look we both gave Daddy when we wished to convey innocent hostility that he couldn't use against us. We called it looking at him daggerously, as if we were throwing mental daggers at him. We had conspired to invent this look and coin the word.

I sniffed. *I am not intimidated by daggerous looks,* I thought. *You can't use a look I helped name against me.*

"Here at Fairvine, we only want the best for Victoria," said Miss Garter, conciliatorily.

My mother didn't reply so I took this as my opportunity.

"I've written a book," I said to Miss Garter. "It's almost finished. And when it is, would you read it?"

They both stared at me as if they had forgotten I was there.

"This book-" my mother began in an irritated tone.

"What kind of book?" asked Miss Garter.

"A mystery," I said.

"Teenage mystery type stuff, it's just fun and games to her."

"You may show me your book after you've improved in your math."

"Well it's not finished yet." I sat back and folded my arms across my chest. So that's how it was. *Blackmail.*

Miss Garter turned back to my mother.

"Try to de-emphasize reading and drawing. Focus on math. And as for writing..." Her voice was doubtful.

"I don't encourage it," said my mother defensively. "She did write her numbers from 1 to 1000 in the second grade."

"Really? That was a waste of time," said Miss Garter sharply, then her voice softened a little as she saw my mother's distress. "I'm afraid that will not help with the new math. The new math is creative, inspirational! It's the way the bright and promising students are being separated now. The aerospace industry, medical technology, those are the careers of the future."

For a moment Miss Garter had a strange hypnotic look, her eyes gazing into the distance combined a slight smile. It only lasted a moment.

"Surely there's something for students good at reading and writing," my mother ventured.

"Oh, well, she could be a teacher. But this is 1966. She doesn't have to settle for teaching, not with her IQ." Miss Garter hesitated. "She's very gifted, there's no doubt. But her gifts have been and are being developed the wrong way. She should be doing extra math problems, working on advanced solutions. I know it is not yet in the curriculum for the lower grades but to expose her to some science would do her a world of good."

The hypnotic look came back over her when she said the word "science". Again she was back to normal after a moment.

"Neither my husband or I have a high school education. I don't know what we can-"

"She is also in severe need of some social skills. She is impolite, sometimes arrogant, and never subservient when she needs to be." Miss Garter stirred in her chair. "And she thinks NOTHING of IN-TER-RUPT-TING."

Miss Garter turned and glared at me as she said that last word and I closed my mouth. And sat on my hands again.

"Well, in my husband's family tradition-"

"Tradition is irrelevant. Tell me, Mrs. Grasso. Does she have any friends besides Julianna Whaels?"

"Yes, - no not really, they play with those new fashion dolls," said my mother. "Otherwise, all she wants to do is be alone and write."

"Fashion dolls," said Miss Garter, as if she had tasted something bad. "Victoria will never do well in this world unless she learns to cooperate with others and work as a team member. She must change her attitude."

So that was it. *They think my success in the world depends on playing baseball!* I knew that wasn't true. Many famous and successful people were not baseball players. They were actors, writers, painters, and politicians. Were the famous baseball players expected to act, write, paint, or be in the government?

Miss Garter is just annoyed that the black girls beat us and we don't play baseball anymore.

I had no doubt that thought was true. We had been lectured about losing at baseball. Baseball was extremely important to all the grownups at school and even some of the parents were upset that the baseball games had to be ended because the black girls always won. They had formed a little protest group and marched into Mr. Qurand's office with a couple of big signs. It didn't work. Baseball was gone, thank God.

Daddy says baseball is not important and people who pay good money to go watch baseball games are really stupid. If only he were here…

"Stop daydreaming, Victoria, and pay attention," said Miss Garter.

"Yes, listen to your teacher," said my mother.

"She is shirking her responsibility in math," Miss Garter was saying. "She is not trying and to put it bluntly is simply being lazy."

That is not true. I did the best I could. Once I started listening to them, they got back to talking as if I wasn't there.

My mother nagged me about math constantly for days after that meeting. At first I tried to ignore it and continued to try my best, but my scores did not improve.

Finally, after about two weeks, I had had enough.

"I'm not doing any more math," I said to Miss Garter in class when she handed out the next math assignment. I handed it back to her.

"Victoria, you will take this assignment or I will have you called to the office."

This really made me mad. I folded my arms and glared at her. Daggerously, I hoped. She stepped back a little. Then she placed the paper on my desk.

"Attention! Class, I will make this a homework assignment," she said loudly, and everyone scrambled to make sure she didn't see them looking at us. "I will expect it first thing in the morning."

That evening I sat in my room staring at the assignment. It was actually a repeat and I knew I could probably do it. But I wasn't. I wasn't going to give in.

There was a knock on the door. That was unusual, my parents didn't normally knock. There was no reason. I always welcomed them into my room. It was my opportunity to show a dressed doll or more of my book or something I had drawn.

Daddy was at the door. He pushed it open but did not come in. I looked at him.

"I hear you are having problems with your math?" he said.

I nodded warily.

"You're going to do your math," he said, "like your teacher tells you. I don't want to hear any more of this."

I nodded again sadly and, looking satisfied, he shut the door, leaving me alone.

He had cause to be satisfied. His word was all it took. From then on I did the math as best I could without complaining. But Miss Garter wasn't happy. She still believed I wasn't doing my best. There was nothing I could do.

They think I'm brilliant. But it's just that I can memorize stuff so easily. As long as it's in English. I can fool them into thinking I'm brilliant as long as I have English to work with. But take the English away and I'm no smarter than anyone else.

It was that simple. I could memorize words, people, pictures, even whole movies. I could go over the dialogue in my mind long after seeing the show. I could see the pictures before me as if they were still there. That is one reason why I secretly thought acting might be a job I could do. I would have no problem memorizing lines, picturing scenes. But take English away and I was lost.

Adding and subtracting were tedious, multiplication was hard even with the tables, and division was just beyond me. *I think if God had gifted me in math life would be harder, not easier. I'd be expected to do that boring stuff all the time, my whole life would be wasted on that.*

I did wish sometimes my memory for words wasn't so good. I could never forget what Miss Garter and my mother said about me. Or for that matter, what anyone said about anything. Sometimes I would go over and over conversations in my mind for hours, restlessly awake at night, wondering why someone said something, wishing I could change what I said, imagining what might be different if I had changed or added something.

Lately I had been unable to sleep at night wondering about God. I wondered if God would hold me responsible for not saying or forgetting to say the right thing.

I wondered if Julianna was right about God maybe not existing. Julianna was, I hated to admit, probably smarter than me. But years ago Ruth Marino had said she heard His voice. And Ruth would never lie or make things up. She just didn't have it in her. But I went to church and prayed frequently and had not heard anything yet. And if God was not real, then the story of Saint Bernadette was not true. And I was sure that the story of Bernadette was true.

I remembered without God, how random the world would be, and how anything could happen. I decided to reread that book and pray harder and pray every day. But despite my prayers, I was soon in trouble again at school. And undeservedly this time.

"I didn't say anything about that at school," I said, defensively. "I just told Julianna. She was bragging about how much money her father makes."

"Julianna's mother complained to Miss Garter. Why would you tell her anything like that?"

"Well, I saw his paycheck, it was $4123.23. And he gets paid every week."

"But you don't tell people things like that. That's a secret. You've always been so good at keeping secrets. I thought you couldn't remember numbers well. How come you could remember that one?"

"I didn't know that was a secret." It had been right there on the green paper that Daddy left on the table. And it was an easy number to remember. And while I had not sworn Julianna to secrecy, we had become so close that I has assumed she did not repeat everything I told her. *Well, apparently I was wrong about that.*

"And he doesn't make that much money every week. It varies with how much overtime he makes. We have to pay taxes out of that too. Your father works hard for every penny he gets. We pay our bills on time and we save all our extra money in the bank."

"I know, I told Julianna here, not school. I don't see where Miss Garter or the school should be in any way at all involved in this."

"Mrs. Whaels is concerned that you are telling tales and she doesn't want Julianna unduly influenced. She spoke to me about it also over the phone. It looks like you were lying and bragging. You have to go to them and tell them you made a mistake. Say your father makes $4000 a month, sometimes, rarely, never that much in a week. You made a mistake. You accidentally saw his pay stub and you got the numbers wrong."

"But I didn't!"

"Yes, but most blue collar workers don't make near that much and - your father's special because he can make the plane engines run. He won't let them promote him. He's too stubborn. So they have to give him bonuses. The unions don't know about them. He doesn't always make that much, it varies."

"You mean sometimes he makes more?"

"Victoria Irene! You are just going to do exactly as I tell you! I haven't used that belt for years but it's still hanging in my closet! You are going to school and tell Miss Garter you made a mistake. They all know the problems you are having with math and how you seem to have trouble remembering numbers. This will support your side that you are not faking it. Miss Garter will tell Mrs. Whaels and that will be the end of it."

"But-"

"Otherwise, see, you may not be able to play with Julianna anymore."

This stunned me into compliance. "Ok. Ok, I will."

My mother was silent for a moment. Then I realized she was not only angry with me.

"They can't stand the idea," she said, bitterly. "That a man with no education, an Italian, could make that much money, more money than them. That his skills are worth more to the airplane owners and the cargo companies than they are worth with all their degrees. The shippers lose tremendous amounts of money when the cargo is tied up because the planes don't fly. And many times he is the only one who can figure out what is wrong. People's lives depend on him. There's no telling what your father might have done in life if he had been able to get an education."

"Ok, I'll tell them I made a mistake," I said.

"You're going to college and get an education if your father and I have to kill you to get you there."

"That won't be necessary."

"If there's more than one broke down at a time they bid for him. He works day and night many times. He comes home exhausted, dirty, filthy, hungry. And he does it all for us, for you. So you don't have to grow up and work in the fields or a store or as a maid in a hotel."

"Ok! Ok! I'll go to college! I'll tell Miss Garter I was wrong." *And I'll keep my mouth shut in front of Julianna from now on. Daddy is right, you cannot trust anybody.*

"And say absolutely nothing about this to your father, we don't need to get him mad or involved."

That was certainly true. "I won't. Believe me I won't." Then I smiled at her. "If you kill me to get me to college, that will make it really hard for me to get a degree."

My mother laughed and I relaxed, crisis over. Even though she was now over 50 she was still really beautiful when she laughed.

In one way she is just like a real fairy princess, just older, I thought.

We had been studying the fairytales in school. I was excited that Miss Garter was teaching literature this week. We were reciting epic poetry in class. Miss Garter was explaining the rules of epic poetry and how it told a story in a song format and had to have a refrain. She said the poem had a mathematical formula and to write one you had to understand math.

"I can write that," I told her. I silently disagreed that the math was important. *It's the words that matter,* I thought, but I didn't say so.

Miss Garter replied that if I could do so and follow all the mathematical rules she would have the class recite it.

"The syllables must have the right count and the poem the right beat," she said.

I brought my poem in the next day and I was showing it around to the class as Miss Garter prepared for the day at her desk, laboriously removing and storing the metal crutches.

"We're not going to have to say this. Miss Garter won't make us. You're just a kid like us. You can't write anything," said Riland.

"Yes, I can. I have. I've written a book too," I said.

"She may get it published when she grows up," said Julianna, defending me.

"Yeah, it'll fall apart by then. What you going to do? Spray paper preserver all over it? You think you'll get this published some day?" said Riland. "That's a laugh."

I was wondering what paper preserver could be, envisioning spraying it all over my book and wondering if it would make the pages stiff, when Miss Garter took my poem from me and read it silently. She put it on her desk and it sat there all during the morning lesson but after lunch she handed it back to me.

"Victoria has written an epic poem and I promised her I would have the class recite it if it followed the mathematical formula. And it does. So, Class, we will recite Victoria's poem." Miss Garter directed Julianna to pass out mimeographed copies of my poem as the class let out a collective moan.

"Class, you are being rude, you will hurt Victoria's feelings. She put a lot of work in on this."

"She doesn't have any feelings!" Riland said in a sour voice. From her expression I could tell even Julianna was a little jealous. She still would not let anyone, including me or her mother, read her work.

"Riland, one more word out of you and you will be on the list to go to the office tomorrow," said Miss Garter. "Victoria has demonstrated mathematical ability in writing this poem. She must have worked very hard on it."

Riland glared at me silently. Most of the others just sulked.

She typed it during lunch and then mimeographed it, I thought, feeling proud but guilty that I had just written the words and not paid any attention to the mathematics involved in the poetry. I didn't understand them. All I did was make my words in my poem correspond to the words in the poem we were studying, using similar length words to create a different story.

She thinks I worked hard but it was easy. I had written it in about 20 minutes. It had not been hardly any work at all.

"Now, Class, we will recite the poem."

Fair Maiden by Victoria Grasso
Trio: Upon a hill sat a fair maiden.
Others: What hair color has she?
Girl: Her hair shines like the high noon sun,
     But no man dare to ask her out for fun,
     For beneath her sash there is a gun,
     Her lips are red as roses,
     And all day long she sets and poses.
     She holds her head high,
     She never utters a word--not even a sigh!

Others: She never speaks?
     Not even a squeak?
Girl: She never moves--not even a smile,
     But she turns her head once in a while.

Others: Where is the hill?
Trio: No one knows where is that hill;
     Only--beside it is a great, shining silver mill.

Others: Is that where she sleeps?
Girl: Oh-h-h, I suppose,
     Nobody really and truly knows.
Trio: She was cruel and mean,
     Clever and keen,
     She had to be seen,
     Or so it would seem.

Girl: But then one day a dragon came along!
     He was great and big and powerfully strong.
     He took her to his home.
     And around her he put a pile of stone.
Trio: The poor, fair Maiden, she cried and wept.
     Oh, how awful she felt
     She was so sorry for her very bad deeds.
Girl: "Oh," she cried. "I was bad, and mean!"
     This is my punishment. "Oh, dragon--set me free.

I am sorry for my sins."
Then the dragon took three spins.

All: And then?

Girl: The dragon turned into a handsome prince!
He took the Fair Maiden to his palace!
She married him in a dress that's hard to find.

All: And after that she was always good and kind!

Girl or Boy: The End

"Have you written any other poetry?" Miss Garter asked, after class when I thanked her for typing my poem and making the class recite it. Especially for typing it, it was so good to see it in print, even if the print was pale purple mimeograph, not black and white like real books and magazines.

"Yes, I have." I told her about *The Statue of Liberty* for Miss Tucker and confessed about *The Miniskirt* for Miss Bridge. I recited both from memory.

Miss Garter laughed. "What did Miss Bridge say about that?"

"Oh, I never showed it to her," I admitted. "But if you think I should, I could find her."

"She's gone, I'm afraid. She went to a bigger school district."

Miss Bridge was not the only one gone from Fairvine. Julianna Wells had moved away just before we studied the poems. Other students were missing also. I reported them missing as each one disappeared to my mother and she said their families had moved away also. Some of the kids at CCD class at church were gone too. I didn't care as long as Kris was there.

Father Schmidt was our new CCD teacher. It was the fourth grade. We now had priests to teach the next two years leading toward Confirmation. Father Braun was assigned to fifth grade. Previously both grades had been combined and taught by Father Mallett. He now took over the post Confirmation classes, everyone in sixth grade and older, called the Youth Class. The younger classes were still taught by parent volunteers. I was glad to escape being taught by Father Mallett for two more years.

We liked Father Schmidt. He was funny and entertaining, not stiff and pompous like Father Mallett. I liked that he didn't think all non-Catholics went to hell. My mother kept reminding me to tell Father Schmidt that I knew Theodore Rossi Jr. and his family but I kept forgetting as soon as I saw Kris. Kris had a negative effect on my memory for some reason.

One Sunday a Protestant guest came to our church to sing a special song at Mass. I missed the announcement of exactly which of the new priests the woman was related to. Kris was not serving. So he was sitting with me when the woman was introduced. Kris was talking away. I did catch the elderly woman saying she was proud her nephew was a Catholic priest even though she was a Protestant and she was going to sing us a Protestant song. I elbowed Kris hard to get him to shut up.

Someone played a violin while she sang. I was enraptured by the flawless verse and the capturing melody both growing more and more wonderful as the song came to an end...

"...*How Great Thou Art!*"

I had never heard anything so astounding.

That song had not been in my piano hymnbook. I had never heard it on television or in the movies. I forgot about which priest was supposed to be the singer's nephew. I didn't follow the Mass as it continued. I forgot Kris was beside me. I was still hearing that song over and over in my mind.

If there are churches in this world where they sing that song then I am in the wrong church.

It was time for Communion. We had to kneel. Kris bent over and put our kneeler down and I knelt down beside him. Impulsively he took my hand in his. I looked up at him and we smiled at each other. Suddenly I felt at home and began to follow the Mass again. *As long as he is here this is where I'll be.* We stood up to go forward. Kris took my hand and looked down at me and smiled. I thought about the majesty and history of the Catholic Church as I looked into his eyes.

Our great religion binds us together, I thought, dramatically, enjoying the power of that thought. But after the service was over, that song came back into my mind and I felt torn.

By Wednesday I was focused on Kris again. We were having a Christmas Party at church for our CCD class with music and dancing. The grownup kids in the church youth group were supervising us. Father Mallett handed them records to play, then left early. Others were complaining but I was delighted the music was old fashioned and slow. I was enjoying Frank Sinatra singing when Kris came and tapped me on the shoulder.

"You've gotten skinny suddenly," Kris told me as we started to dance. I was pleased. I had been trying to lose weight for Christmas. He was still shorter than me but not as much. He put his arms around me and I put mine over the tops of his shoulders and we started swaying slowly back and forth.

I had my eyes closed but suddenly the lights went out as if we had a power failure. Youth group members pushed us slightly to the right.

"Go in here, stay in here," one of them whispered, and the other one giggled a little. And they closed the partition and we found we were alone in darkened section. Below the partition I could see the lights come back on in the other room.

We just kept dancing slowly to the song, not saying anything, but I could tell he was enjoying it as much as me. *This is special,* I thought, *special to us alone forever.* When the song ended, the partition was abruptly pulled open, and the adults came in.

"Song's over," one of them said, and pulled us apart and back into the main room. They were laughing. Kris went off with one youth group member and, as the other released me, I was suddenly surrounded by all the other girls who heretofore rarely spoke to me.

"Tell us what happened?" said Phoebe.

I was annoyed. Phoebe was a nuisance. My mother's friend, her mother/grandmother must have told her to follow me around.

"Are you going steady now!?" asked one of the other girls who had never spoken to me before. I was less annoyed now. "Did he give you a ring!?"

"Did he kiss you!?" asked another, who had only barely tolerated me in the past.

"N-No," I said, wishing he had, now basking in their attention, but wary of their sudden friendship. But I decided they should know. "He held me in his arms, it was wonderful!" And in response, they all cooed appreciatively, so excited they were not even jealous.

I looked around for Kris and he was amidst the boys all paying him attention, too. Then the dance was over and we had to go home.

Soon after school let out for Christmas I issued my usual Christmas list which was just the fashion doll clothes booklet with what I had checked, and what I didn't have marked wanted. But my mother handed it back to me.

"You're not getting any more," she said. "You are getting too old for dolls."

And indeed as I searched the growing pile of presents each day as Christmas approached, there was nothing that looked like it could be doll or doll clothes. Finally, I stopped going into the living room where the tree was. I didn't bother to play the Christmas carols on the piano. My last piano lesson had been before school started. Mrs. Lambert was moving away from her beautiful home in Water Oaks. I didn't see how she could bear to leave it and she did seem very sorry to go.

"I had thought we would stay here the rest of our lives," she told my mother on the last day. "But it was not meant to be."

If only her beautiful home was in our neighborhood, then she would not have to move, I thought. But down the side street, Valery's family also had their house for sale.

"I'm not taking any more piano lessons," I told my mother. "I'm too old for them too."

My mother was slightly distressed by this, much more distressed by my next announcement. But I figured it was a good time to tell her. It was Christmastime. Daddy was off for several days for a change and she wouldn't want any trouble.

"I'm not going to the beauty shop anymore," I told her. "I'm tired of my head hurting, the prickly rollers and sitting under the hot dryer. There's cigarette smoke most of the time. I'm not going back ever."

My mother appealed to my father but he came down on my side. "Why should we pay $6.00 a week for her to go to the beauty shop when she doesn't want to go? She's lost weight. She's pretty now. She doesn't have to go to a beauty shop."

I had lost weight and kept it off and I had grown taller. I knew I wasn't beautiful like Julianna, but I could hear my father say I was pretty and agree with him. Especially when Mama let me darken my eyebrows so I looked more like him. I couldn't do that for school. But for church it was allowed and sometimes she let me use just a little lipstick, too.

"I was beautiful when I was young," she would say. "I had the boys swarming all over me. A little makeup and you can look pretty, too."

I didn't have boys swarming but I wondered if she knew about the dance with Kris.

One place I did have to go was to the eye doctor. Miss Garter had recommended that I get glasses. My parents were both very concerned that I would feel bad about having to wear glasses. I wasn't sure how I would feel.

But when they put the glasses on me, I had no doubt.

The world suddenly looked so clear! I could see way down the road while we were driving home. I couldn't believe it was possible to see so well and I had not realized how little I did see before.

"These are great!" I said.

My parents looked at each other and shook their heads like they were amazed too. There was only two drawbacks to the glasses. Daddy had already put up Christmas tree lights and they had always been so beautiful that I couldn't wait for it to turn dark that night so I could see them with glasses.

That was a major disappointment. The Christmas lights looked much worse with the glasses. I could see the wiring and the paint on the bulbs and the lights did not shine nearly as pretty as before.

"Just take the glasses off when you look at the lights," said Daddy, when I complained.

That did solve that problem but there was nothing to be done about the other. I realized at once, when I looked at my mother, how many wrinkles and lines were in her face that I had not been able to see before, especially behind her glasses which had heretofore blurred them to me. She looked so much older! I had thought she looked in her 30s, but she really looked in her 40s. Although she still didn't look nearly her real age, it sent a pang through my heart.

She's growing older as I grow up. I thought.

Daddy's image was more reassuring. While he did have a few lines I had not seen before, he still looked much the same. He had almost no wrinkles. Aunt Worthrose looked a lot older but I had expected that. She was really old.

When Christmas morning arrived, one more present was under the tree. I grabbed it and tore it open first. Barbie! After all! I didn't even mind that it was a redhead. I never forgot the thrill of seeing her, her smooth bendable legs, striped swimsuit with the aqua bottom, short page boy hairstyle, her lips pale red matching her hair.

"This is the last one," my mother said. "Absolutely the last one. And this year, I know it's early but we need to make plans. If it's Ok with you, no birthday party. We plan to visit Uncle Buford in the countryside instead for your birthday. Take you out of school for a couple of days and have a mini vacation. Uncle Drake and Aunt Talinda may be there. He's due for leave and they may come home."

"Ok." *Wow,* I thought.

"Aunt Nelwynn will make you a cake and we'll have a little party there. You won't get much presents but we will get you what you want - except more dolls- here at home."

"Ok." *Take me out of school! Wow.*

"You can make up any school work when we get back. It won't take the place of our real vacation in the summer. We are thinking of maybe going to Disneyland next year."

Walt Disney had died recently and some people had said Disneyland would close without him.

"It won't close," said my father. "Not just because one man died. Others will carry it on."

My mother looked over at my father who was reading the newspaper, ignoring his Christmas presents, which sat unopened under the tree.

"Have any of your friends been to Disneyland?"

"No, but Juliana Whaels and Kris have been to the fair."

"Hmm, sounds to me like those people are just puttin up a

front," said my father who had been eavesdropping as he read the paper.

"What does that mean?"

"It means they pretend to have more money than they really do," he said.

"Both Mr. Whaels and Mr. Stavich have white collar jobs," said my mother.

"It's what you do with your money that counts," said my father. "The important thing is to put as much money in the bank as you possibly can. If you save your money when you are young, you won't have to work so hard when you are old."

"Vic, will you shut up about money and open your presents."

"All right, all right. If it will get dinner on with any faster." He laughed and she started throwing Christmas bows and crumpled wrapping paper at him. He shielded himself from this paper assault with the daily news.

XVI *Conspiracies*

I was looking forward to meeting Uncle Drake and Aunt Talinda. I knew I had actually met them as a baby but I couldn't remember them. *How exciting to fight the Japanese, then to travel and live all over the world.* I hoped they would like me and tell me lots of stories about their lives.

I mentioned this to Mama during the time between Christmas and New Year's when Daddy had to go back to work.

"I'm sure they will love you," said my mother. "As all of my family that knows you does."

"Will Aunt Talinda ever have any children?"

"She's too old now. Talinda told me she never got pregnant as far as she knew."

"You can be pregnant without knowing?" This year in school they taught us some of the basics of the egg and sperm being fertilized. And Mama had explained that I would soon be having periods.

"Um, yes, at the very beginning you can be, then if the baby-um, dies- early on- you just, well it is possible to not know for sure you were ever pregnant. Many times I hoped but-" She was looking really sad and I was afraid she might cry. So I interrupted her with the first question that came to mind.

"Why didn't Uncle Drake and Aunt Talinda adopt?"

"Oh, they've had an exciting life, living all over the world, and, and I don't think Talinda cared in the long run that she didn't have a child."

"Unlike you?"

She smiled at me suddenly and instead of crying her face brightened and she was as beautiful as I ever saw her.

"I have a child, Victoria. I have you," she said.

Besides looking forward to my birthday trip, the real reason I couldn't wait for Christmas holiday to be over was so I could see Kris again. But I had a terrific jolt when I got back to CCD class. We were no longer in the same class.

A second fourth grade class had been formed with new people

who had started going to our church over the holidays. Volunteer parents had taken over the original class and Father Schmidt went with the new class. I was in the new class. They were very nice and I soon had a new girlfriend. And the boys in this class were certainly dark and handsome. They liked me too. But I missed Kris. I was the only girl taken from the old class to the new. I wondered if Kris and I had been split up because of our Christmas dance.

Strangely enough just like I never saw the new kids at school outside of the playground, I began to realize I never saw the new kids at church outside of CCD.

"At least some of them should come to the same service as us," I told Kris, after a Sunday Mass.

"They don't ever come to any of our services, silly," he told me. "They all go to the new afternoon Spanish service. You were put in the class with all the Mexican kids."

"Oh." *That explains a lot.*

"Didn't you notice they were Mexicans?"

"Well," I said, thinking, but not really remembering them that well. "I must have. I noticed my new friend Juanita is. But I didn't really pay attention to any of the other kids."

"Anyway, I know how we can spend a little more time together," he said. He looked dashing in his white altar boy robe with the dark collar that set off his fair skin, dark brown hair, and blue eyes. He had suddenly grown a little taller and was now taller than me just since Christmas.

"How?"

He related his plan, then said, "You know I'm going to marry you some day."

"I'm never getting married." I told him smugly. "I'm going be a spinster."

"What? Why not?"

"I know where babies come from and I'm never doing that."

"I know too, and it does sound kind of gross."

"If I marry, my relationship with my husband will be platonic."

"What does that mean?"

"We will be like a priest and a nun."

"I know. I'll become a priest and you become a nun and we'll

254

get married."

"They wouldn't let us. Now you're being silly, you know that. They would still think that we were, well, you know. How could they know we wouldn't-?"

"We could try it and see if maybe it wasn't so bad."

I whacked him good across the shoulder.

"Hey, what was that for?" He grinned, rubbing his shoulder.

"I'm never going to marry anybody," I yelled.

"You could just be my mistress then if we like it," he said wickedly.

"You are not supposed to talk to me like this," I told him, sneering. I was trying to act scandalized.

But we put his plan into effect.

It had to be a Saturday morning on a day Daddy went to work. Fortunately he was again working most weekends.

"Now if you tell anyone, even your Aunt Worthrose, I will kill you, your daddy will kill us both if he finds out."

"I'll never tell!"

"You are to go straight into the movie theatre, find Kris and his brothers and sit with them. Don't talk to nobody else. Don't get up and leave for any reason. Go to the bathroom now, here. Don't go in the movie theatre. Take some candy in your purse. Don't go buy anything and call me at once if anything goes wrong. Here's two nickels. Put them in your pocket. I will show you where the pay phone is when we get there."

"Ok."

Kris and his brothers didn't go to either of the beautiful movie theatres we usually went to. And the movie theatre begun in Fairland Addition had never been finished. So we went to a theatre across the freeway closer to Kris's neighborhood. It was connected to a shopping mall but we went in from the street.

I found Kris and sat with him. His brothers were nowhere to be found.

"I sent them to a different show," he whispered. "So they won't pester us."

"But they are even younger than you. They can't be by themselves!"

255

"Sure they can. They are not much younger, and anyway, we go everywhere without our parents and I send them off without me a lot."

We saw **Thoroughly Modern Millie**. It was a wonderful movie, the best I had ever seen. It more than made up for the plain, drab theatre. During the movie, when he could sit still, which was not most of the time, Kris held my hand and told me again we would get married some day. We had time together after the show before my mother got there.

"I'll fetch my little brothers from the other side of the theatre later," he said nonchalantly. "I don't care if their movie's over, they can sit and wait."

"Do you ever go to those movie theaters that look like palaces for kings and queens?" I asked, thinking we could go there and be really romantic.

"Rarely," he said, "they are more expensive. We can't afford them." Then he put his arm around me. But he didn't kiss me. I wondered if I had bad breath.

"What books do you read?" I asked him while we were waiting for my mother to come and get me, wondering if it were possible to let him read my book. But I feared it was a book just for girls.

"Oh, I like science fiction and the mysteries where the guys outfox the villains," he said.

"You ever read mysteries where the detective is a girl?" I asked, timidly.

"Of course not! Those are just for girls," he said. "You don't read Hardy Boys?"

"No, of course not." I did not admit that ever since Matthew Waterston had read from one of them in first grade that I wanted to, was really curious as to how boys' books were written. But my mother wouldn't ever let me touch one.

"Girls can't read boys' books and boys can't read girls' books," Kris informed me with certainty.

So **Barbara Kay Scott Mystery Series -The Mystery of the Missing Persons** was really only going to be for girls. I felt a little sad about that.

"I read lots of real science books, too," he said. "And I like math."

I looked at him, narrowing my eyes. "Time for me to go," I said. "That's our car coming right there."

"I have to see that movie again," I told my mother. "It was fantastic."

"Maybe. When it gets to the theatre we normally go to. I hear the seats are not near as comfortable at the mall and your father needs comfortable seats due to his back."

"They weren't," I said, rubbing my back a little. "But it was worth it."

"You are a young girl," she said. "If the seats hurt your back, it won't last long."

"What is white slavery?" I asked.

"What?"

"White slavery?"

"I don't know. Where did you hear that term?"

"I don't know." I actually didn't know where but somewhere I had recently seen it.

"Maybe on a movie poster? They make movies about all kinds of evil things these days. Probably some violent movie rated R or X. The world is going to miss Walt Disney more than people realize."

"But what is it? I thought only the blacks had been slaves."

"I don't know what they meant by that," she said after some hesitation. "I guess people being made to work in the fields like the black slaves before the Civil War. Maybe in other countries."

"Oh." I reflected. "They would be sold for money just like the blacks were?"

"Why- er- yes, I guess so," said my mother and she left me to go get the laundry. I tagged along, at risk of being made to help.

"Which countries?"

"I don't know. Bad countries. Countries where the bad guys live." She handed me some small towels to fold.

Well, that explains it. I thought, as I quickly folded the towels, then pulling out my book.

I saw it in my mind. *Rows and rows of white girls, dressed in rags and kerchiefs, picking cotton in the hot Russian sun.*

I didn't write anything new right then. But I reread it all, making minor corrections. And I had a plan.

Sunday we were busy visiting the Espositos, whose house was a very long drive away. Monday and Tuesday I was distracted by a new art project Mrs. Hopwell had devised, and I spent the afternoons making posters for it for extra credit. As I did this easy work, I looked forward to Wednesday night in the back of my mind.

A singular secret movie date was not the only plan Kris and I had for getting together. I knew my mother was not going to brave that scene again soon, if ever. We were now meeting before and after CCD and also for the 15 minute break in the middle of the classes. He was not allowed in my classroom and none of my class was allowed in the main building but we could stay outside and talk. And we did so, even when it was bad weather.

This night had been clear and we had talked a long time. We had overstayed the break and it had turned dark. We realized this suddenly and broke off our conversation. He went back into his classroom building. Mine was further away and I had to cross the sidewalk as I stepped onto the sidewalk.

Father Mallett came out of nowhere and grabbed my arm.

"What are you doing out here?" he asked in a whisper, which really wasn't a question.

"I'm on my way back to class," I said. I wasn't afraid of him. But the way he was acting was sinister. It made me nervous. With two assistants, he no longer taught a class and we rarely saw him on Wednesdays.

"I notice you spend a lot of time with Kris Stavich," he said, his voice still low and rushed as if he were being pursued.

"So, we are friends," I said, deliberately slowly, hoping I didn't sound defensive.

I didn't feel guilty and I didn't want him to think I did.

"If I were you I would not spend so much time with him," the priest said in an ominous tone, his hostile face so close to mine I felt his black rimmed glasses lightly touch my frames. "He is no good for you. Stay away from him."

"No, I won't do that," I replied automatically, defiantly, pulling back.

The priest abruptly dropped my arm turned and walked away. I stood there mildly stunned. I was now all alone in the courtyard. I couldn't think of anything else to do except sprint the short distance, bounding up the two steps to the temporary building where my class was. Father Mallett's words burned into my mind and I heard them over and over again at the expense of whatever Father Schmidt was talking about for the rest of the night. *What did this sinister, deadly serious, meant to be intimidating, warning mean? Who was behind it? Was it our parents, or someone that was complaining we sat together in church? What was he saying to Kris about me?* And the hostile priest's square jawed face with the black rimmed glasses and sinister stare remained pictured before me even as the genial cleric lectured on.

Chapter 16
The Face in the Window

Back home Barbara was unusually quiet and abrupt when Ellen asked her what happened at Harold Hall. Actually what she needed was a little encouragement on the case. She knew she couldn't depend on her mother for that. She needed her father. Suddenly Barbara remembered Jane and Belle and the other girls, then she remembered her father's words, "Barbara don't ever give up on anything even if things seem bad, don't give up!"

Suddenly somehow Barbara knew her father was all right. Encouraged by this she went and started to fix dinner.

Ellen smiled.

While Barbara was cooking, the mailman came in with a coded letter from Belle. It said:

BARBARA,
SORRY. THEY MOVED US. MAY COME BACK. DON'T KNOW. BYE.

Barbara called April and asked if she got one, too. She had. It was also in code. It was longer.

BARBARA,
WE WILL GO TO USSR. SOON. WE WILL BECOME SLAVE.
STIFF IS COWARD. PLEASE FIND SOON. COME BACK.
JANE

None of the other girls' families received note except Minnie's. It said:

HURRY B. YOU'VE GOT 3 WEEKS!
MIN!

Mrs. Foster was very upset at that. "Do you think you can find her in three weeks?"

"I'll certainly try," Barbara assured her.

That night when Barbara began to prepare for bed she heard a rapping outside her window. She quickly put on her robe and slippers and hurried to the window and looked out. In the house next door a face peered through the window. Barbara rushed to wake up Ellen who said they should call the police immediately. Which was exactly what they did. Three policemen came shortly after.

All three heaved against the Peers's door. As soon as they got it open they heard a back door slam. Two officers ran after them while Lieutenant Ames stayed with Barbara to untie Mrs. Peers, a young woman of 30, who was tied up on the couch.

"Mrs. Peers, what happened?"

"Well," said Mrs. Peers. "My husband is out of town. I came down to the kitchen to get some milk and suddenly heard someone in the den. I went to call the police when someone clapped a hand over my mouth."

"Where is the phone?" asked Lieutenant Ames.

"In the room next to the den."

"Well, it could have been one person or two."

"Yes," agreed Barbara.

"We will send a fingerprint man out immediately. Meanwhile don't anybody touch anything. Only- Miss Scott what is that?"

"A note. I found it over there by the phone," explained Barbara. "It says:

TELL MISS SCOTT NEXT TIME
IT WILL BE HER HOUSE

"'HER' is underlined 3 times."

"Here let me see," said Lieutenant Ames. He examined the note and put it in his pocket. "Miss Scott, I suggest you have some plainclothesmen as your guest."

"Why I'd be delighted, sir."

"Good. I will assign two of my best men, Lieutenant Ames and Officer Kinson."

The next day as Barbara left the house in Jane's car which April had let her keep at the Scott house, a plainclothesman stopped her. "Are you Miss Barbara Kay Scott?"

"Yes."

"May I see some identification?"

Barbara showed him her credit cards and her driver's license.

The officer smiled and relaxed.

Barbara started to go on when he stopped her again.

Barbara immediately became suspicious.

"Would you like me to escort you?"

"No."

"I think I'd better," he started to get in the car.

Barbara suddenly screamed and two men came running. They quickly grasped the man tightly.

"Who is this man?" asked the elder of the two men.

"He said he was Lieutenant Ames."

"I'm Lieutenant Ames," the other spoke up quietly.

The policeman took the impostor to the police station. Then Barbara drove on to Mrs. Foster's house.

To her surprise Mr. Foster was there, too.

"Carl and I have decided to put off the divorce proceedings until Minnie is found." Although Mrs. Foster smiled, she looked very tired and worried.

"Yes, we have," said Mr. Foster.

For the first time Barbara looked at them closely. Minnie had Mrs. Foster's blonde hair and she had her father's eyes and mouth. Mrs. Foster was about 35 and Mr. Foster was 38. He was an extremely handsome man and any girl would be proud to call him father.

Barbara learned that they had received no message from Minnie so she drove on to Mrs. Horton's house, then she went to Mrs. Bolman's home. There she got results. There was a letter from Emily May.

DEAR MOTHER
WE HAVE FUN HERE. WOULDN'T COME HOME FOR $1,000. DIANA'S BACK. WE WERE NOT KIDNAPPED. HAVE TAKEN A PLANE TO SAN FRANCISCO FAR AWAY FROM DENVER. I'M FOR A TRAIN. HAS BARBARA, OUR DOG, HAD PUPPIES YET? I FOUND HER TOY BONE IN MY PURSE YESTERDAY. LET HER OUT ONCE IN A WHILE.
EMILY

"What does it say in code?" asked Mrs. Bolman.
"It says:

MOTHER,
HAVE COME BACK. WERE TAKEN AWAY FOR BARBARA FOUND OUT
EMILY

"'Have come back?'," said Mrs. Bolman puzzled. "What does that mean?"

"It means," said Barbara excitedly. "That they

262

have come back to Harold Hall!"

"Are there two Lieutenant Ames?" asked my mother, when she had read this part.

"No, there's just one. Barbara does not recognize the policemen when they are not in uniform," I explained. "Like they cannot tell who Superman is when he has on his costume."

"Hmm, I think you have a little more work to do on this section," said my mother.

I disagreed. But later I would look it over. It was time to prepare for our trip and once again I would have to leave the book at home.

My birthday vacation had been delayed because there was so much work for Daddy, we could not go to Uncle Buford's house until late March. We missed Uncle Drake and Aunt Talinda's visit home as he had to go to his new station in the South Pacific before we got there. So I still hadn't met them. Aunt Nelwin baked a wonderful cake but I did not enjoy the trip much. I loved my country relatives but the cigarette smoke once again made my head and my throat ache unbearably.

And my parents were still oblivious to my complaints. I was not allowed to voice them for fear of insulting my aunt and uncle. It was even worse in the cold than in the previous summer visits. They didn't have central heat so it was cold. I couldn't breathe at night at all.

So I barely paid attention to the adult conversations, trying to pass the time writing. But one conversation did prick my ears. It was interesting for its content but also because there was no tension between the adults even though they disagreed. Everybody was much friendlier in the countryside. It was a different world which would be nice to be in if it weren't for the smoking.

Some of Uncle Buford's friends arrived at his house for breakfast. In the countryside the men ate first at the dining table. After serving them, the women could take some food and go sit in the den on the couch or chairs or floor. *Another reason to never get married,* I thought, *especially not to anyone from the countryside.* But the house was so small there were no private conversations. While these men ate, they were suggesting to Daddy he should support George Wallace for the next president.

"I can't," Daddy replied to them. "I just drove through Alabama. The roads there are terrible. He can't even procure decent roads for the citizens of his own state. He is not qualified to be president. If he can't take care of the residents of his own state he doesn't need to try to be president. There was one lane bridges. I mean one lane. And no road signs. No signals. If two people started down the bridge at the same time one of them had to back up. And this was the major highway."

"You went through Alabama?" one of the men asked, incredulous.

"And we detoured through Mississippi as well," said my father somewhat smugly.

"Hell! Vic are you crazy? Going through Alabama and Mississippi at a time like this?" Uncle Buford practically yelled, but was laughing at the same time.

I flinched but Daddy just laughed, too.

"I wanted to see what they were like, what was going on," he said.

"You are damn sure nuts," said Uncle Buford, shaking his head and all the men laughed.

Wow! I thought. *If one of my Italian uncles ever said Daddy was crazy, blood would have been spilled. Their blood.*

"Well, I'm for Wallace," said one of the men. "My union is for him and that's good enough for me."

"Nobody's going to tell me who to vote for," said my father smoothly.

This disagreement did not make anybody mad or even tense. They just kept eating. All the food was disappearing.

"Anybody would be better than that bastard Lyndon Johnson," said one of the men.

"I still think that SOB was somehow behind Kennedy's assassination," said another. "Ain't no way one man alone did that killing."

"He wanted Kennedy dead so he could be president and put the coloreds in power," said still another.

"Ah, the coloreds ain't so bad," said Uncle Buford. "I's damn near raised with 'em. Weren't we June Rosette? Nelwynn? Where's the coffee?"

"I don't like any of the current candidates," said my father.

"We need somebody like Eisenhower," said Uncle Buford.

Everybody wholeheartedly agreed with that. The countryside men all lit up cigarettes.

"We stood in line for hours to vote for Ike," my mother reminisced, with a misty look on her face as she went to serve them coffee.

"Those days are gone. It will never be the same," said Aunt Nelwynn as she started washing the dishes. The women, including me, still hadn't had much to eat.

"You got that right. Hell, I may not even vote myself anyway," said my uncle.

After breakfast the men all went fishing, leaving my mother and aunt to finish cleaning up. We got a chance to eat what little they had left. Although I wasn't left hungry, I definitely felt like I did not get my fair share of the food.

If I ever marry anyone from the countryside, I'm not having this. There will be changes made. Women will be eating equally with the men, I thought.

After Daddy got back from the fishing trip the other men went home, Uncle Buford went to take a nap. Aunt Nelwynn had a Bible study meeting that evening to prepare for. We started home that afternoon.

"Who are you going to vote for, how do you decide who to vote for? Does Daddy tell you?" I asked, after a while when my throat stopped hurting from all the cigarette smoke I had just endured and I could talk again.

Daddy had gone into the gas station store to get some snacks, including some ice cream to help my throat. The gas station attendant was washing the windshield.

"When you go in that voting booth, Victoria, nobody knows who you vote for. I can let your father think whatever he wants to think. When I get in the voting booth he doesn't know what box I check and I don't have to tell him or anybody else. That's the beauty of our system."

"I like Robert Kennedy." He wasn't nearly as ugly as all the rest of them. He had lots of hair. I didn't understand why most men got so ugly as they got older. Except for some of the movie stars. And I suspected actors did something artificial to keep young. Something like all the cold cream my mother wore to bed every night, only much more expensive and more effective.

My mother may not have looked as young and beautiful as she had in her twenties. She said that it was because her skin was so fair that she got wrinkles. Without doing anything artificial, my father looked almost as handsome as when, as a young man, he had been so incredible looking. Perfection. And nobody believed either one of them was over 50.

"You'll never know who I vote for either," she smiled confidently. My father returned, got back in the car, and mercifully the airconditioner was started again.

During the ride home I began a new campaign to go on to Mexico. I had been hearing lots of TV commercials about how wonderful it was to vacation in Mexico and I hoped to get some more ideas for my second Barbara Scott mystery, still untouched since the trip to Canada.

I already had some ideas from my new friend in CCD. Her parents were from Mexico. Juanita reminded me of Carmelita but she was not nearly as shy or as dark. Juanita spoke both English and Spanish. She was surprised I could not speak Italian and had never been to Italy. When I told her that was because Italy was on the wrong side in World War II, she said that was sad. She was glad Mexico had been on the right side. She told me about visiting her grandparents and how close Mexico really was. I had thought it was much farther away.

Just before our trip I had gone to Juanita's birthday party. She had given an open invitation to all CCD fourth grade students. It was at her house across the freeway the Saturday before we left for our trip. With two classes full invited, I had believed it would be mobbed, but it was mostly the other Mexican girls and a few boys that came, besides me. That was good because it was a very small house.

The house was plain on the outside but beautiful and colorful on the inside. The walls were painted bright colors and there were lots of religious statues and candles. There were beautiful pictures of paintings of Jesus and the Virgin Mary on the walls and photographs of two of the popes. But the largest photo, on the fireplace mantel, was of

President Kennedy. There was a small candle burning beside it.

The party had been great fun even if most of the conversation was in Spanish. Everyone was very nice and translated occasionally. The cake was really good and we danced to Mexican music, girls taking turns with the boys as there were so few. I wished fervently Kris had been able to come but he said his mother wouldn't let him. I tried to enjoy dancing with the Mexican boys. It was the shaking type of dancing where nobody touched each other. The Mexican music was fast but not as aggravating as fast American music.

Before the party ended, we had all joined hands and an adult had prayed in heavily accented English, thanking Jesus for the party, the food, the house, and America. I thought that was nice and wondered if the prayer had been said in English just for me. Judging by Juanita's home, the country of Mexico must be colorful and exciting, not dull like Canada was.

Daddy didn't say anything when we got home but the next morning he woke me up early and said, "We're going to Mexico."

"Wow," I said happily and started to repack. Daddy was full of surprises. I had expected a long hard campaign before a trip to Mexico was agreed to, if ever.

"Don't pack much. We're not going to stay long. Just us, your mother's too tired to go. And we're going in my pickup so she can keep the car here."

So I dressed, grabbed a night gown and a Coke and off we went. The pickup had no airconditioning but that didn't matter as it was not too hot, especially that early in the morning, and we rolled the windows down all the way.

I liked riding with Daddy alone because we could talk if we wanted or be silent if we wanted, without any problems. We were mostly silent as the wind was loud, Daddy made fast time on the highway in his truck and I was happily contemplating fun in Mexico. There would be huge bazaars in the street with colorful mariachi bands playing as we shopped among the happy people there. Almost like the fair but with no rides.

Or maybe we'll be lucky and there'll be a carnival, girls in costume dancing, men playing guitars on the streets.

After a long long time, during which it got hotter and hotter, we got to the border and Daddy talked to the border guard for a moment and we were there in Mexico.

He turned off the main road and slowed down.

"You know, many of the men I work with are Mexican and they told me just where to go to see Mexico," he told me, as we turned on some bumpy dirt roads.

"Great," I said. *Inside information, even better. A preview for a longer trip in the future.*

Soon we were there.

We turned onto a road full of shanties and lean-to shacks with beaten looking people standing and sitting everywhere. Stinking mud ran through the center of the street. Little children, some naked, ran through the mud as hostile adults yelled at them to get out of our way. There was no color, no bazaar, no music, nothing but poverty and pain. It had turned very hot and suddenly I was dripping wet with sweat.

"This is Mexico," said my father. "Now you have seen it."

I was silent. This was far worse than the slums in our city where we had sold the house to Miss Trudy. This was unending filth and stench that filled up the truck and covered us like a blanket. There was no air coming into the truck, just an invisible fog of stench.

He turned around the truck and headed back to the highway watching me from the corner of his eye.

"You see, Mexico is made up of a few rich people who keep everyone else poor. The Mexican men I work with send most of the money back to their families so they won't starve. They don't keep hardly anything for themselves only what they have to take out to live in America. Most of the people in Mexico are poor poor people. They don't have enough to eat, no decent place to sleep, no real shelter from the storms or the cold in the winter. I don't ever intend to vacation in Mexico and give my money to the rich people that own the resorts. They may hire a few peons but most of the people never see a dime of the money the tourists spend."

By now we were almost back to the border crossing.

"I see," I said.

"I hope you do," said my father.

"I don't want to vacation in Mexico," I assured him.

"I don't know why it is this way. They have elections there," my father said, less emotional now, after crossing the border. "But they don't really count for some reason. I don't know that much about it but my friends at work say it doesn't do any good to vote. Nothing ever changes."

We drove back towards home, still mostly in silence, stopping at a small motel on the way when it got dark.

The next morning we had a good breakfast and went the rest of the way home. I thought about the Mexican-American kids at Juanita's party, how nice they were.

I remembered the prayer thanking God for America.

I was so glad I was born an American.

"Who are your parents going to vote for?" I asked Kris, when we got back. I had only missed one CCD class while on my trips.

But I was missing another one.

Kris and I had met before class as usual when our parents dropped us off.

But instead of going to our classes, we had slipped behind the buildings into a secluded spot in the woods.

"I don't know," he said. "They vote, but they never talk about it."

"Do your parents talk about money and religion either?" I asked, remembering that most people supposedly did not.

"Never," said Kris. "You aren't supposed to talk about those things."

"We do," I said. "We do."

The nighttime encounter with Father Mallett was still vivid in my mind.

As I held his hand and talked with him I knew there was nothing wrong with Kris. The only thing I could think of that provoked the priest's warning was that there was something wrong with his family.

"What does your father do for a living?" I asked Kris.

"He works for the FAA."

"He wants to be a farmer?" I asked, confused.

Kris looked confused too.

"He works at the airport. My grandfather was a farmer."

Maybe that explained it. "Does your father fly a plane?"

"No. He works on the ground. He works with the air traffic controllers."

"Oh." I explained how my father worked on the engines.

We continued talking and before we knew it, the class was over and parents were coming to pick up the kids.

We had to slip out of our hiding place and blend in with them as they exited the classrooms

If you ever marry anyone it will be Kris Stavich.

This unbidden thought came to me several times before I next saw him, having lain in wait for him and his family before Mass started.

He pulled away from his family and came to my side.

His father waved at me with his free hand. The other was holding one of his little brothers.

His mother glared at me and turned away.

"My mother is torn about my sitting with you," said Kris cheerfully. "She has to balance my usefulness in containing my little brothers against the trouble I might cause her if I stay with the family and misbehave."

"Oh." *I'm glad I'm an only child.*

That thought came often, more and more as I grew older.

"So far, trouble I might cause is winning the day. So here I am with you!"

I sat down in a pew. There it was again. *If you ever marry anyone it will be Kris Stavich.*

I clenched my teeth as the opening procession began and only unclenched them when the song began.

That is unimportant.

I have no intentions of ever marrying anybody, I thought as I began singing **"Holy Holy Holy...***"

Kris and his brothers and sister do not look beaten. Maybe his father drinks. Oooh...Maybe his family are criminals. Maybe Father Mallett had heard all about their criminal activity in the confessional and he was trying to warn me.

Wondering exactly what an air traffic controller did, an excited shiver came over me as I sat there.

My parents had just dropped me off.

They skipped Sunday services frequently now, so other Sundays I sat alone in the pew when Kris was serving as an altar boy.

But when he wasn't, he never failed to leave his family and come and sit with me so I would not be by myself.

I felt safe from any criminals when he sat with me.

XVII *Avalanches*

After the incident at the grocery store and reports of other crimes, including burglaries in Fairland Addition and Water Oaks, the Millers across the street were having burglar bars put on their windows. Aunt Worthrose, Mama and Daddy were discussing doing the same. Daddy had already installed double deadbolt locks that needed a key to open and close them from both sides.

"But there haven't been any burglaries in this neighborhood," said Daddy. "We already got the locks. If there's a fire you can't get out."

"Look how close it's coming," said Aunt Worthrose. "Look how close Fairland Addition and Water Oaks are. Many people already have their house for sale, the blacks are going to move in there. Sooner or later someone is going to sell to them. Then it will be just like a domino effect. Haven't you heard anything?"

"The Guidance Group was only allowed to schedule two meeting this semester. The first was right after Christmas, the second hasn't happened yet."

"Our class was smaller when I went back after our trip," I said.

"We were only out of town a week but since we got back, the mothers I chat with on the phone have been very distant, not saying much, there have been no invitations to visit class for any projects, so I guess I may have sort of lost track of what is going on," said my mother.

"When was the last time you drove down through Fairland Addition?" asked Aunt Worthrose.

"Let's go right now," said my father.

So that weekend we took a drive through Fairland Addition. Aunt Worthrose rode with us in the backseat with me. She had only done that with us one other time years ago to see Christmas lights at night.

"I need to see all this myself," she said, as she got in the car.

It was as if the manicured green lawns of the houses had been brushed by strokes of bright red and green and spotted white and black. In every yard, without exception, were colorful 'For Sale' signs. Like holiday decoration assortments, a set number of identical designs was randomly distributed on each block. Each street had a differing variation on the assortment with a sometime lone plain sign reading only 'For Sale by owner'. And many of the signs, if not most of them had a little addendum that read 'Sale Pending' or 'Sold!'.

"This is blockbusting," said my father.

"What is blockbusting?" I asked, annoyed at another word I was unfamiliar with.

"Blockbusting is when real estate agents convince one person to sell, giving the first seller market price or higher, then once the sale is done, they go door to door warning that blacks are moving in and convincing others to sell at rock bottom prices."

The incredible speed of this change took our breaths away. We knew Valery's family had sold their house to black people and so had the other people living on Foam Meadow. Mama had been a little nervous about this but Daddy said they were far down the street from us and didn't have any teenage children. Then Mama and Aunt Worthrose were relieved when they learned the Millers had decided to stay regardless. They were retired and had no children to worry about. Living outside of the additions, none of us really realized how fast the changeover was going in those planned neighborhoods, until now.

"This's been going on all over America," said Aunt Worthrose. "Mrs. O'Kelley Senior says that Fairland Addition was blockbusted because of a feud between two neighbors over a tree. One sold to the coloreds on purpose to spite his neighbor."

Driving through Fairland Addition now, and seeing the brightly colored 'For Sale' signs in every yard on every home, row after row of signs, it did indeed seem like an avalanche was happening on the other side of Silver Brook.

People had been leaving school before the year ended A couple of classes had been combined in some of the grades. The teachers were indeed all resigning, according to Mrs. O'Kelley Senior, who was looking for another job.

"I hope our neighborhood isn't next."

"They won't be interested in our house." Daddy was sure.

But for once he was wrong.

A real estate agent was coming to talk to us. Daddy had not wanted to let him but Mama had talked him into it. A few weeks had passed since our drive through Fairland Addition and the end of the school year was not far away.

"We have no intention of selling the house. Why should we talk to him?" Daddy asked her.

"Just see what he has to say. I have two or three, every week, stopping here while you and Victoria are gone to work and school. I have to handle them by myself if Worthy is not visiting. They are very persistent and it takes me 30 minutes or more to get rid of them. Sometimes I can't get rid of one of them before another is coming up the walk."

"I told you don't answer the door."

"I'm afraid one of them will break the door down. They just pound on it when I don't answer the bell. If we talk to one, I can tell the others we have already talked to one of them and they will go away. And they're calling on the phone every day they don't come by."

"We got to get an unlisted number. All right. Better make it a man. I don't want to hear no woman agent prattling on."

So Mama had picked a man's name out of the many business cards piling up on the porch. "This one has been a most particular pest," she told me.

She phoned and told him he could come over on a Saturday Daddy didn't work. The agent was prompt and eager. She let the man in and directed him to the chair right beside the front door. I noticed she forgot to lock the door after he entered. But before I could say anything she spoke right up at the man. "Come in! Sit right here!"

We were all in the living room. Mama and I near the hall entry, Daddy further in the room, and the agent now on the chair where Miss Trudy had so recently sat.

The man got off to a good start by showing us pictures of beautiful houses that he would have like to sell us. They were in different parts of the city where the situation was "stable" he told us. We let him finish his presentation.

"Well, we have numerous reasons not to sell," said my mother. "My sister and her husband, who are significantly older than us, live in the next house over and they would not be able to or want to leave. If they did, would you have people interested in their house as well?"

"Umm, the older place on the corner, this side of the street?"

"Yes, that's it."

"I'm afraid not. You see, my buyers want houses like yours here. Relatively new, brick with modern conveniences. You do have a dishwasher?"

"No, we don't."

"Oh well, they can be put in later. But otherwise, central heat and air, I observe. Two bathrooms?"

"Yes."

"Yes, quite. Now for the price you might get-"

"My wife just told you we are not really interested in selling." My father spoke up. "We really just wanted to hear what you had to say. And then maybe you can let all your friends know we said no."

"Um hmm, well, I notice down Foam Meadow already there are two black families so I'm afraid you would not get top price. But still it's early here..."

"What price do you think I might get?"

I heard the challenge in my father's tone and mentally wanted to warn the real estate agent that my parents had spent $11,000 to have the house built. I really wanted to tell him that, I tried to convey that to him via mental telepathy. But it didn't work.

"Well now, Mr. Grasso, the house is six years old, some of the features are a little outdated, the garage on the side makes for an awkward turn on the drive, and the drive isn't paved. But the house is all brick. But that dilapidated workshop in the back-"

"I built that workshop myself, from scrap lumber."

He's warning you himself, I thought desperately toward the man. The man was young and tall, but he was a little overweight and looked generally pudgy all over. *Daddy can take you down with one blow,* I thought hard at him.

"Right, um, I afraid it rather detracts than adds. But if it were taken down-"

"Any of the houses you want me to buy come with a workshop?"

I could not understand how the guy could not hear the menace in my father's voice.

I would stand up and start inching towards the door, if I were you.

"I'm afraid those neighborhoods would restrict such a structure but many of these houses have detached garages and extra storage outside."

"How much do these new houses cost?"

"About- they range from about $18,000 for a simple two bath, three bedrooms to- well anything with extra space you are looking at a range of $24,000 to $30,000."

"I couldn't possibly afford that much money," said my father smoothly and he got up. "So I guess we'll have to stay-"

"Mr. Grasso." The real estate agent got up too. My mother and I involuntarily stepped back a little. "You can't stay here. Don't you know what is happening?"

"What do you mean?"

"Well I mean, we have people who are on waiting lists for houses- um, houses like this- in this school district. And we have to fulfill the demand-"

My father sat back down. "Well, I ought to get a high price for my house then, if people are waiting in line to buy it."

"Sir, I'm afraid you don't quite understand-"

"Well, how much can I get? I know you cannot give me a fixed price but what would it list for?"

"There's no need for a list price. I have buyers ready-"

"Ok then, what price would I get then?"

"I would say, maybe if you'll put in carpet over the hardwood floors and paint the inside- well maybe $4,000."

My father was back on his feet in an instant. "Just $4,000!" he yelled. "Do you know how much I paid to have this house built?"

The man coughed uncomfortably "Possibly $5,000, for the right buyer, with new carpet throughout and a dishwasher- I don't think I could get 6- even if you had the drive paved-"

"You're telling me I've got to sell my house for less than half it cost me to build it. And it's a good house, with nothing wrong with it!"

"But Mr. Grasso, Fairland Addition, the schools, next year all will be all black-"

"Hell yes, they'll be all black if all the white people sell out and leave."

The agent turned to my mother. "Surely, Mrs. Grasso, you know that the teachers at Fairvine are all leaving. The students will all be black. The district's accreditation is in danger due to the mass resignation of the teachers-"

"I'm not worried about the school," my father said. "I can afford to send Victoria to private school."

"But, Mr. Grasso, you- you don't want to live this close, well, the black bastards are right down Foam Meadow already."

"Please, we do not use foul language in front of Victoria," my mother said quietly, but neither man heard her.

"If Mrs. Longhem sells more lots, and she is being sued because she stopped selling, then the bastards'll be all up and down-"

"Oh you think I cannot stay in my house because I am white?" My father sneered. "Well I've got news for you. I ain't white. I'm a dago."

"What?" The agent looked confused. *He doesn't know that word. How strange.*

"I'm Italian. Or as we are supposed to say now Eye- talian-A-Merican."

"Oh, well, that is certainly white and-"

"It is? Well that's sonovabitching damn news to me! I've never been treated like I'm a white man! I'm white only when it puts money into the white man's pocket! When being white would put money into my pocket I'm a dago!"

"Well-um. Well-" the real estate agent did back toward the door a little. *He's got some sense of self-preservation after all,* I thought, but I was wrong, for the next thing he said was-

"Well, Well Mr. Grasso. You may not consider yourself white but - but think of your wife and child. Mrs. Grasso is obviously white and Victoria- you don't want them living with-"

That was as far as it got before my father flew at the man with his fist in the air and the man sort of crumpled back against the wall.

"Get out of my house you damn bastard!" my father yelled, as he pulled back and raised his arm back again.

But my mother had deftly darted around them and pulled the front door open wide. *So that's why she didn't lock it behind her,* I thought.

Somehow the man got part way on his feet and stumbled out the door, shoved a little by my mother before my father got to him again. My mother shut the door behind him and quickly locked it putting the key back in her pocket and slid across the room to the hall.

My father looked at the door, looked at her and looked at me. Outside we heard the agent's car start up and roar off. My father dropped his arm and started to smirk. My mother was now laughing openly and I joined in, although I felt more like applauding than laughing.

"Well now," my mother said lightly. She brushed her fingertips together lightly. "I don't think I'm going to be troubled or harassed by any more real estate agents ever again. I'll get supper." And with a light step she exited the room.

My father sat down on the couch. He was perspiring a little and out of breath. He grinned at me.

"Your mother thinks I'm her bull terrier and she can just set me off whenever she feels like it."

"Oh."

"You understand what I mean?"

"Sort of."

"She forgets I'm 52 years old." He relaxed. "And I have heart trouble."

He must have seen my look of alarm for he added. "Just a little, nothing serious. All the Grasso men have it sooner or later. I knew what they were going to say, that's why I didn't want a woman here. I was afraid I might hit her. A man should never hit a woman. Victoria, go get me a glass of water."

I did. And when I got back, he continued talking. This was indeed rare, he was talking just like Aunt Worthrose did frequently. Talking to me, but also not to me. He had never done that before.

"I never have hit a woman and no woman ever hit me. Well, once right after we were married, your mama slapped me. But that was the end of that. I told her right then there was going to be none of that with us. And she got the message, she's never hit me again and I've never hit her- I know, well- she doesn't hit you with a belt anymore, does she? I didn't know about that until we moved here and Worthrose told me. She hasn't done it since we moved here, has she? I warned her-"

"No, she hasn't," I lied, remembering the one time she had and then promised never again. That had been a long time ago, just after we moved, before my surgery. "And when she used to do that she would always cry and cry afterwards."

"Well I know sometimes you needed discipline, but I didn't know about the belt and well- her family- when she was little- that was their way. She didn't know any better."

"I know she told me her brothers were whipped with a switch."

"Well, I don't think it was just her brothers- but that's her story to tell. My mama punished me when I was young. She wouldn't get me a bicycle. I had to quit school after fourth grade and work in the bakery for nothing. She made me go out in the cold and work all night. She wouldn't even give me 50 cents. Then my little brothers got the bicycles. I hit THEM all right. We brothers hit each other but Mama and Papa never hit us."

I felt guilty. I never rode the bicycle that my parents got me a long time ago. But I didn't like it. I could hardly keep my balance.

"But my mama didn't love me," he continued. "That was all there was to it. That's why she left me out of the will. That's just the way it was. She loved Vince and Chris. But Papa loved me and he was as good a person as any that ever walked the earth. If he had been able to read English and he hadn't died before her, things would have been different." My father sighed.

"Your father couldn't read English?" I thought how terrible for him. Poor man.

"No, Papa could speak a little English but he never learned to read or write. He never knew what he was signing. He depended on Mama for all that." Daddy grinned wickedly. "And she was a snake in the grass."

I didn't reply to that. I was imaging a cartoon snake version of my grandmother sliding through tall grass.

"Papa sent for a bride. Sight unseen in Sicily. He was only five feet tall and by the time he was in his 30s he knew he wasn't going to get any American woman, even an Eyetalian A- Merican one to marry him. So he sent for a bride from the old country.

"It was said that the bride he sent for rejected him on sight and the one who had sent for my mama rejected her on sight. Somebody put them together. She had to find someone or they would have sent her back pronto."

My father seemed to relish the thought of his mother being sent back to Sicily, even though it would have meant he would have never been born.

"You think I'm being hard, do you? You think I just didn't understand her? She was my mother after all. She really loved me but didn't know how to show it?"

Something like those thoughts had been crossing my mind. That was how my mother had explained it once.

"Bullshit."

"Daddy!"

"Pardon my language. I know you've heard some language today but if you never hear worse than today you'll be doing good in life. Let me tell you this. In the 20s when I was a little boy she would get me up in the middle of the night. Papa had worked hard all day and Florrie always slept like a log. Vince and Chris weren't born yet. Anyway, Mama and I would sneak out of the house with an empty suitcase and go to a big warehouse and just sit and wait in the damn cold. Then a furniture truck would eventually come, big with a name on the side too, it varied but all the famous furniture companies from then. And I would have to help unload all that heavy furniture. Then we would be there, alone in the cold again for a while. Now we couldn't sit on the furniture, we had to sit on the cold concrete floor or stand up. And then another truck would come with no name on the side. And I would have help the driver load up the furniture to that truck, just him and me- a little kid, younger than you are now."

I still didn't say anything. I was imagining my father as a young boy in a large dark warehouse, moving furniture with strange men while his mother watched.

"One time I got hold of that suitcase when she wasn't looking and I opened it. It wasn't empty anymore. You know what was in it?"

"No." *Old clothes? Little decorative knickknacks that came with the furniture? Maybe some antique looking dolls...* I tried to imagine other old things that could fit in suitcases...

"Money," he said. "It was stuffed full of money. Greenbacks, smackolas!"

280

"Oh." I now imagined the suitcase overflowing with money, all stuffed in randomly like my paper dolls shoved into my drawer in my desk.

"So what do you think was going on there? All that money and she wouldn't even give me 50 cents." He sighed again, as if he really didn't understand this scenario either. "But all that ended with the Great Depression in the 30s. Nobody wanted any of that fine furniture any more. They couldn't afford it."

"Didn't your father know what was going on?" I had only formed a vague idea so far myself.

"No, he never knew. I don't know what he would have done. I was afraid to tell him. And I've never been afraid of much in this world. But I was afraid to tell him that. He was honest. He was honest and good. He would give food to poor people if he knew they were hungry and couldn't pay. Italian, Mexican, black, it didn't matter to him. He didn't let people go hungry.

"He rarely got mad, but he could get mad. I was afraid to tell him. And as I said, it all ended in 1929 with the Depression. Your Uncle Chris and Uncle Vince were born right after the Stock Market crashed. So there she was with four kids, two of them babies, and the Great Depression just starting. After that she had to work with Papa in the bakery to make a living. I had to quit school to help them. They had put their hard earned savings from the bakery in the bank and lost it all when Roosevelt took power. But my mama had kept her secret money hidden at home. You know what happened to that money?"

"No."

"She hid it in a false water pipe in the basement in the old house. And she never trusted banks again, even with the FDIC. From the 30s on, all my parents' savings went into that pipe. And after Papa died, if she went anywhere she took it out of the pipe and put it in her bosom. That's right. She stuffed down her dress. I saw her do it many times. Every time she went somewhere. If she forgot to do it she had to go back and get it, even if it meant being late, no matter where we were going."

"Really?"

"Really. That's what they went back for the night she died. She had forgotten the money. She was afraid to leave it at the house and they had to go back and get it. It wasn't just money to pay for the dinner. Any one of them would have normally carried that much on them. No, it was money what she had saved for 40 years. She had forgotten to get it out of the pipe that one time. That's when they got hit. That's why she and that beautiful girl died."

I hadn't thought about Alexandria for a long time. But I remembered her now. *Breathtakingly beautiful with her chestnut hair that was later shaved off...*

"How much money was it? Who got it?" I thought maybe it was still in the pipe and if we went over there in the dark...

"Oh, I don't know how much it was. A lot. And Vince or Chris got it that night. They both knew about it too, at least where it was. I doubt they ever knew where it came from. Like I said, they wasn't even born in the 1920s. It was theirs anyway once she died. The will says Florrie just gets so much income every month. I never wanted any part of it. I never wanted any part of the rent houses. I just went along with that to avoid more trouble. Little good that did. I was proud of my hardware store but that, well, didn't last."

"Why did you close the store?"

"Before the war we lived above the store, which was not too far from the house we sold to Miss Trudy. After I was drafted I bought a house for your mother to live in a white neighborhood in case I never came back. That's the house we had when you were born. It was a long drive to the store."

"We sold that house to the Gonzalez family."

"Right," he said. "When the soldiers came back from the fighting, we sold the store. You know, your late Uncle Chris Romano was like a brother to me for many years. He was my partner in the store. I was best man at his wedding. Ha- both his weddings."

He laughed ironically.

"We worked together in the store. We were drafted at the same time. And I understood when he left Florrie when he got back, her being the way she is. But now that I am older and I have you, I can see in one way it was wrong. He knew when he married her she wasn't quite right.

"He took it before the war Ok, but he couldn't handle it after he got back. What he saw during the war made him look at life different, I guess. So in another way he was justified. It was his life too. What happiness he had in life was with Jolene before he was killed in Korea. But my mama never forgave me for being loyal to him when he left Florrie, that's the real reason she disinherited me, I believe."

"Well, I'm glad you didn't get any of the money," I told him.

"Why?" He looked surprised.

"It must be tainted," I said.

He became very contemplative at that remark as if it had never occurred to him before. "Well every dime I have, I made honest myself. I've never gotten anything from anybody and until your Aunt Worthrose gave us this lot, nobody ever gave me anything either. I'm doing pretty good, too. You may be right. I probably make more than Chris or Vince. The Lord has been good to me."

"What do Uncle Vince and Uncle Chris do?"

"They have jobs. Vince works for the city. Chris works in an office somewhere downtown. And they tend to those rent houses, they work hard. Papa raised them right, like he did me. Thank God, he lived to see them grow up. I'm proud of them. They and their families- they're good Christian people. Like I said, they didn't know Mama the way I did when she was young and mean. And they were so much younger than me. By the time they came along, she was older. She treated them good. They thought she was a saint. And when Papa got sick, she took good care of him before he died." He paused.

"She loved Florrie's boy- he turned out to be a good boy. That's almost impossible with no father. Looks like he'll have to go to Vietnam."

"What's wrong with Aunt Florrie?"

"Nothing really. She's mean. She is smart enough to do anything she wants. But she never has understood the value of hard work. She never would do her lessons in school. She refused to ever clean her room. Wouldn't help our parents in the bakery. She refused to learn to cook. When she grew up, she didn't want to get married. She wanted to go off to Hollywood and be in the movies. Well, Papa would never have allowed that.

"When she was married, she wouldn't work in the store like June did. My mama would have to go and clean their house. Chris would make a little money and she'd go out and spend it all on junk she piled up in the closets until they overflowed. Everybody thought she would change when Christian was born, but she didn't."

So they think she is off because she doesn't like to work, I thought. It was hard to understand, but many of the kids in school didn't want to do their work either. *They aren't really off,* I thought. *It's something different.*

"Then when Chris was drafted, she couldn't follow him stateside, like June followed me. June didn't have a baby to worry about so she could just rent a room in whatever town I was camped at. Florrie then up and joined the WACs, leaving Christian with my mama. We knew she was crazy then. When the war was over she wouldn't get a job. Then came TV and she just sat around all day watching it. My mama still had to keep house for her and take care of Christian. At least after her husband left her, my mama only had one house to clean."

So she didn't like being stuck at home with a baby while the world was at war. Adventure and excitement everywhere and she was expected to just change diapers.

"Now it's not my problem. Vince called me the other day wanting me to go with them to meet some psychiatrist about what to do with her. They're all upset because she still won't get a job and won't clean house. It smells. She watches TV all day."

"Why don't they take away the TV? What did you tell him?"

"I told him no. When my mama left me out of the will that let me out of any responsibility towards Florrie. That's the way I see it. Otherwise, I was the oldest. I would have been head of the family and had to deal with her. But it's now none of my business." He laughed. "They are probably scared to take away the TV. She is a Grasso. She's got a temper."

"What will happen to her? What will they do about the house?"

"Christian will have to support her now that he's grownup, I guess. I don't know about the house. My brothers want it clean, I guess they can get their wives to do it. Or hire her a maid," he laughed, again. "June sure won't ever be doing it."

While I was experienced with dirty houses, the idea that anyone would voluntarily reject a paying job was new to me. I thought the only way to leave a job was to get fired or, if you were a woman, get married. The idea of a child having to support a parent seemed strange to me, too. Backwards.

Secretly, though, I had been thinking that I would want a maid when I grew up and moved out. After all my mother would not be there to do it. I certainly wasn't planning to. And I wasn't going to tolerate a dirty house. So having a maid seemed like the best solution.

Better keep quiet about that, I thought. *Maybe a red headed Irish maid like in the movies. I'll leave the house while she works, so the cleaning chemicals don't give me a headache…*

"That's enough about the past, the past is the past and you cannot change it. It's the future that matters. What we do now. I can't live the rest of my life fretting about how my mama treated me. Maybe it was partly my fault. Maybe I yelled at her a bit." He grinned at me. "I yell at everybody. What do you think when I yell at you?"

I shrugged. I didn't want the conversation to turn to me. I wanted it to continue to be about other people.

"That's what I thought." He laughed. "Nothing fazes you."

He paused a moment, then repeated something I had heard before a few times in the past.

"You know, Victoria Irene, that I love you just as much as I possibly can, just as much as if you weren't adopted, as if you were my own child."

For some reason this remark had always made me a little uncomfortable. I didn't know why but something about it rang false. I certainly had no doubt that Daddy loved me as much as possible. But I felt odd when he said that. I hadn't heard it for awhile and after the last time I had prepared a response which I now invoked.

"You know we are supposed to pretend I'm not adopted at all," I said, trying to sound reproving but forgiving.

"Oh." He moved abruptly, looking a little startled. "Yes, I forgot that."

"So," I continued, "you should stop saying that."

"Well," he said, almost meekly. "Ok, I will. I- I won't say it again."

We were silent for a moment. He looked directly at me in a curious way.

I realized there was no one else in the Grasso family I could get information from. No one like Aunt Worthrose who could clarify and embellish what he told me.

I felt sad about that for a moment.

"Um, hmm, I wonder what really goes on in that mind of yours?" he said thoughtfully.

I didn't say anything, thinking how handsome he was and talented with the airplane engines.

And as long as he is on my side I am safe.

Finished with her cleaning, my mother came back into the room. He glanced at her.

I wondered suddenly if she had been listening in the hallway.

"You heard what that real estate agent said about all the teachers leaving Fairvine and it losing its accreditation with the state," he said to me, glancing purposefully at her.

"Yes."

"Do you know what that means?"

"He said I can't go back to Fairvine next year because it will be all black. So what, I like them." *I like some of them a lot better than some of the white kids who made fun of me.* "We don't have to play baseball anymore because they are there."

"The children are not the problem. Apparently the teachers are all really leaving. I can't imagine how they can desert their jobs. You would think they would feel it their duty to stay-"

My mother broke in.

"Are you talking about next year? The Guidance Committee had their last meeting last week before officially disbanding. Only Miss Tucker has not resigned. She is due to retire next spring. She will be 65 by then. The district offered her an early retirement without penalty but she declined. She is sticking to her plans and staying to teach second grade one more year no matter what."

"How could she get early retirement without penalty?" my father asked suspiciously.

"They would agree she was disabled in some way," said my mother. "Apparently they knew a doctor who would sign off on it. But Miss Tucker would have none of it. She refused to be labeled disabled. She said she has absolutely nothing wrong with her."

"Surely Miss Garter will be there next year?" I said.

"Actually," said my mother. "She is getting married. She told us at the Guidance meeting. She is leaving for Wisconsin because her fiancé lives there. We are going to give her a party at school on the last Friday with presents."

A party!

Presents!

Our conversation turned to what to buy Miss Garter and how much to spend.

So much was going on that I was finding it hard to find enough time to write. Time was running out and I wanted to get my book finished in time for Miss Garter to read it before she left town. I wrote an extra long chapter to try and finish but it still was not done.

Chapter 17
Janie White

Instead of going home after talking to Mrs. Bolman, Barbara drove on to Harold Hall.

When she got there Barbara had the uneasy feeling someone was watching her.

Suddenly she tripped over something. It was a girl! She was bound and gagged and badly beaten up.

Barbara half carried, half dragged the girl to the car and sped off.

Halfway to the hospital Barbara was stopped by a motorcycle policeman.

"I'm taking a girl to the hospital," explained Barbara.

The policeman glanced at the girl and said, "Come on, I'll lead the way."

They sped through the city towards the emergency hospital.

The girl later identified herself as Janie White. She said that she could find the other girls with Barbara, when she got out of the hospital. The doctors would release her in one week. They wanted to make sure she had no internal injuries. After that she told Barbara what happened.

"They somehow heard that you were coming. I don't know how but they did. Anyway they were doing something terribly important, I believe they were sending a message to some other country. They saw you coming, so they had to think of some way to detain you. I was the only one with no relatives although I have no idea what that has to do with it, so they tied me up and gagged me and pushed me down the hill. You found me and here I am."

"You mean you have no relatives here?"

"Miss-"

"Scott."

"Miss Scott I have no relatives anywhere!"

"Could you lead me to the place where the others are held?" asked Barbara hopefully.

"Yes, I believe I could," said Janie.

Barbara's eyes brightened at the prospect of solving the mystery. But it wasn't solved yet. The doctors found out that Janie White had internal bleeding. Her arm would have to be operated on.

This caused a delay in Barbara's plans. It would take at least two months for Janie to get completely well. They had only three weeks. Barbara would have to do it alone!

Early the next morning Barbara began to put a plan into action. She had stayed up half of the night thinking it out. She got up before Ellen did and left her a note saying that she had gone to find Belle and Jane.

Barbara did not drive all the way to Harold Hall, she parked her car about a mile away and walked the rest. Upon approaching the old mansion Barbara took extreme caution. She knew that if she was seen it would be the end. This was her last chance.

She slipped quietly around the back. Seeing that there was a trellis she tested its strength. It would do, she decided. It was all she had. Barbara was halfway to the top when she heard the slight murmur of voices. She climbed to the fourth floor before she found a window which was open. It was about 10 inches more than she could reach from where she was.

"I just hope I don't fall," Barbara thought, as she tried for a foothold in the rotten wood.

Once a piece of wood broke and she almost fell, but she barely managed to pull herself up and through the window.

She landed lightly on the floor to find herself in what was once a very elegant lady's bedroom.

It had an oak canopy bed, white with dust and mold. There was an Oriental rug that would have been priceless if it had not been eaten by rats and mice.

The only thing that had not been touched by age was the curtains. They were golden, about 100 years old and made of the finest silk. Barbara figured that they would fall apart at the slightest touch.

Barbara opened the door which creaked loudly. Immediately the murmur of voices stopped. Barbara's pulse quickened. Would she be caught now when she was so close to her goal? But the people, whoever they were, apparently decided it was nothing for they went on with their conversation.

As Barbara ventured into the hall she was faced by a life size painting of George Washington.

The hallway was quite dark but Barbara didn't dare use her flashlight for fear of being discovered.

Suddenly Barbara heard someone coming. She could choose one of many doors to hide from him or her. But she did not know which one he or she was destined for. Barbara made a quick choice. She opened the door closest to her right and slipped in.

Barbara found herself in another bedroom. This was obviously a man's. It had brown curtains which hung in shreds. There was a four poster bed which had not been touched with mold but the dust on it was an inch thick.

There was a closet full of men's clothes stiff with age. There was a big and very thick Bible which the pages were yellow with age.

The footsteps became louder but they did not come in the man's bedroom. Instead they tapped toward another room one door down from Barbara's room. After a few moments the footsteps clicked back down the hall.

Barbara then decided that she wanted to find out what was so important in that room.

She slipped quietly into the dim hallway softly closing the door behind her. She tiptoed to the other door and softly opened it.

She found herself in a very small room with a flight of stairs leading downward and then leading upward.

Barbara descended the downward stairs until she came to a door.

The door did not creak as she slowly opened it. She found herself in another small room with another flight of stairs going down, only this time they curved slightly to the right. Then she understood. The doors were not there when the house was first built. This was really only one flight of stairs. The doors were installed later. But why?

Again she descended the stairs. This time she did not hesitate to open the door that was at the end.

This time she was surprised at what met her eyes. Before her was a very large and beautiful room. It looked as though it was a living room, it had a huge chandelier in the middle. There was a beautiful silk sofa. Everything in the room looked as if it cost a fortune. Oddly though none of it looked as if it had been touched by age.

"Remarkable isn't it Miss Scott? What modern scientists are able to do these days!"

Barbara whirled around but no one was there.

"You can't see me Miss Scott, but I sincerely hope you can hear me!"

Suddenly Barbara detected where the voice was coming from. She flung open wide a door which gave a sudden lurch then crashed in on the man who was in there.

Barbara did not wait to find out who the 'voice' was, she just fled from the room as fast as she could.

The last day of school was a shorter day. I finally took my book, unfinished, for Miss Garter to see. It was my last chance.

I felt a shiver of fear as she took the folder from me without a word. I knew I should have written a copy. But just the thought of so much writing made my hand hurt, plus I never had time. As we did our last assignment of fourth grade, I could see her reading it at her desk. Before the last bell rang she handed it back to me. "Put it under your desk and I'll talk to you about it later," she said without emotion.

We had a great party for her and I saw her talking with my mother. I got closer. I knew she was talking about my book but I only heard the stunning fragments of the conversation that filled me with disappointment and hurt.

"I heard what she said about my book," I said to my mother as we were on the way home. My mother had asked me why I was so quiet.

"She didn't say anything that bad."

"She said I copied it! Or that you wrote it!" I couldn't think of anything more insulting. I felt more insulted by this than anything the kids had ever said to me.

"She only asked me if I was sure that you did not copy someone we might know or if I had watched you writing it and seen you looking at any books while you did. Or if I had helped you write it. In a way it is sort of a compliment-"

"How could she even think that? How could that even cross her mind? That's not a compliment! I would never copy anybody! I made it all up myself!"

"I told her I did not ever write a word," said my mother. "I told her you did it all by yourself and nobody even saw it until it was almost half finished. I told her we knew no one else who wrote fiction and you did not copy any book."

"I don't think she even read it all." I started sniffling. During the time Miss Garter had my book, after the anxiety felt when the manuscript passed from my hand to hers dissipated, I had cautiously fantasized that she would come back to me, beg to edit and type it for me and send it off to be published...

"Oh, yes she did read it, at least some of it. She noticed some of the names you used..."

"I made up all those names! I can't help if I met people with some of those names later on! That didn't mean I had to change them! I thought she was so smart! I thought she would tell me if I could really write or not. It would have been Ok if she said I didn't have any talent, but to say I didn't even do it all-"

"Well she's not the end all," my mother replied, somewhat smugly. "I hear stories about her. If they are true, she is nothing but a fraud. I wasn't going to tell you, you were so crazy about her."

"Tell me! What stories?" We were home by now, just sitting in the car talking. "I wasn't crazy about her." *I just admired her.*

"The rumor is, just a rumor, mind you, that there is no fiancé, she's just leaving because of the black kids coming in, like all the other teachers," said my mother. "She just doesn't want people to know she is just like all the others, prejudiced. Which would make her just 'puttin on a front' as your father says about people. A hypocrite."

Surely that wasn't right. I tried to think back and recall Miss Garter's words and actions since announcing her engagement. Surely she didn't fake that. She had been so happy and proud. I had cautiously asked her one time to show us a picture of her fiancé but she said she didn't have one with her.

Daddy came out to see why we were still outside. He was home that day as he had worked all night before. "Well, last day of the fourth grade!" he said, opening the door for me like a gentleman. "My how time goes by."

"The problem is going to be fifth grade, I was talking to her teacher about what to do," said my mother.

I was hoping Mama would tell Daddy what Miss Garter said about my book and he would go back to school and clobber her.

"She's brilliant, they all say so. She's got a high IQ." My father patted my shoulder. "There's no choice!"

"I know," said my mother. "Let's discuss this inside."

They continued talking while I went and changed clothes. *Aha, Miss Garter is going to get it good from Daddy for suggesting I copied my book,* I thought. But that was not what they were discussing at all.

"I just don't like it, I wish there was some other way. But it's too late for anything else."

"You think I like it! It's the last place I wanted her to go. But if she doesn't go, if she stays here, her high school diploma won't be any good and she won't get into college. She's got to go to college."

"I'm going to college, what do you mean?" I broke in.

"Victoria," said my mother. "Do you understand what is happening to Fairvine?"

I nodded.

"She doesn't have to go to college," my mother said in a lower voice to my father. "She could go to cosmetology school and be a hairdresser."

"She's going to college!" my father yelled back. "She's not going to be no damn hair dresser. She's going to be a doctor or a lawyer."

"The colored kids came in," I said, trying to make some sense of this conversation, hoping desperately to avoid having to fix hair when I grew up. "But I told you both that I like them Ok."

"We understand that but-" my mother began.

"The teachers are leaving. All the white teachers, they don't want to teach-" my father continued.

"Miss Garter is leaving because she is getting married." I defended Miss Garter haltingly, remembering what my mother had just told me earlier and suddenly, against my will, believing it was true. Or was I just angry and disappointed with her? "Do you carry a picture of Mama in your billfold at work?"

"Uh, why no, I don't." Daddy looked confused at the change of subject.

"If he carried a picture of us it would get all dirty and ruined when he worked. Try to pay attention to what we are saying. It's not just her, all the teachers have quit. They don't want to teach Negro children. They cannot hire new teachers. No white teachers want to work there."

"There's colored teachers," I said, thinking of Miss Bridge but remembering she was gone...

"But there's not enough," said my mother, "not enough qualified colored teachers want to work in a small low paying district like this. With this going on all over the country, there's higher paying jobs for them. There won't be any qualified teachers, the district is going to lose its accreditation."

"I still don't understand. Why is accreditation so important?"

"What that means is that every school has to have enough qualified teachers to teach all the students that go there. And if they don't, if they hire unqualified people to teach, which is what they are having to do at Fairvine, the state would take away their credentials. In other words you might go there and do the work but it would not count. And the high school diploma you would get at the end would not be recognized. It wouldn't be any good, so you wouldn't be able to get into a good college, any college."

This all left me feeling empty inside.

"They are trying to hire people, anybody with a college degree, on a temporary basis and get them certified later, but that might not work out. There is talk of merging the district with the city or another smaller district but that could take years to decide in the courts. Meanwhile, there's even talk of closing the school completely."

"If so, there's no telling what school you would go to, how far away it might be," said Daddy. "The other district elementary school is really far from us and it's real old."

"We want you close to us in school, for many reasons. And all of your friends will be gone next year," said my mother.

"Julianna won't be back?" She had been avoiding my questions about next year. I suspected her parents had instructed her not to tell. Her Saturday visits had become less frequent and shorter in duration.

"No, they are moving."

"Sue?" *I could overlook that she cheated sometimes…*

"Moved."

"Janine?" *She had wanted to be friends but she was so backwards…*

"No, moved."

"Pete?" *We had thought it so strange his mother had to work…*

"Gone."

"Marva?" *Even worse her parents were divorced, her mother with a career...*

"Her mother just rented, she didn't even have to sell a house."

"Jayne could come back?" I knew what had happened with Jayne but maybe Mrs. Anderson had come back...

"No, honey, they are all long gone for good, you know that. Dr. Anderson teaches at a college in Austria now."

"Riland?" *I am getting desperate even naming kids I don't even like...*

"Gone."

"Phoebe at church?" *I would try to like her if only she stayed. She could even come over to my house...*

"They are moving too, the other elementary in Fairvine where she went will be mostly all black now, too," said my mother, sadly. "Even though they are retired and it is going to be really hard for them financially. They thought they were set for life where they were but they are going to start over. If they weren't responsible for Phoebe they might have stayed. They were trying to get her in Fairvine since it was technically closer to them than the old elementary but now they don't want Phoebe to go to school with, well, they are going." My mother bit back tears. She was losing her friend, also.

"Most of these people decided to move and were just waiting for the end of the school year, one person sold their house for a high price to Negroes and the others are now selling cheap to get away. The first one to sell makes money, the others all lose," said my father.

"Why do all the black people want to move here? Where are they all coming from?"

"Well, from over the mountains, rural areas, downtown slums where they were all forced to live together for generations," said my father. "They were kept out of subdivisions for years. Developers refused to sell to them. The homeowners formed associations to keep them out. They were kept out of so many places for so long that when they finally got the chance to move into decent neighborhoods, there was more of them ready to move than there was houses for sale."

"I thought they were all poor. How can they afford the houses in Water Oaks?"

"Many of them worked hard. They've been saving their money waiting for just such an opportunity and you can't blame them for taking advantage of it. Who has money in this world is not necessarily who you think has the money. You see a bum on the side of the road in old clothes and no shoes, he might be a millionaire."

"Really?"

"Vic Christopher," said my mother, in a warning tone.

"Well, he probably isn't. But you don't know, so you don't judge just on how he looks."

My mother interrupted. "Phoebe's parents was hoping some of them would change their minds as the prices of the houses went so very low, but they didn't. The only ones left are those who have not been able to sell their houses or are too poor," she said.

"Poor people live in the additions?" I asked, surprised at her words. "I didn't think any white collar workers were poor."

"They are poor now, they now owe more money on their houses than they are worth," said my father. "Many have abandoned their mortgages and will get foreclosed. They'll be ruined. They'll never own a home again." His voice was explanatory but I could hear a tiny bit of satisfaction in it.

Finally tears came to me as I said without much hope. "What about Kris at church?" I asked.

My parents exchanged glances.

"Do you know anything about him?" asked my father.

"I don't know, but I think he lives over in that area that the Whaels are moving. I don't know if they are just renting to wait and see, but I don't think that neighborhood has been blockbusted yet. Supposedly, people in that neighborhood are banding together to fight the blockbusters, welcome the few blacks that have moved in but not sell to anyone else unless they can get a fair price."

"More power to them," said my father. "These cowards in Fairland Addition could have done the same thing if only the SOBs-"

"Honey, as far as we know, Kris will still be at church. He would have to move very far away to go to another Catholic church, ours is the only one within miles of here."

"But- what about that other new church? They won't let us go there."

"Hush," my mother said to him, and then to me. "No telling when the new Catholic church will be finished. Don't worry about that until it happens. Maybe never, like, like our movie theatre."

I paused, that was something. But the question remained.

"Where am I going to school next year?"

My parents exchanged glances again.

"We are going to try to get you into another district. But it may be too late for that. At least for the fall semester."

I thought about all this at once. My friends and enemies I would see no more. What could I do? Maybe keep up with Julianna by writing letters like I did Vickie Bianchi after she moved after first grade. But that had only lasted a short time.

It had not sunk in yet, but dimly I realized I would never go to the junior high with the Roman columns in front, never go to picturesque Hereald High school, that ultimate goal for so long. Already I had unconsciously made plans for the beginning of fifth grade at Fairvine, the thrill of that first day of school, a new teacher, looking around to find familiar faces. When I went back to school next year I had hoped my book would be finished and --- *MY BOOK!*

"MAMA," I screamed. "I left my book at a school!" I burst into hysterics.

"You left it at school?" My mother said, as if this was the last straw.

"Let's go look in the car," said Daddy, in a shaky voice.

"It's not there! I know! I left it under my desk. I know!" I was screaming. I clearly remembered putting it there after Miss Garter handed it back. I did not remember retrieving it.

"IT'S FRIDAY! The last day!" I screamed. "They'll clean the room! They'll throw it away."

"We'll go and get it." My mother consoled me. "I'll call the school. Vic, get the car keys. I put them up already."

We walked down the hall to Miss Garter's classroom. The rooms had already been cleaned but the janitor said if it wasn't there, we would look through the trash. I imagined my book all mangled. All dirty and torn, maybe even pages missing. I would have to write it all again. I had calmed down on the ride over but I could hardly hold back tears of real despair now.

The janitor had let us in. The lights were all dim and my

mother's heels clicked eerily as we slowly walked down the warm unairconditioned hall. She was holding my hand tightly. Daddy followed us silently. It was not yet dark, of course, and cloudy light came through the tall narrow windows, casting moonlike beams as we passed each empty unlit room.

The janitor opened the door to Miss Garter's classroom. It was all empty, most of her stuff gone, her desktop a shiny wood glowing empty slate, the blackboard blank, all the desks clean, neatly lined in their rows and forsaken. The room spotless. And barren.

But my desk was not empty. I gasped. I spotted it immediately. Miraculously there was my book, under my desk, still on the floor where I had left it. Untouched.

I was weak with relief. I could hardly believe it was there.

"You were very lucky. You need to learn to keep up with your things," my father said. "I remember you lost a five dollar bill once."

I grabbed up my book and held it close.

"I will not ever take it to any school ever again," I promised. *Next year if anybody wants to read it they will have to come to my house.*

Next year...

We thanked the janitor who also said I was lucky, somebody had been careless in cleaning the room.

"It's a shame," my father said, after we returned to the car. "A damn shame, this practically brand new school, right around the corner from our house."

"She would have been here two more years. And not much farther to the junior high. I wish I could just keep her home and school her. If only I had the education myself and if it were legal..." My mother made sure I shut the door right in the back seat.

"Damn bastard Congress and that bastard Johnson, they got lofty ideals and rhetoric. They don't give a damn that they are messing with people's lives."

"And, Vic, it was the U.S. Supreme Court too," reminded my mother, as the car reached the driveway. "That son-of-a-bitch Earl Warren and all the rest of them. They don't care what happens to any of us ordinary people."

My mother's rare use of that profanity startled me slightly. And she had come up with somebody new I had not heard of before. But I didn't ask any questions.

I was still a little numb. I didn't care who Earl Warren was.

I had my book.

They didn't say anything else after leaving the parking lot.

I rode home in silence.

End of Part 4

Part 5

XIX *Subterfuges*

We let the first couple of weeks of summer pass without mentioning school again. After almost losing it, I had carefully put my book away and not touched it for awhile.

I pulled it out again the next Saturday morning and took it into the den with me. Breakfast was already in the works. Bacon was frying and eggs were being cracked. Both my parents said "good morning" as I came in.

I asked them again.

"Where am I going next year?"

The expression on their faces said they had been expecting this conversation to resume sooner or later and were prepared.

"Well," my mother explained, as she set the breakfast table, repeating herself somewhat and sounding weary. "You understand we didn't realize they would all move away so fast."

"It's Ok, I can go back to Fairvine," I insisted. "I can get along with the blacks."

"Honey, you can't be the only white person there."

"If there were no white people there, would they kidnap me? Are they all really criminals?"

My parents exchanged looks again. My mother walked back towards the kitchen.

"NO," yelled my father, at the table, still waiting for breakfast. "Listen to me, Victoria. I am no better than no man on this earth and no man on this earth is any better than me. You are born just as good as anybody and anybody else is born just as good as you. Don't you ever forget that!" He stood up and slammed the dining room table with the palm of his hand and the table, solid maple, bounced, the dishes clattering.

We were silent for a moment until the table stopped vibrating.

"You're going to hurt your hand, Vic," my mother commented, as she returned to straighten the table settings. "Victoria, in the countryside, us kids played with the black sharecropper kids and thought nothing of it. In the 1930s when your father and I first lived above our store, everyone around us was black. We had no problems. Did we?"

"I never did," said Daddy, sitting back down, rubbing his hand a little. "I had more trouble with the white people then."

"Did you go to school with the blacks?"

They looked at each other. "In the city they had their own school," said Daddy.

"In the countryside, the black kids didn't go to school, many of the whites didn't either," said Mama. "We only had so much space. Only the smartest kids were let in. It was just one room." She sounded apologetic, as if the limitations of educational space in her childhood country school were her fault.

"Today is different. We would not know what to do if there were trouble," said Daddy. "And it's not good to be the only one of any kind of person in a group of people that's totally different from you in some important way. People do things in groups they wouldn't do individually."

"So all the white kids are really gone? Even the ones in this neighborhood?"

"Yes."

"Cindy?" I recalled how just a short time ago I had hoped for more kids my age to move in our neighborhood, so I didn't have to go play with her or Alyce.

"So far they are not planning to move," my mother said. "But I heard the school age children in the family are being sent across town to live with their grandparents when school begins next fall. That's just for next year. I think long term they plan to move but cannot afford to right now."

"There's a 'For Sale by Owner' sign in their front yard," said my father. "If they have to get a fair price, it will take them a long time to sell it."

"The O'Kelleys are not moving," my mother said hesitantly. "You can still play with Alyce."

"No," I said, stubbornly. If she was all that was left it wasn't worth it. "She's not in my grade. I'm not going to her house EVER again. I wish they would move."

"They cannot afford it, they had too many kids, they couldn't afford-" my father began, somewhat sarcastically, then my mother silenced him.

"Vic, we'll talk about them later. That's enough about that."

"Yes, forget it. They're not important."

"What about where I am going to school?" I persisted. "I want to know."

My mother sat down at the table and shifted her chair closer to Daddy.

"It is too late to get you into another district, you will have to take tests to see if they want you."

"They'll want her, June. You know that as smart as she is-"

"Hush." My mother silenced him again. "No matter how much we talk about this, it won't change anything. Right now for next September the only alternative we have," she hesitated, "is Catholic school."

"What? No!" My eyes felt like they would pop. "CATHOLIC SCHOOL!?"

"There are no other private schools within reasonable driving distance and they all have long waiting lists anyway," my mother explained. "Aunt Thelma convinced me to put your name on the list for this school years ago when Father Mallett baptized me, even though I never intended for you to go there. I did it just to please her. Every year they called and I told them not yet. But when they called this time I told them yes, just in case. So you have a spot for the fifth grade class. Now calm down. It won't be so terrible and maybe only for a short time."

"Where is this Catholic school?" *It has to be too far away. It just has to.*

"Just across the freeway and down north a little. It's the closest Catholic school to us. It will be about a 20 minute drive to and from-"

"Ruth does not go to a Catholic school!" *Why would Aunt Thelma want me to go when her own daughter didn't?*

"I know but-"

Ah ha! "Aunt Thelma thought I needed to go there because I am BAD!" I yelled. "That is where they send the kids who are BAD! I'm not bad!" It was obvious. I was furious. *She isn't even a real aunt! How dare she!*

"See, I told you," my father began. "We didn't need to tell her yet."

My mother interrupted. "Now that was just boys that go to Catholic schools because they are bad. Girls go there too- just because- they want to."

I glared, wishing Aunt Thelma could see how mad I was at her. *Catholic school… Nuns…Nuns like those who tormented Saint Bernadette…*

I shuddered.

"And," added my mother, in her 'I'm trying to be more helpful' tone. "You won't have to go to CCD anymore, you'll take religion right there during the day with the nuns. We won't have to take you every Wednesday night."

"But, but, I won't see Kris anymore then!" I started crying.

"We can still go to church at our regular church. You'll still see Kris then."

"I want to go to CCD." We hardly ever got to talk much on Sundays. It was our stolen time on Wednesdays that was precious. With all the extra priests he had now at the church, Father Mallett had decided to extend CCD for the whole summer instead of stopping it when school let out. I was looking forward to a summer of stolen Wednesday nights with Kris.

"Maybe you can still go to CCD." My mother looked at my father for an answer. He shrugged. "Certainly, you can keep going in the summer since they've extended it."

"I don't know," my father replied. "Knowing this church they might not let her. They'd like to get rid of us, me anyway."

I cried some more.

"I don't see why you cannot go to both. I'll talk to Father Mallett. He doesn't know about the Catholic school yet."

"Probably have to pay him," said Daddy, sneering. "Make a special contribution."

My mother glared at my father. Her reassurance was comforting somewhat. I knew Father Mallett liked her a lot. Everyone liked her a lot. She had so many friends she talked to on the phone. *If only I could be like her, I'd be so popular my life would be wonderful.*

"I won't tell him," she said.

"He'll find out. They probably got some rule against it," said my father. "That jackass Mallett would never make an exception. Wait until I tell everyone about that bastard Schmidt."

I sighed. I was like Daddy, not Mama. I knew that. The priest did not like him, or me much either, I suspected. *But what is with Father Schmidt? I thought he was Ok.* He seemed to like me. I was thinking of showing him my hymn to the Virgin Mary soon.

"All the more reason to keep quiet. I'll handle it, Vic," said my mother firmly.

"Depends on how far it goes," said Daddy ominously.

"We're still going to our church on Sunday?" I needed affirmation.

"Yes," said my mother, glaring at my father again. "We are going to stay there, no matter what. If we don't go, we will be happy to take you there."

"Damn hypocrites, wait until I get finished with them."

"You aren't going to do anything." My mother's look was daggerous now.

"Wanna bet?"

"You need to take my feelings into consideration some of the time." She was almost hissing. "Remember divorce is really easy these days, getting easier all the time."

"You'd never divorce me." My father sounded only half confident, a little disconcerted by this unusual hiss.

"Ha! That's what you think!"

I went to my room then, not wanting to see them argue again no matter what it was all about. I shut the door so I couldn't hear them at all.

I was still clutching my book. It was almost finished. I had so wanted Miss Garter to read it and like it… but, no that was over. With bitterness, I recalled her asking my mother if I copied it.

I cried again. They must have heard. They came down to my room to see if I was going to be Ok.

I stopped and said.

"It's Ok. I'll eat breakfast later. I'm going to write on my book," I said.

"Ok, honey, you know how much we love you."

"Yes, Daddy."

"Mama, too."

"Yes, Mama."

I thought about all the people I would probably never see again, missing from my life forever.

"Mama and Daddy will always be here," said Mama.

"Always," echoed Daddy.

"I know. Ok," I said, wanting now to get rid of them so I could be alone and write.

"That book," I overheard Mama say to Daddy as they went back down the hall. I peeked through the door so I could see them. I watched them walk away, following just a little ways down the hall.

"She's only 10 years old and she's written a book," said Daddy proudly. "Have you read it? Do you think we could send it to a publisher?"

My mother looked at my father and shook her head.

"No, no, don't be ridiculous, Vic, she's just 10 years old. Nobody would be interested in that. And she mustn't get the idea that she can be a writer. She's got to get a job and make a living, you know that."

My father looked crestfallen. "She's not like Florrie. She might not get fat again. Even if she does, look at that teacher. She found a husband. Anybody can. Victoria might get married someday."

"Look at Pamela," my mother countered. "She's not crippled, makes good money. But no prospects in sight. We don't really know the truth about that teacher. Maybe she is engaged. But we just don't know. Look how old she is anyway. We have to accept it. For at least part of her life, if not all of it, Victoria is going to have to work for a living when she grows up. We have to prepare her."

"Hmm," said my father. "She's going to college. I can afford to send her, if she can just get accepted. I got the money saved. All this demonstration bullshit will be done by the time she's grown. You can't tell me there's many kids writing at a young age like her."

"But we mustn't encourage her too much. All the teachers agreed that if she gets sidetracked by thinking she can be an artist or writer, or God forbid, an actress, it will ruin her life. If she goes to college, her best bet is to actually become a schoolteacher herself," said my mother. "That's what all the teachers said, more or less."

"Well," he said stubbornly. "She's going to college and get a degree and maybe be a college teacher. Or maybe a doctor or a lawyer or something."

I slipped back down the hall, into my room and shut my door silently. I was glad they were just talking now, having forgotten their argument. I was proud Daddy thought I could do anything. I figured he was right and Mama was wrong. And I knew I was not going to be fat when I grew up. That was for sure. I would just starve myself first. But I didn't think I wanted to be married either. I certainly didn't want any children considering the way most of them acted.

That persistent thought- that if I ever married anybody it would be Kris Stavich- was a darned nuisance. I swiped it out of my mind every time it popped up, just like a song that wouldn't go away. *Maybe he would make a good date for the prom someday,* I told myself instead. At this moment I still irrationally envisioned a prom at Hereald High School, the big old mysterious looking building now lost to me forever.

I wanted to be single like Pamela and make a lot of money. She seemed to be having a good time in her apartment in the city. She was down to just one roommate, hoping to afford to live alone soon. And there were going to be boys at the Catholic school… I would find a school boyfriend to replace Matthew…And hopefully a new best friend to replace Julianna, as she had replaced Jayne, as she had replaced Vickie…

I opened up my book. I was still so proud of the title **The Mystery of the Missing Persons**. It was the most perfect title ever. *Now where am I? And what is going to happen next?* I had been undecided if there were going to be any more mysteriously vanishing persons in the book. No, I decided now, *it is almost finished. Time for everybody to be found.*

I got out my pen and a blank sheet paper.

Chapter 18
Meeting the Enemy Face to Face

When she fled, Barbara chose the nearest door she could find. She knew that the 'voice' would be right behind her. The doorway led to a short dark hallway. In panic Barbara saw that the end of the hallway was a door.

"You're trapped Barbara Scott!" The flashlight was coming closer.

Desperately, Barbara pounded on the door. It was her only chance!

Suddenly after Barbara literally threw herself against it, the whole door heaved forward. Startled, Barbara went with it. As she fell she struck her head hard on something and then everything went black.

When Barbara awoke, drowsily she heard the faint murmur of voices. She slowly put her hand to her head. To her surprise she was lying on a small army cot. She tried to get up then she laid back and moaned. Her head felt 10 times its size.

Her moan brought the attention to the other people that she was now conscious.

"She's alive," a small weak female voice whispered.

"Of course she's alive." Another female scornfully retorted. Barbara did not have to open her eyes to know who that was.

"Addie Jones," she called out weakly.

"That's right, honey! And now I'm going to pay you back for all the misery you caused in the jailhouse. But you won't have anyone to rescue you!"

Then Barbara opened her eyes. Standing there was a small child, a strange man, Addie Jones, and Dr. Andistone! But the strange man addressed him as Stiff when he asked what he was going to do with Barbara. It was the other voice she had heard in the cabin in the woods! And Dr. Andistone was Stiff Jones! But who was the young man, the child, a girl?

"What you going to do with me?" Barbara asked meekly.

"That's for us to know and for you to find out.

Which you will do very soon. But I doubt if you'll tell anyone about it. Ha ha Ha!"

Barbara sat up suddenly. "Where's Belle, Jane and the others?"

"You'll find out soon enough."

"Why are you kidnapping them?"

"So we can sell them of course!"

"Sell them!" Barbara was horrified. "As slaves!"

"Why of course!" said the man. "How else would we sell them? They bring a tidy sum in Russia."

"Russia! You mean you work for Russia?"

"We work for anybody if the price is right, lady."

"Why would Russia want teenaged girls?"

"We don't ask questions, we just follow orders."

"What did the sign mean?"

"It meant that Stiff was supposed to get rid of you! But he didn't make it!"

"And the snake?"

"That was an accident. It slipped out of the bag."

"Who lost the shoe?"

"Addie."

"Who posed as Sergeant Memoy?"

"My brother."

"Who mimicked my voice to Mr. Horton"

"Stiff did. He's good at that sort of stuff."

"I see."

"No, you don't see. But you will." He jerked her roughly to her feet. "Come on Barbara Scott, we're going to see the girls."

Barbara went along willingly across the room to a padlocked door. Stiff Jones unlocked the door which he swung wide.

There on the floor huddled together were the kidnapped girls. Jane was eating. She was the only one untied.

Suddenly Barbara swung around and kicked Stiff

Jones in the face. The others, surprised, ran to help him. Jane dashed out the door and down the stairs. Two more floors and she was free!

Now that I was a lot slimmer, Mama liked to take me shopping at the mall with her and Aunt Worthrose. I no longer had to wear chubby girl's sizes so I didn't complain. One trip, I meandered into the toy department, well, into the doll section.

"What are you looking at in here?" My mother caught up with me.

"Oh nothing," I said, picking up a fashion doll dressed in an orange swimsuit ensemble.

"Well, look at that, they have changed her face," said my mother. "She's beautiful. She - she really looks kind of like you. Except her eyes are still blue."

"Yes, and her waist twists, too." I looked up at her with an unspoken request.

"They certainly have changed the clothes!" My mother picked up a loud print pantsuit.

"Yes they have. They are terrible." I tossed aside a crude mini skirted outfit with ugly boots. "But this doll could wear the old clothes."

"She had such beautiful clothes. Such beautiful clothes," said my mother, softly.

"I don't need more clothes, I don't have enough dolls to wear all the clothes I have," I said.

"You're too old for this," she said.

"I know. But this one is so different," I said wistfully

"You've agreed to put them all away. Will you stand by that?"

"Yes, if I can have this one more? I really don't play with them anymore. I just look at them."

"You'll put them away soon? And this is the last?"

"Yes, I promise. I will put them away and this is the last."

So I got the last Barbie of my childhood. Different but wonderfully similar. I was thinking of trying for a blond just like her next Saturday but, to my surprise, Daddy was home and Mama took off with Aunt Worthrose, leaving me with him. About midmorning there was a knock on the side door coming from the garage into the dinette. The garage door must have been left open, as it only was when we were expecting friends or family. I had no idea anyone was coming.

"You don't tell your Mama anything about this," said Daddy, as he went to open the door. "You hear?"

Daddy unlocked the deadbolt. To my surprise, in came Uncle Vince, Uncle Chris, and Uncle Chris Marino. I was so astonished that I half expected Uncle Vince Vaccaro to come around the den corner. But he did not.

"Victoria, you remember that you don't tell anybody who came over today," said Daddy.

I nodded.

"Hello, sweetheart!" Uncle Vince greeted me enthusiastically with a hug.

"Hello, Vickie," said Uncle Chris Marino.

"It's Victoria," I reminded him.

"Hello, Victoria," said my real Uncle Chris softly and deliberately. He held out his hand and shook mine same as he did the day of my surgery years ago.

I solemnly shook his hand.

"Victoria," said Uncle Vince, "we have to talk to your father about something very important. Why don't you go to your room and play?"

"Yes," said my father. "Go play dolls or write your book while we talk. And remember, this is a secret."

I made a big show of obeying immediately, went down the hall, and audibly closed my door. I waited a very short time and slowly turned the handle and silently opened it again. As usual I knew just how far I could creep down the hall and hear everything they said.

The three visitors were nervous. My father spoke first.

"Try to look at this from my point of view. This is a dying parish, the whites in Fairland Addition and Water Oaks are gone. Flat gone, all of them. So they close the Mexican church and in comes all the Mexicans that live in the area. And a few blacks that happen to be Catholic. Ok. No problem. But then my daughter's taken out of her class and put in the Mexican class but that's neither here nor there. Ok.

Ok, that's all right. I still don't complain."

He stood up to better gesture with his hands.

"But all these years we have just one priest. But suddenly, as the number of people DECLINE, he gets two assistants! They send him priests that just happen to come from a parish across town where some of the members of my family happen to belong to. Out of hundreds of Catholic churches in this city, they send- happen to send them here."

As soon as my father paused, they started in and the conversation went quick and fast from there. I couldn't always follow who said what. Except for Daddy's, I was only vaguely familiar with their voices. And they all sounded a lot alike. I had to listen sharply to keep up and get the plot.

"They were trying to send him as far away as pos-"

"They sent him away because he's having an affair with one of the women in his parish, one of the married women-"

"He seduced her, she just wanted counsel-"

"Oh, yeah, it's always the man's fault isn't it?!" *That was Daddy.*

"The bishop thought the situation was in hand, no need to get mad, Vic-"

"He seduced her? She's a middle aged woman! He seduced her, my ass!" *Daddy again. One against three, yet he is getting in every other line.*

"That is totally irrelevant. Please, no hostility is necessary here. We are four adult civilized men discussing a social problem-"

"And the bishop sent the other priest here too! For what? To keep an eye on him? Spy on him?"

"Vic, they were hoping to put some distance-"

"No need to get mad? Did he get sent to your parish? Is he preaching morality to your wife and daughter at Mass while thinking about-"

"The bishop never dreamed anyone in your parish would know-"

"Would know anyone rich!? I know a helluva lot of people richer than-"

"Now Vic that's not-"

"Than Theodore Rossi's wife! My own cousin's wife. And how do we find this out? Oh, well, my wife says to your wife, 'Guess what, we got two nice new priests, just transferred from your parish. One is teaching Victoria the CCD'. And you wife says 'Oh, no! Which one is Victoria's teacher? It cannot be that they sent him to YOUR parish? Surely he's NOT teaching the children? Let me tell you what's been going on HERE!' "

"It was believed if the -uh- involved- uh, that if he was separated from her by distance, the affair would fade."

"Yeah. Right! And it's not that he DID have an affair. The damned affair is still going on. After the Wednesday night class is over, he's meeting Theodore Rossi's wife in a motel. What kind of a sick situation is that?"

"You know, Vic, he was a convert."

"That ain't got nothing to do with it. Hell, Vince, don't you have any sense?"

"It does make a difference, he was not one of us-"

"Not one of us? I haven't seen an Italian priest in years! They're all Irish or some type of foreigner, except in the old Italian parishes, where the old rich folks demand them. The church took that man and made him a priest and said he was just as much of a priest as any of them-"

"But, Vic, Vince is right. His family was some kind of German Protestants or something."

"I don't give a damn if he came from a family of Hindus! It doesn't matter-"

"Not as many men want to take holy orders as used to be-"

"They stood him up in front of me and everybody else in the church and said- 'Here is a priest! Here is a holy man of God, better than you and me!' "

"Well, they didn't know what he was doing."

"They did know by the time he got here! Even now that they know what he is, they are standing by him! But me? I'm no good! I'm not good enough for them because I don't bow my head to no man on this earth!"

They all stopped there to get their breaths. During all this the three visitors has risen and drawn defensively closer together and were on one side of the room while my father was on the other. I could see his back and glimpse their faces which were all a little pale.

They are all taller than him, not much, but taller. And they are all younger, especially Uncle Vince and Uncle Chris.

"I didn't know you ever considered the priesthood, Vic," said Uncle Vince drolly. He smiled a little and shifted nervously.

The others looked down. Daddy took a step towards them and they all flinched. He turned adjacent to them, leaned against the counter and almost, not quite, but almost, cracked a smile.

"There's a helluva lot of things you don't know about me, Vince." He did smile then. But a dangerous light crept into his eyes.

"Now, let's keep calm," said Uncle Chris. "No one is saying there is anything right about this. Vic, you should understand-"

"Oh yes I should understand!" He stepped forward into the middle of the room and faced them, his arms spread wide, his voice more sarcastic than ever. "I'm so bad, I'm such a sinner!"

They had all jumped when he started moving. When he stopped, Uncle Chris began hesitantly, "No one is saying-"

"The sonavabitching damn priests are sonavabitching damn hypocrites! They tell me I'm wrong while they're doing worse! I ain't never taken no other man's wife- broke up no man's family. And I don't present myself as any better than any other man. I don't stand up in front of an audience and proclaim that I am holy. I don't stand up in front of a class of children and tell them I know all about religion."

"You have to think about the good of the church as a whole-"

"The good of the church? Where after my mother's funeral they told me I had to pay $5000 or she was going to go to purgatory? That church?"

"They told you that too? They said I was executor of the estate so it was my responsibility-"

"Dammit Vince! You didn't PAY them?"

"Well, I could not let Mama-"

"They told me the same thing, Vic," said Uncle Chris softly breaking the pattern of dialogue. "I paid, too."

"So we both paid?" Uncle Vince looked at his younger brother, disconcerted. They both looked at the floor.

Daddy laughed genuinely now, the dangerous light went out of his eyes. "You two neither one got the sense you were born with."

"Vic, Vince, Chris," said Uncle Chris Marino. "Let's not get into this any further. You three can resolve your differences some other time. No one is saying the church does not fail from time to time. The church is composed of people and people fail. The point is- we're trying to avoid a scandal. For the sake of innocent people that would be further harmed by this being revealed. Theodore, Jr., his grandmother, people just going to church. Take June's feelings-"

"Yeah June's feelings- Y'all think she is so nice to you! Hell, I wouldn't be surprised if she called you all! You don't know what she says about you behind your back. June ever tell you about her hero brother-in-law, the one with the bastard son that he and her sophisticated sister wouldn't even acknowledge or support?"

"Oh, Vic! Please listen to reason!" said Uncle Chris, with more emotion in his soft voice than I had ever heard before. "We've spoken to the bishop. Another transfer is already underway. You won't be sorry if you back down. Just this once. This one time. For once in your life."

There was another silence, all four men were breathing audibly.

"My daughter stays home from CCD until he's gone."

Of course I get the brunt end of this. Cheated out of time with Kris.

Kris and I were planning another evening in the woods as soon as we felt we could get away with it. There had been a little trouble as our slipping away had attracted the attention of some of the other students. One Wednesday, when Kris had been home sick, one of the Mexican boys, with two of his friends beside him, had asked if I wanted to go to the woods with him. When I declared Kris was my boyfriend, he showed me an open pocket knife and said something threatening in Spanish, while his friends moved closer around him. Juanita intervened then and shoed them away, scolding them in Spanish.

Later I told Kris, but he said not to worry, he knew the boy was just a bully and they were all just bluffing. Thankfully they were gone for the summer. But we were more careful after that, getting Juanita to keep an eye out for us. Juanita warned us the Mexican boy and his friends would be back in the fall. At least if Father Schmidt left, that would be one less person to worry about catching us.

It had been quiet on the home front while I had fretted about my boyfriend, but now Uncle Vince's voice brought my attention back to the four men in the den.

"So he'll be gone in a week, if you just keep quiet. Will you please not say anything?" said Uncle Vince.

My father looked at them and narrowed his eyes. I knew his silence was acquiescence, the most he usually gave.

"It's for the greater good, Vic," said Uncle Chris Marino.

"They'd better get rid of him soon. If it gets out any other way then I'm going to speak my piece loud and clear," Daddy warned, but in a quieter voice.

You've won, drop it now and go home, I thought hard at them. But it did no good.

"The priest is going to be gone. At once. Pronto. Good to get that out of the way," said Uncle Vince. He sat down in a chair as if exhausted.

There was a pause in which some of the tension started to evaporate but they couldn't leave it be.

"While we are here, we did want to mention one other thing. Thelma told me that June told her that you were thinking of supporting George Wallace," said Chris Marino.

Boy are you pressing your luck, I thought. *You're just a cousin, you know.*

My father walked around for a moment causing the men who remained standing to shift out of his way. "That's her people talking. I just listen politely."

"We want to say-"

"Anyone of you ever been to Alabama?" My father folded his arms and surveyed them. *Almost affectionately,* I thought with surprise. *All so like him but yet all so different. They have some type of restraint on what they say and do that he doesn't have.* I didn't quite understand it. But I knew I was right.

The three visitors took a few minutes to think about this and it was unanimous, no one of them had ever been to Alabama.

Daddy gave them same speech about the bad roads in Alabama that I had heard in the countryside. They took this to mean he would not support Wallace.

"Well, Vic, that's a big relief to hear you say that," said Uncle Vince, using more motion than necessary to get up from his chair and go to the door leading to the garage. "I need to get going soon. My better half is having some ladies over tonight and I'll be watching the kids." He laughed nervously.

"I don't necessarily tell anybody who I'm going to support. That's my business. I listen to what everybody has to say. It was a problem for you all in 1960 when I supported Nixon over Kennedy-"

"That's all in the past," said Uncle Vince quickly, his hand on the doorknob.

"You're not thinking of supporting Nixon again?" said Chris Marino, apparently still not realizing that if it was none of the other two's business, it was even less his.

"I haven't decided, and when I do I will not tell anybody but June. That's the beauty of the voting box. It's a secret. I don't have to tell nobody how I vote." My father was speaking calmly now.

"Could you consider supporting Robert Kennedy?" said Uncle Chris.

"Robert Kennedy?" My father's voice was less calm, a little incredulous.

"He was our President's brother. We would much like to see the President's brother in power," Uncle Chris said, with conviction.

"Have any of you been listening to what he actually says? And don't tell me it's because he's Catholic. I don't want to hear that." The calm had all gone.

Uncle Vince laughed nervously. He turned the knob and opened the door. "Chris, I think we've made our point."

"I have to go. Goodbye, Vic, Vince, Chris." My not real uncle Chris Marino, maybe realizing at last that he was not really my father's brother and had no say in this subject, slipped by Uncle Vince and out the door. I heard the garage door rattle.

"But what about June? Is she planning to vote Wallace?" Uncle Chris persisted, stubbornly.

I flinched but Daddy made not a move.

Uncle Chris gets away with things with Daddy that other men don't, I realized.

"June will vote for whoever I tell her to vote for," my father said confidently. This declaration of secure masculine authority finally silenced both my uncles. They looked satisfied. I wondered if they thought they told my aunts how to vote. It looked like they actually believed Daddy really did tell Mama what to do. Surely Daddy knew better.

I wonder what kind of actor Daddy would have been if he had gone to Hollywood? I thought. I pictured him in my mind, surrounded by admiring, glitteringly dressed people. Wearing a tuxedo himself. Proudly holding a little gold statuette.

Both his brothers now followed their cousin out the side door into the garage.

Daddy walked outside behind them.

I went to my room.

"So you knew they were coming."

I was waiting in ambush for my mother when she got home.

Daddy was now out back in his workshop.

We could hear some occasional hammering even through the brick walls.

Bam, bam, bam....BAM!

"Of course. I called them. Why shouldn't I have used them? He wasn't going to listen to me. We don't really go that much anymore but I still know a lot of people there. You still want to go to CCD. I didn't want a scandal. And I knew there wouldn't be any trouble here if they all knew you were home with him. They would all keep their tempers in check and be civil with you in the house."

I said next, "So Father Schmidt is having an affair with Theodore Rossi, Jr.'s mother?"

"Yes," she sighed in exasperation. "He was her priest and she went to him for some kind of counseling and they fell in LOVE." She said that word as if it was synonymous with the word "MUD".

I kept quiet.

"Damned bastard men. And of course, of all the churches in town, they had to send him here to try to get him away from her. I hear it has backfired, he's actually going to leave the priesthood and marry her when she gets a divorce. But that's likely to be some time away. It's going to be a nasty battle."

"And Father Braun is some kind of spy?"

"I don't know anything about him," said my mother.

"And Uncle Drake has an illegitimate child!" I folded my arms against my chest. "You knew about that! And you never told me!"

"I knew there would be a price to pay for this." She stared at the ceiling, then looked back down at me. "Men! They're all cheats! Yes! My family included. They all cheat!" She grimaced a little but smiled a little at the same time and nodded slightly, unconsciously putting a finger to her lips. "Yes, in the Orient during the war."

"And you never told me!" I repeated, more outraged by this failure to report the sin than the sin itself.

"He was never sure it was really his baby. Aunt Talinda said she would divorce him if he supported it. This woman had slept with several men in his unit but the company commander officially accused him so he got the blame socially. He fought it legally though, and won. But you might as well know the rest, someone will tell you one day anyway."

"What happened?"

"The woman harassed and tormented them in civil courts, tracked down all of Drake and Talinda's family, including us, writing letters and sending us pictures of this child over the course of several years, demanding money. She moved to wherever Drake was stationed, and even moved here for awhile. The scandal just grew and grew as the child got older. So finally the family all got together and just paid her off a few years ago, without Drake and Talinda even knowing we did it. Mercifully, the child came of age recently and would have none of it all. So that was the end of it. Good thing, too. Drake will retire next year and he plans to come and move back to the countryside and run for Congress."

I will bet I know who got stuck paying most of that blackmail, I thought.

But I said nothing.

Daddy would not have cared about his brother-in-law's future political career but he would have done it for Mama.

"It's these modern times. Before the war, before the discovery of penicillin, people used to have some restraint when they thought they might get the gonorrhea or the syphilis, but with antibiotics they can just carry on without fear."

"Aunt Worthrose says God is going to send a plague on people who-"

"Your Aunt Worthrose is always talking doom and gloom." Her

319

voice acquired an impatient sharpness. "Nobody knows what is going to happen in the future. There is enough trouble in the world right now. I don't want to hear about Aunt Worthrose and her predictions. Premonitions never come true."

I wasn't so sure about that.

Sometimes things I thought about ahead of time came true later.

Just little things, like when the phone rang who it was.

Sometimes I had strong thoughts about or dreams of seeing people and then the next day they would show up.

I had feelings about how people felt and sometimes they confirmed my suspicions one way or another, by what they said or did.

Right now I could see in my mind's eye Uncle Drake's son looking just like his father did in the photo on our living room end table.

But...

"Was the woman Asian? Was it a boy or girl?"

"No of course not. Drake would never. She was white. And the baby was a boy." She hesitated.

"And?"

"And the boy did look just like Drake," she admitted, not too grudgingly.

Um hmm, got that right, I thought.

"What was his name?"

"I don't know." She took a deep breath. "That's truly all I ever knew about it. And you don't say anything about it. It's a secret. It's over. Let's change the subject. What else did they talk about?"

"Oh, politics, boring stuff."

"But they did convince your father not to cause a scandal? You're sure?"

"Oh yes."

"Because if they didn't, he still has one aunt alive on his father's side. She's the widow of his father's brother, doesn't speak English and must be a hundred. But I'll bring her into it if necessary. He would have to listen to her out of respect, whether he wanted to or not."

"Does Daddy speak Italian? Really?"

"Yes. No. He could. But he won't. Says he can't anyway. His whole family vowed to never speak it again when Italy sided with the

Nazis in the war. So maybe he cannot speak it anymore. But he can still understand it. He would understand his aunt."

"Was that the really really old old woman I had to kiss at the Catholic festival?"

"Yes."

"I think you won't need to get anybody else's help," I said.

XX *Skirmishes*

It seemed like a long time ago since we had actually driven toward the direction of Fairvine. With me beside him in the front seat, Daddy sped down the familiar road, passing the boarded up ice cream parlor, the abandoned theatre construction site. I knew when Mama and Aunt Worthrose went shopping, they now went the opposite direction.

The grocery store looked the same though it had a different name and was owned by a national chain, not a family like Matthew Waterston's. The doors still swung open as we approached, its bright glass front wall of windows still let sunshine flood the front area even if they were not quite as clean. The floors were still bright beige even if not as shiny. The colorful groceries still arranged the same about the store on neat aisles segregated by type of product.

All the other people were black, the checkers and the customers. They stared at us curiously as we walked in. The mild hum of conversation between shoppers who knew each other slowed but did not stop. The checkers continued with the click click of the registers. We went part way down an aisle and Daddy picked up a few cans of soda.

We said nothing to anyone or each other as we approached the register. The checkers were all busy with their immediate customers and each register had a small line. We picked the shortest and stood behind an elderly man wearing a fancy 1950s hat, white shirt and tie. My dress rustled. He glanced behind.

"Oh. Sir. Excuse me. Sir, go right ahead." The man stepped back to allow us to advance. He feebly raised his arm to touch the brim of his hat.

"No, that's Ok," said my father with a half smile. Some of the younger people in the store turned to look.

"No. Sir, no. Sir, you go ahead," said the elderly man loudly, as if he were a little deaf.

My father glanced around the store. Some of the younger people continued to stare but some dropped their gazes.

The elderly man looked at my father with mild anxiety tinged with a strange type of admiration.

"Well. Ok. Ok. Yes. Thank you." Daddy pushed me forward and deposited the soda on the counter before the checker who was now ready for her next order.

"Thank you, suh," she said, barely glancing at us as she took the money and sacked the drinks.

By this time most talking had stopped and more people were watching us. But other people continued coming and going. Those just coming in obliviously greeted their friends and chattered amongst themselves.

"Thank you," said my father loudly.

As he took my hand and pulled me toward the exit, I turned around to see the elderly man take our place and put his few groceries on the counter. I wanted to say goodbye to him as he made his purchase but he did not look at us again.

As we drove back home I asked, "Did you know that man?"

"No," said Daddy. "I never saw him before. You know why he let us go in front?"

"Yes, I think. Because we were white?" I knew it was only a half question.

"Yes, that's the way it used to be. He's old and can't or won't change," said my father. "In an odd way it would have been insulting him if we had not gone ahead. But the younger ones didn't like it."

I could see that. Except it seemed to cause the elderly man immediate intense anxiety when he thought we might refuse to usurp his place in line, there was no sane reason why we should have gone ahead. Yet when the elderly man had stepped aside to us deferentially, I had felt an odd sense like pleasure that was not really pleasure but gave a similar satisfaction.

How odd that he should have been anxious for us to displace him and how odd that it made me feel sublime.

"Those times are gone, for better or worse," said my father. "There will be no deference from the next generation. Don't expect this to happen again."

We went onto the bank. I was expecting great changes at the bank also. I had not been there since that bright day in 1964 when I had discovered the inner criminal within me, only to have my life of crime thwarted by God. I smiled at that recollection of my childhood.

"What are you laughing about?" my father said, as we pulled into the parking lot.

"Oh, just thinking back to when I was a little girl," I said.

"Oh, when you were a little girl," he mocked me with fondness. "You are only 10 but you are thinking back to when you were a little girl?"

"You know what I mean," I said. "Besides I'm almost 11."

"In six more months." He was still laughing at me as we entered the bank.

To my surprise the bank looked much the same. It was still as clean and its formal design still delightful. There were a lot of customers and I counted only three blacks. Maybe one or two Hispanics. The tellers were all white still, maybe one was Hispanic. It was hard to say. Everyone was friendly, although I didn't get a formal greeting this time. *I must be too old for that,* I thought. I did notice that while still being better dressed than people in general these days, the employees were not quite as well dressed as in the past. And the customers were significantly less well dressed. Most of the men did not have on coats or ties. A number of the women wore pants with tight blouses.

"That bank is on the other side of the freeway," said my mother, when I mentioned all this to her later. "That's the dividing line now, not Silver Brook anymore. It's all the same on this side of the freeway now."

But it wasn't. She was wrong. Almost none of the elderly people without children had moved or were planning to move. A couple of them had died further down and their houses sold to non-whites. I wasn't sure which kind.

Despite being annexed by the city earlier this year, our little area remained the same except for one change a little further down the street. Mrs. Longhem, stubbornly still not yet dead of the cancer she didn't yet know about, had sold a little more of her land.

She had sold a lot directly to a black family. In fact, four lots. We watched the progress of the houses being built each time we left the neighborhood, having to deliberately drive a little out of the way to see.

This was, of course, a matter of discourse among the longtime neighbors. Many were very angry at Mrs. Longhem but basically couldn't do anything about it.

"The blacks are moving in after all," said Aunt Worthrose. "There'll be trouble. Especially if they have a lot of teenage boys."

"The two black families down Foam Meadow have caused no trouble," said my mother.

"But they don't have young kids."

Four nice brick houses, larger than ours, were being built on a small square block with newly paved side streets. In no time the houses were finished. On the way home from the mall one Saturday afternoon, Mama and I saw them moving their furniture inside. The people were all black all right. We were taken aback by the distinct vehicles in their driveways.

My mother called Aunt Worthrose to come over. My father was sleeping late from working most of the night before so we got him up. Then we told them what we saw.

"You might be mistaken," said my aunt.

"We both saw the same thing," said my mother. And I nodded.

"I'll go find out," said my father. He got dressed and walked down the road to make the acquaintance of our new neighbors.

"June and Victoria, you were right, that is the type of cars y'all saw. They get to bring them home because of their jobs," my father reported to us when he came back.

"Glory be," said Aunt Worthrose.

"Five black police officers, all in just one family," he reported. "Two are brother and sister. They are both married and each has two small children. Their father and mother will live in the biggest house and are helping the son and son-in-law build their houses. The father is a police sergeant and the mother is a city secretary. The son-in-law is a cop with some other department, Jacksonville, I think. Got a bit of a drive from here. The brother's wife stays home and looks after the children. The other little house belongs to a cousin who is a sheriff's deputy. He's single. I spoke with the father. He said they like to live close together and kind of away from other people. But if we ever need anything, we can feel free to call on them."

325

My mother and my aunt were speechless.

It had been a year since we had gone to the slums and Daddy had fixed Miss Trudy's roof. She was now coming over to our house.

She had an elderly man with her, not nearly as old as her, but he also had gray hair. He held her arm as she came through the front door much as Claudia's grandfather had come with her and held her arm years ago.

I thought how few people came through the front door and how the majority of those that did, like Claudia, seemed to eventually go away and never came back.

We had not spoken of her since the nighttime conversation in 1964 when I had been told the adoption had fallen through, there would be no sister, until the month she turned 18. I had almost forgotten all about her. As her birthday, which happened to be a Saturday late in the month, approached, my parents began to sporadically discuss what they might do if she came back or called. She would be legally entitled to contact them, if she desired. And perhaps she had been waiting for that day. Especially since she had never been allowed to say goodbye.

That Saturday my mother had waited all day by the phone in case she called. I had worked on my book all day, half listening, then jumping when the shrill sound of the phone ring tone permeated the house. But it was always one of Mama's friends and she would get them off right away, telling them she was anticipating an important call. Daddy had been at work all day. Aunt Worthrose came for a while to help Mama wait but she left before Daddy got home.

He came in late that night with an expectant look but when Mama silently shook her head, he said, "Well, that's that."

We never mentioned her again.

"Victoria, come say 'hello' to Miss. Trudy," said my father, as he took her arm away from the other man and led her to the couch so she could sit down.

"Hello, Miss Trudy," I said.

"Lawd almighty! Looks at you! You look just like your daddy!" said Miss Trudy as if she were seeing me for the first time.

My mother came in with some Cokes and gave one to me and one to Miss Trudy. The man with her declined.

"I have my granddaughter in the car as the other witness. She's a little feared to come in. I hope that's Ok, Mr. Grasso."

"Fine with me, my part's done."

Everyone except me signed the papers.

"Be sure and have it recorded at the courthouse," said my mother.

"Oh yes, ma'am. We knows to do that right away," said the man.

"I can't tell you how much this means to me, Mr. Grasso." Miss Trudy started to cry. "Owning my own home. Free and clear. No mortgage. My own home! I can pass it on to my grandchildren. I'm so grateful to you."

"She's the envy of everybody on the street," said the man. "None of the other landlords will sell."

"I'm proud for you," said my father. "I'm sorry you had come all the way here. But I've been working so much I just haven't had time to make it downtown."

"Oh, that's all right. You've got a lovely home and I'm pleased to see it. But I can't stay. These old bones can't take too much activity so I need to be on my way home. To my house. Again I thank you from the bottom of my heart. God bless you."

She stood up, tottering really, still sniffling some. And the man took her slowly out the door. Outside I saw a big car with several other people, all peering out the windows at our house.

"I know it was hard for her to make that trip all across town," said my father.

"Well, if she wanted the papers finalized, that was to her advantage. She made all the payments. There was no reason why we have to go back there," said my mother.

"I don't think she minded," I said, thinking so we had sold Miss Trudy that little tiny house in the dirty neighborhood. I wondered aloud why anybody that old would care about owning such a house.

"It was her home," said my father. "She has lived there 50 years. She wanted to keep it. She wanted to own it."

"If it meant so much to her, why did she wait so long to buy it?"

"Most of those houses are never put for sale. People that own the houses in that type of neighborhood want to keep them, thinking they're so close to downtown they will be worth a lot of money someday. Maybe they're right. I could have made more money had I sold it to a landlord, but I wouldn't do that. I sold it to her for what she could afford to pay for. If I hadn't then she wouldn't have been able to make the payments. But I made a little money, added to my savings, so I'm satisfied. I'm done with it."

"Now when she dies her grandchildren will inherit it," I said, imagining Miss Trudy's grandchildren moving into the house when she died, all still grateful to us.

"They don't want old houses, just new houses like ours and those in Fairland Addition and Water Oaks. Most of them, the younger ones, especially have had enough of old houses."

"Then Miss Trudy's grandchildren won't live in her house when she dies?"

"Oh no, they'll sell it, and probably make a lot more money on it than I did," said my father. "But owning property, even if they sell it, that will give them a better chance in this world."

Chapter 19
Jane's Chance

Jane flew out the door of Harold Hall as if she were on fire. About a mile away she spotted her car. Out of breath she climbed in and roared down the road.

Meanwhile the kidnappers were recovering from Jane's mad dash to freedom. By the time they got Stiff to his feet Jane was 3 miles away in her car. Freedom felt wonderful to Jane. Her first thought was to get something to eat. During the time she was a prisoner she had lost 20 pounds. She was no longer fat. She was now actually pretty. Then she remembered the girls she now called her friends. She must help them. Jane drove immediately to the police station.

Barbara, back at Harold Hall, was having inner doubts about Jane. If only it had been any of the other girls untied. Then she could have depended on them to go straight to the police station. But suppose Jane decided that now she was free she might as well enjoy it or suppose she decide to get out of the state altogether. Well, Barbara decided, it was a chance they all had to take. It was also Jane's chance. Would she take advantage of it?

The kidnappers came back then, their efforts to catch Jane were in vain.

"You took one chance too many Barbara Scott." The man Stiff called Harry jerked Barbara's wrists and feet together tightly and bound them. Then he shoved her in with the other girls.

By some miracle, Belle was not tied up and she jerked till her fingers were blistered and bleeding before the stubborn knots came loose. Finally Barbara was free. The two girls hugged each other and Barbara asked Belle how come she was untied.

"Well," began Belle. "I was so good that they said if I didn't untie any other girls that they would untie me. I promised, so they did."

"But you untied me."

"I know."

"Didn't you break your promise?"

"No. It just dawned on me that you weren't among the girls I promised not to untie!"

Barbara giggled, "Oh Belle, you're a genius."

Barbara quickly set to work on untying the other girls. After they were untied Diane Bolman told the story.

"They kidnap us, then they sell us to Russia for $100 apiece."

"The price of a human," murmured Barbara.

"Yes," Diane went on. "They were getting a message from their employer the day they beat up Janie White. In three weeks there will be a plane from Russia to pick us up and bring the money."

"The letters?"

"That was Jane's idea and Stiff Jones was stupid

enough go along with it," said Emily May.

"At first we thought it was a gag," said Mary Watson. "Then Belle explained about the code."

"Yes and it helped a lot," said Barbara.

"They tied up Aunt April because they were receiving one of those messages," added Belle.

Suddenly the door burst open and Stiff Jones called out, "I'm ready for you Barbara Scott! Come right this way!"

He led her through several doorways and then he blindfolded her and began to turn her around. Then he led her into a room stacked high with newspaper.

Suddenly she heard the soft crackling of fire from the far end of the room. Then the realization shocked her so that she stood there trembling. They were going to burn her alive!

Barbara had given such an accurate description of Jane and the picture of her two years ago that the Chief of Police on duty nearly jumped out of his chair when Jane walked in and said, "I am Jane Kape."

Father Schmidt did leave our church late summer. A parent volunteer took his place. They dismissed the extended classes for two weeks before Labor Day. So for 14 days Kris and I had no contact and did not know if we would ever see each other again. It was torture.

Catholic school was nothing like I or my parents had thought it would be. My class, all white except for a few Italians and one or two Mexicans, was almost 44 students out of which only nine were girls.

But those eight other girls were a vicious group. They didn't just make fun of me because I was smarter than them and couldn't play baseball. They hated me at first sight just because I was new. Far from being taught by nuns, the teacher wasn't even a teacher. She was just a tall large boned housewife who only had a high school diploma. She was mainly a disciplinarian for all those boys and ignored the girls. The work assigned was so easy I had it done an hour after school began and spent the rest of the day drawing, reading, starting new Barbara Scott stories or staring at the clock which mercifully never stopped.

Time never stops passing, was the one lesson I learned at that school. *No matter how slow it drags or what is happening, it never stops.*

My parents were already making plans for another change. I had taken a test and if my score was high enough I could get into the city district at the beginning of 1968, second half of fifth grade.

"Can't I go back to Fairvine?" I begged in a moment of weakness. I was picturing everyone back in class there.

All of us including Michelle and Carmelita, Julianna and Matthew, even Jayne… a little older, in the fifth grade with a new young pretty teacher… And full fantasy now- *Vickie returning and Kris would move into my district and be there, too…*

"No one sends their children there if they can find any alternative. Even the O'Kelleys got all their children into Catholic school on a hardship charity. They just have to take them across town to an older Catholic school that used to be empty," said my mother. "Even your friend Carmelita went into that Catholic school, I heard. They are carpooling."

"I wouldn't care," I said, thinking about Michelle.

"Your friend Michelle would not be there. She was bussed in. She didn't live in the district. They don't need to bus black kids to Fairvine."

"What about the new girls across the street?" Mrs. Miller's husband had died unexpectedly and she had rapidly sold her house to a black family. There were now two little girls just across the street from me, Wendy and Wanda. Unfortunately they were both younger than me, twins, age only eight. I had already been over to their house to play and had a good time. The house was clean. Their mother was nice. Their fashion dolls were just a little messed up. Wanda seemed to be almost as smart as me, but Wendy was not, and she was rough on them. Plans were in the works for Wendy and Wanda to come over. I wanted to play with Wanda again but Wendy was a question mark. I was just worried about my dolls…

"They would not be in your class, they are younger. Their mother is trying to get them a district transfer anyway. The smarter one has been accepted but she is trying to get the other one to improve her scores so they don't have to be separated," my mother continued.

"Fairvine has no teachers to speak of, the entire district is on probationary accreditation. They may lose it completely. All the work you would do in school could be lost and you would have to repeat the grade. If your test scores are high enough, you can get into the city elementary because we can petition that this district does not have the resources to teach you. You'll start in January. It's about 40 minutes from here and I can drive you."

"Won't that one be all black, too?"

"No, the city is fighting desegregation and there is no bussing in their schools yet. That school's neighborhood has not been blockbusted."

"What about Kris's school? It's much closer," I asked, thinking how wonderful it would be to go to school with him.

"No, they are not accepting transfers of any white students. The federal government is suing them for not having enough blacks. That's where Wanda and Wendy's mother hopes they can go. They are just a small neighborhood school district like Fairvine and they don't have the resources to fight like the city. They would only take you if you were black."

My score was very high. The city school district wanted me. I would have to endure Catholic school and the hateful girls for only a couple more months. None of the boys seemed to dislike me. But they were so busy fighting with each other they didn't have time to pay much attention to girls.

And we got to go to Mass every morning. The prayers were nice and we got a short time in airconditioning, but there was no music at these services, just talk. And it was over so quickly and back to the boring stuffy class and the hateful girls. P.E. was sheer torture as there was no supervision outdoors. Girls were separated from the boys and they could taunt me all they wanted.

I lived for Wednesday nights. CCD had resumed after the two weeks and I was now in the fifth grade. Father Mallett had made an exception and let me come to CCD even though I went to Catholic school. I was even back in the same class with Kris. There were no longer enough white kids to make a separate class so we were all together. Father Braun taught us.

Kris and I still had not gotten caught when we missed class and slipped off to the woods or else they didn't care. The Mexican boys were back but Juanita kept them in check. Since Kris and I could sit together again in class, we only slipped out when the weather was really good. All we ever did was talk and hold hands. He still had not kissed me yet. I kept hoping.

But Kris had very bad news for me this Wednesday in early October.

"You know they are building a new church closer to me," he said.

"I know." We both looked at the ground, leaned on one foot and moved small pebbles and pieces of dirt around with the other. Then looked at each other in the eyes intensely for a few seconds. He had grey-blue eyes I realized with surprise. With dark brown hair I had always thought they were brown.

"My parents say we'll have to go there. We have no choice. They think it will open over the Christmas holiday."

"Couldn't they just drop you off here and go there just themselves?" I asked. While I was at Mass, my parents were trying out Protestant churches on Sundays now, although they didn't talk about it. I didn't think they had yet found one that would accept us.

"No, they won't do that," he said sadly. But he brightened. "It isn't finished yet. Maybe a tornado will take it out, at night of course so nobody gets hurt."

I did not hear it as often but I still heard sometimes.

If you every marry anyone it will be Kris Stavich…

I sort of wished I could hear it now.

"What are you going to be when you grow up? Where are you going to college?" I said, suddenly thinking if we both went off to college, it might not be the same one. What were the odds the same college would accept us both?

"Oh, I'm not going to college," he said.

"NOT GOING TO COLLEGE?" I realized for the first time I knew nothing about Kris as a school student, only as a church member. He read the same level of books I did, so naturally I assumed he was very intelligent and a good student like me.

"Naw, one of my brothers might go, not me."

"Don't your parents want you to go to college?"

"They don't care. Why should they? They didn't."

"How did your father get a white collar job if he didn't go to college?"

"He knew somebody. That's how it's done anyway. College doesn't matter. You need to be in the upper class anyway to get in."

"Aren't you in the advanced class at school?"

"Heck no! I'm in the normal class, sometimes in the behind class!"

"Oh my God! Why! How can that be possible?"

"I don't like schoolwork, it's boring. I never do it unless I absolutely have to."

"Don't you care? What kind of grades do you make? Your future will be ruined!"

"Naw, I don't care. I only make Cs and Ds, just enough to pass. I'm going to go in the service. Grades don't count for anything. My father was in the Air Force. I am going to the Navy."

I was horrified. What kind of people were his parents to let him get away with making such bad grades and not caring if he went to college? I had not really thought about it, but from the way he talked and interacted with me, I had taken it for granted that he was smart like me, Julianna, at least as much as Matthew Waterston. I would have sworn he was.

"Cs and Ds!? How? The Navy!?" I thought of the song from President Kennedy's funeral- *For Those in Peril on the Sea.*

He will probably be drowned right away.

"Yes, out on the ocean," he said, with great anticipation as if he had good sense. "On a submarine, if possible."

"You want to go off in the Vietnam War on a submarine? Are you crazy? Surely your parents won't let you do that," I said. "You'll get killed."

"Of course, I'm crazy, and we all gotta go someday!" He laughed happily. "You know that. Besides I'll be drafted if I don't pick out a different branch than the army."

"Vietnam will be over by then. Wars only last four years. World War I and World War II were over in four years. Didn't your father tell you about World War II?"

"World War II? He's not that old. My grandpa was in World War II. My father was in Korea. He went into the Air Force rather than get drafted."

"Korea?" I had forgotten about that one. "It only lasted four years too, I think."

"Vietnam is surely lasting longer. It's already been four years almost."

"It can't last another eight years."

"It might be over by then. Or if not, I'll go fight." He made fists and punched the air, pantomiming a boxer, and jumped around on the ground. This pitiful attempt at comic behavior did not help matters as far as I was concerned. I folded my arms and turned away from him.

"If you go to college, you can get out of going, I heard." I was still trying to appeal to his common sense, if he had any. I had heard that Christian Romano had tried to go to college but it had not worked out for some reason. He had gone in the Marines instead. And now he was missing in action.

"I don't want to get out of going. I don't want to go to college. If there's no war I'm still going to volunteer."

This was going nowhere fast. I was utterly dismayed. Kris's determination was disconcerting.

"What about afterwards, what kind of a job will you get?" I asked, trying to think ahead. If he survived he wouldn't have to be in the Navy forever.

"Oh, I won't get a job, I'll just lay around and be a lazy bum." He began saying "lazybum" again and again as if it were one word instead of two and he really liked the sound of it.

"Lazybum, lazybum." He deteriorated into a singsong before continuing. "Anyway, who knows what will happen? Right now, I am trying never to grow up, like Peter Pan. Let's just have fun. Can I call you on the phone after I go off to the new church?"

Oh my God, I thought. *What would my life be like if I did marry him?*

I would have to stay Catholic and have as many babies as possible because I couldn't take the pill. We would wind up like the O'Kelleys...Or worse if he stayed in the service like Uncle Drake, we would have to travel all over the world but dragging lots of little dirty children along...

I just couldn't marry him. I could never allow my life to wind up like that. I was going to have a career and make a lot of money.

"I never talk on the phone. I don't like to talk on the phone," I said.

"Why not?"

"Well, I just don't. My mother talks to her friends all the time but when I get on the phone I can't ever think of anything to say. And when I call people I always think I am disturbing them."

"Oh, well you probably are," he said nonchalantly. "We'll think of something, someway to be together until we get married."

I didn't say much else, I felt like I was surrounded by a fog that I could not find my way out of. I had a whole new dilemma to sort through and figure out what to do.

"Whatever made you think you might marry Kris Stavich?" my mother asked when I related this conversation to her, wishing she could do something.

Talk to his parents, something. Get Daddy to talk to them. Call the police. The government. Anybody.

"I don't know," I said. Mentally I was panicking. *His life is going to be ruined and there's nothing I can do…He doesn't care about the grades he makes…he doesn't want to go to college… he is going to wind up a criminal or an alcoholic…with dozens of children… or a ditch digger, poor, lonely, sad, sick, abandoned, homeless…except he'll get killed first in the war…his body will be missing at sea…*

"Maybe I could go to the new church when it opens," I said, still hoping there was a way to save him.

"No, it's too far away," my mother said. "And we don't know anyone there. The last thing I need is to have to listen to your father complain about another Catholic church. And they would never let you go there alone."

I knew she was right. Why would they? They wouldn't want me.

"You are not quite 11 yet. There are lots of boys out there. Just as good fish in the sea that's ever been caught out of it. You don't want to get married too young. Take your time, date lots of boys. You want to marry a doctor or a lawyer, at least someone with a college degree and a good career ahead. You want a good provider like your father."

I could see that.

Mama had it good.

She kept her house just as she wanted.

She had the daily housekeeping done by lunch.

After that she was free to do whatever she wanted until I got home from school. Even then all she had to do was fix supper and talk to me.

She had plenty of time to read books, paint, and write.

Of course she did none of this but if she had wanted to, she could have. She could have watched TV if she had wanted. But I knew she rarely did that either.

She did still talk on the phone a lot and go to the hairdressers every week. Sometimes she and Aunt Worthrose still went shopping but not often. Aunt Worthrose used the mail order catalogue instead now.

Daddy and Uncle Clyde worked and made money so they could do all these things. But I didn't see how this way of life was ever going to happen for me.

"Daddy will never let me date."

"Oh, he will someday. You are going to have to prove you are growing up before he's going to give you any privileges. A good start would be putting away the dolls like you promised. You are too old to play with dolls. It's embarrassing!"

"Some girls date at 12." *I have to have some consolation if I give up my dolls forever.*

"You can forget that, 16 probably, 14 at the earliest. If you put your fashion dolls away, you will not have to worry about them if Wendy and Wanda come over. You can play games. Wanda's smart like you, her mother told me. Only not in English but in math. She's got a high IQ just like you. Wendy is just normal, but you have to play with her, too, as they are sisters."

"Yeah, I know. I'll be happy to play with them both," I said without much enthusiasm. *Wish I could go back to the time when avoiding playing with younger kids was the only problem I had.*

I suspected my mother's desire that I visit with the new neighbors came as much from her social isolation now as mine. She no longer had a church and there was no school group to belong to. Other than an occasional visit with the Espositos and their brain damaged son, we rarely saw the Italians anymore. My parents had lost contact with Aunt Jolene, Eva and Victor in Saudi Arabia. Uncle Vince Vaccaro, and whoever he was now married to, were strangers. Aunt Concetta and Connie had never resurfaced. Uncle Chris Marino and Aunt Thelma were angry that my parents were trying Protestant churches so they had broken off contact with us. Oddly though Ruth had sent me a card about God's blessings at the start of the school year. I suspected her parents did not know she did that. I did not know how to reply to it, so I didn't.

We did get occasional wedding invitations. Daddy still wanted to go to every memorial service of any Italian he ever had known. Members of his parents' generation were in their final years so there were frequent funerals to attend, sometimes for several weekends in a row. Each funeral had a Mass, so in one way my parents were still quite often attending the Catholic church after all.

At those occasions we often saw Uncle Chris or Uncle Vince or both, but they never brought my cousins, just sometimes my aunts. I was glad Mama and Daddy always took me. When my aunts attended, my cousins were with babysitters, I was told. Other than Aunt Worthrose, I had never had a babysitter. I supposed they were too expensive.

Wanda said their parents could not afford babysitters either. In her family, little was spent on luxuries, in hopes the twins could afford college someday. I really was looking forward to seeing Wanda again.

There really wasn't anyone else left. Julianna and I were sporadically keeping in touch by writing letters. But she was now getting very active in her new school, which she really liked. They had let her conditionally skip a year. She was now in the sixth grade on probation. So she was very busy trying to excel as much as possible. I was happy for her. Plus I knew she was less likely to run into Kris that way.

At least Wanda and Wendy don't come with any lifelong problems like all my past friends and Kris who wants to go off to war and get himself killed.

The military was almost sure Christian Romano was dead in Vietnam.

Numerous witnesses had seen his helicopter crash behind enemy lines.

There had been no memorial service yet. Aunt Florrie still hoped, we heard, for definite news.

But his body remained still missing.

"Look what I got your aunt for her seventieth birthday. I took an old photo I had and the studio made it bigger and sharper," said my mother. She showed me a custom framed photo of Aunt Worthrose and her first husband when they were young. The man was in a World War I uniform.

"I thought he was a pacifist. Why is he in uniform?" He reminded me of Gary Cooper more than Mama's brothers or Uncle Drake.

"He went and served anyway," said my mother. "He did his duty to his country. Many people did things during the world wars they never would have done otherwise."

I had seen **Sergeant York** by now. I thought it might be something like that. I picked up the photo. The handsome soldier in his uniform. Aunt Worthrose in a simple dress and a big hat that somehow emphasized the plainness of her proud features. The frame was metal and engraved "Sam and Worthy Rose Harp 1921".

She was proud she got such a handsome man, I thought.

"Do you think she'll like it?" my mother asked hopefully.

No I really don't, I thought. But I said, "Oh, her name really is Worthy Rose? Worthy is her first name and Rose is her middle name?"

"Yes, that's right. How could you not know that? Worthrose is just a shortened version of her name that she came to be called over time. Like Aunt Nelwynn is really named Nelwa Lynn and Aunt Talinda is actually Tara Linda. It's just those country names get spliced like that. Mine just didn't lend itself to be shortened." She bit her lip. "I didn't like it if they tried. No one was going to call me Junsette or something like that. I wasn't going to have it."

"Well, I just I always thought you were kind of mocking her when you referred to her as Worthy. I mean she says she is such a sinner. And roses are beautiful. She is so plain."

"Don't be silly, I would never do that. I love Worthrose. She's hard to deal with sometimes but I love her."

"What did she do? Why does she say she is such a sinner and cannot go to church?"

"Well," my mother hesitated. "I don't know for sure but I have heard rumors about the 1920s, maybe actually- the- before the 20s-"

"Yes?" I began to get excited. I hadn't really expected Mama to know, much less tell me. Was I going to find out? I tried to imagine what criminal activity Aunt Worthrose could have done when she was that young. *Perhaps a WWI spy for the Germans! After all her father was German!*

The distress in my mother's voice interrupted my imaginings. "I think- I heard- That she- she- in the 1920s or even earlier- she had an- ah-um. She did something to not have a baby." She said the last sentence very quickly and turned away.

Oh, that doesn't seem so bad. "There was something you could do before the pill?"

"Yes, yes, there was. Lots of different things." She sounded impatient. "Listen, you're too young for me to be talking about this with you. Help me wrap this present. Listen, I've been meaning to ask about the latest chapter of your book. Why did the bad guys keep the girls so long and not just send them on to Russia as soon as they kidnapped them?"

"They had a plane and were waiting to get it full before flying the girls to Russia," I explained, glad to talk about **The Mystery of the Missing Persons** but slightly annoyed at her for trying to change the subject.

"Also," she continued rapidly. "You have it that Jane and later Belle are inexplicably untied. Why would the bad guys untie them?"

"They had to eat and it would be safer for the bad guys to untie and feed them one at a time, plus they believed Belle when she promised not to untie the others. They were really dumb," I said. *I thought I had made that clear.*

"Ok and what about-"

"Oh, it was before she was married!" *Ah ha, that explained it!* "Aunt Worthrose had a boyfriend before she got married so she tried not to have babies!"

"Yes, yes, that was it, so I heard. Just let's leave it at that. And don't ever tell her I said anything. Please, please."

"Of course not." I filed this away in my long list of grownup secrets to be kept as we began wrapping the special present. I was certainly not going to have any babies before I got married. *Or afterwards either, if I can help it,* I thought determinedly.

I planned to go back and check on the points my mother raised about my book when I got a chance, but right now I was more concerned with my future relationship with Kris.

"I'd say 18 at the earliest," said my father about dating, when I asked him later. "Really, 21 would be better. Better forget about dating, concentrate on your education. You want to be a doctor or a lawyer or have your own business so you can make lots of money and take care of yourself when you grow up. You won't have to be dependent on no one. You won't have to work for nobody but yourself and you can be your own boss."

Well, that's final. When Kris goes off to the new church I'll never see him again. He'll sail off for years to war in foreign lands, have a girlfriend in every port, drown in the ocean and marry young and have lots of little children and babies.

Somehow, in my distress, I saw no conflict in Kris being caught up in all those events simultaneously and taking them all in stride.

And I'll never go to the prom with him.

That stark fact left me cold inside.

That settles that, I might as well not worry about him anymore. I'm done with him.

Two tornadoes had struck overnight and as a result I got the welcome news that I did not have to go to school one early November day in 1967. I welcomed the tornadoes as long as they did not strike our houses, hoping maybe they would strike my school and demolish it.

If it took a few of my fellow female classmates with it, that would be Ok too, I thought.

"Your school only has minor damage," my mother reported midmorning, after a few phone calls. "It will be open again Monday."

"Mrs. O'Kelley Senior says Fairvine was severely damaged. Yet it hardly touched my flowerbeds," said Aunt Worthrose. She had arrived early in anticipation of lunch.

"I thought Mrs. O'Kelley Senior was getting another job," said my mother.

"She hasn't found anything. Anyway she says it's been terrible so far this year at Fairvine. They're desperate for teachers, hiring housewives with nothing but high school diplomas. So she thinks they may not rebuild-"

"I don't want to hear about Fairvine!" I announced loudly. And Aunt Worthrose went silent.

I didn't want to imagine it smashed to bits. The clear glass doors cracked. Its walls huge splinters of jagged wood and crumbled bricks strewn about the playground.

I want to remember it the way it was.

I wanted to remember it exactly as it was the morning and brief afternoon hour before we knew President Kennedy had been murdered while I was painting teepees. I wanted to remember our cheerful room with all the big windows. The cool music room with the sound of patriotic and religious songs. I wanted to remember the halls as they were draped with that partially finished colorful mural about the history of America. How we prayed that morning and then did our lessons with confidence and optimism, looking forward to the upcoming bright holiday and long-term secure futures.

"Since I am home, this is a good day to put my Barbies away," I said, gritting my teeth.

I am strong, I thought. *I can take anything.*

"We'll do it after lunch," said my mother quickly. She started towards the kitchen.

"These tornadoes are just the beginning of the end of time," said Aunt Worthrose ominously, after a pleasant lunch. "But they should be the last storms for this year. I'm going to be giving the hydrangeas their fall fertilizer this afternoon. That's going to take some time. So I'll be on my way."

Aunt Worthrose went home to her flowers. I went to my room and brought out all my dolls. I dressed them all in their favorite dresses. I did not have enough dolls to wear all the clothes so I had to select carefully. The rest of the clothes were wrapped in white tissue paper. And all the accessories were put in a small box.

My mother opened the cedar chest in her bedroom.

"They'll be safe in here." She paused. "I'll try to make room. You sure you don't want to give them to the O'Kelleys? Alyce's little sisters would love to have them. I'm sure they never have anything so nice to play with."

"NO!" I was getting angry again. Was I going to have to fight this battle all over again? "Why do you hate my dolls? Give away those stupid baby dolls I never wanted. They take up much more space."

"Ok. Ok." My mother sighed. "I don't hate your dolls. They are just dolls with lots of beautiful clothes. Better clothes than I ever had. I'll make room in the chest. Bring them here."

I gently placed them one by one, side by side, staring at them on top of everything else in the cedar chest, memorizing exactly what they looked like. Suddenly, I had a thought.

"Don't close it yet! I want take a picture of them," I said, and ran to get my new Kodak 105 camera. I snapped a shot of them peacefully resting in the cedar chest. I put the clothing on top and pushed the accessory box down beside them. Then I spotted something interesting.

"Ooo- look! Some pictures," I said, and snatched up the large brown envelope before my mother could stop me.

"Be careful with those, they're old. And fragile. Handle them gently. I'll be right back." She left the room.

I knew my mother didn't really like looking at old pictures and would have preferred it if I had left them alone. I pulled them out anyway. There was this familiar 8-by-10 of my father's parents taken when they were gray haired middle aged people in their fifties. There was a familiar photo of Rosalind Renee in her coffin, dressed in her christening gown and a little bonnet. Her eyes closed, her face sunken but with unmistakable Grasso features.

But there were some smaller pictures in the envelope I had never seen before. I pulled out two pictures, one of a child about my age, dressed in a white lace and a veil, and the other of obviously the same girl a little older as a real bride. In the old photo of the bride and groom, the bride was slightly plump, obviously short but still little taller than the groom who was very thin and small. The bride was wearing a very simple A-line dress, with a simple veil held in place by flowers, pulled back to expose her face and lightly tracing down her shoulders. The groom was wearing a formal suit that appeared to be a little too big for him. Behind them was a photographer's backdrop, carelessly placed, so that you could see the edge of it on one side of the picture. Both bride and groom stared unsmiling, looking a little shocked, facing the camera dead on.

My mother returned with an armload of baby dolls from my closet and dropped them on her bed.

"Who's this girl?" I stared at the faces.

My mother glanced quickly at the photo and looked away. "That is your Grasso grandparents." As if distracted by something, she went over to the window. "That's their wedding picture. The old lady, she had just got here from Italy and didn't speak a word of English. The other is her also, her First Communion picture. It must be more than 60 years old."

"And that man is Daddy's father?" I continue to examine the photograph.

"They said he had black hair, blue eyes and a red mustache. By the time I ever saw him he was all gray. But he did have blue eyes."

Well, I thought. I had said that to throw her off. I wasn't looking at Grandpapá's face. Watching my mother out of the corner of my eye, I looked in the dresser mirror and quickly held the photographs up, covered the groom with the photo of the younger girl, comparing my mirrored image to both. *Wow. How about that. Well, well.* And then I giggled at my next thought that just popped into my head without any warning- *Glory be!*

My mother made a sharp movement then. I quickly dropped my hand, trying to control my giggles, dropping the photos as well. My mother rapidly came towards me, bent over and quickly snatched them up and put them back in the envelope, along with the other pictures, and dropped them back in the cedar chest. She closed the heavy lid which dropped into place with a loud click.

"Anytime you want to see the dolls, just tell me." Her voice sounded upset, nervous. She continued speaking though.

"You know, your grandmother had a hard hard life. Her father drowned in the river when he was a young man, leaving her mother and brothers and sisters starving in Sicily. She came to this country at 18, alone, and not speaking English, to marry a stranger. When I married your father she still could hardly speak English, just understand it.

"When she first got here, she told me, she couldn't afford lessons and didn't learn any English until the movies stopped being silent. Then whenever she could, she used what little extra money she had to go to the theatres and sit there all day long, watching the movies over and over again, memorizing words before she even understood them. That taught her to understand. But it wasn't until the 1950s, when she had television, she learned to speak right. Then she would spend hours repeating the words she heard on television until she could speak fluently. I saw her myself many days talking to the TV, practicing, trying to get the words pronounced right. By the time she died she could speak English as good as me.

"She went to Mass every day of her life. She was a devout woman. Early in our marriage I was alone, away from all my family with no car back then, she would come over and keep me company. She taught me how to make spaghetti sauce from scratch. She would come and get me and take me to church with her even though I couldn't understand a word of it.

"And your grandfather was a real good old man. Good to me, good to everybody he ever knew. She was so devastated when he died. She cried and told me 'I'm so all alone in the world again'.

"You should never be ashamed they were your grandparents. I

know she would have changed the will if she hadn't been killed so suddenly. She told me a lot of things you father never knew. She had gotten closer to us after you were born. That will was made long before then, over trouble long past, more about your father staying close to your late Uncle Chris Romano after he left Florrie and other things, just lots of things, more than she could bear, I guess. She just hadn't gotten around to changing it. We all think we are never going to die."

"Ok." I was still avoiding looking directly at her as she spoke. I didn't care anything about that.

"Your grandmother was both bad and good like most of us. Don't let your father tell you she was all bad. He doesn't really think that, either."

"Daddy didn't exactly say she was all bad. He said she was good to her other children and her husband." I spoke deliberately casual, still suppressing the laughter which I didn't want to explain, even to myself. But I was glowing inside, feeling not at all ashamed but quite proud actually. Someday I would get back in that cedar chest and take a look at the rest of those pictures.

One picture I was sure was missing. There had been no duplicate of my parents' wedding picture Aunt Worthrose had snapped the day they eloped.

I'm going to swipe that one from the credenza next time I visit Aunt Worthrose if she won't give it to me, I thought. It was justly mine. I wouldn't have the least bit of guilt in stealing it if necessary.

Mama and Daddy belong to me.

They are my only parents. I am their only child.

But that could wait. It was almost time to go to CCD and see Kris again.

Then my mother quickly put as many of my old baby dolls with some small pillows on top of her cedar chest, intricately arranging them so that it would be a lot of trouble to take them off again. I lifted my camera and snapped her picture. And snapped some more. I was planning to take a lot of pictures in the future. I was proud she was still so beautiful and Daddy still so handsome...

I slept soundly that night. I always fell asleep face down where I would stay until morning, if my allergies did not prevent my breathing and cause me to have to turn. My arms were thrust forward under my pillow.

I was awake suddenly. But not from lack of breath. Instead it was as though someone had directed a beam in my eyes. I began breathing excitedly and my eyes flew open wide in darkness. There was an energy pressing me down to the bed. I could not have raised my little finger if I had wanted to. I did not want to.

I had known the instant I awoke that God was in the room.

There was light, the greatest most powerful light. But I could not see it. All I could see was darkness, not ordinary darkness of clear nights with figures outlining themselves as the pupil adjusts, but total blackness. No moonlight from windows, no headlights from passing cards. Nothing.

The light that I could not see had obliterated these weaker lights. It was as if there was light and I knew it, but I could only feel it. It was energy and it surrounded me, pressed me to the bed, pressed with equal force against all parts of my body. I felt buoyant and light. Floating on air instead of resting on a mattress. Suddenly I could move my left arm horizontally out from under the pillow. I felt my hand go across the sheet.

It's a dream, I thought. But the thought vanished as I felt the cool rough sheet slide under my palm. My hand reached the edge of the mattress and slid down along the side with no difference.

If I can reach the headboard and feel the second board underneath the wider top, I'll know it's not a dream, I thought. Cautiously my arm moved back, passing my head. Mindful of the fact that I could not rise at all, I strained to reach under the headboard. Down in between the boards my hand gripped the lower one tightly. It was slick and cool and wooden. I felt its sharp edges. My fingers gripping hard, holding reality. It was not a dream.

Yes, I had known from the instant I was awake that God was in the room. The source of the invisible light, the energy, was standing behind me in the back right corner of the room. The One who possessed the power that dominated and filled the room was waiting patiently for me to settle down and decide I wasn't dreaming.

I drew my arm back under my pillows. God was paying me a visit and I might as well accept it. I thought about God the Father, the

Creator whom I should fear. I wasn't afraid, only excited. And He was still waiting patiently.

Well what do You want? I asked silently, not without reverence, but to get to the point. I could still see nothing.

I heard you were having some problems about Me. I thought I'd come by and let you know I exist.

I heard no voice. These words, this idea, expressions- were conveyed to me somehow. They just came into my mind. And I knew.

You will not be allowed to see Me. I am here for one purpose only. To let you know I exist.

How logical. I accepted this irrefutable logic that God had simply come to prove His existence before my doubts. An act of kindness performed with little effort and ending my anxiety, a cleansing of my heart, peace granted. I accepted it without question.

Why didn't this happen sooner? I asked myself as He still stood there.

The energy changed. No less powerful, nevertheless I knew I was free to move. The air I breathed was unlike ordinary air. It was pure and cool to the point of vibrancy. My heart beat fast and happy and it was made boundlessly strong by the pure air that it received through my bloodstream. I was still.

I will stay with you as long as you need Me. You are free to turn now but you must not catch even a glimpse of Me. As soon as you begin to turn, I will be gone.

Immediately, I was seized with the most urgent desire to turn. I had to fight this. Once I turned, I knew the invisible light would not become visible, it would be gone. But how it urged me to rise and look! I used my will to remain rigid. A standoff was reached. Part of my strength was occupied fighting the urge but the rest of me savored the Presence. I wanted to enjoy this for a few moments more.

This will have to last me a lifetime.

I closed my eyes. In my mind's eye I could see a form. One shade of black over another. The tone on tone outline of a head and shoulders identical to a man.

I was growing tired. And I didn't want to seem greedy. *He must have so much else to do ....*

I hung on for a few more seconds. Then I took a deep breath. I paused. I turned, as fast as I could but not fast enough. I knew it would not be. He was gone. Taking with Him the invisible light, the energy unlike any other.

I sat up in bed. Moonlight seeped from behind the curtains. My furniture took form as my eyes sharpened. Physically I felt like I was in the middle of a day. I was as fresh as if it were noon.

I got up silently not wanting to wake my parents. I walked up and down the hall, still feeling vibrant for a long time. I committed it all to memory, every second.

I must remember the feeling. I must lock it into my mind forever. I am loved. And I love Him.

I felt a surge of joy.

As the experience faded, I thought about reaction if I told anyone. *A dream they would say. Or she's crazy.* I decided to keep silent and tell no one.

I was also glad He had told me He had come just to let me know He existed. No miracles, no missions, no calling, or sainthood for me. I was glad of that considering how they treated saints like Bernadette. The next day I was as fresh as if my sleep had never been interrupted.

The Barbara Scott and other stories were going into the cedar chest with my dolls, I decided. In the many titles I had started but never finished, Barbara, Belle, and Jane had solved many more mysteries in unexplained ways and found romances and each gotten married. Barbara was considering having her first child (after rescuing her husband when he mysteriously disappeared).

I was too old for them now. They sounded childish and juvenile when I reread them. And they needed so much more work. They would never be finished. But first, I wrote one more part for **Barbara Kay Scott - The Mystery of the Missing Persons.**

Epilogue

Jane, of course, brought the police in time to save Barbara from death by fire and free the other girls who were all happily reunited with their parents. Jane was able to quickly lead the new chief to the girls through the secret passages, having become familiar with them during her captivity. Dr. Andistone was just an alias of Stiff Jones. He was actually a young man and not a doctor. He and his wife Addie, his brother and their associate Harry were arrested and properly punished.

A tragic thing about their crime was that the fire destroyed the scientific process they were working on which could remove all trace of age from furniture and home décor. They had been planning to cheat people by passing off old antiques as new. But the process could have been used for good by keeping antiques and old houses from ever deteriorating. But it was tragically lost to the world in the fire.

The small child with them turned out to be Janie White's lost sister, so after her full recovery in the hospital from internal trauma, she had some family to go home to after all. Chief McBlend was found in the lowest basement of the ruins of Harold Hall, protected from the fire by a mound of dirt. He returned to duty and promoted Officer Brownlee to Captain.

And Barbara's father Christopher Scott, who knew nothing about any of this because he had been working undercover on a case of his own, came back safely and praised Barbara for her fine work. Jane and Barbara became close. Jane kept off her lost weight and was able to straighten out her life.

Barbara, Belle and Jane then went on to more and more adventures and they were the subject of lots more good titles and beginnings if not any more endings!

It was a satisfying epilogue. It didn't go into too much detail. The main plot and characters were generally wrapped up. Readers were smart enough to figure anything else they wanted to know themselves.

Next year would be 1968. I would start a new school and start over with completely new people. I was not going to write kid stuff anymore. I was starting a new serious book about love, life, and death. Maybe some sex. No more juvenile stuff. I was going for realism.

No more happy endings!

I had easily been able to hide all my old writings in Mama's cedar chest secretly one day when she was occupied helping Aunt Worthrose over at her house. After opening and closing the chest, I had used the photos I took the day my dolls were put away to guide me in carefully replacing the baby dolls on top as if they were undisturbed.

The only sad part about the future would be that the new Catholic church would open and Kris would have to go there. Before I would ever be allowed to date, he would be gone to the Navy. I would miss him, as I missed all the persons who had already disappeared from my life.

On the plus side, I would be away from the tormenting girls at Catholic school, leaving them behind, as I had left behind those at Fairvine that didn't like me. I would start over with regular kids and I would be popular this time. Once I got back into a normal mix of kids, I wouldn't let any of them know I was smarter than them.

Once Kris was no longer there, I would not go back to our Catholic church. When I got grown I would find a church where they sang **How Great Thou Art** and other good songs like that. In one way, I wanted to stay Catholic. I would miss the Catholic Mass very much. I really loved it, even though the songs weren't so good. When they said the part about lifting up your hearts, I never failed to picture my heart being lifted to Jesus.

Knowing Father Mallett didn't like me was sort of hurtful, but most people didn't like me, so I didn't hold it against him. And I didn't really care at all that Father Schmidt had run off with Theodore's Rossi, Jr.'s mother. But to make Kris go to another church and not let me go there, just because of where we lived, well that was the final straw. I wasn't going back.

More important, no matter what school or church I went to, if they liked me or not, I would still have Mama, Daddy, and Aunt Worthrose. Our homes had not changed and our neighborhood remained much the same. We just never went back across Silver Brook for anything. Whenever we left home to shop or run errands we went across the freeway. Daddy said that our neighborhood had survived the blockbusting and was even getting better now.

We had not gone to Disneyland in the summer of 1967 because of all the riots all over the country. But maybe we could go on another real vacation in 1968. Everybody said that Lyndon Johnson would not be president much longer. Maybe the new president would be Robert Kennedy. Having President Kennedy's brother for president would be nice. He would end the Vietnam War. It would be safe to go to college again.

And America would have peace...

But whatever happened I had my own kind of peace now. I wasn't going to be an atheist or an agnostic. I had written about that special experience that night and hidden the paper in the midst of all my old writings that were now put away in the cedar chest. It was safe from prying eyes, though not easily accessible to me as well. But I didn't need to read it again to feel that wonder.

I had long memorized every moment of that encounter.

I knew God would always be there for me. No matter what happened.

The Mystery of the Missing Persons
Cast of Characters

The Grasso family
Victoria Irene Grasso - a child of six at the beginning of the novel
Vic Christopher- her father
June Rosette- her mother
Rosalind Renee- their (late infant) baby

June's extended family in town
Aunt Worthrose- June's older sister
Uncle Clyde- her husband

Vic's extended family in town
Uncle Chris- Vic's youngest brother
Uncle Vince- Vic's younger brother
Uncle Chris Romano (late)- Vic's ex brother in law
Aunt Florrie- Vic's sister, Chris Romano's first wife
Christian Romano- Florrie's teenage son
Aunt Jolene- Chris Romano's second wife
Eva Romano- Jolene's daughter
Vic Romano- Jolene's son
Uncle Chris Marino- Vic's first cousin
Aunt Thelma- his wife
Ruth Marino- their daughter
Uncle Vince Vaccaro- Vic's first cousin
Aunt Concetta- his wife
Connie- their daughter
Uncle Theodore Rossi- Vic's first cousin
Mrs. Rossi- his wife
Theodore Rossi, Jr.- their son
Grandmamá- Vic's mother

June's extended family out of town
Aunt Talinda- June's younger sister
Uncle Drake- her husband
Uncle Buford- June's brother
Aunt Nelwyn- his wife
Pamela- their adult daughter (moves to town)
Cliff- their older teenage son
Cousin Clark- their younger teenage son
Honor Clarkson/Lind Patterson (late)- June's father

Vic's family out of town
Uncle Leo Esposito- Vic's first cousin
Aunt Theresa Esposito- his wife
Leo Esposito, Jr.- their son

Non-family
Alma- A friend of Grandmamá's
Alexandria- her adult daughter
Father Mallett- a Catholic Priest
Mrs. Anderson- a first grade teacher, English
Miss Tucker- a second grade teacher, English, Math
Mrs. Choy- a third grade teacher, English
Miss Bridge- a third grade teacher, English
Miss Garter- a fourth grade teacher, Math
Mrs. O'Kelly Senior- a school cafeteria worker

Victoria's friends and classmates
Claudia- Victoria's teenage friend
Alyce- lives on Victoria's street, Mrs. O'Kelley Senior's granddaughter

At church
Kris Stavich- an altar boy, CCD classmate
Phoebe- CCD classmate
Juanita- CCD classmate

In school
Vickie Bianchi- classmate
Jayne Anderson- classmate, Mrs. Anderson's daughter
Matthew Waterston- classmate
Julianna Whaels - classmate
Julianna Wells - classmate
Carmelita- classmate
Michelle- playground friend

Also
Cindy- lives on Victoria's street, not in her class
Valery- lives down another street in Victoria's neighborhood
Glenn- classmate
Riland- classmate
Pete- classmate
Rita- classmate
Dr. Plunkett- a family doctor
Dr. Anderson- a college professor
Mr. Gonzalez- a renter
Miss Trudy- a renter
Father Schmidt- a Catholic Priest
Father Braun- a Catholic Priest
Mrs. Lambert- a piano teacher
Mr. Qurand- a school principal
Mrs. Hopwell- an art teacher
Mrs. Longhem- a neighbor, property developer
Mr. and Mrs. Miller- neighbors
A politician's daughter
A real estate agent
A janitor at the school
Friends visiting Uncle Buford

Victoria's books
Titles with Table of Contents

The Mystery of the Missing Persons
Barbara Kay Scott Mystery Series
Book 1 (began circa 1963, finished 1967)

The Mystery of the Lost Painting
Barbara Kay Scott Mystery Series
Book 2 (Began 1966, unfinished)

The Ghost of Anita Rosbeck-
Barbara Kay Scott Mystery Series
Book 3 (Began 1966, unfinished)

Characters in Victoria's books

Barbara Kay Scott Mystery Series
Book 1
The Mystery of the Missing Persons

Barbara Kay Scott- amateur teenage detective

Her family
Jane Lee Kape, Barbara's cousin,
Maria Isabel Maine (Belle), Barbara's cousin
Christopher Scott, Barbara's father
Ellen Cobbler Scott, Barbara's mother
Aunt April Cobbler Kape, Ellen's sister, Jane's mother
Uncle Raymond Kape, April's husband. Jane's father

The police
Chief McBlend
Lt. Anderson
Lt. Wayne
Lt. Ames
Sgt. Tom Memoy
Sgt. Fred Sackle
Officer Brownlee
Officer Kinson
Several other unnamed policemen

The other teenage girls
Diane Bolman
Emily May Bolman
Sarah Horton
Mary Watson
Kelly Denson
Minnie Foster
Janie White
Sandy Andrew

Their family members
Mr. Horton
Mrs. Martha Horton
Mrs. Fran Denson
Mr. Watson
Mrs. Carolyn Watson
Katie Watson (child)
Mrs. Fay Bolman
Mr. Carl Foster
Mrs. Foster
Mr. John Andrew
Mrs. John Andrew
Little boy Andrew

Possible Suspects
Mrs. Peers - a neighbor
Dr. Grasson
Dr. Andistone
Stiff Jones (Steven)
Addie Jones
Harry
Brother of Stiff Jones
Various postmen

And
An unidentified child
Bleachy- Jane's dog

The Mystery of the Lost Painting

Active Characters
Barbara Kay Scott
Maria Isabell Maine (Belle)
Jane Lee Kape
Señor Garcia- the grandfather
Maria- the granddaughter
Señor Roberto Garcy
Señor Peter Camblen

Family Flashback
Ellen Cobbler Scott- Barbara's mother
Christopher Scott- Barbara's father
April Cobbler Kape- Jane's mother
Raymond Kape- Jane's father
Anna Cobbler Maine- Belle's mother (deceased)
Frank Maine- Belle's father (deceased)

The Ghost of Anita Rosbeck

Barbara Kay Scott
Maria Isabell Maine (Belle)
Jane Lee Kape
John Roy Sands Cape
Dave Scott
Jim Main
Anita Rosbeck
George Hancock

Also by Deborah DR Kralich

The Mystique Woven in Our Land
Murder as the Organist Plays
An Innovative Murder for the Season
The Ruler of the Toys
A Kaleidoscope of Masquerades
The Unknown Puppeteer
I Lift Up My Heart

Author's Note: With the exception of public figures mentioned, all characters are fictitious and any resemblance to anyone living or dead is unintentional and coincidental.

Except for major American cities and states mentioned in context with historical events, all other locations and events are completely fictitious and any coincidence to actual locations or events is unintentional and coincidental. The world of Victoria- her neighborhood, Fairvine Elementary, Water Oaks and Fairland Additions, her church, bank, stores, entertainment facilities and all other places Victoria frequented- is completely fictional.

HOWEVER- The adventures of Barbara Kay Scott and her compatriots presented herein as the work of a child during her elementary years were actually written by a child.

While the portions of the original manuscript written prior to her eighth year did not survive, what did survive includes the second draft of the original complete *Barbara Kay Scott Mystery Stories - The Mystery of the Missing Persons* and the subsequent unfinished stories, *The Mystery of the Lost Painting* and *The Ghost of Anita Rosbeck*, intended to be the second and third books in the series.

This fictional story of the Grasso family was originally conceived as a device to present these childhood writings in such a way as to make them entertaining and understandable. As sometimes happens, the newly created fictional characters took over the project and ran with it. But, true to the author's original purpose, they never were allowed to tamper with the actual Barbara Scott stories. These are presented in their entirety taken from the original unaltered handwritten manuscripts except for the following:

A few character names were changed due to the writer forming relationships with persons coincidentally having those names many years subsequent to the 1960s.

Grammar, spelling and punctuation were corrected to 1960s standards to minimize frustration for Twenty First Century readers. They were cleaned up to the extent that the writings demonstrated what the author's skills at that time would have produced if she had taken time to correct all the errors herself back then.

Due to the complexity of presenting the story in real time, the very few plot and character inconsistencies were fictionally explained inside the fictional story of the Grasso family. An attempt was made not to change dialogue unless it was a glaring error. All original ethnic dialect is presented exactly as written more than 50 years ago.

The author hopes the preceding explanation will convince readers more interested in the social historical fiction presented in the contemporary text of the book not to lightly skim or even completely skip the work of the child, even though doing so would not compromise the historical fiction much. While sometimes tedious and confusing, the childhood fiction, especially the first *The Mystery of the Missing Persons,* is for the most part action-packed and when viewed in the context of time, surprisingly focused, insightful, complex and complete.

www.ingramcontent.com/pod-product-compliance
Lightning Source LLC
Chambersburg PA
CBHW051131030726
47504CB00004B/819